Nathan awoke with his location firm in his mind, but a vague uneasiness about the time of day.

He looked around for a clock and saw a water glass on the table. He tried to reach it with his right arm without moving the rest of him.

"What is it?" a soft voice asked, as Margaret came close to the bed.

"Margaret, you should not be here," Nathan said, suddenly aware of his bare shoulder and arm.

"What do you need?"

"A drink. I'm devilishly thirsty."

She put the glass in his hand and held his head up until he was finished. The touch of her hand and arm sent an unexpected thrill through him that nearly choked him.

"Thanks," he whispered, taking a better look at her.

"It's the least I could do after nearly getting you killed...."

Dear Reader,

November brings us another great month of historicals, all by your favorite authors!

Our big book pick this month is the long-awaited reissue of *Pieces of Sky* by Marianne Willman. In this dramatic and emotional novel, Norah O'Shea flees her isolated past for freedom and adventure in the Wild West. But she is not prepared for the harsh reality of the American frontier—or the sensuality of Comanche Indian Scout Sergeant LeBeau.

In *Deception*, Ruth Langan—author of the popular TEXAS and HIGHLAND series—brings us the provocative story of nobleman Shane Driscoll and street urchin Claire Fleetwood who become partners in a royal jest, but wind up in the midst of a deadly conspiracy.

Laurel Ames made her debut as a 1993 March Madness author with *Teller of Tales*. We are delighted to bring you her latest book, *Castaway*. Sea captain Nathan Gaites gets more than he bargained for as the unexpected "heir apparent" of his estranged family, especially when he falls in love with his prickly "cousin" Margaret in this charming tale.

Grieving a lost beau, Catherine Caden makes a desperate attempt to find her true love by seeking the aid of the infamous river pirate Patrick McLendon.

We hope you enjoy these titles, and look for our 1993 historical Christmas short story collection, *Christmas Keepsakes,* with stories by Curtiss Ann Matlock, Marianne Willman and Victoria Pade.

Sincerely,

Tracy Farrell
Senior Editor

Castaway

LAUREL AMES

Harlequin Books

TORONTO • NEW YORK • LONDON
AMSTERDAM • PARIS • SYDNEY • HAMBURG
STOCKHOLM • ATHENS • TOKYO • MILAN
MADRID • WARSAW • BUDAPEST • AUCKLAND

ISBN 0-373-28797-6

CASTAWAY

Copyright © 1993 by Barbara J. Miller.

Books by Laurel Ames

Harlequin Historicals

Teller of Tales #163
Castaway #197

LAUREL AMES

Although Laurel Ames likes to write stories set in the early nineteenth century, she writes from personal experience. She and her husband live on a farm, complete with five horses, a long springhouse, a carriage house, and a smokehouse made of bricks kilned on the farm. Of her characters, Laurel says, "With the exception of the horses, my characters, both male and female, good and evil, all are me and no one else."

Chapter One

Bristol, England, 1818

"Are you sure you should be up, Nathan?" The dignified, gray-haired man half rose as his young guest entered the sitting room and moved rather stiffly to the bow window looking out over Bristol docks and the Avon River. Nathan's left arm was in a sling, so his coat was only half on, and draped over his left shoulder.

"I just came down to read for a while, sir. The walls were closing in on me."

"I made sure the doctor said another week at least before you should be about." Captain Hewitt settled himself into his armchair again with a slight frown creasing his brow. "A broken shoulder is nothing to fool with, not to mention what you have done to your hand. Can you move it at all?"

"Not yet. But don't worry. I won't go crawling about the quays for a bit, not when getting dressed knocks the wind out of me."

"Here's a volume you might enjoy, an antique I picked up in Spain, for the illustrations, mostly. Can you make it out?"

Nathan moved over to the captain's pipe table, picked up the book and let it fall open in his right hand. "Some of it.

The type is very old." He settled himself on the window seat and became absorbed for a time in the work.

The captain watched the blond-haired lad with a certain amount of pride. He was not related to Nathan, but he would have been happy to call him his son. He had taken the boy in at fifteen, taught the lad all he knew of commerce and seamanship and, what was more important, awakened in Nathan a longing for knowledge more passionate than his craving for adventure. They were more or less partners now, the business having prospered by Nathan's hard work and enterprise. When Hewitt died it would all belong to Nathan. Hewitt's only regret in all this was that, like himself, Nathan was alone in the world.

Nathan squinted his eyes, sighed and looked wistfully out to sea. Captain Hewitt's house was located only a short walk from the Bristol quays, in the long mouth of the Avon River, but it was high enough to command a good view of the comings and goings of the ships.

"Too bad you had to break your good hand. Otherwise you could have sailed with Marsh next week."

Nathan looked up in surprise. "He's bound for the West Indies and America. You know I have no taste for such trade."

"True, true. Well, I shall need a navigator for the *Mary Anne,* but she will not be refitted for two or three months yet. Perhaps it's good that you shall have a long rest."

"What are you getting at?" Nathan knew that his mentor's aimless conversation usually had a point, arrived at sooner or later.

"Me?" The captain ruffled his iron gray eyebrows in wounded innocence. He made a great task of choosing a tobacco from one of the several Oriental jars on the table beside his chair, before filling his pipe.

"I know you, sir. You have got something up your sleeve." Nathan closed the book and waited expectantly.

"Certainly not. I just thought you might be bored kicking your heels here till the ship is ready."

"And what have you in mind for me to do until then?"

"Why, nothing. You might do many things, perhaps even go to London for a few weeks. By the way, I hear those Chinese antiques you brought back fetched a handsome price."

"The genuine Ming usually do."

"Your dealer has no idea you save the best pieces for me." The captain looked at the assortment of jars on his pipe stand.

"No, and I hope he never finds out." Nathan laughed. "He would have an attack if he knew you kept your tobacco in them."

Hewitt chuckled. "Of course, there's no question of real trade with China yet."

Nathan smiled and shook his fair head. "We have got nothing they want except gold and silver. It's as simple as that."

"You keep no pieces for yourself," the captain complained.

"I take no particular delight in them."

"Nor in anything else since your mother died."

The smile retreated from Nathan's eyes and he looked out to sea again.

"She has been gone a long time," Captain Hewitt said gently. "I knew her, Nathan. She would not want you to grieve like this."

"Of course not." Nathan turned to face him, smiling sadly. "But it is so often difficult to listen to reason when it runs counter to your feelings."

"I know." Hewitt lapsed into silence for a minute, then roused himself again. "Let me see, there was something else I was meaning to tell you when you got better. Now, what was it?" The captain's mind seemed to wander off absently. Nathan waited patiently, resting his aching head against the window embrasure while Captain Hewitt puffed to relight his pipe. "I know. There was a fellow here looking for you. In January it was. Name of Matthew Gaites."

Nathan turned a suspicious eye on his old friend. Although Captain Hewitt had almost thrice Nathan's twenty-five years, they got along amazingly well. Nathan made Hewitt's home his own when in port and, since Hewitt now tended to manage rather than captain the four vessels he owned, he was glad for the companionship.

"Gaites, a relative, do you suppose?"

"Yes, your cousin, in fact. He said you had never met him…" Hewitt seemed to be dredging his memory. "But he is your youngest uncle's son, or one of them. He quite lost me."

"Did he say what he wanted?"

"It seems your uncle Talbot died."

Nathan wrinkled his brow in an effort to remember names he had not heard since he was ten. "Father never spoke of his family much since his father cast him off, but I believe that would have been his elder brother."

"Any road, he wanted me to let him know when you returned."

"And did you?" Nathan stood up a little tensely.

"I don't know but what I may have slipped him a line in the post while you was lying feverish with your broken bones."

"But why? You cannot imagine I have any interest in those people."

"Nay, I know you have not, but he did make me promise him."

Nathan chuckled in spite of himself. "Nobody has ever made you do anything you didn't choose to do. Well, I suppose I shall have to see him, if he comes again while I'm in port."

"Take it from an old bachelor, it's well enough to be alone when you are young, but nice to have a bit of family, however distant, when you get older. I wish now I had married and had some children to comfort me in my old age."

This surprised a bark of laughter from Nathan. "You can't expect me to believe you are past your prime. I live in daily expectation of hearing that you may have to wed Sally Masefield.''

Hewitt himself chuckled.

''She is quite taken with you. I believe it's your eyebrows she finds your most attractive feature.''

Hewitt was just recovering himself when the housekeeper came up with a card for Nathan, presenting this rarity with a flourish.

''Oh, Lord. Show him up, Mrs. Beckley. I will get you for this, Captain,'' Nathan said, turning to the still chuckling conspirator.

The captain stayed long enough to introduce the two young men, who eyed each other so warily they looked to be about to wrestle.

Matthew was a head taller, well built with dark hair, but he was rather too dainty looking for Captain Hewitt's taste. He thought Nathan with his fair hair lightened by the sun, his hard muscles and strong hands, the better looking of the two.

When Matthew had originally asked after Nathan Gaites and been directed to the tall well-kept house near the harbor, he had assumed Mrs. Beckley to be the landlady of a lodging house for sailors, and that Nathan was merely one of her tenants. The noticeable lack of servants did nothing to dispel this impression. So when the captain had served up some canary wine and then volunteered to leave the two alone, Matthew begged him to stay, reluctant to drive him from what he perceived to be the common sitting room.

''Oh, I have some business down in the harbor,'' Hewitt said, and sauntered out with his walking stick.

''The captain tells me one of my uncles has died. Not your father?'' Nathan was prepared to be mildly sympathetic.

''No, Uncle Talbot never married. My father, that was your uncle William, has been dead these fifteen years. You are probably wondering why I have come so long after Uncle Talbot's funeral. You were off somewhere when it happened.''

"The East Indies. I seem to miss a lot of funerals." Nathan set his glass down grimly.

"The fact of the matter is, Grandfather wants to see you," Matthew said in a rush, then peered at Nathan for his reaction.

"Good Lord, is he still alive?" Nathan was conscious of Matthew's gaze and turned to face the window. "And all his sons dead before him," Nathan mused.

"Perhaps you are thinking God has fittingly punished him for disowning your father."

Nathan gave a start. "Why should I think that? Life punishes us enough without God taking a hand in it."

Matthew took it the boy spoke from experience. Nathan was a year younger than Matthew but did not look it. The creases around his eyes, the weather-beaten face, let alone the sling and bandaged hand, spoke of hardships Matthew could only guess at. He knew a moment's jealousy of Nathan who had seen so much more of the world than himself. But since he disliked being hot, cold or hungry, this passed quickly from his mind to be replaced with a vague sort of sympathy.

"Well, he has only the three grandsons left—you, me, and my older brother, Jared. Is it odd that he would want to make your acquaintance?"

"Left it a bit late, didn't he?" Nathan chided, in some amusement.

Matthew scarcely knew what to say and was so obviously discomforted as he fumbled with his wineglass, that Nathan hurriedly said, "I'm sorry. That was uncalled-for, and unkind. Would you like some more wine?"

Nathan moved toward the side table and Matthew rose to present his glass. "It does rankle then, being ignored all these years?"

"It should not," Nathan said, carefully refilling the glasses, one-handed. "I have no claim on my grandfather."

"He wants to make amends," Matthew said sincerely. "Is it so much to ask that you would at least come to meet him?'' Nathan's indecision showed in his face. ''I will drive you there myself,'' Matthew offered. ''It's no more than an hour away.''

''So close?'' Nathan seemed surprised. ''I wonder if Father was ever tempted to go back.''

''So far as I know, Uncle Robert never returned after marrying your mother, at least, not that I heard of.''

''No, he would not.'' Nathan drained his glass. ''She may have been the chandler's daughter, but she was a remarkable woman.'' Nathan pulled himself back to the present. ''I cannot make out how you even knew about me.''

''Your mother wrote Grandfather when she was certain your father had been lost at sea,'' Matthew answered. Nathan looked distressed. ''She mentioned a son,'' Matthew continued, ''and your name is not exactly common.''

''Did she ask for his help?'' Nathan whispered tensely.

''I suppose. What is the matter with that?''

''If you had known her, you would have known what it cost her to write that letter.'' He carefully put the glass down without thumping it. ''She never told me.''

''If Grandfather had come then, when he should have...'' Matthew dropped his eyes ''...you might have grown up at Gaites Hall with me. I don't know why... '' Matthew was looking miserable again.

''Don't concern yourself,'' Nathan said. ''It's certainly not your fault. The old man himself may not know why he did not come.''

''The old man?'' Matthew managed a wry smile.

''That's what Father called him, when he spoke of him at all. You would have liked Father, he was a jolly fellow, full of the devil, and never sad, except when it came time to leave us. In between voyages he was here for weeks at a time, and I felt myself the luckiest boy alive. We were together, the three of us. Those are the times I remember, swinging on his hand as he walked the hills with Mother by his side.'' Nathan was not consciously aware of his attempt to comfort Matthew, except for thinking what a damnable task the old man had set for him trying to wipe away a wrong so long neglected.

He was, however, adamant in refusing to take up a connection he had absolutely no wish for, but he reckoned without the intrepid captain.

That night Hewitt called on Matthew privately at the Full Moon Inn to warn him not to carry Nathan off until the doctor had pronounced him fit.

"You mistake, sir. It does not look as though he shall be going with me at all. I have failed to convince him of my grandfather's sincerity in wishing to make amends."

Hewitt sampled the claret Matthew poured out for him and pronounced it satisfactory. "Perhaps you have not dwelt on the perilous state of your grandfather's health."

"But my grandfather is not ill," Matthew said in some surprise.

"Never?" Hewitt looked at him meaningfully over his glass.

"Oh, I suppose an occasional fit of... oh, I see."

Hewitt was pleased to find that Matthew was not dense in the slightest.

"You will find that one of Nathan's few flaws is an over-ready compassion. He would not let his worst enemy die unabsolved, if it was in his power to set the man's mind at peace."

"How long have you known Nathan?"

"Nearly all his life, I suppose. His mother kept a ship chandler's shop while his father was at sea. Nathan was not more than thirteen when he begged me to take him to the East Indies. Some idea of finding his father, no doubt."

"And did you take him?"

"No, I refused him, for his mother's sake. A mistake on my part, I'm afraid. He stowed away on Rayburn's ship. That voyage left its marks on the boy. He was lucky to have survived it. When he returned, his mother was dead, so I took him with me after that."

"It appears we owe you a great deal of thanks for looking out for him. You seem to favor this reunion with his family." Matthew fished for a motive.

"I merely do not wish to see the boy alone in the world as I am." Hewitt observed that Matthew himself was not incapable of compassion. "Never mind me, though. Come this afternoon to take your leave of him, your excuse being the urgency of returning to your grandfather's bedside."

"But Nathan gave me a firm answer. He does not look to see me again."

"Then he will be sure to be at home."

Matthew laughed with the captain, and enjoyed another glass of wine with him before seeing him off.

Nathan had been imprudent enough to visit the *Mary Anne* that day and, because of slipping on the gangway and setting off the pain in his shoulder again, he was still lying down resting when Matthew arrived.

"Is he badly hurt?" Matthew asked.

"Just overdid it, I think. I rely on you to get him to the country for a rest. I cannot keep him off the quays, and he's a danger to himself in his condition. Let us go up to his room."

This was a third-floor garret with a commanding view of the river and docks. Matthew noticed only its small size and almost passionate neatness. Nathan had kept the same room since he was fifteen because he liked being the first to announce the arrival of the ships.

Hewitt laid a hand gently on his forehead and Nathan awoke with a start that wrenched a grunt of pain from him. "What is it?"

"Just your cousin come to say goodbye. I will leave you now."

"I thought you had gone already, Matthew." Nathan got his right arm behind him and pushed himself up with some effort, swinging his legs down off the edge of the narrow bed.

"It appears I must now. Grandfather's health being what it is, I don't like to leave him for long."

"What's wrong with him?" Nathan tried unsuccessfully to twist into a more comfortable position.

"Old age. There's nothing much to be done for him." Matthew thought he might be laying it on a bit thick, but Nathan, in pain himself, took the news at face value.

"He's not . . . dying."

"We are all dying," Matthew said truthfully. "Some of us just have less time left than others."

Nathan rubbed his forehead and squinted up at Matthew. "Are you sure he really wants to see me?"

In the end Nathan agreed reluctantly to stay at Gaites Hall for a month, a long-enough obligatory visit, he judged. Having once made his decision, Nathan would have been inclined to leave the next day and get it over with. Matthew, however, made the need to supply Nathan with evening dress his excuse for lingering in Bristol another week.

Matthew accompanied Nathan to the tailor, the barber, the boot maker, and somehow induced him to visit the haberdasher, as well. Nathan insisted on buying all his new finery out of his own pocket, so much upsetting Matthew that Nathan finally agreed to let his cousin pay for his hats. He hated hats and had no intention of wearing them, but Matthew insisted they were a necessary part of any gentleman's wardrobe.

Matthew reflected he could have done much better outfitting Nathan in London and was disappointed that his cousin insisted on roomy, rather than close-fitting, coats. But he supposed allowances had to be made for getting them on over his bad shoulder. He flattered himself that, with the modish haircut he had gotten the boy, and the apparel he had selected, he would not have to blush when presenting Nathan to his grandfather.

Nathan certainly did not grudge the expense. He could afford to pay as much for his coats as he wished. But the repeated fittings and Matthew's fussing about details of apparel that Nathan considered inconsequential were beginning to wear on even Nathan's good nature. By the time they finally set forth on a Saturday afternoon near the end of May, Nathan was anticipating the projected visit with nothing but foreboding. He comforted himself with the thought that a month, no matter how long it seemed under certain conditions, would eventually pass, and that he could then return to his more rational life.

Chapter Two

On the drive to Gaites Hall, Matthew filled Nathan's head with as much family history as he thought would be useful, and Nathan listened with half an ear, being more occupied in keeping his left shoulder from getting shaken. Apparently Matthew's mother, Eleanor, also lived with his grandfather, acting as hostess. Matthew's brother, Jared, preferred to stay in the London house most of the year. There was also a litter of grandchildren left there by the old man's sister, Jocasta.

Jocasta's improvident son and daughter-in-law had both succumbed to the influenza. When word came of Jocasta's death, Eleanor had forced Sir Owen to bring the children to Gaites Hall, making it a matter of family pride. The Westons now called Sir Owen "Grandfather" for convenience' sake. Nathan wondered idly if Matthew's mother had anything to do with him being summoned there, as well.

As they turned in past the gatehouse, the curricle wheels bumped over a rut and Nathan was jostled against the seat. A gasp escaped him and Matthew reined in.

"Are you all right?" Matthew asked in some concern.

"That depends on how much farther it is."

"The house is not in sight yet. It's past the woods."

"I am sure you are an excellent driver, Matthew, and it is the condition of the road that leaves something to be desired. All the same, do you mind if I walk the rest of the way?''

''Of course not,'' Matthew laughed, helping him down. ''I will walk with you. Kerry,'' Matthew said to the groom who came off his perch to take the reins, ''take the team up and, if anyone asks, tell them we are looking at the home wood.''

Matthew pointed out different species of trees as they walked. Nathan nodded and even asked him to identify one or two he had not seen before.

''And what have we here?'' Nathan inquired, ''A wood nymph?''

''No, your youngest cousin, Boadicea.''

''Boadicea?'' Nathan turned to gape at Matthew.

''Don't blame me. I did not name her,'' Matthew said defensively. ''Dicea, over here.''

The girl in the white frock stood still, with a tree between her and the house. Her long dark hair was escaping from the blue ribbon that held it back, and her brown eyes wore a hunted look. Nathan thought she could not be more than nine or ten.

''Escaping from your governess again, I see,'' Matthew remarked as they approached her.

The child looked up at them imploringly. ''You won't tell on me, will you, Matt?''

''Of course not. Say hello to your cousin, Nathan.''

The child remembered to curtsy and tried to hide her rather grubby hands behind her. Nathan knelt, smiling, and took one of the hands to his lips. ''Your majesty. It is such a lovely day for an escape. I'm sure no one could blame you.''

''What did you call me?'' Her eyes grew wide with wonder.

''You have not given me leave to use your name,'' begged Nathan.

She withdrew her hand and said passionately, ''I hate my name!''

"Really!" Nathan pretended surprise. "Is it possible you do not know?"

"Know what?" she asked uncertainly.

"Boadicea is a very ancient name for one so young. Your namesake was one of the very first queens of this island we stand on. And she ruled alone. Have you never heard the story?" Nathan asked in mock surprise. Matthew found himself somewhat beguiled by Nathan's soft voice. The effect on Boadicea was magical.

"No," she whispered in awe. "Will you tell it to me?"

"Yes, of course. May I rise now, your majesty?

"Oh, yes, and you may call me Boadicea. It sounds almost pretty when you say it."

Nathan rose with a little effort. "You are hurt." The child looked all concern and took hold of his right hand as though to help him.

"Just a trifle. Please don't regard it. Besides, I'm sure I will be well again soon now that I am here." They walked off toward the house talking so naturally that one would think they had known each other all their lives.

Matthew was truly puzzled. He would not have thought a bachelor sailor would take much notice of children, let alone be able to charm such a strange one as Dicea.

"Queen Boadicea's story is a long one and I will have to save it for when we have more time. For now, why don't you tell me something of your wood."

"My wood?"

"Yes, I have the feeling you know it better than anyone else who lives hereabouts. Which are the best trees for climbing, for instance? That is what you were doing today, is it not?"

"Yes, over here. This is my favorite." She led him to a very old willow within sight of a stream and showed him the first few handholds.

"I will try it when I am able."

As Boadicea and Nathan discussed the rival merits of various trees from the standpoint of hand- and footholds,

Nathan reflected that the child was not much different from a child encountered in any of the lands he visited, except that, in this case, he did not have to learn her language. When he traveled inland he made friends with the children first, learning a few words and perhaps exchanging presents. Their curiosity drew them to him. And it seemed natural to him, since he had been little more than child himself when he began trading.

The children were able to open doors for him he would not otherwise have entered. Parents the world over were proud of their offspring and flattered by the attentions shown them. Even if he did not desire trade, Nathan attempted to make at least one contact wherever he landed.

By the time they were walking up the house steps, Boadicea and Nathan were on the road to being fast friends. Matthew walked behind listening to their chatter in some amusement.

"Dicea!" a harried-looking woman called from the side terrace. "Where have you been?" she asked as she came around to take charge of her pupil.

"Oh, Miss Prin, meet my cousin, Nathan."

"Forgive the child for imposing on you, sir."

"On the contrary, it is I who should beg your forgiveness for detaining her. She was showing me the home wood." Nathan took Miss Prin's hand in a warm clasp.

"You are too kind." She curtsied, then towed Dicea away.

"You do well enough with children and governesses," judged a grinning Matthew. "I wonder if you will charm the rest of the family so easily."

"What do you mean?" asked Nathan innocently. "Why should I wish to charm anyone?"

The door was flung open in their faces by a nervous old man. "Hello, Gregson." Matthew handed his hat to the butler and suddenly noticed Nathan was not wearing one. "Where is Grandfather?"

"In the billiards room pacing. He thought to see you with your curricle. He is not best pleased at being kept waiting."

"Thanks for the warning. May as well get it over with," Matthew said almost nervously.

"Billiards room?" Nathan queried as Gregson opened the door and Matthew thrust him ahead.

Nathan's first impression of his grandfather was that he looked remarkably healthy for someone reportedly on his deathbed. His upstanding eyebrows and gray hair, thinning at the temples, seemed to be bristling with their own wrath. When he threw up his head, his predatory nose and dark, flashing eyes gave him the look of a bird of prey. Nathan cast a suspicious glance in Matthew's direction. Matthew had the grace to look abashed.

"So, you have brought him at last. What's this nonsense about dallying in the home wood? I swear we have been kept waiting an hour or more. I'm Sir Owen, your grandfather." The bony hand that grasped Nathan's still had remarkable strength. "You don't look much like your father, or any other Gaites I ever saw."

Nathan scarcely knew how to reply to this so he confined himself to, "Really?" His grandfather's pronouncement had the effect of drawing everyone's eyes to Nathan's face. Nathan could not remember being so conspicuous since he had wandered into the exotic baths in Lisbon. The thin figure next to the old man looked the image of him with forty years shaved off. Matthew filled the embarrassed silence by introducing Jared, his brother. Jared was taller even than Matthew, so looking down his nose at Nathan was no trick, but Nathan suspected height had nothing to do with Jared's sneer of contempt.

"Are you sure you have not brought us a changeling, Matthew?" Jared asked, meticulously taking snuff. Jared's left eyebrow soared, lending emphasis to his expressed doubt.

"Well, he has not the Gaites nose, but neither have I really, or Jeremy," Matthew defended.

"Perhaps he looks like his mother," suggested a hard but unmistakably feminine voice. Nathan noticed for the first time that one of the figures standing about with a billiard stick was a tall, thin, humorless-looking girl in a dark green walking dress. He was thankful, for her sake, that she too had escaped the Gaites nose, but she had their dark hair and eyes, and a sharp, piercing look to match the old man's. Yet she was not ugly by any means. Nathan was just thinking that if she would only smile she might be quite pretty.

"This is Margaret Weston." Matthew did the honors and noted with interest that Nathan found Margaret's expression so forbidding he did not even attempt to shake her hand, but merely bowed. "And this is her brother, Jeremy." Jeremy also was dark and brown eyed, and aside from Matt, the only friendly face Nathan saw in the room.

"Matt says you have been at sea half of your life," Jeremy started, "I should like to—"

"Later, brat, later," the old man commanded, but not unkindly. "I have had Matt look up the papers, birth certificate and marriage license. You are a Gaites all legal and proper. Whether you can live up to the name remains to be seen." The old man handed his stick to Jeremy, apparently declaring an end to the game, and went to sit in a leather armchair near the empty fireplace. "Well, sit down," he commanded.

Nathan took a few moments to walk to the opposite chair and get his temper under control. It would not do to go cutting up at the old man even if he did seem to be in high health. Then he was struck by something his father had said years ago, how the old man liked a good quarrel better than a fine wine or a pretty woman. At that moment Nathan determined to give him no satisfaction, and when he sat down and looked across at his grandfather he smiled good-humoredly and said, "So good to see you in high force after your recent illness."

There was dead silence in the room except for Matthew nearly upsetting the wine decanter. He glanced at Nathan in mute appeal and nearly caused him to laugh out loud.

"Illness! I have not been ill . . . well, except for a bit of stomach trouble now and again. Don't you go thinking my number's nearly up. I have got a good few years left in me yet."

"Of that I have no doubt," Nathan said.

"Well, here we all are," Matthew said unnecessarily, handing both his grandfather and Nathan a glass and then going to sit on the edge of the billiard table as though they were going to have a cosy chat. Nathan had been raised to not seat himself while there was still a lady standing, so he kept glancing uncomfortably at Margaret who leaned on her billiard stick as casually as any man and returned stare for stare.

"Perhaps Miss Weston would like a seat," Nathan suggested finally.

"I will stand, thank you," she bit back with so much rancor that Nathan wondered what he could possibly have done to anger her so. Sir Owen glanced at her sharply and she cast her eyes down.

Margaret realized that the tumult of emotions at war in her was bound to spring out like that at an innocent bystander. If only they had not all just been teasing her about marrying this stranger she might not have bitten his nose off. Bad enough that her grandfather had proposed the match to her, but to do so in the presence of the sneering Jared and her giggling younger brother made it seem more like the sale of a horse than anything else. She scrutinized Nathan under lowered lashes. He was not ugly but wore the uncomfortable aspect of a little boy who had been dragged in from play, scrubbed up and tricked out in a new suit for company.

Margaret would have been startled to know how much her own impression matched the way Nathan felt at that moment. He was used to loose and comfortable clothes and had never worn a neck cloth capable of strangling him before.

"What sort of vessels have you served on?" Jared asked as though it were the first question on an inquisitor's list.

"Trading ships, mostly to the East Indies, or to British Guiana."

"Went to sea at thirteen," the old man grumbled. "I don't believe it."

"Actually, I stowed away that first cruise. When they found me, it was a toss-up between throwing me overboard, or making me cook's helper."

"I thought you were going to say cabin boy," Margaret put in boldly without drawing a reproof from her great-uncle.

"Oh, no, I didn't advance to cabin boy until next voyage," Nathan said blithely, and smiled at Margaret engagingly. This seemed to put her even more out of temper, the fact that he was not stupid and could give as good as he got.

"Well, Matt, you took your time about it, but you did get him here," the old man acknowledged. "The chestnut colt is yours."

Matthew blushed and cleared his throat. He glanced at Nathan and read a look that warned of future vengeance of a hideous sort. Nathan could not really be angry at him. There was no question about Matthew's heritage. It seemed the whole family was rude and unscrupulous. No doubt it had to do with their upbringing.

"Enough talk for now," the old man announced abruptly. "It wants but half an hour to dinner. We have barely enough time to change, thanks to you two. Gregson will show you to your room."

The note of dismissal was emphasized by his grandfather rising and giving the bell rope a vicious tug. Gregson popped through the door immediately as though he had been waiting in the hall. Nathan followed him obediently, but jerked his head at Matthew who went with him out of the room.

"Well, he doesn't look so ill," Sir Owen observed with the door barely closed behind Matthew. "He could be taller, mind you, but we may make something of him yet."

"No, Grandfather." Jared shook his head sadly. "You may be able to keep him here on a leash like a country squire—I can't bring myself to use the word *gentleman*—but you'll never be able to pass him off in London, I'm afraid."

Sir Owen had never aspired to the height of fashion Jared kept up, even in his younger days, so Jared's pronouncements on such matters did not weigh that heavily with him.

"At least, he dresses well enough, which is more than I can say for our young coxcomb here." Jeremy only grinned at his grandfather's condemnation.

"I'm afraid I perceive the style of Matthew in Nathan's dress, and I would bet my grays that Matthew tied that neck cloth for him."

"I will find out," said Jeremy mischievously, and slipped from the room.

"Well, we are stuck with him so we may as well make the best of him."

Jared was too sensible to show his disapproval of this idea to his grandfather, but he felt confident that, even with no interference from him, Nathan's obvious ineligibility would soon be apparent to all.

They both left the room and Margaret sank forlornly into a chair, still clutching the pool stick. She was used to being talked about as though she were a piece of furniture. She had to be blunt and forthright to get the attention of her rude relatives and to let then know how thick-skinned she was, but it cost her. She took a few shuddering breaths, threw the stick across the room and rose, but she did not cry.

"We have put you in Mr. Talbot's room, sir, that was lately occupied by Mr. Jared," Gregson explained as he threw open the door to a huge, chilly apartment on the east side of the house where a nervous-looking footman was unpacking Nathan's new clothes. Nathan was scarcely listening, since he was trying to convey to Matthew that he wanted an immediate conference.

"Have to go change," said Matthew. "We'll talk later. Gregson will tell you where the drawing room is." Nathan had grabbed Matthew's shoulder with his right hand, but Matthew skilfully wrenched himself free and slipped into the next door down the hall.

"Being as you have not brought your valet with you, I have assigned Fields to do for you. If there is anything you need, you have only to ring." Gregson bowed himself out.

"Well, Fields, have you got a first name?" Nathan asked as the young man assisted him out of his coat and boots.

"Tim, sir, but you had better call me Fields."

"Oh, right, I was forgetting. Well, I am called Nathan."

Fields managed to get his disabled employer through the washing up and dressing without discomfort to his injuries. He even fashioned a fresh sling from a neck cloth.

"Do you think you can tie this thing for me?" Nathan begged.

Fields achieved a simple cravat for his temporary master and remarked how difficult it would be one-handed.

"For me, impossible even with two. You must know, I'm just a seaman."

"Uh, yes, sir." Fields was unused to any Gaites addressing him as an equal.

"Well, I suppose if you are to be my valet you will need a raise."

"Sir?"

"If you want the job, that is, and mind I don't know how long it will last. Shall we say two shillings less than the old man's valet, whatever that may be. I'm sure you can discover it."

"The 'old man,' sir?"

"Sorry, my grandfather, I mean. All I need is to make that slip."

Fields grinned in spite of himself. "Really, sir, there's no need . . ."

"I insist."

"If you think I will give satisfaction..."

"The question is, can you put up with me? You won't always have to baby me, of course, and I don't imagine myself demanding. I'm not a fop, like Jared."

"No, sir." Fields allowed himself another smile.

In spite of Fields's best efforts to turn Nathan out early, the encumbrance of a taped shoulder and bandaged hand required more time for everything. Fields managed to ease both Nathan's arms into his coat, and although it was tighter than Nathan liked from the standpoint of being able to breathe, it did help hold the pieces of his shoulder together.

Matthew opened the door and poked his head in on his way downstairs. He nodded approval at Fields's efforts. Nathan exited, looking forlornly back at his valet as though he would by far prefer to spend the evening in his company. Fields was already experiencing a lively sympathy for his new employer and vowed that he would never be the reason for young Mr. Nathan falling into disgrace.

"What do you think of Grandfather?" Matthew inquired on the way downstairs.

"Pretty crusty," was Nathan's verdict. "I would not want to serve under him."

Matthew laughed and once again pushed Nathan into the room before him where, this time, he encountered the previous stares plus two more. Matthew introduced his mother, Eleanor, a formidable woman, tall and stately with a dignified graying at the temples of her dark brown hair. Her dark eyes measured Nathan speculatively, but he could not fathom what she was thinking. He tried the effect of kissing her hand and she actually thawed enough to smile at him. So too did Cristine, Margaret's sister, but shyly, and her curtsy was obviously taught her by the same Miss Prin who had been working on Boadicea. Her eyes were soft and doelike but did not hold his attention, at least not with the fulminating stare of her sister upon him.

Since he had already encountered Margaret, he wondered if he should greet her the same. Usually nothing was better for thawing women out. He did venture to take her hand, at least, and murmured, "Margaret," a gaffe, he supposed, since she snatched it away again immediately. He was rescued by Matthew, who did not seem surprised at Margaret's treatment of him. Matthew indicated a chair for him, but his grandfather was already rising.

"No time to talk now. We will go in." His grandfather led the way into the adjoining dining room, a dark and awesome place of red velvet drape and highly polished mahogany. Before Nathan knew what was happening, Jared had taken his mother's arm to escort her, and Matthew had hold of Cristine. He was left standing in the middle of the room with Margaret and a giggling Jeremy. Nathan approached the girl warily, almost fearing she would reject him, but she merely cast him a withering glance before laying her left arm stiffly along his right and accompanying him into the room.

There were two empty chairs to Sir Owen's right and Margaret stopped at the second, which Nathan slid out for her. She pulled it up to the table herself and Nathan sat down clumsily next to the old man.

Nathan caught Eleanor casting a speaking glance at Margaret, who immediately dropped her eyes to her plate. She was being admonished for her rudeness to him and Nathan felt instantly sorry for her. There was something going on with the girl. He could tell by the way her breasts rose and fell in the confines of her dark evening dress, as though she would burst into tears at the next word. Instead she bit her lip, put her chin up, swallowed, and managed to eat her food better than he did.

The strain of the meal was not alleviated by Nathan's rejection of so many of the dishes, either on the score of them being too difficult to eat one-handed, or because they were covered in cream sauces, which he knew better than to try. He had no tolerance for any type of milk, cream or butter, although he could eat some cheeses without getting deathly ill.

"You have a French chef, I see," Nathan observed, more as a mental note to himself than as an attempt at conversation.

His Aunt Eleanor stared at him as though she had been slapped. *Lord!* he thought, *a new enemy every time I open my mouth. No need to ask who insisted on a French chef in the West Country.*

Nathan's dinner consisted of soup, what few vegetables were served plain or vinaigrette, and a piece of chicken breast he managed to cut with his fork. He tried to fill up on several apples but let the nut dish pass by. The desserts all looked fatal to him.

With each refusal, his grandfather became more and more incensed. Nathan was actually beginning to feel the heat emanating from his left. Turning his head to the right brought him into the contemptuous gaze of Margaret. Sweeping his eyes around the table, he did not encounter one friendly look. Even Matthew thought he was being purposefully difficult. But short of asking the footman to cut his meat for him, which he was sure would draw fire from the old man, he could not see that he could have helped matters any.

"God's death! Have you had your ear pierced?" His grandfather raised his quizzing glass and scrutinized the side of Nathan's head in a most embarrassing way. Suddenly the absurdity of the situation struck Nathan, and he laughed in spite of being tired, hungry and possibly a bit feverish from the drive.

"Why, yes. It's a sort of ceremony," he explained. They all looked blank.

"When you cross the line," he added.

"I agree that it crosses the line of good behavior," his grandfather fumed.

"I meant the equator."

Nathan's explanation was frostily received.

"Surely you don't actually wear an earring," Jared sneered. "Such things went out decades ago."

An idea had sprung into Nathan's fertile mind. "Oh, no," he said jovially, smiling in his most piratical way, "not when on land."

Margaret choked on a bit of cream cake and turned a startled and somewhat suspicious look on him. Nathan began to see a chink in the iron maiden's armor. If she was really shielding a sense of humor under there somewhere, it would require investigation.

Conversation was not aided by the exit of the ladies. Nathan refused snuff but accepted the port, one glass only. He was not sure of its effect on his half-empty stomach. He was in a brown study trying to plot an escape when he became aware of being addressed and started guiltily.

"I said," his grandfather raised his voice as though addressing someone deaf, "I would have thought someone who survived ship fare would not be so nice about what he eats."

"Sorry, but I cannot eat milk or butter, and most of the dishes tonight were pretty well swimming in it."

His grandfather stared as though his son Robert had spawned some strange religious fanatic.

"I don't know what it is, they just make me sick," Nathan offered by way of further explanation.

"I never heard of such a thing," the old man grumbled.

"I have," piped up Jeremy helpfully. "Joan Marshall's baby nearly died of it...until they got a goat." Jeremy seemed not to mind the disapproving stares he drew. "Are we going to get a goat, Grandfather?"

"No, we are not."

Nathan would not have guessed that Jeremy could be more than sixteen or seventeen, but he took his turn at the port with the rest of them, and perhaps that was why he seemed a little giddy now.

"Shall we go in to the ladies?" The old man rose without waiting for a reply, and Nathan heaved a sigh of relief.

If he thought the evening was drawing to a merciful close, Nathan was mistaken. It appeared he was to endure a piano recital before getting any rest. Cristine made it through her piece, but just barely, and Nathan hated to think shyness of him was the cause of her uncertainty, for he knew she would pay for her mistakes later from the way Eleanor was staring at her.

Margaret played a not-very-feminine work, a march almost. He really enjoyed it. In keeping with her character, she played fiercely. If any other girl had tried it the thing would not have worked, but she almost seemed able to speak of her frustrations, her courage, her indomitable spirit through the keys of the piano. All this he felt without even knowing her. He wished he had been attending better when Matthew had told him about her.

She got up with a challenging look, but the old man just nodded dismissal of her. Nathan could not make out what was going on between them. It was almost as though she were being constrained to perform.

Aunt Eleanor did not wait, but remarked on the mistakes of each performer within earshot of everyone. Cristine blushed, but Margaret merely looked at her as resentfully as she looked at everyone else. Matthew started a conversation with the men about crops and livestock, Nathan thought, to cover Cristine's embarrassment. Not part of either group, Nathan merely looked from one to the other until Gregson entered mercifully with the tea tray.

Eleanor poured and called their names as through they had assigned cups. Jeremy served his grandfather first. To Nathan's surprise, he was served next, he supposed, because he was a guest. To Eleanor's "Cream and sugar?" Nathan replied, "Just plain, thank you." Even this brought him a severe look.

"I would have thought, after so many years at sea, you would wish to enjoy the elegances of life, Nathan, not sneer at them."

Nathan was busy trying to manage a cup and saucer one-handed with no table by him. Finally he turned his left hand palm up to hold the saucer and winced as the bones twisted. The challenge seemed to require an answer. "Well, after all these years, I pretty well can't tolerate milk or cream."

He had meant all his years at sea, but could tell from Eleanor's slight gasp and look of shock that she must be thinking he had suffered a very deprived childhood. The idea that had germinated at the dining table suddenly came into full flower in his mind. If they thought he was offensive now, just wait till they found out how really impossible he could be. A month—he would give them a week before they sent him packing.

"Yes, I daresay many of the things you eat every day of the week would nearly kill me," he said rather sadly.

"Indeed," Eleanor said so softly that he almost relented out of compassion for her. She must be thinking of the family's abandonment of him and his mother, and what she assumed to be their years of privation. Cristine looked almost tearful and the men all rather uncomfortable, except his grandfather, who was staring at him under menacing brows. Only Margaret was unmoved. He felt her glittering look on him and dared not face her for fear it would penetrate his charade. As soon as he had downed his tea he carried the cup and saucer back to Eleanor and said he thought he would turn in, since he had had a long day. He could almost feel the stares on his back as he left the room. He imagined they would appreciate a chance to discuss him in private.

He entered his room tugging unsuccessfully at his cravat. "What a night! Fields, help me off with this thing. It's choking me." Fields obliged him and also eased him out of his coat. "I think I can manage the rest. What a crew! And close as a bunch of oysters where I'm concerned. They can't possibly want me here. Have you any idea why I have been sent for?"

Questioned point-blank on an item he had no business discussing, Fields hesitated, but his liking for Nathan overcame his normal reserve. "As I make it out, sir, they have no choice but to accept you, or won't when Sir Gaites dies."

"What do you mean? Why should they even bother about me?" Nathan sat on the bed and leaned thankfully back against the bank of pillows.

"Don't you know, sir? The estate, at least Gaites Hall, passes to the next male heir." Since this brought only a puzzled look from Nathan, Fields added, "That is you, sir."

"Me?" Nathan sat up with a jerk that made him wince. "An entail?—damn. So it makes no odds how I treat the old man. He has no choice but to leave me with this moldering pile." Nathan cast his eyes resentfully around the room with its faded hangings and gloomy Jacobean furnishings.

"The next in line is Mr. Jared, then Mr. Matthew. There's really no way out of it for them."

"Unless Jared murders me in my sleep, which I don't doubt he would like to do, or they manage to poison me to death. That puts me in mind of what I wanted to ask you." Nathan stood with an effort. "Do you think you could find me something to eat, plain fare, I mean—cold meat and bread and a bit of ale? That swill they served up tonight, all laced with cream and butter, would have killed me."

Fields chuckled and said, "I will see what I can find, sir," and left Nathan to ponder his fate.

When Matthew thumped on Nathan's door a few minutes later, he responded to Nathan's simple, "Come," as though it were an order, and found his cousin perched on the windowsill in his shirtsleeves. The night air flowing in the open window seemed chill to Matthew but did not seem to bother Nathan.

"I wanted to explain . . ." Matthew started.

"Livestock!" Nathan said, turning to face Matthew. "Much better than taking cold cash for such a job."

Matthew sighed and seated himself on the edge of the bed. "I wish he had not said anything. I could see it set your back up."

"Why should it? It certainly was not the worst insult I suffered tonight."

"You do not understand," Matthew entreated. "The chestnut is not just any horse. It's the best Grandfather ever bred here. And he would not sell it for money, not even to me."

Nathan's soft laugh came across to him with the night breeze. Nathan stood up, shaking his head, and pushed the window closed.

"You are not angry?"

"No. Your price was pretty high after all. I suppose I just don't understand about horses, I mean how you value them."

"You may not believe this," Matthew said, standing up, "but I would have searched for you even if Grandfather had not offered the horse."

"I believe," said Nathan, "that there is very little you would not do to put Jared's nose out of joint."

"Whew, you don't miss much." Matthew began to pace the length of the room. "It's true, there's no love lost between us. I do all the work around here, and he does nothing but run into debt and have to be rescued by Grandfather. He's twenty-eight. He should be past such pranks by now. Once I had met you, I decided I would much rather have you inherit than Jared. At least you would not run the place into the ground."

"In fact I might even leave you in charge, since I have other interests," Nathan guessed.

"Is that an offer?" Matthew asked hopefully.

"Yes." Nathan laughed. "You may consider it a firm offer, if it's true that I inherit Gaites Hall and," he added as a rider, "nobody murders me in my bed."

"They don't like you much, and that's a fact. But it looked to me like you were deliberately trying to provoke them, refusing almost all the dishes, and reminding them all the time of your background.''

"Have you ever tried to manage a knife and fork one-handed?'' Nathan leaned his good shoulder against the wall and massaged his still-numb left fingers with his right hand.

"Oh, I had not thought of that.''

"Besides, when everyone in the room was prepared to expect the worst of me, whatever I said would have been taken amiss. I am just sorry I agreed to come for an entire month.''

"About that,'' Matthew drawled, looking at his boots. "Grandfather actually expects you to make your home here.''

Nathan jerked upright. "Ouch! No, Matthew—sorry, but no, even if it costs you your precious horse. As it is I shall be skin and bones in a week. You had better tell him the truth. I'm not staying.''

"I will tell him, but he won't like it, and it is important that you try to please him.''

"Whatever for?'' Nathan asked tiredly.

"It is not yet certain how things will be left. You get the house and the surrounding acres, not much more than what the stables and the home wood stand on. The rest of the lands, what the rents come from, he can leave as he chooses, plus what's in the funds. It's no good having Gaites Hall if you cannot maintain it.''

"Matthew, even I could maintain it better than this,'' Nathan said, shaking the dust from the bed hangings.

"Well, at least, promise you won't go out of your way to insult him.''

Nathan seemed to be considering Matthew's plea, but he was actually still plotting his escape.

"If he were your captain, you would respect his orders,'' Matthew said hopefully.

"If he were a ship's captain, I would never sign on. He's such a cross old bugger he would take the vessel to the bottom out of pure spite.''

Just then Fields entered with a tray laden with cold beef and potatoes, bread, cheese and a wedge of meat pie. "Ah, provisions. Join me, Matt," Nathan invited. "All that rich food is bad for you."

"No, thanks, I'm for bed."

Matthew did return a moment later, but only to bring Nathan a decanter of brandy to complete his feast.

Nathan sent Fields off and took his time over the servants' leftovers. He finished his repast with an extra glass of brandy to assure himself that his aching shoulder and hand would not keep him awake. He washed up, stripped off his clothes, leaving them, for once, strewn all over, and slid on the expensive nightgown Matthew had picked out for him. For someone who often had to sleep in his clothes in a hammock, the feather bed was sheer luxury. He did not like much about Gaites Hall, but he could get used to being waited on. He was just planning on how he could take Fields with him when he drifted off to sleep.

Nathan was not normally a sound sleeper since he had for years been used to being awakened to stand a watch. So when he heard the bed creak he thought someone must have come to arouse him for this purpose. He was startled to see by the faint moonlight coming in the window a woman slip off her nightdress and crawl under the covers with him. It suddenly occurred to Nathan he had not the foggiest notion who she was or even where he was, and he was generally very careful about such things. Then the previous evening slid into place in his memory. "Oh, my God!"

Nathan recoiled with such violence from the girl that he slid off the high four-poster and fell over the table with all the crockery on it. The resulting crash in the silent house would have been enough to bring everyone running, without the girl letting out a scream, as well. Nathan had banged his knee and was still sitting on the floor nursing it when his grandfather came in holding a candle and demanding, "What the devil's going on here?"

Nathan looked up helplessly at Sir Owen in the uncertain
light. The girl's cries had died to a whimper under Sir Ow-
en's baleful stare by the time Jared and Jeremy, still dressed,
and finally Matthew, in his nightclothes, entered the room.
There were four faces looking from the blushing girl holding the covers up to her chin to Nathan, who saw no possibility of getting to his feet and looked sheepishly back at
them from his position on the floor. "What—? What—?"
his grandfather sputtered as he took in the enormity of the
scene.

"I think that's obvious," stated Jared coldly. "He's se-
duced the kitchen maid." Jared looked menacingly at the
girl, who cowered even lower behind the covers. Jeremy
started to giggle. Nathan opened his mouth to protest, but
the evidence against him was so damning that he could tell
even Matthew leaped to the obvious conclusion. Then Nathan remembered that Gregson had said this room was lately
occupied by Jared. He looked at Jared speculatively. Quite
a gambler was Jared, to bluff his way out of this?

Suddenly and for no good reason, Nathan found himself
admiring Jared, fighting in the last ditch as it were. Some
devil in Nathan made him ask, "Well, who do you sleep
with until you are married?"

His grandfather fumed and turned an alarming shade of
red. "How dare you! No one in this house!" Matthew's eyes
grew round, and Jeremy so hopelessly succumbed to his
laughter that he had to lean against the wall to catch his
breath.

"Get to your room, girl. I will deal with you in the
morning." Even Nathan did not see how the poor woman
could obey him, but Matthew, coming out of his trance,
whipped a coverlet off the bed and held it up, averting his
eyes, while the girl drew it about her. He very courteously
handed her the nightdress that was lying on the floor and she
slipped out the open door. Nathan was still lost in admira-
tion of the grace with which this was accomplished when the
old man said, "As for you, sir, even making allowance for

your upbringing, this is outrageous. What if your aunt should come to hear of it?''

''Perhaps I had better leave in the morning, sir,'' Nathan said with feigned disappointment.

Sir Owen breathed heavily several times and seemed to master his impulse to throw Nathan out. ''If you have such overwhelming needs, you take yourself off to the Half Keg in the village. Ask for Rosalind. She will take care of you.''

Nathan stared, as did Matthew and even Jared. Jeremy lost the battle to recover himself and sank to the floor in helpless mirth. Nathan had never expected his impertinent question to be answered, and in such a way. He found himself liking the old man for his frankness, but could not resist adding, ''I see. You have an account?''

''You can call it that if you like.'' The old man turned to Jared and commanded, ''Get Jeremy to bed. You have let him get drunk. And as for you,'' he stabbed the now-grinning Matthew with a bony finger, ''I'm making you responsible for Nathan's conduct. I rely on you to tell him how to go on. Is that understood?''

''Yes, sir.'' Matthew came to attention and took the candle his grandfather thrust at him as the other three exited. He closed the door on them and turned back, laughing, to Nathan. ''You don't suppose he still goes there, do you?''

Nathan was by then sitting on the bed and shook his head. ''I was not about to ask him that, as well. What a family. I thought surely this would be enough to get me cut loose from here. Just what do I have to do in order to disgrace myself?''

''You planned this?''

''Don't be stupid, Matt. She thought she was crawling into bed with Jared.'' Nathan slid under the covers again and arranged a pillow under his hand, which was aching in good earnest now.

''That's right. He's used this room since January. But why didn't you speak up? You wanted Grandfather to throw you out!''

"That thought did cross my mind, but also...well, I thought it would go easier on the old man thinking I would do such a thing than to find out Jared was capable of it."

"That Jared has the devil's own luck. I promise you he won't thank you for the favor."

"I don't imagine he will, especially if the old man turns the girl off."

"Oh, I don't think he'll do that. I would think he would want to keep it as quiet as possible."

Sir Owen's wishes notwithstanding, the servants, at least, knew all about the goings-on, if Nathan was any judge. Fields could barely keep a straight face as he helped Nathan dress.

"All right, out with it. What are they saying about me belowstairs?"

"Why only that it's a shame you got the blame for Mr. Jared's devilment. Mrs. Tomlin will keep Molly well in line from now on. She won't be bothering you again."

"Good God. I hope no harm comes to the girl."

"Less than she deserves, probably," was Fields's verdict.

"Fields, you are a valuable man. Come, what else can you tell me about the household?" Fields hesitated. "Margaret, for instance," Nathan continued, "why does she take me in such dislike?"

"I'm sure I can't say, sir. She was engaged to Mr. Talbot when he died, and she has been in a taking ever since."

"But he would have been twice her age."

"More, sir. Then we heard that she was to marry Mr. Jared, but nothing ever came of that."

"So she would have been Lady Gaites one way or the other, if not for me. That could account for it. I think it would suit her much better to run the house herself than to be under Eleanor's thumb."

"Very likely you are right, sir, especially since she was in charge of her grandmother's house, that was Sir Owen's sister, Jocasta."

"Why was Margaret in charge?"

"Jocasta Weston was a famous invalid who lived in Bath. After her mother and father died Miss Margaret was said to have run her grandmother, Jocasta's house. It sounded, by what I heard, to be a hard task, there not being much money."

"How old was she then?"

"Seventeen, I make it when her parents died, and nineteen when Mrs. Gaites went to Bath to get the Westons. Sir Owen would only take them in if she would put herself in charge of them. He said he knew naught of raising girls."

"Neither, I perceive, does my Aunt Eleanor. She's turned Margaret into a termagant, Cristine is too shy for her own good, and little Boadicea is the loneliest child imaginable."

"Perhaps you can put things to right, sir." Fields gave Nathan's sling a final adjustment.

"That would be meddling, Fields. Still," Nathan mused, "someone should do something. I can't hope that Matthew sees what's going on. All he cares about is farming and horses."

Judging by the frozen stare Nathan received from his aunt as he entered the breakfast parlor, the look of wide-eyed interest Cristine shot at him and the blush that touched Margaret's cheeks, the events of the previous night must have become common knowledge throughout the household. Nathan chuckled inwardly. At least Margaret was not scowling at him. She had an oval face, slanted eyes and eyebrows, and quite pretty lips. For his money, she was more taking than Cristine when she was not angry.

"Tea, Nathan?" Eleanor asked coldly.

"Is there any coffee?"

"We don't drink coffee here. Sir Owen says it is foul stuff and he will not have it in the house."

Not about to argue with her, Nathan merely said, "Tea is fine, then, just plain. Thank you."

Margaret wrinkled her nose at Nathan's preference for dry toast and plain tea, but among the scones and rolls served up for the ladies' Sunday breakfast, that was all that Nathan thought might be safe for him to eat. Matthew had told him no real food was ever to be had until eleven, but Nathan found he could not lie abed any longer than eight.

Margaret stole another look at Nathan. He did not seem at all discomposed about being caught out in a compromising position. She wondered if he did it purposely to offend them. She even wondered if he ate almost nothing to embarrass them, or if he just was not used to anything better. She had hoped that the incident with Molly would put Nathan beyond the pale and stop all this talk of her marrying him. Instead Eleanor had merely said that Margaret must work to improve his morals, although she did not elaborate on how a virgin lady should broach such a topic with a man of Nathan's obviously free and easy life-style.

When Margaret protested to this effect her grandfather had told her to get used to Nathan and make the best of him. This did nothing toward reconciling her to the match. She didn't care that Nathan was rather handsome, in a common sort of way, with his brown skin and flashing eyes, or that he smiled at her even when she scowled at him. She felt trapped and frowned at the food on her plate and at Nathan picking at his toast and making crumbs all over the cloth.

Nathan noticed her regard and smiled sympathetically at her as though they were both prisoners. That dazzling smile, so easy for him, startled her and she glared resentfully back.

Eleanor noticed the byplay and interrupted ruthlessly. "Do you go to church, Nathan?"

Nathan swallowed. "Why, yes, I planned on it." At her raised eyebrows, he could not resist the urge to bait her. "You seem surprised."

"Certainly not," Eleanor said with dignity, "I'm quite sure no one needs it more." Margaret choked on a laugh and pretended it was a crumb. Nathan cast his eyes down at his plate, managing not to smile, and vowed to get to know Margaret better. Cristine blushed, either for his behavior, or his aunt's.

"I was surprised to see you up so early…after last night."

Nathan wondered what Eleanor wanted from him, an admission of guilt? He would have thought she would not even acknowledge the event. He began to be a little afraid of her tongue himself.

"I just got used to attending services, from when we were at sea," he hedged. "We were, what you might call, a captive audience."

"I see," Eleanor said acidly.

Nathan pretended to look downcast and asked with some foreboding, "Do you drive to church, or walk?"

"We walk when the weather permits." Eleanor rose, pulled on what looked to be an inadequate shawl and led the way out into the hall.

"Oh, good, may I walk with you then?" He waited for Cristine and Margaret to precede him.

"If you are determined to go, you may accompany us."

Boadicea's governess whisked her down the stairs as the party prepared to depart, and the child confidently took Nathan's hand for the short walk to the village church. Cristine and Margaret stared at each other in amazement as the unlikely pair walked ahead of them down the lane chatting happily about trees and frogs, treasures and princesses.

"Dicea is not usually so outgoing," Margaret observed.

"I think perhaps Cousin Nathan is still a little innocent," Cristine ventured.

"Innocent!" Eleanor whispered fiercely, "after last night—ignorant more like."

"Quiet, he will hear you," Margaret warned, though why she would care she did not understand.

"I'm sure he just did not know it was wrong," Cristine said with some passion. "It is not his fault, the way he was raised." Being so unlooked for, this plea on Nathan's be-half was actually heeded by Eleanor.

"I suppose," Eleanor conceded, "you may be right. Be-lieve me, if I had known of the boy's existence before Tal-bot's death, I would have had him brought to Gaites Hall and raised him here. I don't know what Owen was thinking of, keeping the boy a secret."

"He probably thought he would never have to worry about him," Margaret said.

"Yes, if you and Talbot had married and had a son, I bet Nathan would never have been sent for," Cristine guessed.

Margaret looked quellingly at her sister, who subsided into silence, but Eleanor tended to agree. "It's just like Owen to put off his duty, merely because it's inconve-nient."

Nathan more or less ignored this whispered conversation as Boadicea pointed out Talbot's stone in the churchyard and several other Gaites stones. "Your father does not have a stone here," she remarked.

"No, nor anywhere else," Nathan said softly. "He lies at the bottom of the sea."

Boadicea clutched his hand a little tighter and changed the subject. "When can you tell me my story?"

"What about today?" Nathan brightened. "What do you do on a Sunday afternoon?"

"After church, Miss Prin and I have lunch, then I study my Sunday lessons, then there's tea at three, and some-times I go for a drive with Cristine and Margaret."

"Does everyone take tea at three?" Nathan asked in contemplation of another dull meal.

"Oh, no, only Miss Prin and me, because she says I can-not be expected to wait the whole way till six for dinner. Of course I get no tea at nine."

"Believe me, you are not missing much. But don't you ever actually eat with the rest of the family?" Nathan fi-nally asked.

"No, not until I'm civilized, Cousin Eleanor says."

Nathan shook his head. "That's ridiculous." Boadicea stole a fearful glance at Eleanor to see if she had heard.

"It's all right, Nathan," Boadicea whispered. "The cakes are fresh at three. Mrs. Tomlin makes them especially for me."

"In that case, your majesty, may I come to tea at three today?" Nathan executed a gallant bow.

"I should be delighted, Sir Nathan."

"What, a knighthood already? And I have not even slain any dragons for you yet."

"Would you two get in here?" Eleanor spoke from the door of the church as to a couple of dawdling children. "You are late."

Boadicea raced Nathan to the doorway, where they both slowed to a circumspect walk. To Eleanor's relief, Nathan appeared to pay attention during the service and, except for staring at the ceiling once or twice, did nothing to embarrass them.

She would have been distressed to learn that his thoughts were very far from holy matters. He had never known many women, either sexually or socially, but it did occur to him that, even in the dark, Molly should have been able to tell the difference between himself and Jared, especially if she had been Jared's lover for some time. Perhaps she came with the room, Nathan thought bitterly. Jared had been the heir apparent. Now Nathan had assumed that position. Had Molly decided to give herself up to him without so much as an encouraging look on his part?

Nathan had not often sought relief in such quarters. His physical need had to be overwhelming before he would buy such an encounter, for it left him feeling empty and desolate. And there was a real danger of disease even in the best houses. Except for his mother he had encountered only two kinds of women, those who were cheap and those who were expensive. What it cost him never made him feel any better about the experience. He supposed that there were women who did not sell themselves, but he had never bothered to think much about them.

Now he was living under the same roof with three of them. He could take the lashings of his aunt's sharp tongue. Cristine was an innocent, full of compassion for even one as undeserving as himself. Margaret was something else. That she held him in contempt was obvious, but was it just himself or all men? Why she intrigued him more than Cristine he could not say.

When they rose to sing he held the other half of a hymnal with Boadicea, but Margaret noticed that he never glanced at it. He seemed to know the words by heart. And his voice made even the vicar stare. He was a powerful tenor, assured and unembarrassed to sing, like so few men. He had definitely practiced somewhere. After the service, Nathan hung back to talk to Vicar Denning on the doorstep while Eleanor and the girls went out to chat with friends.

"You have sung in a choir somewhere. I am almost sure of it."

"The Cathedral when I'm in Bristol."

"We could use you here. We are a small congregation."

"I'm only supposed to be staying a month. Tell me, do you get as much rain here as we do in Bristol?"

"Why, yes, I suppose, but what…oh, the roof. Yes, I'm embarrassed to say you did see daylight through it. We simply get out the buckets. The repairs are beyond us, I'm afraid."

"It did not look to me like any of the beams were ruined yet. If you had a new roof now you would be all right and tight." Nathan turned his back to the crowd and slipped a stack of bills from his wallet. "This may not quite cover it if a scaffolding has to be built. Can you come by the workmen locally?"

"Why, yes, there are plenty of men about who could use the work, but are you quite sure? This is so much." The vicar was the next thing to being overwhelmed, but the money had been presented without embarrassment, as though Nathan did that sort of thing all the time.

"Oh, I'm pretty flush, right now. But I would appreciate it if you did not say where it came from. It might embarrass Sir Owen that he did not think of it first." The vicar raised an eyebrow at this but merely thanked Nathan in the warmest way.

"I wish I could help you with it," Nathan said as he backed up a little to look at the eaves, "but I'm not much good for anything right now."

"Go up there, you mean?"

"Why, yes. It's no higher than a ship, and I bet it does not sway about much."

"If I may ask, how did you come by your injuries?"

"We got caught in a storm a day before we made Bristol. Some rigging fell on me," Nathan said simply. "The shoulder's mending nicely, but I don't have much use of the hand yet. You know, I begin to wonder if Captain Hewitt did not ship me off to the country to keep me from crawling about the ship."

"I hope you shall get well quickly here with us. I was wondering if you would like to come to tea this afternoon."

Just then Boadicea came and confidently took Nathan's hand since their party was leaving. "I thank you, but I am engaged for tea already today. Dicea has invited me to the schoolroom."

The vicar chuckled. "You must not disappoint her then. How about Wednesday at three. You come, too, Boadicea. My wife bakes again on Wednesday."

"We would love to come, wouldn't we?" Nathan looked down at Boadicea. "I'm sure Eleanor will say it's all right." Boadicea nodded but looked a little scared at what Eleanor would say.

At lunch Eleanor interrupted Nathan's suspicious scrutiny of the omelet to ask what he and the vicar had been talking about for so long. Nathan thought for a moment and finally answered, "The weather."

Eleanor seemed satisfied, but his grandfather looked at Nathan menacingly. Nathan thought this might be because he had dared to go to church at all, but he turned to the old man with innocent pride and said, "I thought it was a safe topic."

Jared gave a snort of laughter, which brought the beetling gaze to bear upon him instead. He had already gotten a trimming for sitting down to the meal late, but nothing was said about the events of the previous night.

"Oh, I almost forgot." Nathan drew their attention away from the sulking Jared. "Dicea and I are invited to tea at the vicarage Wednesday. I already accepted for her, so I hope it's all right."

Sir Owen heard Nathan out and only commented that he was glad to see him mending his ways.

"Whyever would he ask you to tea?" Eleanor was startled into asking.

"Perhaps he wants to get to know me better." Nathan was not sure Eleanor would lose sleep over the invitation, but he thought it would not improve her digestion.

"Well, you shall have to be careful at the vicar's," Jeremy warned.

A dead silence ensued, broken at last by Jared's muttered, "That goes without saying."

Nathan turned toward Margaret to hide a smile from his grandfather, and surprised a genuine look of amusement on her face.

"No, not that." Jeremy laughed. "I mean about the food. I had tea there once. Mrs. Denning is an excellent baker but, as they have a good cow, she uses cream a lot."

"Thank you, Jeremy. I shall watch my step," Nathan replied ruefully.

"I still think we should get a milk goat for you."

"What is this about a goat?" Sir Owen demanded.

"You can drink goat's milk, can't you, Nathan?" Jeremy asked with enthusiasm.

"I have had it, but I do not like it overmuch."

"Do you think we should buy a goat?" Matthew asked seriously.

"No, I beg of you, not on my account." Nathan's reply was a disappointment to Jeremy, who had begun to enumerate the virtues of having a goat about.

"Oh, for God's sake, why don't we just hire him a wet nurse?" Jared remarked acidly.

"Ha—very good!" Nathan drawled before anyone could register shock.

Sir Owen glared at them both. Having Nathan appreciate the cut took away from Jared all the pleasure of saying it.

"I have had enough of you, Jared," Sir Owen growled. "You know better than to make a remark like that in front of the ladies." Eleanor was stiff with indignation, Cristine was blushing, and Margaret was trying to contain herself behind her napkin.

Normally only Sir Owen was safe from Jared's tongue. Jared especially enjoyed setting his grandfather against his brother, and Matthew invariably rose to the bait. But Nathan never took offense at these remarks. This time Nathan's quick riposte had turned Sir Owen's anger back on Jared and he was not used to being at outs with his grandfather. He began to wonder if Nathan was as stupid as he appeared.

A stolen moment with Molly had assured Jared that her visit to Nathan's bed rather than his own had been an accident. Jared could only guess that Nathan had not been smart enough to figure this out. Otherwise he would have apprised Sir Owen of the truth. Jared spent the rest of the meal in silence, plotting his revenge.

By the time lunch was over, a light mist was falling. Jared volunteered to play cards with his grandfather to begin the

process of placating him. Matthew and Jeremy towed the
reluctant Nathan off to the stables to introduce him to the
horses. These were mostly blood chestnuts out of Sir Ow-
en's old stud, Cinnamon. Ember was the fiery young colt
Matthew had earned for himself. Margaret's mare was
named Titian. Grandfather's current favorite was a lusty
Roman-nosed brute named Trafalgar. Nathan thought there
was a bit too much of the workhorse about the creature's
head but said nothing for fear of ridicule.

"I hope you ride, Nathan."

"I have ridden, but usually mules or horses not much
bigger than ponies, compared to these."

"You will have to get used to horses," Matthew warned
him.

"We brought a cargo of Andalusians over from Spain one
time. I don't think I slept the whole voyage for fear they
would kick a hole in the hull."

"You took care of them?" Jeremy asked.

"I was by way of being the expert since I had touched a
horse before."

Jeremy chuckled but volunteered, "I will teach you to
ride."

"First, who's going to teach you?" Matthew cuffed the
boy playfully.

Nathan kept his appointment in the schoolroom and was
accorded royal treatment. Mrs. Tomlin came through with
honey and jam for their rolls instead of butter, and the tea
was not bitter, being made a little weaker for Boadicea.

"Boadicea was an exceptional woman, even for a queen,"
Nathan began. "The Romans spelled her name Boudicca.
She fought with her husband when he accepted the Romans' permission to rule for them such that their kingdom
was conquered without a struggle. She warned that they
would all come to regret his weakness, and she was proven
right."

Dicea listened attentively and even Miss Prin, who had heard the story before, was irresistibly drawn into the tale. Nathan's phrasing was somewhat archaic and he spoke slowly with expression and there was something else about his voice. It was as though he were speaking to you over a great distance of time, out of the very heart of the past where he was a privileged observer of the events.

"When King Prasutagus came to die he left no male heir to the throne, neither did he attempt to appoint his queen. He felt nothing would lead to war more quickly than that. He left half his lands, cattle and goods to the distant emperor thinking to flatter the Romans into leniency. He left a quarter of the rest to each of his two daughters, and nothing for Boadicea. If he sought to leave her powerless he was mistaken, for her people had great regard for her sense, and were as angered as she over their king's subservience to the Romans. Better to be plundered and killed, they thought, than to submit willingly to slavery.

"The king's bequest had the opposite effect that he desired. The Romans took everything. All of the lords of that day were stripped of their possessions. Even lowly farmers were driven from their houses and lands to provide homes for Roman settlers. When Boadicea complained to the Roman procurator that he had overstepped his authority, which he had, Catus Decianius had her tied in front of her house and publicly whipped. Her daughters were given to the soldiers.

"That was all that was needed to raise the revolt. Queen Boadicea convinced the neighboring tribes to join them. They also were being treated like a conquered enemy. They captured the town of Camulodunum in two days and butchered the survivors. The hated Claudian temple was destroyed.

"Then they marched on London. The legions there deserted the town and it was destroyed by fire. The Roman inhabitants were slaughtered. So also with the Roman city Verulamin. The rebel tribes returned north to meet the massing Roman army under Paulinus. The Britons had the Romans vastly outnumbered and perhaps their overconfidence spelled their downfall. They even took their wives to the battle plain to watch the victory.

"The Romans were seasoned troops and experts in the art of warfare. The Britons, exhilarated over their victories, were not taking the battle seriously and Boadicea drove back and forth in a chariot with her daughters trying to impress on them the absolute necessity of winning. 'It is not as a woman descended from noble ancestry, but as one of the people, that I am avenging lost freedom,' she shouted. 'Roman lust has gone too far! In this battle you must conquer or die. This is a woman's resolve. As for men, they may live and be slaves.'

"Those that did hear her were whipped into a passion of vengeance, but she could not be everywhere. She saw the front rebel ranks fall to the expert javelin throwers of the Romans. Wedge-shaped phalanxes of Roman infantry and cavalry split her forces like spears piercing the body of an enemy. The Britons were thrown into disarray and killed. Those that tried to retreat were blocked by the wagons loaded with women. The Romans had no mercy even for these. The Romans reported eighty thousand Britons killed to their four thousand.

"Queen Boadicea would have stayed and died there if not for having her daughters with her. That night she made provision for their escape to the north and, after they had gone, she took her own life by poison, for she would not live as a slave either in Rome or in her homeland."

"What do you think of her story?" Nathan asked of the wide-eyed child.

"I think she did what she had to. It's so sad. There was no way out for her." Dicea stood up and went to the teapot.

"You have put your finger on the essence of tragedy," Nathan remarked. "She may have realized that they could not fight off the might of Rome forever, but she had to try."

Miss Prin was relieved that Dicea was not frightened by the gory tale and was less impressed by the martyrdom than the tragedy of it.

"What is this wonderful jam?" Nathan's normal voice broke the spell, and he accepted another cup of tea from Dicea, who was playing at serving today.

"Bramble berry. You can help us pick them this year. I forget when they are ripe. Miss Prin—?"

"We always looked for them the first of July."

"Oh, I'm afraid I won't be here then. I have only come to stay a month."

Boadicea's disappointment was palpable. Even Miss Prin was upset. "But I thought you had come to live here," the governess said.

"No, I have no such intention."

"Not even when . . . I mean, don't you plan to live here even when you inherit?"

Poor Miss Prin, thought Nathan, she had probably been looking forward to teaching his children after Boadicea was too old.

"I really cannot stay," Nathan pleaded. "Seriously, I don't think it would be good for the old man's health to have me always causing a stir."

"But where will you go?" Boadicea came and sat by his chair.

"Why back to sea, your majesty, on voyages of exploration, and to bring home treasures to lay at your feet," Nathan said grandly.

For once Dicea refused to be lured away into the world of make-believe, and caught at his hand. "I would rather have you here by me than all the riches in the world."

Nathan's smile slowly faded as he remembered the last time someone had said such a thing to him. "If anyone could keep me here," he whispered, "you could, my queen."

"Then you will stay?"

"I cannot promise. Perhaps Sir Owen won't want me to. The way things have been going, I'm surprised he has not thrown me out already."

Miss Prin blushed, but, since Nathan had no idea what version of the story she had heard, he changed the subject and asked Dicea if she could find Brazil on her globe.

"Where have you been?" Matthew asked as they went down to dinner together.

"A tea party." Nathan chuckled at Matt's puzzled look. "Dicea and Miss Prin invited me to take tea in the schoolroom this afternoon. I must say they fed me better than I am used to lately."

"Well, I think you will notice an improvement."

Nathan should have asked what Matthew meant ahead of time. Then he would not have been caught off guard when the footman cut his meat for him. He swallowed his pride and thanked the fellow, but he could see Sir Owen starting to fume, so it was another uneasy meal. He tried to say little so as not to draw any fire, and everyone pretty much ignored him. He longed to have two good hands again.

The only thing he had to look forward to was Margaret's playing, and his disappointment must have shown in his face when he learned it was to be a card evening. Apparently Sir Owen had trounced Jared and was still feeling lucky. Nathan denied any knowledge of cards and was left to sit watching the women sew.

"Does Dicea ever join you for tea?" he spoke out loud, longing for the child's animated conversation.

"She is just a child. The drawing room is no place for children."

"No, I suppose she would not have much fun here," he said, thinking how subdued the child became in Eleanor's presence.

Eleanor looked at him sharply. "Why don't you entertain us, Nathan? Tell us about some of your voyages."

"What would you like to hear about? I have been to Spain, Italy, the Indies, China, and South America."

"Oh, South America," Cristine said.

"The jungle was not at all what I expected it to be. I suppose I pictured a Garden of Eden, full of animals and colorful birds. But you cannot see any of that. You can scarcely see the sun, the trees are so high and so completely fill in the sky. The vines grow the size of trees and coil up their trunks like monstrous snakes."

"Didn't you see any animals?" Cristine asked eagerly.

"We scarcely even heard any. We could tell there were birds up on top of the canopy, but what we saw were only dark silhouettes. Some of them might have been monkeys. We saw lots of insects, huge ones, but you don't want to hear about those. The strangest part was the darkness of it. It was like walking into night as though it were a physical place, not a time. It is rather dangerous trying to set a course through the jungle. Trails grow over quickly and you are always making detours, so it's easy to get lost. The best you can hope for is that you will come either to a river you can follow, or rising ground so you can get above the treetops. Walking up a mountainside into the sun again feels like ascending from Hades."

Jeremy had been trying unsuccessfully to divide his attention between the game and what Nathan was saying. After being called to book for two errors, he was finally thrown out of the game and came over with Matthew to sit around the fireplace.

"It must have been very dull while you were at sea, with nothing to look at but the flat ocean." Margaret did not like Jeremy's fascination with Nathan's adventures and feared he would put ideas into her brother's head.

"The sea could never be boring. It's even a different color every day, since it takes on the color of the sky. And we had the clouds building mountains in the sky for us with new shapes hour by hour. Of course we had our storms to face, too.'' Nathan stopped then and his eyes clouded over with remembrance.

"Did you have any battles with pirates or natives?" Jeremy prompted.

"It would be a compliment to call those French privateers pirates." Nathan suddenly caught a menacing stare from Margaret and was in the midst of wondering what he had said to offend her when he was rescued by the arrival of the tea tray.

This time Eleanor startled Nathan and his grandfather by asking, "Coffee, Nathan?" Eleanor was looking quite pleased with herself.

"Yes, yes, thank you. Black, please." One gulp convinced Nathan that the beans must have been grown before he went to sea.

"How is it?" Eleanor asked.

"Very . . . strong."

"Nathan, may I come in a minute?" Matthew asked through the door after tapping on it.

"Yes, I am quite alone tonight."

Matthew entered, chuckling. "That is not what I was thinking. Did you send Fields down for more provisions? You looked like you got more to eat tonight."

"I had forgotten that. I'm surprised you didn't reach over and cut my food yourself. No, I sent Fields for something to dilute that coffee your mother gave me. Without some brandy or something I will not sleep all night. Was that your idea or hers?"

"Acquit me on that score. I knew nothing about it." Matthew lounged back on the bed, since Nathan occupied a chair pulled up to the window, where he braced his feet.

"You did not tell him yet . . . that I'm leaving?"

"Damn you, Nathan. How do you know what I am thinking? I have to pick the right time to break it to him. And with Jared around, it's hard to get a moment alone with him when he's not been stirred up against me."

"It didn't seem to me like Jared was much in his favor, either."

"Not lately. It almost seems like . . . almost like Grandfather is punishing him."

"Is he in debt?"

"Probably, but he's been in tick before. I think it has to do with Talbot. Last year Talbot convinced Grandfather to let him have a farm to manage for himself, Tenwells, just adjacent to this place. Talbot complained that the reason he drank and gambled so much was he had nothing of his own to occupy him. That's why Grandfather deeded Tenwells over to him, so he could rebuild it—with what I don't know. He said then he would marry Margaret and set up house there."

"But he never did."

"Never even asked her to marry him. He went off to London with Jared."

"Why?" Nathan was beginning to look interested.

"I have no idea, but Talbot and Grandfather had a terrible fight when he came back. It seems that Talbot had lost Tenwells in a card game to a Captain Vilard."

Nathan whistled. "Pretty stiff stakes."

"That set plays high. I'm sure Grandfather blames Jared for luring Talbot into bad company."

"Oh, really, now. Talbot was his uncle."

"And barely competent when he was sober, let alone drunk. Although I don't see why Jared would willfully do such a thing, hurt the family finances in that way. He may be a troublemaker, but what advantage would he gain from it?"

"Did Talbot stay home then?"

"Yes. In January he shot himself in the home wood."

Nathan grunted as his feet slid off the windowsill and hit the floor. "An accident?"

"Most likely. He was drunk as usual. There was some talk of suicide, but I don't believe it. Talbot had not the guts to do himself in."

"Surely the old man does not blame Jared for that."

"Who else has he got to blame? Quite a comedown for Jared. He was used to being Grandfather's favorite, especially when it looked like Talbot would never produce an heir."

"He does not seem to take much notice of his fall from grace."

"He's pretty cool on the surface, but I have a feeling the shoe is beginning to pinch. He has not had any money out of the old man since—oh, Lord—you have got me saying it."

"What?"

"Old man. If I get caught at that, I will not soon be forgiven."

"How did Margaret take all this?"

"She was as mad as fire. She would have liked to live at Tenwells, I think, even if she had to swallow Talbot to get it."

"I can readily believe that. If she was managing her grandmother's house when she was little more than a child herself, it must chafe her to be here under your mother's thumb."

"You mean Grandfather's."

"You may be ruled by your grandfather, but I have a feeling he follows Eleanor's directions when it comes to the girls."

"He does say he knows nothing about raising females."

"Your mother appears to know little about it, either."

"I suppose you will set her straight," Matthew concluded with a smile.

"I can, at least, tell her that they are, none of them, happy, especially Margaret. I wish there was more I could do."

"She may be all right when Grandfather dies. I think he plans to leave her the bulk of the estate that's negotiable."

"She looks to have sense enough to take care of her sisters and brother."

"I think Mother's idea was to lure Jared into marrying her—to keep it all in the family. Of course, that was before we knew about you."

In the short pause that followed, the gears of Nathan's mind slipped around to catch on Matthew's meaning. "Good God! Never tell me Margaret expects me to offer for her."

"I do not know what she has been given to expect, but Margaret is not stupid. She knows how things are left."

"And I suppose the old man is not too delicate to tell her to make herself pleasing to me. No wonder she's been looking like she wants to cut my liver out. What a position to put a young girl into!"

"She's not that young—twenty-six, I think. Besides, she should be used to it by now."

"Being manipulated?" Nathan asked. "Not her—not ever. Don't you know her better than that?"

"Frankly, I have always been a little put off by Margaret. She always seems so...unapproachable."

"I still think the best plan, when the time comes, is for you to live here and manage things. Margaret can reside where she chooses."

"It is not likely anyone else will offer for her."

"After the way she's been treated, I'm surprised she doesn't consign us all to the devil. If I had known all this in Bristol, I might have shabbed off and not come."

"I am sure of it."

Nathan decided to deprive himself of early tea the next morning so as not to run the danger of Eleanor's coffee again. Instead he had a hot bath and talked Fields into changing his bandages. Fields would have been ready to call the doctor to perform this service, but Nathan assured him he had tied everything up tightly enough. Nathan was actually feeling fairly comfortable when he wandered into the morning room to stumble upon Margaret at the desk, working over what looked a household inventory.

"Oh, there you are." He tried desperately to think of something to say to her, but her uninviting scowl would have put a braver man off. "I was just looking for you," he lied.

"Why?" Margaret asked with foreboding.

He nearly fell over a chair then when it occurred to him what she might be expecting. He looked down, caught sight of his broken hand in its sling and blurted out, "I was wondering if you could write a letter for me."

She said nothing but looked at him suspiciously.

"To Captain Hewitt in Bristol. He's a friend of mine," Nathan continued without encouragement. "He will want to know that I arrived safely."

"Who usually writes your letters?" she inquired acidly.

Nathan thought she meant since he had broken his hand. "Well, he does."

"I see your problem." She put her chin up and managed to look down on him while remaining seated. "But I would think Miss Prin could help you out as well as I could."

Nathan said nothing, just heaved a sigh of relief at the prospect of escape and was about to ease himself out of the room. Margaret thought she had embarrassed him and did not feel any satisfaction in the accomplishment. She suddenly realized that Nathan might be reluctant to let a future employee of his, especially a governess, know that he could not write. Some crumb of pity in her stopped him as he got to the door.

"Wait, I have some time this morning, and there is no point in having Dicea's lessons interrupted." Nathan turned hopefully at the change in her voice. It was the nicest thing she had said to him yet. He seated himself in a chair beside the desk as she drew a sheet of paper out, dipped her pen in the standish and looked at him expectantly. He thought, at that moment, with no emotions at war in her face, that she looked quite lovely.

"Well?" Even her neutral tone made him jump.

"Dear Sir..." He gulped and desperately began composing a letter that would, no doubt, surprise Captain

Hewitt. "We arrived safely enough on Saturday. This is the most amazing place. The woods and fields go on forever. I have not explored the tenth of it yet. And the house is enormous. I still lose myself in it. The food is rather strange to me. I don't know what I am eating half the time."

Nathan noted a self-satisfied little smile on Margaret's face. "Everyone here has been very kind to me, especially my cousin Margaret, who is a lovely girl..." Nathan stopped because the pen had quit scratching across the paper. "Am I going too fast for you?"

"I have not been kind to you and I am not lovely."

"But it's my letter. May it not contain my opinions?"

"I will not write that." She threw the pen down rebelliously.

"May I at least say you are comely?"

Margaret's lips twitched in spite of herself. "No. You are not allowed to say anything of me."

"Oh, very well—especially my cousin Margaret, whom I am not allowed to talk about."

This surprised a laugh from her. "I can't write that, either. What will he think of us? Besides, no one has been kind to you except Matt and Dicea."

Her voice had a lilt to it when she was not being surly, and he thought he would like to hear her sing. He shook himself and replied. "I know that. But I don't want him to think I have been thrown into a nest of vipers. Besides, it's a matter of comparison. Everyone here has been kinder than my first captain."

"Which is to say..." she prompted suspiciously.

"That I have not yet been beaten."

"That may come, too," she threatened, "if you do not stop being so provoking."

"Perhaps, we can say everyone has been kinder than I deserve," Nathan negotiated. "Yes, a great deal kinder than I deserve."

"That, at least, is true," remarked Margaret, thinking of his exploit with Molly. "Do you really want to send a letter?'' she asked him point-blank as though it just occurred to her he might be making game of her.

"Why, yes," he replied innocently. "What did you think?"

"Nothing." Margaret resumed her task and obediently took down his words without further editing.

"I have met the most delightful child here, Boadicea, by name. You would like her. She loves history as much as you do. The old—my grandfather reminds me of Captain Ainsley. I shall write more about the rest when I know them better. If you care about me at all you will send me a pound or two of that good Brazilian we just brought over. You would not believe what they drink here for coffee."

Margaret chuckled. "I thought you were not enjoying that much. Why did you drink it?"

"It's a poor guest who complains about the food."

"Refusing to eat it is complaint enough."

"Is that why you look so crossly at me all the time?" Nathan said it lightly enough, but it brought the mulish look back to her face. "I was only joking. But tell me what I have done to offend you."

"Nothing. Sign this and I will see that it is posted."

"He will know who it's from."

"Surely you can at least write your name," she said impatiently.

He got up with a heavy sigh so as not to anger her further and laboriously drew his name with his right hand. The process seemed to be more of a bother to him than an embarrassment but, by the time he was finished, Margaret was sorry she had insisted, for it put him close to her. Even though he smelled of fresh soap and water and did not try to physically touch her, she had to put down the impulse to recoil from his nearness.

If Nathan's experience of women was limited, it was no way as deprived as Margaret's knowledge of men. She had never had a season in London, never known any eligible man who had not a monetary motive for his interest in her.

It was not just Nathan who repelled her. Talbot's clumsy attempts to get near her she had found truly disgusting, and the only time Jared had stolen a kiss from her, years ago, she had slapped him so hard he had never touched her since except with his scathing remarks. Matthew, of course, was too terrified to approach her. She liked him the best of all the men she knew.

She had been willing to marry Talbot, in name only, if he agreed never to touch her. When he died it was almost a relief, for she placed no dependence on him living up to their agreement when he was in his cups. Then when she realized Eleanor expected her to marry Jared, she was terrified. He was so brutally unkind she could not imagine living with him even if there was no intimacy. She and Eleanor had fought for weeks about it and finally, when Eleanor offered Matthew in place of Jared, it had made Margaret sick. Cristine was in love with Matthew. That's when Grandfather had sprung news of Nathan on them. Margaret had scarcely ever been touched by a man, yet she felt used and worn-out. Of love she never considered the possibility.

Nathan had sensed her aversion and was careful to thank her and extricate himself without touching her. He was not used to being taken in dislike, not by women anyway. He began to wonder if his pride was a little hurt. He joined the others in the breakfast parlor for another dreary meal. Since it had begun what looked to be an all-day rain he could not even get away for a walk. He filled in the day watching the others play at billiards or cards.

"Don't you know any games?" Jeremy asked him.

"Sometimes we would play at dice—hazard—when we had any money."

"That is not a gentleman's game," his grandfather condemned.

"I thought not." Nathan looked mischievously at Matthew.

"Is that all?" Jeremy prompted.

"Well, sometimes, if things got a bit slow, a bunch of us would stand in a circle back to back and throw our daggers up in the air."

"And what?"

"And run, of course."

Matthew burst out laughing and so did Jeremy.

"God's death!" exclaimed his grandfather. "What next will you be teaching the boy?" Matthew was immediately ordered to take Nathan off somewhere and teach him the rudiments of whist and piquet, at least. These two escaped to the library where Matthew discovered Nathan could play if he chose.

"Why do you deliberately provoke him? I should think you would try to get on his good side."

"Has he one?" Nathan had to lay his hand facedown to pick out his discard.

"Not really, I suppose."

"Then it's hardly worth the effort."

"But he may tumble to the fact that you go out of your way to make him angry."

"Don't worry. They all think me far too stupid to be capable of such subtlety."

Matthew looked at him sharply for a moment then resumed play.

"About our talk the other night," began Matthew, "if you decide to stay, you may change your mind about me taking care of Gaites Hall. I won't hold you to our bargain."

"I'm no farmer. Nor am I likely to become one overnight. Gaites Hall will fare much better with someone who was raised here in charge."

"I can't but agree with you there," Matthew commented as he discarded.

"Best have a care the old man doesn't get wind of it though. He might not be best pleased to find us making such provisions with him still in his prime."

"True." Matthew chuckled.

"If you want something in writing, we can go to Bristol to have an agreement drawn up."

"No, your word is good enough for me."

At three o'clock Nathan took himself off to the school-room, where he was welcomed and possibly even expected. Nathan was prevailed upon for another recital during tea. He chose the legend of Merlin this time, which was not really history, but Miss Prin did not seem to mind that. When he said after half an hour that Boadicea must return to her lessons, Miss Prin seemed to look with special approval on him. He ventured to ask if he could stay and observe. He even helped Dicea a little with her numbers by turning the problems into stories so that she could see some point in learning her arithmetic.

As he lay on his bed later, watching Fields brush off his evening dress, he reflected that the high point of his day had been the time he spent with the child. He had always wondered what it would have been like to have a sister or brother. He now began to wonder if there was some point to getting married after all. If only one could be sure one's own children would be as charming as Dicea, it would certainly be worth it. To marry just to have children he would have thought absurd a few days ago. There should be more to it than that. You should feel something for your wife. He tried to imagine being married to Margaret and almost shuddered. Not even for the sake of ten children like Dicea.

What Sir Owen did get wind of through the efficient grapevine of Jared and Jeremy was Nathan's appellation for his grandfather. As Jared passed this tidbit on to his young cousin, he reflected that it was going to be easy to dislodge Nathan if he continued to make such blunders. Oh, Nathan would get Gaites Hall eventually, much good it might do him, but Jared intended to get the bulk of the estate. He had only to keep Margaret and Nathan apart to drive Mar-

garet out of Sir Owen's favor when she refused to marry
Nathan. That end of it looked to be taking care of itself.

"So you think I'm old?" Sir Owen thrust at Nathan as
they began the meal that evening.

"I'm sure I don't know how old you are," Nathan said in
some confusion, wondering why these arguments always
coincided with mealtime.

"You call me 'old man.'"

"Oh, that." Nathan looked surprised. "That was a pet
name my father had for you. I'm sure he meant no disre-
spect by it."

"And just what do you mean by it?"

"Why nothing," Nathan said innocently. "It was the only
thing I heard you called most of my life. It's a bit hard to
change now."

"And I suppose that is my fault?"

"What?" asked Nathan absently as he scrutinized a
platter of fish.

"That you were not raised here where you should have
been." Sir Owen seethed at Nathan's dullness as an opponent.

"I can't but be glad for it," Nathan answered after a
moment's thought, selecting a fillet for himself.

Matthew gave up trying to signal Nathan and moaned
audibly.

"What?" Sir Owen shouted menacingly.

"I have a life of my own which I would not have had
here," Nathan said proudly.

"A seaman? You call that a life? You know nothing of
estate management or any gentlemanly sport. You are rude
and belligerent. You seem determined to insult me—all of
us. Is that something to be proud of?" Sir Owen was standing by now.

"No," Nathan said quietly, looking up at his grandfather in mock defeat. Of all those present, only Jared smiled,
and Jeremy felt a particular pang at being the agent of Na-

than's downfall even though he had meant it in fun. "You are right. It would be better if I left."

"You cannot!" Sir Owen brought his fist down on the table, then subsided, smoldering, into his seat.

Nathan looked an amused challenge at Sir Owen. "Why not, sir?"

"Because you are my heir, and there's not a damn thing I can do about it."

"If I had known that before..."

"What? What would you have done?"

"I would not have come for one thing."

"Then it's good Matt did not tell you."

Nathan's look of surprise was genuine. "You told him not to tell me?" Nathan accused Sir Owen.

"I had a feeling you might be like your father." Sir Owen did not expound on this cryptic judgment and left Nathan to muse over it.

"What's to keep me here now?"

"Duty. One thing you must already know about. You will have Gaites Hall sooner or later. It's best you learn how to handle the responsibility now."

Nathan was so stunned by the truth of this that he made no reply.

"I have got you there, have I not?" Sir Owen crowed.

Nathan chuckled grudgingly. "I suppose you have. It looks like we are both trapped."

"And no good to be got from moaning about it. We may as well make the best of a bad job."

Sir Owen and Nathan went back to their dinner as did the rest of the family. But Jared scarcely ate another thing. To have Nathan acknowledged and actually accepted nearly choked him. How could things have twisted back on him so? If Matthew had been caught out like that, there would have been a terrible row. Jared could only conclude that Sir Owen was making extreme allowances for Nathan's ignorance, out of guilt at his neglect of him.

Tuesday's boredom was unalleviated by sunshine of any kind. Nathan was so desperate to escape the house he walked out in the light mist testing how well one of Matthew's expensive hats would protect him. He was perfectly comfortable half-wet, but was beginning to be conscience stricken about making work for Fields, when he heard an altercation by the lake.

There was a plank footbridge thrown up over the neck of the lake inlet so that walkers—and, Nathan supposed, even riders—could avoid the swampy woods at that end. It was from there that the cries were coming. When he recognized Dicea's voice in distress, Nathan began to run. She was wrestling with a man in rough clothes. At first Nathan thought she was being accosted and swore at the fellow, but as Nathan drew closer, he realized Dicea was trying to wrest a sack away from the man.

"Sir Gaites said to drown 'em, miss. He will be sure to ask if I have done it, too." The pathetic mewing from the sack was silenced when his superior strength won and he tossed the sack off the bridge into the dark water of the lake.

Dicea screamed. Without giving a thought to his current shortcomings as a rescuer, Nathan plunged off the bridge and swam underwater with his eyes open. The sack was still floating to the bottom. He grabbed it in his right hand and surfaced, then immediately sank again. He put the sack in his teeth and swam one-armed underwater until he could stand. He plunged ashore and Dicea met him on the bank crying pitifully. He couldn't untie the knot, but Dicea held the sack while he slit it with his penknife.

"You're mad, the pair of you," the old servant growled. Dicea hovered protectively over the lifeless forms, but the servant did not attempt to get them away from her again. Nathan massaged each of the kittens in turn, but only a tiny black one commenced mewing. This one Dicea cuddled in her apron like a baby, the tears still streaming down her face. The rough man stomped off, grumbling.

"I'm sorry, Dicea. If I could have got them out faster, we might have saved them."

"Nathan, I forgot your arm. You might have drowned yourself."

"Never, I bob like a cork. But we had better get this little fellow dry and fed or we may lose him yet."

"What shall we do with the others?" she asked hopelessly as Nathan checked the three soaked forms again to make sure there was no life.

"Water burial is best," Nathan advised. "It's what I'm used to anyway." Dicea nodded sadly.

He solemnly replaced the dead kittens in the sack, carried it out to the middle of the bridge and released it into the depths of the lake. By the time he got Dicea to the back door, they were both soaked but she had stopped sobbing. They went instinctively to the comfort of the schoolroom, which Miss Prin fought to keep warm for the child's sake.

They were not amiss in turning to her in this case, either, for Miss Prin cooed over the tiny mite and laid it in cotton wool almost before she realized how wet her charge was. She then took Dicea off to change her. Nathan was drying the kitten when the maid brought the tea tray and, for once, he found a good use for the cream.

By the time Miss Prin returned with a restored Dicea the kitten had drunk its fill and was contentedly purring in the box on Nathan's lap.

"Why, sir, you are even wetter than Dicea," Miss Prin observed from the puddle he was creating on the floor. "You must go and change before you catch your death of cold."

"Being wet never bothers me much. Sometimes I don't get to dry out for days at a time. But I suppose I am ruining the wood." He sneaked down the back stairs and made it to his room unobserved. Apologetically he rang for Fields, who helped him strip off his wet clothes and redid his bandages.

"Why don't you crawl in bed for an hour or so, sir? No point in dressing and then having to change right away for dinner."

Ordinarily Nathan would have scoffed at such an idea, but the cold swim had rather exhausted him, and he was feeling deliciously lethargic now that he was warm and dry again. He must have needed the sleep, for he was out as soon as he lay down, and did not awake until Fields returned to help him dress for dinner.

The storm that broke over Nathan's head when he entered the drawing room made it apparent that somehow the news of his adventure had gotten back to his grandfather. He did not suspect Miss Prin or Fields, or even the maid, so it must have been the gardener who funked on them.

"When I give an order I expect it to be obeyed. Were those cats drowned or not?"

"There are three little corpses at the bottom of the lake. I'm afraid I was not fast enough to save them."

"Except for the black one," Jared corrected, and received a look of such measured resentment from Nathan that it startled him. "Bates said you revived one. I wonder what you did with it."

"You mean you have not had the house searched?" Nathan shot at him, then subsided. He had better get his temper under control if he was going to be any use to Dicea in this matter.

"In the house! I won't have it, I tell you. I won't have my orders flaunted and I won't have that filthy thing in my house." Sir Owen said much besides and Nathan heard him out in respectful silence until the old man stopped to catch his breath.

"Yes, you are quite justified in what you say." Nathan almost smiled at the stunned look on his grandfather's face. "Unfortunately, at the time, I was unaware of all this. I saw only a despairing child and a way to mend things for her. It was the impulse of a moment to suggest Dicea keep the kitten."

"And if you had known what Grandfather's orders were?" Jared inquired like an unusually astute barrister.

Nathan was silent for a moment, putting down his anger again and deciding on the truth as the only way out. "I do not believe I would have done anything differently."

A fresh storm broke and Nathan really began to be concerned the old man might go into an apoplexy. "I won't have it under my roof, I tell you. What do you intend to do about that?"

Nathan waited to make sure he was expected to answer this. "There is only one thing to be done." Jared hated the way everyone hung on Nathan's words. "I shall have to take him to Bristol. I know Captain Hewitt will like to have him now that he is home most of the time. Mrs. Beckley likes cats, as well. She's his housekeeper," he explained.

"But I thought she was your landlady," Matthew said in confusion.

"Oh no, Captain Hewitt has owned that house since before they redid the harbor. He used to live on Welsh Back, but now that they built the floating harbor he can almost see his ships from his bedroom window. Well, it is getting late. May I borrow a carriage and team for the drive, and a groom, as well?"

"Now?" his grandfather demanded.

"Why yes, you said . . ."

"I will not have you running off in this havey-cavey way to Bristol at the drop of a hat and I will not have dinner interrupted. We'll deal with this in the morning." With that the old man closed the subject and led the way into the dining room, where Gregson was poised with a more than normally worried expression. Margaret, who did permit Nathan to lead her in each night, nearly laughed when she saw Nathan wink at the old retainer. Pretty thick with the servants, she thought, but what else could one expect.

For a meal at Gaites Hall, the dinner could be said to be going moderately well. No one stirred the coals of Sir Owen's wrath either accidentally or, in Jared's case, intentionally. Nathan speculated in silence about Jared's motives for such malicious acts and they seemed little enough on the surface. It was not as through Sir Owen could disinherit Nathan, so Jared had to be acting out of pure spite. Nathan had done Jared out of a title, a mere "sir," and Gaites Hall, such as it was, in all its disrepair. Apparently Margaret was supposed to be part of the bargain. Nathan looked sadly at her. She was too magnificent a woman to be bartered this way. She had a mind of her own, and Nathan did not believe Jared wanted her anymore than she wanted Jared.

In a lifetime spent among men, Nathan had seen many of them act viciously: bullies, rogues and troublemakers of all sorts. He knew there did not have to be a reason for meanness, not a conscious one at any rate. Jealousy, competitiveness, maleness itself, that ever-present need to best someone, was reason enough.

Jared would certainly resent Nathan getting in Sir Owen's good graces, especially if it meant fewer favors for him. That had to be the sum of it then, although Nathan would have thought Jared intelligent enough to be above such petty motives.

How to turn Jared around was the problem. Matt and Jeremy had been easy enough to win over. The others tolerated Nathan pretty well now, but Jared did not give his loyalty easily, if at all. He would be a hard case, but Nathan did not doubt he could bring him over in time, as he had the surliest seaman. Suddenly it occurred to Nathan that this was not a ship and there was no reason to win anyone over, because he was not going to stay. Yet he did want to, and not for any reason he could put his finger on.

He must have been staring at Jared with a puzzled expression, for Jared glanced up and shot him a sudden, vicious look that made Nathan remember the helpless kitten. To deliberately hurt a child, now that was not just idle meddling. Perhaps Jared was more dangerous than he thought.

The time to fill in before the tea tray was hanging heavy on their hands until Margaret went to the pianoforte. She played for nearly an hour, not in anger but passionately. Her playing spoke of courage, of an indomitable spirit. Her face, when she stopped, was far away in a place, perhaps, where courage and endurance meant something. Nathan thought he learned more about her in that single hour than the whole three days he had been at Gaites Hall.

"Why don't you sing something, Nathan? You can sing," Eleanor suggested kindly.

Margaret looked up at Eleanor warningly. In one of her arguments with Eleanor, Margaret had used Nathan's illiteracy as an excuse not to marry him. Eleanor had let it slip to Jared, who had, of course, carried the tale to Sir Owen. Margaret had hoped the argument over the cat would put the other matter out of everyone's mind. Just like Eleanor to forget and bring it to the fore.

"I'm afraid the songs Margaret knows how to play and the ones I can sing probably don't jump with each other, but then on the ship we sing without music." He sang "Sails of Silver," "The Daemon Lover" and a particularly sad song about a shipwreck. He sang without hesitation, embarrassment or accompaniment. Margaret thought his voice, so startling in church among so many others, sounded even better when he sang alone. She listened raptly, trying to memorize the words, and realized she was smiling at him. When he finished he returned the look with warmth, and for once she did not recoil into her shell like a turtle poked with a stick. She liked his singing. Not to acknowledge that was an insult he did not deserve.

"Your songs are all so sad," a misty-eyed Cristine said. "All about drowned sailors and sinking ships. Are there no happy songs about the sea?"

"Only drinking songs. Let me think...no, that's no good...hmm."

"Expurgating the lyrics?" Jared guessed.

Nathan grinned in spite of himself. "Well, I would hate to have to quit halfway through if I came to something I could not say in a drawing room."

"Your search is likely to be fruitless considering your music belongs in a tavern?" Jared observed.

"Give me time. I will think of one," Nathan assured him.

In the meantime Jared began a discussion with his mother, and Margaret breathed a sigh of relief.

"I have just been reading the most interesting book by Sir Walter Scott," Jared commented out of the blue. "Perhaps you would like to read it, Nathan."

"No, thank you." Nathan scarcely noticed how he answered, but he had read all of Scott. What did puzzle him was why Margaret should be blushing so furiously.

"No," said Jared coldly, "I did not think so."

Everyone was looking uncomfortably at Jared, except the old man, who was staring at Nathan in a menacing way. "Is Scott a favorite author of yours, Grandfather?" Nathan ventured in an attempt to start a conversation.

"No, he is not!"

Jeremy rushed into the breach with, "Matthew says you can play cards." Nathan found himself inexorably drawn into a game played for chicken stakes, in deference to him, he suspected. It made for a boring end to the evening but, at least, he made no gaffes hideous enough to draw censure from his grandfather. Why he had begun to dread displeasing him was a puzzle to himself. He thought he had better put the old man in a passion again soon just to assert his own independence.

As Nathan feared, the combination of a nap and another dose of bitter coffee made it almost impossible to sleep even after a couple of brandies. He slid on his breeches and shoes, tucked his nightclothes in and went in search of a book.

The sound of a door opening and closing caught Jeremy in the act of crawling into bed. He eased open his door to see Nathan creeping down the hall with a candle. He followed out of curiosity to try to discover which of the housemaids, as he supposed, had fallen to Nathan's charms, for he had not remarked Nathan going near any of them.

But instead of ascending the stairs toward the servants' rooms, Nathan went softly down the main stair and into the library. Jeremy watched from the darkness of the hallway as Nathan surveyed the roomful of dusty volumes in the faint hope of finding something of interest. There was nothing modern to be had but that did not deter him since it was sleep he wanted anyway.

On a lower shelf he did find a large folio on English manor houses and one on English country gardens. Since he knew less about his native country than many of the foreign lands he visited, these looked to be improving volumes. He spread one open on the desk and began leafing through the plans, ink drawings and occasional color plates.

Jeremy got a queer sensation in his chest when he realized Nathan must be trying to learn to read all on his own from picture books. Nathan might pretend he did not care what they thought of him, when actually, Jeremy supposed, Nathan felt his deprivation quite keenly. Jeremy began to wonder if, part of the time Nathan spent in the schoolroom, he was not there as a secret pupil of Miss Prin's.

For Jeremy the sensation was like turning a corner in his life. Up until now his natural mischievousness was unconsciously being honed by Jared into a malevolence that might one day match the man's own. But Nathan awoke the latent compassion in the boy, who vowed now to help his underprivileged cousin in any way he could. He crept away in the quiet hope that Nathan would get something useful out of the picture books.

The next morning at breakfast, Nathan asked his grandfather if he could put his trip to Bristol off for a day, since he did not want to return too late for the vicar's tea. Sir Owen assented gruffly and said no more about it. The rain had at last let up, so Nathan and Dicea walked the mile to the vicar's house, chatting the whole way about how best to hang on to Sir Kaye, the black kitten.

"I have a plan, but if it does not work, I may have to do as I promised and take Sir Kaye to Bristol."

"Just so he is alive somewhere." Dicea looked up at him expectantly.

"It all hinges on whether you would like to have a horse or not."

Dicea looked confused. "I would love to have a horse, but Cousin Eleanor won't permit it. She says I am still growing and she won't be paying for a new riding habit for me every year."

"That's no problem. I have plenty of money. If we get your measurements from Miss Prin, can we send to Bristol and get one made for you?"

"Yes, I know we can." Dicea brightened.

"And I have plenty of money to buy the horse, too, so I don't think Grandfather will object."

"But what has this to do with Sir Kaye?"

"You will see."

Jeremy was correct in warning Nathan about the rich food but, since Mrs. Denning recited the recipe for each delicacy as she presented it, Nathan did not run afoul of any milk or cream. Dicea confided to Mrs. Denning very adultly what Nathan's problem was, and he and the vicar sat smiling as the two ladies discussed various remedies for a touchy stomach and shot cryptic questions at their potential patient.

Finally Nathan laughed. "You know, in the greater part of the world no one drinks cows' milk or cream, not even children, so in fact, I am never unwell in other countries."

The vicar led Nathan on to talk of his travels, which he did more freely in front of a friendly audience. He had dealt in everything from horses and lumber to cloves and medicines. "Aside from antique china, the spices are where you make the most money, and coffee and chocolate. They take up the least room and you can always fill up the hold with exotic wood and fruits. The fruits are risky, as it is hard to predict ripening time. Sometimes you must dump half of it before you reach port, or eat fast."

They all laughed at that. "So you learned navigation from your friend, Captain Hewitt?"

"Yes, I still do navigate for him, of course, but we are more or less partners in the spice and coffee trade we have got going to South America. He owns the ships and I handle the cargoes."

They went on to talk of many things, including great literature. Thanks to Miss Prin, Dicea held her own valiantly where the classics were concerned. They examined and exclaimed over the vicar's library and he invited them to borrow from him if they should run out of reading matter at the hall. By the time they left, Nathan was already late to be changing for dinner, so they sprinted partway back and ran breathless up the house stairs.

"I must be getting out of shape, Fields. I cannot even keep up with Dicea, and all this changing purely wears me out."

Nathan did not get to the drawing room until nearly six. His grandfather rose mutely after his entrance, to lead the way into the dining room. Everyone breathed a sigh of relief except Jared, who smirked. Nathan really was not hungry so he did not pay much attention to what was put before him and tried to follow what Matthew was telling his grandfather about the cattle. He did look suspiciously at the beef tips in dark gravy and hesitated.

"Surely, that has no cream in it," Eleanor remarked with irritation. He really could not tell from the taste. It was fine.

But before the next course was finished, a searing stab of pain in his stomach gave notice he had made an error. In another few minutes he was feeling feverish and visibly sweating. "Excuse me," he said quietly, and, without waiting for acknowledgment, left the dining room none too steadily. Matthew also excused himself, under his grandfather's baleful stare, with the intention of helping what he thought was a slightly drunk young man to his room.

Nathan did not get much further than the bottom of the stairs before another slash of pain brought him to his knees. Matthew half carried, half supported him to his room, where Nathan cast up his accounts into the washbasin. In between bouts of retching, Fields managed to get him undressed and put to bed with a wet compress on his forehead.

"Well?" Sir Owen demanded when Matthew returned to his seat, smiling sheepishly, as the dessert was being served.

"I have not seen anyone quite so sick since Jeremy got into the new cider."

"Did you send for the doctor?" Margaret asked, rising.

"Sit down," Sir Owen commanded.

"He says he doesn't need one, that he will be fine by morning."

"I shall go up to him." Eleanor rose with a challenging look at Sir Owen, but he said nothing.

The cloth slipped off Nathan's forehead when a paroxysm half raised him off the pillow and made him gasp. Fields was trying to hold him down as gently as he could so that he would not wrench his shoulder.

Eleanor thought he looked much like Matthew the few times he was sick as a child. She sat on the chair by the bed. "Nathan, I am sorry. I had no idea."

"What? Eleanor? You should not have come."

"We must get the doctor for you." Even to his bleary vision she looked more kindly than he had yet seen her.

"Oh, there's nothing he can do anyway. The worst is over now." He chuckled weakly and wondered why he thought it so important to set her mind at rest. "I know I must look pretty ghastly now but, I promise you, I shall be fine by tomorrow morning."

Nathan awoke to full sun and a ravenous hunger. He had missed breakfast and luncheon, but Eleanor would not pronounce him fit to rise until he had swallowed some gruel she said was sure to settle his stomach and she had assured herself that no fever lingered. Nathan was stunned to learn, as Fields dressed him, that the French chef had been dismissed, and by Eleanor herself. He sought her out in the morning room to protest this sacrifice on his behalf but she was adamant. "I spoke to him twice about cooking more dishes you could eat. The third time, last night, in fact, he was insolent, and so I discharged him. There is no more to be said."

Margaret was also in the morning room and Eleanor quite pointedly left them together, recommending that Margaret show Nathan the gardens. Margaret had almost looked at him sympathetically when he entered the room, but once she realized that Nathan was perfectly healthy again, she resumed her normal coldness. "Do you want to take a walk or not?" She rose and preceded him through the conservatory out onto the lawn. The turn around the garden was achieved at such a pace, with Margaret rattling off the names of dozens of plants, that Nathan pulled up, rather winded, by a bench near the rose arbor.

"You go on, if you like. I have to rest a minute."

Margaret looked mutinous for a second, then conscience stricken, so she came to sit in sudden silence on the bench at the other end from him.

"Have they told you that you have to be nice to me?"

"How did you know?" she asked in surprise.

"Just a guess. You need not regard them, you know. You can be as rude to me as you like and I won't say anything."

"You would hardly notice, in fact, after the way you have been treated since you have been here," she acknowledged.

"I seem to have offended you somehow and more than once. Was it something I said?" Nathan's ingenuous frontal attack caught Margaret off guard. For a moment she was tempted to tell him the truth, but it was not in her to confide in anyone, let alone a stranger.

"You are not capable of offending me," she announced, staring into the shrubbery.

"Well, I imagine I could, if I put my mind to it, but that is not my aim."

"Stop trying to be nice to me," she snapped. "I mean I take no notice of you."

"What a bouncer!" he exclaimed. "When you are forever looking daggers at me if I so much as open my mouth."

"It has nothing to do with you," she asserted.

Margaret did not, in fact, know why she was so angry with Nathan, except that it did no good to be angry with Eleanor, Sir Owen or Jared. They came right back at her. Nathan, on the other hand, took her snubs and cuts without offense or argument. There seemed to be no insult that he would not swallow to win the Gaites fortune.

In an attempt to wound him as much as possible, she added, "It is your very existence which has ruined everything. In a word, I wish you had never been born."

Nathan looked sadly put out. "I see." He produced a penknife, opened it and began to unbutton his left cuff with some difficulty.

Margaret stared at him suspiciously, "What are you doing?"

"Opening a vein. It's said to be the easiest way, better than shooting yourself, at least. But you know—" he hesitated as she stared at him in fascinated horror "—it won't bring Talbot back."

The shock spurred her into action. "You must be mad, or feverish. Put that knife away. Why would I want Talbot back?"

"I thought you were in love with him."

"No—never." She rose from the bench and clenched her hands.

"Of course, my death would clear the way for you to marry Jared." He brought the knife close to his bare wrist again, below the bandages, wondering what he would do if she called his bluff.

"Stop it!" She snatched the penknife away and hurled it into the bushes. "I don't want to marry Jared, either," she spit at him.

"If you are sure?" Nathan thought she looked well with some color in her face, but hoped it would not take this to put it there every day. He struggled ineffectively with his cuff and she came over impatiently to do it up. He discovered that he liked having her touch him even when it did not mean anything.

"I must get back," she said desperately, but did not flee from him. She walked dutifully with him through the rose garden.

"Lovely," he said. She looked crossly at him, but he seemed to be addressing a flower.

"You may pick them if you like," she offered.

"Most of the young ladies of my acquaintance don't care to be encumbered with bouquets on their walks."

"And do you know many young ladies?" She was beginning to regain her composure and also beginning to resent the scare he had given her. On reflection she did not believe he had been serious, but he was still an unknown factor. She had no idea what to make of him. She was sure his vacant smile did mask a rather reprehensible intellect, but there were times when she was just as positive he was not pretending and she could take him at face value.

"Not in this country," he said, after a pause. She cast him a blighting look as Dicea came out to ask him to tea.

There was an extraordinary difference in dinner that night. It included many of the plain foods Nathan was used to: boiled cabbage and carrots, roast hens, baked ham and fresh green peas served plain. He made a good meal since he was still rather hungry and he noted the fare found favor with Sir Owen, as well. For dessert there was a bread pudding with apples. Since the fruit dish that night contained bananas, oranges, guavas, and was crowned by a pineapple, Nathan concluded Captain Hewitt's hamper had arrived from Bristol. Sir Owen merely stared at the mound of fruit and let it pass by him without comment, so Nathan was disinclined to call it to anyone's attention. Cristine took a guava, but then did not know what to do with it until Nathan took one, managed to quarter it with his knife, secretly retrieved from the rosebushes, and ate out the sweet fleshy pulp.

Sir Owen's good humor lasted through the evening, and he even listened attentively while Nathan talked of his trading ventures with Captain Hewitt. "We made several trips to the East Indies for coffee and spice plants and seeds and traded those to smallholders in the inland of Guiana. Some we even gave away just to get them started." When Nathan said "we," he was speaking of himself and Captain Hewitt. His family interpreted "we" as the crew of the ship of which they assumed Nathan to be a common member. "Because we pay them a fair price for their crops, they save the spices and the best of the coffee crop for us. Also, we are willing to go inland to pick up the goods."

"That's all very well, but it's in the past now," was his grandfather's only comment. "I hope you will take as much of an interest in farming in your own country. The fields have dried up. Dress for riding tomorrow and we'll take you around the estate."

Nathan had just settled down to let a cup of rich Brazilian mellow him after the meal when he was startled into saying, "Riding?"

"You do ride, don't you?" Jared asked.

"Yes, of course, but not for a while now."

"That's something you do not forget, once you learn it," Jared observed.

"Don't worry, Nathan," comforted Matthew. "We'll put you up on old Hannibal—don't you think, Grandfather? He won't run off with you."

Nathan was slightly mollified but began to regret casting off his sling that morning. His shoulder was strapped tightly enough though. He would have to take a fall, he thought, to do it any harm now. He looked forward to the next day with few misgivings and the rest of the month with something approaching complacency. Beyond that he did not think. There was still the puzzle of Margaret to solve, and he would hate to not see Dicea every day. He began to consider other possibilities than he had thought of only a few days ago.

Chapter Three

They brought out a dark bay for Nathan to mount, an older horse, not quite as tall as the others, but with a reputation, they told him, for taking fences squarely and never losing heart over a hedge. This cheerful reassurance from Matthew began to worry Nathan. All he wanted was a horse that would not trip and fall on the road. He did not want anything to do with fences or hedges.

Since he could not use his left hand to hang on to the saddle and reins, he went around to the right side of the horse and managed to crawl on. This solecism brought stares from the whole party and the unexpected wrath of his grandfather down on his head.

"Don't you know the first thing? Always mount from the left."

"I cannot see that it matters, unless you are riding side-saddle." He nodded at Margaret. "The horse cannot possibly care."

"It matters to me. I won't be made a laughingstock at the first hunt we take you to."

"Oh, I see. I will remember."

Avoiding Tenwells, they managed to cover most of the estate and the leased lands, but not very quickly. Nathan wasted so much time pushing through hedges rather than jumping them and getting down to open and close gates that they were all out of patience with him and he was purely worn-out. Every time he crawled back on required more effort even if he could use a rail of the gate to step up on.

"I thought you claimed you had ridden before," Jared said critically.

"Well, I have," Nathan grunted as he clambered back on the left side, "but I never went about the country leaping over things like I was being hounded by the law."

"You will have to learn to jump if you are to stay here," his grandfather commanded. "I won't have the villagers sniggering about you."

Even Nathan thought this was an unreasonable demand to make on someone with a broken shoulder, and opened his mouth to say so.

"I don't want to hear your excuses," Sir Owen growled. "I'm out of all patience with you. Margaret, see him home. We are leaving."

Since Margaret's impatience with a poor rider was as great as Sir Owen's and she suffered the further stigma of being so obviously thrust at Nathan's head, Nathan soon learned he was not being let off easy. She cantered away scornfully. Nathan thought she never looked better than when on the back of a flying horse with her color up. She did keep to wooded paths and trails rather than the hedged and ditched fields but always at a canter. She shook her horse up into a gallop on a straight tree-lined lane and Nathan laughed and followed. He was determined not to lose sight of her. Galloping was really the easiest pace on his shoulder since it just involved rocking with the horse. The staccato effect of the bars of sunlight shooting through the thin tree trunks, across the road and across his eyes, had him half-blinded but he followed her in good faith.

To do Margaret justice she did not really mean Nathan any harm, but she had forgotten that the gate at the end of the lane was often closed, and she jumped it. Nathan could not bear the thought of pulling up so he went over, clinging to Hannibal's mane and the reins with his right hand. He was not prepared for falling ground on the other side.

Margaret looked back to see Nathan lose a stirrup and get bounced off Hannibal's left side. It was not a hard fall, so she turned and rode back to catch the loose horse, then went to see to Nathan.

Something about his still face frightened her. She tied the horses and knelt to touch his cheek and speak his name. In terror she unbuttoned his coat and felt for his heart. It was beating steadily enough, but his breathing was much too shallow and rapid, and he was deathly pale in spite of his sun-browned skin. Just when she had begun to fear he had broken his neck, he rolled his head sideways and moaned. It was then she realized she had been crying. Odd for her to lose her grip in a crisis. She composed herself and called his name.

Nathan thought he was back on the *Mary Anne*. A whole spar must have come down on his shoulder. And there was something stabbing him in the ribs. Nathan was desperately trying to sit but gave up in exhaustion and finally looked at the girl who was loosening his neck cloth.

"Don't try to move," Margaret whispered.

He could not imagine what a girl would be doing on a ship. "Are we in port?"

"What? No, you are not on your ship. You are home—remember—Gaites Hall."

By the vague look in his half-open eyes she knew he was still stunned. Nathan tried to focus on her face, which seemed familiar. The voice he did not recognize. He raised his head at last and, after staring at her, finally guessed, "Margaret?"

"You have had a fall, Nathan. Lie still and let me go for help."

"No, I think I'm all right. I just landed on a rock. Must have knocked the wind out of me. But I don't think I can sit up on my own."

"Are you sure this is a good idea?" Margaret asked as she got behind him and raised him to a sitting position. He stifled a gasp as daggers of pain shot through his shoulder and chest.

"That's better," he lied. "Is Hannibal all right to ride? Bring him closer." Nathan tucked his left thumb securely into his belt to fake a sling, grabbed Hannibal's stirrup and pulled himself to his knees. Then he stood shakily, leaning against the patient horse. He was red faced and sweating with the effort. The air tore audibly in and out of his lungs.

"You can't possibly ride like this." Margaret was close to tears again.

"I can if I can get on. Don't tell Grandfather," he begged as he scrambled up Hannibal's right side with Margaret's help and collapsed across the horse's withers.

"If you can just hang on I will lead him home by the road." Margaret leaped up onto her horse with easy grace and gathered up Hannibal's reins.

When Nathan could talk again, he said, "Do you mean there is a road we could have taken instead of crashing over all these hedges and gates? You must be mad—all of you."

"You may be right." Margaret kept looking back to make sure he was still holding on.

"Don't worry," he tried to reassure her, "I will tell you if I'm going to pass out." He shut his eyes to lock out all distractions and concentrated on hanging on to the handful of mane. It was no different than hanging on to a rope when the waves were crashing over you and your life depended on not letting go.

After a time darkness moved overhead. He heard Margaret call out, "Kerry, help me with him!" Nathan opened his eyes to find he was in the stable, and slid off the right side of the horse and went to his knees. Margaret rushed to hold him up as Kerry led Hannibal away.

Nathan's face was glistening with sweat and he seemed to her about to faint. "Sorry," he mumbled into her skirt.

Kerry almost grabbed his left arm. "No! not that way. Get his right arm around your neck and don't touch his left side."

"What all did he break, miss?" Kerry asked in awe.

"I have no idea," Margaret said in despair.

"What we need is a litter, miss."

"No." Nathan seemed to come awake again and started using his legs. "It will be worse if they try to carry me."

Kerry steadied him by holding his belt. Margaret dispatched an undergroom for the doctor and ran ahead into the house to warn Fields. Even with Kerry doing most of the work, Nathan's breath was rasping in and out of his lungs by the time they got him into his room and lying down on the bed. Nathan coughed weakly, and Fields resolutely escorted Margaret to the hall so they could begin cutting away his clothes and assessing the damages. They slid him unconscious between the sheets and waited impatiently for the doctor.

Nathan awoke to a plaintive voice asking, "What the devil are all these bandages?"

"That was from before, Dr. Stewart," Fields supplied.

Nathan flinched as cold scissors slid under the strapping and opened his eyes to see a harassed, middle-aged man cutting away the bandages. "So, you are awake. Tell me what all is broken here."

"Couple of ribs, I think," Nathan whispered.

"I can see that for myself, can't I? I mean from before."

Nathan laughed weakly. "Shoulder blade, collarbone, shoulder dislocated, and . . . two broken bones in the hand. That's all."

"Would you be so good as to tell me what you were doing on a horse?"

"I didn't think it was such a good idea, but I figured as long as I didn't fall, I would be all right."

"Well, you did fall—lift him up, Fields." The doctor bound his ribs and retied his shoulder bandages so tightly Nathan complained he could not move. "Good, that should keep you out of trouble for a while. Now drink this." Whatever it was tasted foul but did the trick since Nathan could feel himself slipping off to sleep again.

* * *

As hard as Dr. Stewart was on Nathan, it was nothing to what he said to Sir Owen in the drawing room in the presence of his family. "What the devil were you trying to do, get the boy killed?"

Matthew poured the doctor a sherry, "How bad is he?"

"Oh, he will mend, eventually. I just cannot believe you put that boy up on one of your great brutes in his condition."

"But he only has an injured hand," Jared complained. "I don't see—"

"His whole upper chest was held together with bandages," Stewart exploded. "Now he has two broken ribs to add to the lot."

Eleanor looked stunned. "But Nathan never complained of it."

"By God," said Sir Owen, raising his glass, "he's a Gaites, after all."

Jared scowled into his wineglass.

Waking up was like surfacing from a great depth of water. Nathan swam toward the light, holding his breath, and gasped for air as he opened his eyes. Everything was blurry, but he finally made out a brown-haired young fellow who looked familiar and a rather pretty girl. He wondered what could be wrong to make her look so worried. He felt warm and comfortable and nothing even hurt very much, as long as he did not move.

Nathan stared at Margaret so vaguely that he prompted her to ask, "Nathan, do you know where you are?"

"England?" He guessed from the language. His two interrogators looked at each other helplessly. "Not Bristol, though," he mumbled. "I know—Gaites Hall. I went in the lake. Did the cat live?"

"Yes, sir. But that was Tuesday. Today is Friday. You also fell off a horse and broke some ribs," Fields informed him.

"That's right. Margaret?"

"Yes?"

"How did I get back here?"

"You rode. Don't you remember?"

Nathan opened and closed his eyes slowly half a dozen times, then gave up the struggle and went back to sleep.

The next time he woke up he thought he saw Captain Hewitt, which did not make any sense, because he had it set in his mind that this was Gaites Hall.

"Grandfather? Have I been asleep long?" Nathan made as if to rise, but the old man got up from his chair and gently pushed him back.

"All day, you young scamp."

"Oh, the cat. I forgot. It may be a few days before I can take him."

"Don't worry about that now."

"The thing is I promised Dicea a horse instead."

"A horse. Does she want a horse?"

"Oh, yes, for years now. I expect she would be satisfied with the cat though. And I don't exactly know where I will come by a horse. But I suppose Matt had better help me pick it out."

"I should think so."

"She should learn to ride while she's young," Nathan said earnestly.

"Yes, yes. She can ride one of ours. Don't tax yourself now."

After Sir Owen left, Fields looked suspiciously at the chuckling Nathan. "Sounds like Miss Dicea will end up with the cat and the horse, and you could pretty well ask for the moon."

"He does seem to have developed a soft spot for me. If I had known this was all it would take, I would have contrived to tumble off a horse the first day."

* * *

Nathan awoke with his location firm in his mind, but a vague uneasiness about the time of day. He looked around for a clock and saw a water glass on the table. He tried what he could do toward reaching it with his right arm without moving the rest of him.

"What is it?" a soft voice asked, coming to the bed.

"Margaret, you should not be here," Nathan said, suddenly aware of his bare shoulder and arm.

"What do you need?"

"A drink. I'm devilishly thirsty."

She put the glass in his hand and held his head up until he was finished. The touch of her hand and arm sent an unexpected thrill though him that nearly choked him.

"Thanks," he whispered, taking a better look at her. She looked softer somehow, but terribly sad.

"It's the least I can do after nearly getting you killed."

"What are you talking about?" Nathan asked in some concern, for the girl sounded nearly choked with tears.

"I knew that gate was there," she confessed.

"So did I. I saw it. I could have pulled up. What happened, anyway?"

"There's a steep path on the other side. Anyone might have fallen off if he had not known the ground dropped."

He smiled. "You needn't make excuses for my horsemanship."

"You should not have been riding at all," she said passionately. "Why didn't you tell us how badly you were hurt?"

"Don't take on so. It's only a couple of ribs. I will be fine in a day or two. I scarcely even feel them."

"Don't lie to me," she accused. "I know they hurt you."

"I can see you have been under a bit of a strain lately."

"What are you talking about?" she almost shouted.

"Not being able to fly into a passion. It must have been terrible. Don't you feel better now?"

"Did you deliberately—?"

"Margaret!" Eleanor admonished as she entered the room. "I could hear you halfway down the hall. What do you mean by ranting at him in his condition? If you get him upset, you'll bring on a fever."

Nathan grinned at Margaret behind Eleanor's back.

Rather than trying to defend herself, Margaret just cast him a seething glance and left the room.

"Are you all right, Nathan?"

"Yes, if only you can send Fields to me."

"Just coming, sir," said Fields as he pushed the door open with a tray.

"You are feeding him that?" Eleanor inspected the tray. "Where is the broth I ordered?"

"Right here, Mrs. Gaites. I thought I would have my lunch up here to save time."

"Very well." Eleanor exited with the feeling she had everything under control.

"Hungry?"

"Starving, but help me up first. I'm about to burst—don't worry, I won't fall apart the way they have me strapped together."

After he had relieved himself and slid back into bed, he asked, "Why is Margaret nursing me? She should not even be in here."

"She does usually manage most of the sickroom work. We would be hard-pressed to do without her."

"So would Eleanor, but she doesn't know it."

"It's true Miss Margaret is not appreciated as she should be. Do you want me to try to keep her out?"

"Yes—no. It's only that she blames herself. She might feel better if she does help. But, for God's sake, get me some clothes."

"Dr. Stewart says it's easier to work on you like this. He will be changing the bandages every day." Fields ignored Nathan's suspicious look. "Also, he told me to hide your clothes so you would not go out riding again."

"Ha. All right. I will be good, so long as you don't desert me. What a mess for you to take care of. Sorry about all this."

Nathan apologized to Fields every time he had to ring for him or ask for his help. "No need to apologize, sir," Fields said ruefully. "Actually you are easier to take care of when you are laid up. You don't do any damage to your suits."

"I'm glad to know you have the sense to stop me being a dead bore."

Not being used to coddling himself, it was hard for Nathan to get used to lying abed so long over what he considered a trivial injury, but everyone, except Jared, seemed so anxious to make up for his previous treatment that he had not the heart to tell them he felt fine.

Even Miss Prin and Dicea visited him. Dicea obviously did not expect him to exert himself to amuse her since she brought a book and solemnly read to him for half an hour while Nathan played with Sir Kaye on top of the covers.

Sir Owen just looked in on him as Sir Kaye made a rush and somersaulted off the bed onto the carpet with a squeak. Sir Owen picked him up by the scruff without a word and restored him to the bed, then stood talking to Nathan for a few minutes. Dicea and Miss Prin breathed a sigh of relief when he had gone.

Nathan could not make out why it bothered him to be lying there half-naked with Margaret in the room when it did not bother him to have anyone else around. He was not particularly shy of women. It just did not seem decent for Margaret to be there. Then it occurred to him that he was strongly attracted to her. When this realization hit him, Nathan looked at her so helplessly she thought he was in pain and came to fix his pillows. He bit his lip and rode it out as best he could, but the flush that had crept up into his face caused her to feel his forehead and cheek, then go off to look for a fever medicine.

Nathan was still breathing heavily when Fields came in. "Have you been up? You look awful."

"Just trying to get over Margaret's last visit."

Fields chuckled. "I can't very well keep her out if I don't tell her why."

"Don't you dare! She's been so nice to me lately I do not want to scare her away."

If Nathan had trouble dealing with Margaret's proximity, she had none at all dealing with him. As long as he was helpless in bed he was no threat to her. And if thoughts of his muscular, sun-bronzed arms came into her head more often than was proper, they were quickly dispelled by her caretaker instinct. Margaret was intelligent enough to realize that she and Nathan were being thrown together on purpose. She had no intention of giving anyone the satisfaction of seeing her make a fool of herself over a man. She did quite well without them.

She had had no strong father figure, in fact no very clear memory of her father at all. It was as though she had blotted out her whole childhood, she thought of it so little. The past was a closed book; the future a trap she must avoid. She was a creature thrown back on surviving for the moment, and she could not have been more alone if she had been a red deer hunted through the wood—always in flight. That was her recurring nightmare, running, from what she could never discover, just running, and finding no rest anywhere. In her waking life she was satisfied if she could only make it through another day.

About the time Nathan had learned to control himself enough to enjoy Margaret's familiarity, Dr. Stewart announced, "You have been malingering long enough. You can get dressed tomorrow, but do not leave the house." Nathan stretched this to include the large stone terrace that opened off the drawing room and dining room at the side of the house. He was comfortably ensconced there in the warm sunshine when Miss Prin brought Dicea out for her watercolor lesson.

"We don't want to disturb you," Miss Prin apologized.

"On the contrary, I'm perishing for some company. May I watch?"

He was delighted to find Miss Prin was an excellent watercolorist. Her study of the garden, which she explained as she worked so that Dicea could follow at her own easel, was alive with color and light. Dicea's picture looked not at all like Miss Prin's, and Nathan could see that the child was embarrassed. "Watercolor is the most difficult of the arts," he assured her. "It takes years to master it. Perhaps you should do pencil studies for a while to practice."

"That's a good idea and you would understand light better if you had to show it only in shades of gray," Miss Prin added. "Mrs. Gaites insists I teach her watercolor," she added to Nathan. "I just hope I don't put her off it forever."

Dicea sat down then to take the now-sleepy kitten onto her lap.

"What a picture she makes. Have you done any portrait work?"

"I can try." In half an hour Miss Prin had achieved a likeness of Dicea that Nathan thought admirable. Her dark hair curled over the shoulder of her white dress. Nathan particularly liked the way the black kitten stood out against her dress and her white fingers spread to hold the sleeping cat.

"That's the way I see her, too, caring and wise beyond her years."

The more back to normal Nathan got, the more coldly Margaret treated him. It was as though the sensitive, compassionate girl he had come to love had fled. Nathan could not understand the transformation, since he had made no overt advances toward her.

He was making his way along the edge of the stream that fed the lake when he came upon her sitting morosely near a deserted building. He had never walked this far upstream before and looked with some interest at the stone structure.

"I wish you would quit following me around like a dog," Margaret said so forcefully Nathan almost staggered. There was, however, some justice in the remark since he had seen her leave the house and wondered if she should be going off alone.

"I'm sorry. I don't mean to be so stupid." He sat down at a safe distance. "Won't you tell me what I have done to make you so angry with me?"

"Nothing."

"That's right. I forgot. I was born."

"Don't try that stupid knife trick again. It won't work. I know you better now."

"It seems I don't know you at all." He was silent then, watching the moving water, afraid to say anything.

"Are you going to let them keep you here—buy you, like the rest of us?" she asked bitterly.

"What do you mean?"

"Sir Owen will make you an allowance and you will run at his heels like Matthew and Jeremy. Even Jared caters to him."

"I don't need an allowance," Nathan said indignantly, "and no one can make me stay if I make up my mind to leave."

"Are you going then?" she asked in a tone that did not tell him what answer she wanted.

"I think I am making you miserable. Do you want me to go?"

"Yes—no." She looked away. "If you leave now they will say I drove you away, which is no more than the truth. I'm so confused," she almost whispered.

"What?" He tried to look at her face.

"I don't know what to do about any of it." She rested her head on her updrawn knees.

"But surely you are the only one who does know what's going on," he blurted out. "I just assumed—I mean women always do seem to know what they are doing."

"Perhaps the women you know understand what they want," she said scornfully.

"Tell me then why you are afraid of me," he begged. "Perhaps it's something . . ."

"I'm not afraid of you. It's just that you are weak like the others. They will make you offer for me and when I refuse they will make my life even more unbearable."

"Oh, is that all?" Nathan said lightly, getting an idea.

"Is that all—I cannot stand it now."

"But if I do not offer for you, they cannot blame you."

"I never thought of that." She looked almost mollified.

"So there is nothing to worry about. We can be friends then, can't we?"

"You are sure they will not be able to force you into it?"

"I would never marry and then go away to sea. It's too cruel to leave someone waiting at home wondering if you are alive or dead. I saw my mother go through it. I will never again do that to someone I love."

"So it will all go to Jared then anyway, if something happens to you," Margaret said, ignoring the word *love*.

"You did mean it when you said you would not have him?" Nathan hurried to reassure himself.

"I think Jared is despicable. Why don't you stand up to him? You are not so stupid that you don't know he's cutting at you."

"But he's such an amusing fellow. I never know what he will come up with next."

"You cannot be serious. You don't actually like him?" She stared at Nathan in disbelief.

"I could like him well enough if he did not stir up so much trouble. Why does he hate me so?"

"Jared doesn't like anybody very much. Grandfather likes you. That is a strike against you. You have bested Jared once or twice by slithering out of the traps he set for you. That must have annoyed him. Also he cannot draw you into an argument. Are you sure you are a Gaites?" she asked on a sudden thought, turning to scrutinize his face.

"What brought that on?" Nathan smiled sheepishly, not at all offended by the import of her question.

For an instant Margaret smiled back at him, at his boyish face with his sun-bleached hair falling over his forehead.

It was at that moment Nathan decided he must marry her, no matter what it took. He very nearly blurted out a proposal, but remembered in time to stop himself from doing what he had promised he wouldn't only a moment before.

Margaret shook her head as though to clear it of confused thoughts. "Our family have such wretched tempers."

"Neither Cristine nor Dicea do, and I have never seen Eleanor anything but calm," Nathan said.

"You have never seen her..."

"What?"

"She argues with me more than anyone else," said Margaret, yanking out some grass by the roots. "Not violently, but... inexorably. She knows she will win in the end. She always does." Margaret's lips trembled and she sounded so much like a tearful Dicea, Nathan wanted to fold her into his arms for comfort. But he guessed it was too early for that sort of thing yet. Instead he rose and reached down his hand to her.

"She can't win this time," he said. "Come." His hand motioned again toward hers. She looked at it dumbly for a moment before her hand came up, almost against her will, to clasp his. He pulled her lightly to her feet, then let her go. "You have only to tell her that I have not offered for you."

"Then she will pressure you instead."

"I can handle Eleanor," Nathan assured her.

"Or else she will say I have not made myself pleasing to you. That also is true."

"You should not have to please anyone you don't like," Nathan said almost in anger. "But to be glaring at me for no reason may not best serve your purpose, either." He began walking along the bank and she followed him.

"Where are we going?"

"I wanted to see this building. What is it?" he asked to divert her. "No one has spoken of it."

"The gristmill? It's part of Tenwells farm. We no longer own it. The house is just down there."

"Can we see inside the mill?" Nathan asked, carefully sliding down the bank toward the dam.

"I think the door is locked. Jeremy says he's been inside though. He went across the weir by the wheel and crawled in the window."

"I'm game." Nathan led the way to the two-foot-wide dam wall. It was not submerged at the moment, but the stones were slick with wet moss.

"We really should not even be here."

"Are you afraid?" he was inspired to ask.

"Of course not."

"The stones are slippery," he said, reaching back for her. "Take my hand."

"To keep me from falling in, or you?"

"We both go in together. That way you cannot blame me if you get wet."

They made it to the window, which Nathan thrust up with his right arm. He stepped inside. Margaret sat on the sill and swung her legs inside without his assistance.

"It does not look to be in such bad shape," he said, looking at the great grindstones and the arrangement of huge gears that drove them.

"It has only been idle for two years. That's when the old miller died. His wife stayed at Tenwells another six months, then went to live with her sister's family in Bath. That's when Talbot asked Sir Owen for Tenwells. I imagine you know the rest.''

Nathan went up the stairs to the second floor. His boots echoed overhead on the oak floor. He came back down to say, ''It all looks to be in pretty good order. Why has no one started it up again?''

''The new owner lives in London. He doesn't care. In fact, I think he is trying to sell the farm.''

''Can we see the house?''

''If you like,'' Margaret said resignedly, ''but I doubt you'll find an unlocked window there.''

She was right, but Nathan seemed content to walk around it through the overgrown gardens. ''It seems to be made of the same stone as the mill.''

''Yes, the fireplaces, too. I always liked it here. The girls and I visited Mrs. Morton when we came for flour.''

''Oh, what's that smell?'' he asked suddenly.

''It must be one of the herbs—here, lavender,'' Margaret identified.

Nathan knelt by the patch and drank it in. ''It reminds me of Mother. Strange how a scent can be so powerful,'' he said as he crushed one of the flowers and sniffed it from his palm.

''I scarcely remember my mother at all,'' Margaret said indifferently.

''How old were you then, sixteen?''

''Somewhere around there.''

Nathan looked at her strangely, for he remembered his entire childhood quite vividly. It never occurred to him that everyone did not.

Nathan did not seem to be able to get enough of the scent so Margaret suggested, ''We can pick some and take it with us. There is no harm in that.''

''Where is the plaguey boy?'' asked Sir Owen of Eleanor for the third time. ''It's after five. Doesn't anyone keep an eye out for him?''

"Here he comes," Eleanor said from her vantage point by the terrace doors. "Margaret is with him and they appear to have been picking wildflowers." She raised an eyebrow.

"Well, do you think they will make a match of it?" Sir Owen asked impatiently as he too rose to watch the approach of the young couple.

"You just bring Nathan up to scratch," said Eleanor. "I will take care of Margaret."

"I can't deny I like the lad. He has spirit. Needs a bit of town polish, of course."

"We should open the London house and bring Cristine out next season, anyway. We would have until April to get him ready."

"We should be able to whip him into shape by then," Sir Owen decided.

Chapter Four

If Nathan thought he had finally gotten close to Margaret he was mistaken, for the next morning she treated him as coldly as ever. He knew he had said nothing to offend her after their walk. She had even played for him the night before. He imagined it was for him alone, since no one else seemed to appreciate her playing as he did. Now she appeared to have had a change of heart, for she snubbed him brutally enough at early breakfast to draw a reproof from Eleanor.

After breakfast the ladies usually retired to the morning room at the side of the house, where they sewed or wrote letters. From there Eleanor could also supervise work in the adjoining conservatory, which she had convinced Sir Owen to add to Gaites Hall. Nathan had often seen the sour-faced gardener who had murdered Sir Kaye's siblings toiling away in the steamy room, and he had felt no sympathy for the man.

Nathan strolled down to the stables and back to give Margaret a chance to cool off, then presented himself in the morning room only to find her missing. Eleanor took pity on him and said she thought Margaret had gone for a walk in the garden. Cristine hid a smile behind her sewing frame, but Nathan was not embarrassed by his pursuit of Margaret, only by his lack of success.

He came upon her on a bench in the arbor where she had evidently been dismembering roses. "Lovely—the morning, I mean," he said at her defiant look. She was wearing a particularly becoming cream muslin dress that just then was decorated with hundreds of loose pink rose petals. Nathan drank his fill of her. Even angry she looked beautiful. He did not sit down but stood looking at the flowers. "Do you ride this morning?"

"It will be too hot by the time the others get up."

"We could go now," he suggested.

"Are you sure you trust me, after I nearly got you killed?"

"That is the second time you have said that, and once again I assure you, I knew what I was doing. Margaret, what's the matter?"

She looked at him resentfully. It was so like him to bluntly ask for an explanation. "It's what Eleanor says."

"Stop listening to what Eleanor says."

"I was right. She says it is my fault you have not offered. She puffed off all your advantages to me and recommended that I make a push to catch you since I really have no choice in the matter."

"Damn! It's time I had a talk with Aunt Eleanor."

"No!" Margaret said, jumping up as though she would restrain him and littering the ground with rose petals. "You will only make things a thousand times worse."

"Do you realize how few women would have told me this outright?"

"I don't know why I said it," Margaret blurted out, "except that it is your fault."

Nathan went back to his contemplation of the fragrant beauties, sorry now that he had spoiled the lovely picture she made by causing her to stand.

"You may pick them if you like," she said as though to a schoolboy.

"One flower only—" he picked a single perfect rose "—will I risk. So, please, if you are going to do something dreadful to it, don't let me see."

She held the bloom in the palm of her hand, half-minded to crush it.

"I'm sorry," he whispered.

"About what?" She hit him with her challenging look.

"That no one has ever given you anything." He walked on without seeing the puzzlement in her eyes.

Nathan did not know quite what to make of Margaret. Even when she was cruel to him he wanted her to like him. That she would sooner or later relent and be kind to him again he was sure. Beyond that, her hot-and-cold nature was something of a puzzle, since her moods seemed to come and go without any action on his part. He could not believe that Eleanor could upset her so. He found Margaret exciting as no other woman had been, and there was something else. He truly cared about her in a way that had nothing to do with loving her. He admired her and wanted to help her out of her predicament.

She treated him passably well the rest of the day and, if apologizing for things that were not his fault was all it took, Nathan was quite willing to keep Margaret happy in this way.

It was on one of these days when Margaret had been blowing hot and cold on Nathan that Sir Owen broached the subject of his proposed education. Margaret scowled at these plans for the further entrenchment of Nathan, who did not even seem to be struggling to free himself.

"You can rely on Matthew to show you how to ride and drive. Cristine can teach you how to dance and Eleanor will mend your manners," decided Sir Owen.

"I will teach him fishing and shooting," Jeremy offered eagerly.

"Jared, you can help, too," said Sir Owen. "You instruct him in boxing and fencing." Jared was too stunned at the prospect to reply.

Nathan grinned at Jared and drew a venomous stare in return.

"What will Margaret teach him?" Jeremy asked innocently.

"Humility!" Nathan blurted out, then regretted it. Even Jared chuckled as Margaret rose and stalked from the room.

Nathan ran her to earth in the conservatory. He had never haunted the place, having had his fill of steamy jungles on his voyages. He had to admit there was something about the hot, pungent earth odor that was stimulating, and something else today, a sweet scent. Margaret was sitting on one of the warped wooden benches by the rustic table in the center. Nathan supposed the furniture had been placed there for the casual stroller, but the area now seemed to be given over for the purpose of potting and transplanting. Margaret was struggling with a small mimosa tree and Nathan picked up the root ball for her while she exchanged the tub it was in for a larger size.

"It smells like someplace I have been. I wish I could remember where," Nathan said lightly.

Margaret watched his clear eyes as he looked intently at the surrounding plants and searched his past catalog of memories. "Is not one jungle much like another?" she asked.

"No, the plants are all different." He wandered up one of the side paths of herringbone brick. "It's this flower—frangipani."

"We call it a temple-tree. It is poisonous, you know."

Nathan let go the flower he had been holding. "So many lovely things are," he whispered almost to himself.

Margaret turned her back crossly.

"What do you do in the winter?"

"What do you mean?" she asked, taken off guard.

"About the heat."

"Oh, there is a stove over there. The gardener keeps it going most of the time."

"And you the rest of the time?" Nathan surmised.

"I come down to check on it. No one else would think of it," she said tiredly.

"I'm glad you do. This is too lovely a place to lose." He had drawn closer to her. "I am sorry. I did not mean to make game of you."

"Why do you act such a fool? It is not very complimentary to us."

"When all of your expectations are so low the temptation to satisfy them is overwhelming."

"How long do you mean to stay here?" she asked bluntly.

"I don't know. I had not thought about it. Why?"

"I don't want you here."

She was not jesting, Nathan thought, as he looked into her eyes. He had seen women seductive, calculating, even angry, but he had never seen the kind of repugnance Margaret was projecting now. It surprised him that it hurt so much. He had written off the Gaites family years ago. Why now feel so crushed at Margaret's rejection? He turned to go, lost inside himself. That so few words could slice the joy out of his day and send him off to sit on a rock amazed him.

Margaret would have preferred Nathan to fly into a rage with her. Instead he just wandered away with that lost, puzzled look, like a dog that cannot fathom why it has been kicked. He could not know it was not even his fault. Why did she abuse him so? Even in the short time Nathan had been there, she had come to like him better than anyone she had ever met. If only he were not so docile. He should stamp his foot, consign Gaites Hall and all its inhabitants to perdition and storm out. It was the kind of exit she would make if she were a man.

But even as she thought about wanting him to leave, she felt bereft at the prospect. He talked to her and drew her out of herself, how she did not quite understand. She would miss him when he left.

But leave he must. He was too good to be trapped here, too innocent to be corrupted by greed. She did like Nathan. She did not like the idea of what he would become if he stayed here, hanging on Sir Owen's sleeve. For his own good she must send Nathan on his way.

Jared was pretty much trapped at Gaites Hall until he got some financial relief. His actual living expenses were minimal, since he kept a few rooms of the London house open with a skeleton staff. But the debts he owed tradesmen were a point of embarrassment. Even when quarter day came he could not afford to pay the lot without beggaring himself for the next three months. And these were nothing to his gaming debts. Not everyone insisted on immediate payment, but it was damned embarrassing to meet someone you owed money to, hence his enforced stay at Gaites Hall.

His grandfather was always the one to rescue him from these predicaments. Whether he refused to do so this time to punish Jared, as Matthew thought, or to keep him in the country, even Jared could not say.

His chief amusements at the hall were the fights he started among the family. He had a masterful way of setting them against each other, then sitting innocently back and watching them thrash themselves into knots of rage. For some reason this did not work as well with Nathan, who simply refused to be provoked.

Jared could not make out if Nathan was really the ignorant boy he appeared to be. By the way he parried some of Jared's thrusts, he was neither innocent nor stupid. The thought did occur to Jared that he might be an impostor hired by Matthew to impersonate the missing Nathan, but he discarded this. In his opinion Matthew had not the intelligence to invent such a scheme, nor the nerve to carry it off.

Jared knew that sooner or later his grandfather would unbend toward him. If he could be in his grandfather's good graces before Sir Owen died, and inherit the bulk of the unentailed properties, the rents would keep him at his ease.

Let Nathan try to scrape by at Gaites Hall with no income. Jared might not be able to unseat Nathan, but he could make sure he had a very rough ride of it.

"Are you going for a walk?" Dicea called to Jeremy and Nathan from the terrace one morning.

"No, silly, fishing. Do you want to come?" her brother called back generously.

"I better not. Miss Prin might be mad if I get muddy."

"Perhaps she would let you come with us if she knew you were going to practice your sketching," Nathan suggested.

"I suppose I could tell her that." Dicea looked conspiratorial.

"I don't mean lie to her," Nathan chided. "I mean you could sketch while we fish. Go and ask her for a blanket to sit on, as well."

"Will you tell me a story, too?" Dicea asked as she opened the terrace door a few minutes later.

"Unless the fish in these parts have ears, I don't see why not."

Miss Prin's permission had been easily obtained. Since Nathan had arrived, not only had the child's behavior improved but her spirits had risen, as well. Dicea had really begun to delight in learning, if only to please her new friend.

Jeremy tolerated his sister's chatter as well as a boy his age might be expected to, and he got so interested in Nathan's story about the Spanish Armada that he nearly missed a tug on his line. Jeremy had caught enough perch to make a side dish for dinner and he was just thinking how pleased Sir Owen would be. Nathan had seemed more interested in commenting on Dicea's sketch of the bridge than in concentrating on fishing. When he pulled in a tiny perch, he said, "At last."

"That's pathetic," Jeremy scoffed. "Throw him back for a few years. What are you doing?"

Nathan had freed the fish but reinserted the hook under the jaw so the tiny creature lashed about alive but captive. "Bait," Nathan said darkly.

Whatever struck at Nathan's line then nearly pulled the pole out of his hands. "What the devil have you got in this lake, a whale?"

"It must be Old Hunchback," Jeremy said excitedly. "Whatever you do, don't lose him."

"Who's Old Hunchback?" Nathan asked as he pulled in the line slowly hand over hand, tugging against a great weight.

"A monstrous pike we have all been trying to catch for ages." Jeremy ran for the net. "He won't fit."

Both Nathan and Jeremy were muddied and wet to the waist by the time they dragged the huge fish up the bank and stood back to watch it flopping desperately in the sun. Dicea's eyes were wide with shock. "Grandfather will be so proud of you," Jeremy said. "He's the only one who has even gotten a hook into Old Hunchback."

Nathan saw the distorted spine that gave the creature his name, many other scars, and for some arcane reason, a resemblance to his grandfather. He looked at Dicea and knew she was thinking of Sir Kaye. "Quick, help me get the hook out," Nathan said to Jeremy.

"Why, what are you doing?"

"We have to get him back in the water quickly or he will die," Nathan said, as he freed the huge fish and began to drag it back down the bank.

"Are you mad? The whole idea behind fishing is to catch them, not let them go." Jeremy was jumping up and down with frustration.

"Not this one. This one is special. You should have warned me." One last tug and Nathan landed in the lake with the fish. He held it upright in the water and began to walk it around until its gills started pumping water again. When it was strong enough, it left him of its own accord and dived for deeper water, almost knocking him over with a flip of its tail. "We did it!" Nathan slapped the water and Dicea cheered.

"All you have done is convince me you should be clapped up in the attic. How am I going to explain this to Sir Owen?"

"Simple. Don't tell him," said Nathan, slogging up the bank and picking up the discarded tackle. "You understand, don't you, Dicea?"

"Oh, yes. Don't you see, Jeremy? Fishing would never be any fun again if Old Hunchback were gone. It's more important that he be alive than that we have him for dinner."

"Well, I suppose it does mean I will get a chance at him yet. I won't forget that trick you used, either, Nathan."

At least Jeremy could lay claim to all the fish they would be eating that night and, although he did not tell Sir Owen, he did relate the story to Jared. The fish was just being served that night when Sir Owen pounced on Nathan.

"And what the devil do you mean by catching Old Hunchback and then letting him go? We have been trying to land that old pike for years."

"Perhaps you will one day, when the time is right for him to die."

"What the devil do you mean?"

"It just felt wrong to me, sir. I did not even know he was in there and I used a seaman's trick to hook him. It didn't seem fair. Besides, it would have been too much like killing a legend. You don't do that sort of thing any day of the week."

Nathan's grandfather looked searchingly at him but said no more on the subject.

Margaret had been enduring an almost daily lecture from Eleanor on the imprudence of letting Nathan get away. She also had to watch Dicea and Jeremy practically worshiping him and Cristine sighing over his kindness. Everyone seemed to like him except Jared, who had good cause not to. She also felt that they were all watching her to see when she was going to succumb to Nathan's charms. They would all be surprised when he left at the end of June without ever proposing to her. Somehow this thought was far from comforting.

Jared had hinted to Jeremy that he should ask Nathan to get him a position on one of the vessels he knew of in Bristol. Of course, Jeremy broached the subject at dinner, but Nathan merely said he did not think Jeremy would care for a life at sea. Sir Owen began to seethe as Jeremy persisted.

Finally it was Margaret who stood up and stated, "Are you forgetting that I know what it's like aboard those ships—the beatings, the filth, the wormy biscuits. I won't have you dragging my brother off to sea and that's final." She left the room, and Eleanor and Cristine rose to withdraw, as well.

"Your sister's right. We'll have no more talk of it." Sir Owen ended the discussion.

They spent an uncomfortable evening with Jeremy pouting and Margaret fuming. No one dared ask her to play anything that evening. When the ceremony of the tea tray finally released them for the night, Jared hung back in the main hall with Nathan to say in a confidential manner, "One good thing about your coming, at least now, I won't be expected to marry that damned shrew, Margaret."

Nathan looked searchingly at Jared. "Were you going to marry her?"

"Why not, since Grandfather wished it?"

"But you cannot possibly pretend to love her."

"Margaret and I had an understanding. You see, Grandfather plans to leave the bulk of his estate to her."

"She is certainly competent to manage it," Nathan parried.

"He's doing it to get her married, of course." Jared started up the stairs. "Gaites Hall would be of little use to me without the money to maintain it. We planned to pool our resources, financially speaking, but she was to have this house and I was to live in London."

Nathan stopped on the bottom step, looking horrified. "Sounds damned cold-blooded to me. I can't believe she consented to such a scheme."

"Actually," Jared drawled, his eyes half-veiled by his lids, "she suggested it." The hurt look in the blue eyes gazing up at him was quite satisfying. "You might be able to make a similar arrangement with her."

Nathan's stomach lurched and he knew a strong momentary wish to lash out at Jared's sneering, aristocratic face.

"Of course," Jared continued, "she would never condemn you for any little affair you might have so long as you were discreet and did your duty at home."

Nathan set his jaw. "I suppose such arrangements are common among your class. Forgive me if I cannot stomach them." Nathan brushed past him and went on up the stairs. Jared chuckled to himself. He never wanted Margaret himself, nor had he ever any intention of marrying her. But if he could keep Nathan and Margaret apart, Sir Owen might be displeased enough to leave the estate to him. Sir Owen might hold the purse strings at Gaites Hall, but Jared felt that he pulled all the others.

What Jared did not realize was that Nathan had not believed Margaret capable of an alliance with someone she held in contempt. Desperate as she was, she would sooner starve, he felt, than stoop to such an arrangement. What upset Nathan was having lies told behind her back. He wondered if there was anything Jared would stop at to amuse himself, and he began to worry about what Jared might be telling Margaret about him.

Nathan lay low the next day, determined to give Margaret time to cool off. He was beginning to despair of ever winning her. Margaret, on reflection, realized she had allowed Jared to use her again and spent a good bit of the day surreptitiously looking for Nathan to apologize. She could still see his stunned face as she accused him of luring her brother away when Nathan had said nothing culpable.

After dinner Nathan did not enter the drawing room with the rest of the gentlemen. Margaret waited a decent time, then made an excuse of needing to look for more thread. "Gregson," she said, swallowing her pride, "where is Nathan?"

"I believe he stepped out on the terrace, miss."

"Thank you," she said, proceeding toward the stairs. But when Gregson had left the hall, she reentered the dining room and went to the open terrace door. She looked sideways at the doors that led into the drawing room, but they were closed and she could just catch the murmur of voices within. Then she saw Nathan, standing on the terrace, peering out into the sleepy darkness. The peeping of frogs was loud enough to cover her approach. Margaret saw and felt and heard the night but dismissed it all as useless information, unlike Nathan, who seemed to be fascinated by it. She watched him for a moment, for he was not his normal, relaxed self. He was tensed, as though watching something.

"Nathan."

He jumped and half turned to her. "Look at those," he almost whispered. "What are they?" His voice was full of awe.

"Where? I don't see anything."

"All those little lights moving around out there."

"Oh. Fireflies. Surely you have seen those before."

"No. I have heard of them, of course. But I had no idea. It almost makes you believe in fairies."

Margaret watched them for a while, trying to imagine fairy folk flitting about with little lanterns. She found herself wishing she could believe, or even just appreciate, the loveliness of the lights floating about, winking on and off at random. Dicea would understand and join him in this magical spell he seemed to weave. Leave it to Nathan to turn an ordinary thing into a mystical experience. She felt herself to be far too prosaic to cross over into his realm. Yet she was reluctant to speak and break the mood.

"Amazing, oh, what did you want?" Nathan asked at last.

"To apologize, for ripping up at you last night. I'm sure it was Jared who put those ideas in Jeremy's head, not you."

"You see through him, too?"

"I suppose we all do, but never in time. And it's no good saying anything to Sir Owen about Jared. The damage is done, but the thought of Jeremy going through what you did was too much for me. He's not strong like you. He was ill the better part of his life, so he has been more sheltered than most boys his age."

"It was not such a bad life. At least I had only myself to look after. It would have worried me to death if I had had sisters and a little brother to take care of as you did."

"You needn't tell me it was not a bad life. I have seen the scars."

Nathan cringed as though once again feeling the stroke of the lash on his back.

"I'm sorry. I should not have said that." She sat down on the bench by the terrace wall.

"It's all right." He joined her on the bench. "That was Captain Rayburn, a slave trader and a great believer in the whip. There were few men who served under him who did not come away with some stripes. I remember thinking it was a hard thing to be beaten just for stowing away, but there was a chance there would not be enough food. They gave me the job of feeding the blacks and I did the best I could for them, but I was little better than a slave myself."

"Was there enough food?"

"Yes, but some of them died anyway."

"Sickness?"

"Not so much that as despair, I think. Families were torn apart. Mothers lost their children. The men had been warriors in their own land, one of them a king by what I could understand. Any of them could have killed me with one hand, but they knew it was not my fault."

"Thank God it has been outlawed."

"Yes, but only in England, and only the selling of them. What's to become of all those still captive in a strange land with no way to find their families?"

"It makes me feel I have little to complain of."

"Me, either. I was lucky Captain Hewitt took me on then. What a difference. You could take a crew of ordinary seamen, put them under Rayburn, who would beat them to get their respect, and they would act like a pack of curs. If you put the very same men under Captain Hewitt, he would tell them that he knew he could rely on every man to defend the ship with his life and you could see the courage flow into them. They would face the ugliest storm or privateers and never flinch."

"That's what you do for Dicea, is it not?"

"Something like that. I suppose we all act out the role other people have cast us in. Perhaps, unconsciously, we do what other people expect of us."

"You mean I am ill-tempered because people expect me to be? That's silly."

"I would call you volatile, not ill-tempered. Now Grandfather is ill-tempered. Everyone expects him to be and that is how he acts."

"Ha, you are wrong there! We expect him to act like that because he always has."

"Then it's high time someone changed him."

"You cannot be serious. That's impossible."

"I will show you. It won't happen overnight. But he will mellow, if I show him that's what I expect from him. I'm the only one who can change him, since I'm the only one who has not cast him in his old mold."

"Oh, no, the tea tray," Margaret gasped, as she heard the rattle of cups from inside the drawing room.

"I'm sorry. I have made us late." Nathan advanced toward the terrace doors.

"I can't go in that way," Margaret said desperately.

"I forgot you don't like to be seen with me." Nathan grinned. "You flit back through the dining room and come in through the hall. I will go in this way." He kissed her cheek and was gone. In her flight back to where she was supposed to be, Margaret almost did not realize what he had gotten away with.

Nathan was already seated and looking smug by the time Margaret came in and cast him a vengeful look. He appeared so puzzled that she could almost think the kiss an automatic parting response, but by then she was beginning to realize how subtle he was. Other than drawing a disapproving look from Eleanor, who was forced to distribute the tea out of order, she was not censured for her tardy entrance. Either Sir Owen was in a benign mood, or he suspected that she had been dallying with Nathan.

"Hell and damnation!" Sir Owen spit out with a mouthful of soup at dinner the next night.

Nathan eyed him with concern. "Whatever is the matter, Grandfather? It's not like you to lose your temper over nothing."

Since this statement was so patently untrue, the entire table turned to stare at Nathan and waited for the head of the family to blister him for such audacity. Sir Owen, though not always acute, was preparing just such a retort, but the ingenuousness of Nathan's expression made him pause. Whether he considered Nathan an unworthy prey or whether he saw some justice in the remark—he had been trying to keep his temper with the boy—he merely said, "The soup's too hot."

"I quite see how that would put you out. Fortunately we have only to wait a minute to mend that. Now if it were too cold, we should have to send it back."

"Are you finished?" Sir Owen disliked senseless chatter, but since he detected no sarcasm in Nathan's innocent nod, he proceeded with the meal in peace.

* * *

Nathan's next opportunity came when they were waiting for the horses to be saddled the next morning. Sir Owen looked critically at Trafalgar's hind foot, picked it up and said, "Damn it all!"

"Is it serious, Grandfather? It's not like you to be put out unless it is." Nathan peered stupidly at the hoof, while Jared and Matthew, already mounted, waited for an explosion.

"He's loosened a shoe. I can't ride him like this."

"Oh, is that all? Lucky you have so many other horses to ride."

"Ferrow! Ferrow! Where is that groom? Here, get him shod today and saddle Samarkand for me instead." Ferrow led the beast off with a look of fear in his eyes and almost instantly produced what Nathan considered to be a much prettier horse, a tall dapple gray. As Nathan did nothing to disgrace himself on the ride, did not ask any stupid questions about the wheat or barley, and even scrambled over one or two hedges, Sir Owen came back in a tolerably good mood.

Two days elapsed before Nathan caught his grandfather at another bad moment. They were just riding past the lane to the cow barn when a crash and a great deal of yelling heralded the exit of a nasty-looking bull with lopped horns.

"Damn!"

"What is it, Grandfather? It's not like you to swear over nothing."

"Can't you see, you idiot! The bull is loose."

"Oh, is that all?" Nathan had not much experience with domestic cows, but he had seen wild ones driven. He rode over to a tree, broke off a forked branch of leaves, and kicked Hannibal. He cantered toward the bull, who was standing uncertainly in the lane between the hedges. Nathan twirled the branch over his head so that it emitted a tremendous whooshing. Hannibal, his name not withstanding, had never done anything like charge a snorting evil-eyed creature his own size, but the bull had never been

confronted by such a sight, either, and the strange sound
made him start nervously backward. Seeing the creature give
ground was enough for Hannibal. With Nathan urging him
on, he would have ridden right into the bull, if the animal
had not finally turned and fled back into the barn. The
astounded cowmen clapped the door shut, barred it and set
up a cheer.

"You idiot! How dare you use a horse of mine like that?
He might have been killed, and you along with him."

"Oh, no, I don't think so, sir. You had only to look at the
old beast to tell he was all bluff and bluster."

"Bulls are dangerous and unpredictable. Don't you forget that."

"Yes, sir. I will remember," Nathan said dutifully.

Sir Owen let Nathan go on thinking he was displeased
with him, but that did not prevent him from telling the tale
in the drawing room that night to the amazement of Eleanor
and Cristine. Margaret's reaction, part anger and part worry
that he could have been gored or trampled, confused Nathan.

It was a special night. Nathan had convinced Eleanor that
Dicea had a good enough piano piece ready to perform for
them, and there was no harm in letting her stay up for tea
just this once. Dicea was in her prettiest dress. She played
confidently and, so far as Nathan could tell, without error,
the simple yet elegant work chosen for her by Miss Prin.
Even Eleanor deigned to smile and nod as Dicea curtsied
after her performance. Except for the way she looked at
Nathan, Margaret was on her best behavior so as not to
scare Dicea and they had a charming evening.

When Eleanor began to serve the tea, she said, "Dicea,
will you give this cup to Sir Owen?" Dicea obediently took
the cup and saucer and carefully transported it across the
room. Sir Owen, who was explaining something to Matthew, must have bumped the cup with his hand, for a little
of the hot liquid splashed on his knee.

"Damn!" he said. Dicea leaped back as though she had been struck.

"Sorry, child. I should not swear in front of you. It's not like me to lose my temper over such a trifle. Thank you."

Everyone in the room looked at him in astonishment as he blotted his handkerchief on his knee. Dicea had the aspect of one reprieved from the ax. She came to sit beside Nathan after her close call. Margaret was taking an unwary sip of tea when Nathan winked at her. She choked and looked daggers at his self-satisfied smile. She should know better than to put anything in her mouth with him in line of sight.

So he had made good his boast. He had turned the naggy Sir Owen into an old lamb. He did not have to be so smug about it. And what did it prove after all? Nathan could not change her, especially since she knew he meant to try.

Dicea was begging for the legend of Merlin again. Nathan began the tale almost in a whisper, as though it was for Dicea's ears alone. That brought the room to dead silence except for the compelling sound of his voice. Like Merlin he wove a spell about them, not of spider webs and potions, but of sound and imagery. One would not have thought a bedtime story would hold the interest of adults, but there was not so much as a cough for half an hour.

"And so," Nathan finished, "the greatest magician ended his life as we all begin it, in childlike simplicity. It is the regression we are all compelled to face if we are lucky enough to live so long. His clearest memories were those bright ones of early childhood, untrammeled by worry, fear or responsibility. In the end all that was left to him was what he first wrote down in his memory—the golden warmth of the sun, the clear sweet smell of the spring air, and the calling note of a merlin."

"Where did you hear that?" Jeremy asked.

"My mother told it to me when I was little," Nathan said, finishing his coffee. "I suppose I have added to it."

Margaret had felt the oddest sensation, a suspension of care, a taste of the childhood she had never had. Worry and duty had become such habits she could not until that moment imagine life without them. She did not regret her life though: what she had gone though had been necessary and had made her a better person. But it would be wonderful to live her life backward like Merlin and become a child now.

Margaret was going easy on Nathan. It was the last week of June and she wanted to part from him on peaceful terms so that she could not be stigmatized for having driven him away. Besides, she had to admit she rather enjoyed his company. He was like no one she had ever met before. She would almost be sorry to see him go, but she supposed he would come to visit them at Christmas, at least, for Dicea's sake.

They were riding together before breakfast and she playfully evaded him in the home wood. By the time he saw her break cover on the road headed for the village she had a vast lead. But he guessed her destination and cut through the woods, riding like a maniac, to cut her off at the turn in the road. Seeing him coming from an unexpected direction, she felt a moment of panic, like she did in her dream, and almost spurred her mare to run from him. She quickly realized it was childish and dangerous to play these games. He might take another fall, he was so careless.

"You caught up to me."

"Yes, in more ways than one," Nathan announced proudly. "I just remembered I have had a birthday this month. I'm the same age as you now. Will you marry me?" he asked as though on impulse.

"What! You promised you would never ask me that." She jerked her mare to a halt.

"No, I said I would never go to sea again if I were to marry."

"You tricked me," Margaret accused, her color heightened. "You mean to stay after all and you must not. It will ruin you."

"But we have been getting along so well lately."

"I have been tolerating you. That's all. If you stay I will come to detest you as much as I do Jared."

Nathan looked so downcast at this that she almost relented. But she knew she had to dash his hopes once and for all.

"What made you think your age had anything to do with it?"

"I made sure that was it."

"But in two months I shall be twenty-seven. Then where will you be?"

"I had hoped to be married by then," he said dismally.

"There are a hundred reasons why I won't marry you." She urged her mare on.

"But what are they? Tell me. Maybe I can put them right." He trotted by her side, trying to see her face.

Margaret thought desperately, trying to come up with any excuse, something that would discourage him forever. "You really cannot expect me to marry an illiterate, can you?" she lashed at him.

Nathan was so shocked he almost fell off his horse. "What are you talking about?"

"You don't even know what the word means, do you?" she said in exasperation. She truly was angry with him now. "Perhaps Miss Prin can enlighten you, or even Dicea. But I doubt they can mend the deficiency no matter how much time you spend in the schoolroom."

Nathan had taken cuts from Margaret before. But he had never seen her so deliberately vicious. He searched her eyes, hopelessly, and there he saw it, behind the black pain and resentment, a look of terror. Why should Margaret ever be afraid of him? He had been careful never to give her cause.

Then she was gone in a flurry of hoofbeats and he let her ride away. He began to wonder if he would ever get inside her defences. He rode back slowly, trying to make sense of her strange comments and her fear. He supposed getting her to write that letter for him might have suggested the idea, then he remembered Jared's antics with Sir Walter Scott, and chuckled in spite of his disappointment.

Probably only the servants and Dicea had any idea he could read and write. But the others all accepted him anyway, even his grandfather. It was quite touching when he thought about it. For some perverse reason he thought Margaret should be at least as charitable. A hundred reasons, she had said. He feared to think what the other ninety-nine might be.

Margaret did not ride to the village but went on a solitary cross-country gallop that would have terrified Nathan, perhaps even Sir Owen. She pulled up in the home wood an hour later to walk the steaming and trembling Titian into a cooler state. She was too embarrassed to take her horse back to the groom in this condition.

She could not forget the look in Nathan's eyes, the change in him. He had been smiling, his blue eyes alight with laughter. She had said the cruelest things she could think of to be rid of him. His eyes had turned murky and troubled like the sea he found solace in. At least she might have driven him away from this prison. But then she remembered that hurt look and wept.

It was not playing fair to cut at Nathan, for he would not defend himself. She could never remember seeing him angry. May as well slap Dicea as to lash out at Nathan. One was as innocent as the other. Yet she could see no other way to spring him from the trap. Her mind snatched wildly at the idea of going with him. Had she been alone, responsible only for herself, she might have done so. But there was Dicea and Cristine to think of. Even Jeremy still needed her.

It took her so long to compose herself that Nathan had long since returned, walked about the garden waiting for her, and was on the point of saddling up again to go look for her. She ignored his presence at the stable and Nathan knew better than to try to talk to her immediately, but followed her meekly into the house. She kept herself under tight rein until she got to her bedroom where she quite deliberately smashed a vase. Her maid escaped without helping her undress, and Margaret threw herself down in her riding habit for a frustrated cry.

"What the devil did you do to Margaret?" whispered Matthew, trotting down the stairs to breakfast.

"I asked her to marry me," Nathan said dryly. "She did not take it well."

Nathan was wrong in thinking that all of the family were ignorant of his education. Dicea and Miss Prin had taken to having afternoon tea and lessons on the terrace on fair days, another innovation of Nathan's. Eleanor rather liked it since she could monitor Dicea's progress without making Miss Prin nervous. If she and Cristine chose to work in the adjoining drawing room in the afternoon for the light, she was sure no one could think it odd of them.

The history Nathan related during tea and the questions he answered convinced Eleanor that he was well-grounded in both ancient and modern learning, not to mention languages. She could only suppose his education self-acquired, but he most certainly knew how to read to have come by so much information. It was none of the sort of thing she imagined sailors discussed of an evening.

She rather enjoyed her eavesdropping, and she frequently observed tears in Cristine's eyes when one of Nathan's characters was doomed but fought valiantly on. Nathan's stories were compelling. Whether they were factual recitals of great events and battles or whimsical tales full of elves and fairies, he dressed the characters in the threads of his own imagination. He even mimicked the voices, and Eleanor barely escaped laughing out loud at some of the accents he used for his villains. She could now understand Dicea's devotion to him. By treating Dicea as an equal he had turned a lonely, rebellious child into the most delightful and inquisitive creature. If only he could work the same magic on Margaret.

Nathan was making a midnight foray to the library when Matthew caught him in the act.

"I couldn't sleep," Nathan apologized, shutting the book he had been perusing.

"Was your room too hot?"

"What?"

"That you should need such a large book to prop open your window." Matthew screwed his head sideways to read the title. "They will never miss that one."

"It should, at least, cure my sleeplessness."

"May I ask why you led everyone to believe you an imbecile?"

"Why, I never did so," Nathan claimed innocently.

"You certainly never attempted to dispel the notion."

"You must recollect my reception here was less than warm. I admit I tried to give them all a disgust of me, but I had no idea I succeeded so well until Margaret informed me she could not possibly marry an illiterate."

"It made no difference to me if you could read or not."

"I know, and thank you."

"But you seem to be caught in a trap of your own making." Matthew leaned against the bookshelves. "Why don't you set her straight?"

"Not yet. She may come around anyway. Sometimes I think all I have going for me is her conscience and compassion."

"I can tell you it fairly tears my heart out to see you moping about after her. If you are not careful you may find yourself in another trap of your own making. She may accept your next proposal."

"Are you warning me off?"

"Certainly not, if you are serious. I may not get along that well with Margaret, but she's had the devil of a lot to put up with from everyone, and I will not have her hurt."

"Since you ask, then, I am not trifling. I mean to marry her if she will have me. If not, I mean to at least provide for her so she does not feel so trapped here. She called this place a prison."

"I had no idea she hated it so."

"What can I do for her? Do you think she would rather have a house in town?"

"I would not think so. She would not be able to go tearing around the countryside on that horse of hers. You had better ask her."

"The direct approach? That usually ends in disaster, but I will try it next time I'm feeling lucky."

Dicea was playing on the terrace with Sir Kaye and a ball of yarn when Sir Owen came out to take the air the next afternoon. She gathered the kitten up protectively, curtsied silently and made as if to leave.

"Don't run off, child. Let's have a look at him."

Sir Kaye was no fool. When the old man sat down and drew him onto his lap, the cat immediately started to purr and groom himself. The old fingers unconsciously began to stroke him.

Dicea sat on the bench next to Sir Owen's chair.

"So you and Nathan seem to get along fairly well."

"Oh, yes. I'm so glad he came to live here. He knows how to climb trees, catch frogs, and tell his position from the stars. And he is the best storyteller."

"Sea stories, eh?"

"Not many. I don't think that was a happy time in his life. They are mostly stories from long ago."

"Well, you understand that they are not for real, don't you?"

"Most of them are. He always tells me first if it's a true story or a fairy story. The fairy stories all have happy endings. In the true stories sometimes people die."

Sir Owen nodded.

"But even in the fairy stories true things happen. I mean the characters are true. They do not fail each other, like Nathan jumping into the lake to save Sir Kaye." Dicea's eyes grew big when she realized that might not be a good incident to bring up.

"That was brave of him," was Sir Owen's only comment.

"He was underwater so long, I feared he had drowned himself."

The maid was just bringing the tea tray out onto the terrace and Nathan and Miss Prin were following her through the dining room. They both halted stock-still in the doorway when they saw Dicea sitting talking to Sir Owen, who kept stroking the now-sleeping kitten.

Nathan wiped the surprise from his face with an effort. "Is Sir Owen joining us today?"

"Oh, yes, please do, sir. We get the cakes freshly baked," Dicea confided to him.

"I'm a bit old for a tea party."

"Please stay, Sir Owen," Miss Prin encouraged. "Nathan is going to tell us about the battle of Trafalgar."

"I must warn you though, sir. We cover some pretty gory ground during teatime. I hope it does not put you off the cake."

"Lead on, Nathan," the old man said, laughing.

Sir Owen not only made it through tea, but sat contentedly listening to the geography lesson. Dicea ran upstairs for Nathan's sextant, clock and charts. To Nathan's surprise she gave Sir Owen a rather lucid explanation of determining their latitude and longitude if it should become necessary.

"This is a navigator's rig," Sir Owen commented.

"I had Captain Hewitt send mine out to us. Did you think I was still a common seaman?"

"I don't know what to think of you."

"I should not bore you then."

They spent so long over Dicea's lessons that Nathan and Sir Owen had to go directly up to change so as not to be late for dinner.

"Come up to my room. I want to talk to you." To his aged valet he merely said, "Leave us for a few minutes, Heron," and waited for the door to close behind his retainer.

"I suppose you have wondered why I waited so long to send for you." He poured them each a brandy and handed one to Nathan.

"You don't owe me any explanations, sir."

"Sit down. You are going to get one anyway." Nathan blinked and complied. "When your father defied me I told him I never wanted to see him again. He didn't defy me in a nasty way. He just smiled and laughed and took himself off to marry your mother. You often put me in mind of him, by the way. But I thought he knew I did not mean it." He took a drink. "That was the last time I saw him. When your mother wrote to me, I had already had Jared and Matthew here snapping and snarling at each other for two years. Your mother said it was her duty to tell me that Robert was lost at sea, but she would brook no interference from me where you were concerned. Damn fine woman. I wish I had got to know her."

"Thank you, sir."

"Once I had the Weston children here, with Jared baiting Jeremy into all kinds of scrapes and Margaret always storming at Jared, I seriously did not think I could stand any more. Margaret used to be very nasty tempered."

Nathan looked up at him in surprise and smiled. "I see, not like she is now, you mean?"

The corner of Sir Owen's mouth twitched. "Take my word for it. She is much improved, especially since you have come. I want to know if you mean to stay or not. Matthew said you only promised for a month.''

"There is much to hold me here, you, and Dicea . . .''

"What about Margaret?''

"I told her I would never marry if I intended to go back to sea,'' Nathan hedged. "Yet I cannot abandon my good friend, Captain Hewitt. His health is not as good as yours, I fear, and I must at least look after our interests in Bristol and London.''

"Your interests? What do you mean?''

"We are by way of being partners in several trading ventures. I shall have to look for a substitute to do the traveling for me. I would like to make my home here if you want me and if you don't object to me spending a good deal of time in Bristol.''

"If things stand like that, I have no hold on you.''

"Oh, but you have. I think I rather used to like being an orphan. But when you cut yourself off from everyone, while you may avoid worry and heartache, you also miss out on all the good things, as well. Now I find I rather like having a family.''

"I do want you to stay.''

"Thank you, sir.'' Nathan was just wondering if this was a good moment to offer to invest in the estate, but was as reluctant to push Sir Owen as he was to rush Margaret.

"You know, Margaret could prove quite useful to you.''

"Useful? I want her to be more than useful.'' Nathan had risen and was walking toward the door.

"I mean by taking care of your correspondence.''

"Why should I need her for that unless I break my hand again?'' Nathan gave him a blank look.

Sir Owen froze, thought a minute, then burst out laughing. "You young scamp. Why didn't you tell us Jared was mistaken?''

"Why, what did you think?'' Nathan asked innocently as he opened the door.

"You know very well what we thought.''

"Well, not right away." Nathan grinned. "But Margaret enlightened me. By the way, let's not tell Jared. It should be interesting to see if he catches cold over that."

Dicea's riding habit arrived the next day and she begged Nathan to teach her to ride once she was tricked out in it.

"I hope we can do better than me for a teacher. Let's go ask Sir Owen which horse you can ride."

"Look at my outfit, Sir Owen," Dicea said, tripping into the library.

"My, what an elegant young lady you are turning into."

"May I borrow one of the horses so Nathan can teach me to ride?"

"Nathan teach you to ride?" Sir Owen laughed in genuine amusement. "I'm sorry, Nathan, but I really think I had better take charge of these lessons."

Since this was exactly what Nathan had hoped, he was content to smile sheepishly.

"I think we had better put you up on Hannibal," Sir Owen decided as he surveyed the hot-blooded stock in his stable. "Nathan has not managed to ruin him yet. Nathan, you may ride Samarkand."

After the horses were saddled, Sir Owen instructed Dicea on how to mount and dismount, while Nathan made the large gray's acquaintance. Samarkand was Sir Owen's older hunter. "A bit contrary and hardmouthed" was the only introduction Nathan had to the horse. He had seen him rigged out before, military fashion, with two bits, but had never himself ridden with two sets of reins. He remembered that the curb bit was for braking and the snaffle for turning, but wished to heaven he had paid more attention to how his grandfather had held the reins. Finally he just took the curb reins in his right hand, which still had more strength in it, and the snaffle reins in his left hand. Sir Owen must have been observing this indecision out of the corner of his eye, but merely glanced at Nathan's arrangement and mounted without comment.

To Nathan's surprise they did not just ride around a pasture field, but took to the lanes and roads immediately. Sir Owen proved himself capable of a great deal of patience, not only in correcting Dicea, but in answering her endless questions. Nathan rode slightly behind so as not to distract them.

"Ready to try a jump?" Sir Owen asked.

"Oh, yes."

"Good girl," he said as she landed safely on the other side of the low wall. Nathan felt Samarkand fighting him as they approached the wall so he gave him a kick. Consequently they cleared the wall with feet to spare and landed raggedly on the other side. Sir Owen merely shook his head and Dicea giggled.

"Well, I didn't fall," Nathan said, laughing.

"That's something, I suppose," Sir Owen grumbled.

Sir Owen was strong in praise of Dicea that night at dinner. "She's a natural, I tell you. I have not seen a girl take to riding so well since we first threw Margaret up on a horse."

Margaret looked at Nathan with something like gratitude. If he read her right, she might be on speaking terms with him again. She volunteered to play after dinner, so he knew he was forgiven. There was no opportunity to speak to her that night or the next morning, for directly after breakfast Eleanor discovered a virulent kind of wilt among the conservatory plants and enlisted Margaret to root out and destroy the contaminated specimens.

"It looks like a real crisis," Nathan observed to Cristine.

"I take it the gardener forgot to open the windows yesterday afternoon and this is what comes when it gets too hot in there. I don't know much about it," Cristine said helplessly.

"Neither do I," said Nathan. "Let's stay out of their way." Nathan and Cristine seated themselves where they could observe the frantic efforts in the steamy room, and

Nathan said, "In some countries they would think it quite odd to build houses just to keep plants in. Of course, they have no winter. But the whole idea of bringing plants indoors, except flowers perhaps, is totally foreign to them." Cristine went on to question him about his travels and he told her what he knew about the daily life of the people he had encountered. "But tell me about your life."

"There's nothing to tell."

"Well, I have never been to Bath, so it seems as exotic to me as China does to you."

"We never went about much ourselves with Grandmama being so ill. Before she was bedridden we used to go with her to the pump room at the baths. It was funny to watch the quizzes all in their costumes just come out to stare at one another."

"What were your parents like?"

"I don't remember them very well except that they were always making jokes. They wore the gayest clothes and went to all the dances. I don't think Margaret quite approved of them."

"What?" Nathan sat up. "She could not have been more than seventeen."

"Yes, but she always worried about money, even back then."

Nathan shook his head. To his surprise he learned that Jeremy was the second oldest, not Cristine.

"He was a very delicate baby," Cristine told him solemnly. "Margaret said he nearly died half a dozen times in his first year."

"I suppose I don't have to ask who pulled him through."

"Margaret is a wonderful nurse. Dicea was just a baby when Mother and Father died. Margaret raised her almost single-handedly."

"More like a mother to her than a sister, in other words."

"To all of us, really. It was not too bad until Grandmama got very ill. Margaret stayed with her night and day.

I could watch Dicea by then, but Jeremy was always into trouble.''

"Didn't the servants do anything?''

"They started leaving when Margaret could no longer pay them.''

"My God! You didn't go hungry, did you?''

"No. Margaret always managed. She sold all of Mother's trinkets and even some of Grandmama's jewels. They were left to her anyway. But when Eleanor and Sir Owen came to arrange the funeral I think they were shocked at the state we were in. We came to live here then. Now we are comfortable with no worries. I am so grateful to them. I don't understand why Margaret is not. She has the most reason to be.''

Nathan hoped that Cristine would always find someone else to do her worrying for her. More puzzle pieces, but no real answers. Did Margaret enjoy struggling so much that she resented being carefree? Or was she so used to being martyred that she could not enjoy the luxuries provided for her? Finally Nathan decided that she, most probably, resented the loss of authority. Even though she had been standing on the deck of a burning ship, so to speak, it had been her ship. When Eleanor had transported them all here, Margaret had lost her authority over her sisters and brother. Cristine obeyed Eleanor. Jeremy was ruled by Sir Owen. Now he had lured Dicea away from her. No wonder Margaret had trouble masking her resentment from time to time.

Margaret had been seeking an opportunity to talk to Nathan, as well. She wanted to apologize for cutting up at him, but she also wanted to be careful not to reawaken his hopes. He had been such a pleasant companion when she felt there was no possibility of having to marry him. She would like to get back on that footing with him again. But being constantly spied upon made it difficult to meet him alone. Nathan usually walked in the garden or by the lake after Dicea's lessons and before it was time to change for dinner.

She supposed she had gotten into the habit of walking there, too, for they met each other there every day that she was not avoiding him.

She looked up expectantly when she heard footsteps but, when she recognized Jared, her change of expression from one of interest to one of disapproval must have been so sudden as to make that dandy laugh.

"I disappoint you, dear Margaret. I'm not Nathan. Forgive me, but I cannot go about with that hangdog expression, even to win you."

"What are you talking about?"

"That Nathan really has no competition. You know Matthew is not bold enough to offer for you, and I do have some standards."

He was prepared for violence and intercepted the slap by grabbing her wrist. "I didn't mean that, silly. Under other circumstances you would make me an admirable wife." She wrenched her hand away.

"What I cannot stomach is being constrained to marry in order to gain an inheritance. I give Nathan credit for seeing what he must do. No doubt Grandfather hinted him on. Has he begged for your hand yet?"

The flash of her eyes answered him.

"I thought so. Were he more adroit he might have succeeded by now. Who knows but what he may pull it off yet. You both must study to please Grandfather now." Jared sauntered off, more than satisfied with his results.

Margaret tramped down to the lake, hoping to work off her anger and frustration before she had to face everyone at dinner. She was in such a brown study, hardly watching where she was going, that she had started across the footbridge before she realized Nathan was there leaning on the railing.

"Margaret! What is it?"

"Get out of my way!"

Nathan had the misfortune to not listen to her. She looked so distraught he made the mistake of trying to detain her and inevitably received the blow earned by Jared. Nathan had thought he could handle himself pretty well when it came to a scrap, but the surprise of the assault overbalanced him, his weight broke the top rail, and he fell in. When he came up for air he saw only Margaret's retreating back.

Resignedly he threw his boots and coat up on the bridge and swam about for a while. No point in wasting a dunking on such a hot day. When he judged it was time to change for dinner, he wrung himself out and sneaked into the house through the back door.

"Don't tell me," Fields begged, receiving the dripping coat, "Margaret again."

"What a fist she can make!" Nathan felt his jaw. "I think she grazed me."

"You may have a bruise there," Fields said, scrutinizing his chin. "Are you sure it's going to be worth it, sir?"

By dinnertime Margaret had calmed down enough to realize that Jared had trapped her again. She really did not believe Nathan to be as mercenary as Jared supposed. That Jared believed it himself she could almost credit. But Jared had planted the seed of doubt and she could not help wondering what Nathan did want. She had little to recommend her, except her playing. She was silent through dinner as her mind spun in circles. She did not even look in Nathan's direction. He could not be in love with her after the way she treated him. He must be after the money. This thought sent her to bed with a headache directly after dinner.

Margaret was trying to avoid Nathan the next day by staying close to Eleanor, so he gave up playing cat and mouse with her and went to sit on the terrace, while they sewed in the drawing room. He was not good at sitting idle and was thinking he might have to take a bolt to Bristol when he realized with a jolt that his month was nearly up.

He heard a shot and some cries from the direction of the home wood. It sounded like a wounded bird. Suddenly Dicea emerged from the edge of the wood, running and stumbling. When she saw Nathan she started screaming his name. Nathan bolted down the steps and across the lawn before the women even got onto the terrace. From the blood that was streaking her apron he thought Dicea had been shot, but it was the weight of Sir Kaye that was encumbering her. Jared broke out of the woods with a shotgun and ran to her.

"Help him, Nathan, help him." Dicea was almost incoherent with tears.

"Where are you hurt?"

"It's not me. He's shot Sir Kaye."

Nathan took the black burden from her, but the young animal's eyes were already set. "I can't help him, Dicea." Nathan laid Sir Kaye on the ground. Margaret tried to get hold of the child, but Dicea flung herself into Nathan's arms and cried.

"It's only a cat, for God's sake," Jared said. "I didn't mean to shoot it."

"But we saved him and now you've killed him!" Dicea cried.

Nathan hugged her. "It's not just a cat."

"It was only a cat," Margaret said coldly as she pulled Dicea away from Nathan, "until Nathan turned it into something else with all his stories." Of all the cutting things she had said to him none had wounded him as much as this, because he feared it was true.

Dicea still clung to Nathan's hand. "He didn't do it on purpose, Dicea," Nathan said.

"No?"

"He would not dare. Jared knows about cats, and how they come back, sometimes. He would not take the risk of making Sir Kaye angry."

"Stop it, Nathan." Margaret did drag the resisting child away.

"Sir Kaye, I want him." She broke free and came back to stroke the still-warm fur.

"Leave him, Dicea. He's dead," Margaret said coldly.

"I will take care of him, Dicea." Nathan gathered Sir Kaye up gently in his arms, disregarding the blood he was getting all over his jacket.

Dicea sniffed and said bravely, "Water burial is best, I suppose."

Nathan nodded as Miss Prin came to help with Dicea. The governess looked horrified and seemed on the verge of tears herself.

Jared was still trying to recover from the shock of Margaret taking his part against Nathan. "Why did you tell her it was an accident?"

"She just had something she loves die in her arms," Nathan said in a cold fury. "She doesn't need to learn to hate all in the same day."

Nathan was not as confused by Margaret's reaction as Jared was. He thought over the incident as he watched the sack he had prepared with a brick and Sir Kaye's corpse slip beneath the cold, murky waters of the lake. Dicea had not run to Margaret when she was in distress, but to him.

After putting Dicea to bed, Margaret went to have it out with Nathan. He saw her striding ruthlessly toward him across the lawn with an expression like that of one or two first mates he had known. He put down an impulse to run.

"I want you to stay away from her." Margaret folded her arms.

"The only way for me to do that is to leave."

"That's up to you." She turned to go.

"If she had been hurt, or hungry, or cold, she would have run to you, not to me." Nathan saw Margaret hesitate and he continued, "because you have always been the one to feed her, clothe her, make her well. She would go to you for that. It's only because I saved Sir Kaye once that she came to me. She doesn't love you any less."

Margaret realized with a shock that she was jealous of Nathan's hold over Dicea. She turned to look at him, trembling. The expression on her face was impossible to read.

"Having to do all these things for her has made you a very strong person," he continued. "That's why it's hard for you to play with her, or do anything else that's trivial," Nathan pleaded.

"You mean like love her?" Margaret's lips trembled, but she set her jaw.

"No, she knows you love her." Nathan took a step toward her.

"She has never been hungry or wanted for anything. I have seen to that," Margaret said almost proudly.

"I know. When I think of what your life must have been like . . . it's one thing to be cut loose on your own, quite another to be responsible for three children into the bargain."

"I did what I had to do."

"I know. I think you deserve Boadicea's name more than she does. You would never have given up."

"But I have only taken care of her physical needs, and she has other needs."

"Perhaps it is impossible to be her mother and her friend. I don't know. I do know that she needs me in a role no one else has filled."

"You are right." Margaret blinked, swallowed and turned toward the house.

"Wait, don't go like this."

Margaret had herself under such perilously tight control she actually shook, but her mouth remained set. "You can stay for all I care."

"I didn't mean to hurt you. If you knew how much I admire you . . ." Nathan actually touched her arm.

She flinched. "Leave me alone." He took his hand away and she walked blindly toward the house.

What was said to Jared that night by Sir Owen was heard by everyone in the house except perhaps the sleeping Dicea. Nathan had never heard anyone's character ripped up and down so thoroughly even by the foulest of captains. He wondered how Jared could stay in the library and take it.

Every transgression major and minor since Jared had come to live at Gaites Hall was trotted out. Nathan imagined Jared was having a taste of what judgment day would be like.

Nathan was waiting in Dicea's room when she awoke the next morning. As soon as she saw him she remembered what had happened and looked so forlorn he asked, "Will you be well enough to start on our quest today or should we put it off until tomorrow?"

"Quest, what quest?"

"Why, to find whatever kitten Sir Kaye may have come back into. I don't think I can go alone. You know Sir Kaye so much better than I do. You will be more likely to recognize him."

"We can't put it off. He will be confused and lonely. Let's go now."

"As soon as you have breakfasted."

When Margaret checked on Dicea, she found not the sobbing child she expected but a little creature full of plans for setting a wrong right. Margaret almost condemned it as a bunch of nonsense, but clamped her mouth shut on the words and merely nodded.

An hour later Margaret was at the stable waiting for the gig to be hitched up when she saw Nathan and Dicea walking down the driveway talking like two children, while Nathan consulted a map he had drawn from directions the servants had given him. She caught up with them before they reached the road. "If we are going to find Sir Kaye, we may as well travel as fast as possible."

"Oh, Margaret, are you coming with us?" Dicea asked as Nathan handed her up.

"Yes, if you like."

"More than anything." The hug Dicea bestowed on her sister surprised Margaret. "Now I know we shall succeed."

"Leave it to you two to start on a quest without even a basket to put the kitten in," Margaret chided.

Nathan picked up the basket and got in on the other side of Dicea, then peeked under the lid. "This basket is already full."

"That's because our lunch is in there," Margaret announced.

"Nathan," Dicea asked, "did they used to take a picnic lunch on a quest?"

"Now that I think of it, they were sure to have taken provisions."

"I think Margaret knows more about quests than you do, Nathan."

At the first cottage they visited, the kittens were much too young to take away but, since they were all gray tabbies anyway, none had much resemblance to Sir Kaye. At the farm they had been directed to, Mr. Milner led them down to the cow barn where thirty or more cats of various sizes were gathered around a shallow trough, lapping milk still steaming from the cow. Dicea's eyes grew big at the sight of every describable color and marking of cat.

"The littlest ones are over here." Milner showed them a stall with several nursing cats bedded down in the straw. One worried-looking calico counted her brood, evidently found someone missing, and went to the trough to carry the stray back.

"Are there any black ones?" Dicea asked.

"I believe there are one or two in the haylofts, but they are a bit hard to catch."

"You stay here and study these, while I go look," Nathan volunteered. "Remember," he called from the ladder, "Sir Kaye might not be the same color, so concentrate on personality." Nathan's invasion of the loft caused the exit, by various routes, of half a dozen adolescent cats, several of which were black, wild-looking things. Dicea giggled at the sheer delight of so much movement and color.

Nathan returned looking abashed and holding his handkerchief around his thumb.

"Sorry, sir. I should have warned you they bite. I can't get near some of them myself," Milner said.

"How bad is it, Nathan?" Margaret asked, putting down the kitten she had been examining.

"Nathan, you have been wounded," Dicea said with delight. "This is a fine quest."

Margaret rewrapped Nathan's hand, saying it was borderline for stitches.

"Nathan, Margaret thinks Sir Kaye would definitely come back as a boy cat."

"I never thought of that." Nathan watched in amazement as the old calico dragged back into her nest a resisting juvenile who, neither by appearance nor size, looked to belong to her litter.

"Aye, Bess is such a good mother, she tries to steal all the kittens."

"Sorry for the trouble, Mr. Milner."

"That's quite all right. I hope you find what you are looking for."

The next stop was a cottage in Kernwell Abbey, the next closest village after Little Chewton. There they found a large litter to a white mother who purred contentedly as the white and gray kittens seethed and sucked at her. The smallest of the white kittens sat forlornly in a corner of the crate, looking about him with innocent blue eyes.

"Now he looks familiar." Margaret picked him up. "I know, he reminds me of Nathan," she teased.

"The poor little fellow will be deaf, won't he?" Nathan said.

"Why?" asked Dicea.

"I was told blue-eyed white ones always are. It is not likely he will make it on his own."

Dicea's ready compassion was awakened. "He's not Sir Kaye, of course, but someone should take care of him. He will never get enough to eat otherwise. We could call him Gawain."

"I see, pure in heart." Nathan handed the kitten to Dicea.

As she stroked the kitten, it looked wonderingly up at her. "You are right, Margaret. He does look like Nathan."

"Thank you," Nathan said dryly to Margaret, who looked sideways at him, smiling, and made his heart thump.

Dicea almost didn't notice a black kitten that had just awakened and run out of a corner of the room to hook a claw into the hem of her gown. He finally cried up at her in a demanding voice and she glanced down to see him tugging at her for attention. "Sir Kaye! There you are."

Nathan and Margaret looked at each other in amazement. Nathan felt something like a chill. The old cottager went on rocking happily. "The shyest and the boldest—they would make a good pair."

"May we take them both?" Dicea begged. "If Sir Kaye has someone to play with, he might stay out of the woods."

"We can certainly take them both," Margaret decided. "Whether you get to keep both of them is between you and Sir Owen."

Since they had not yet emptied their basket, Nathan and Dicea had to each hold a kitten until they came to a good spot for a picnic.

"Oh, look!" exclaimed Nathan, much as Dicea would at some delightful surprise. "What is it?"

"Just a field of oats," Margaret said, driving the horse onto the verge of the field.

"But it looks like the ocean. Look Dicea, how the wind kicks up waves on it, like on the sea. I suppose it's because the heads are different colors from the stalks that it has the ripple effect when the wind ruffles it."

"Is that really what the sea looks like?" Dicea asked, hugging Sir Kaye.

"Very much so, except for the color."

Nathan got down and led the horse under some shade and then assisted his companions. Margaret spread a blanket where they could look out over the field and unpacked ham sandwiches, a bottle of cider, and some fresh seed cakes. The kittens were put to bed in the basket and Nathan and Dicea walked down closer to watch the golden ocean move.

Margaret tried very hard to see the same beauty that Nathan and Dicea were seeing. She wondered if she ever really saw anything. She tried pretending she was only ten again and seeing such a sight for the first time. She emptied her mind of everything except the color, movement and sound of the grain blowing in the wind. For just a second she was down there, swimming in the golden sea, laughing and being tossed about by the wind. For a moment only, she had a taste of carefree happiness, and tears started to her eyes.

"You see it, too," Nathan said in delight. But the spell was broken. Much more quickly than she had let herself go, she pulled back into the safety of her shell.

"Yes, I saw it."

"It is beautiful, isn't it, Margaret?" Dicea asked, taking an enormous bite of bread and ham.

"Yes, it was."

On the drive home Dicea fell asleep between them, but never loosened her hold on the basket. Margaret took the turns gently so as not to wake her.

"I have been thinking about what you said," Margaret started. "If I had been more of a friend to Dicea, I would never have been able to take care of her as I did, making her swallow foul medicines, cleaning her scrapes. I would have felt her pain too much."

"I know that. I didn't say I blamed you. I just said it must be hard for you, because you have missed out on the most delightful side of her. You could be less serious more often, like today. Just try pretending you are quite someone else. It will give you a different perspective."

Margaret glanced at him in surprise. "I did try that. It almost made me giddy."

"Good for you. Next time do it for a little longer."

"I cannot pretend to be someone else."

"Of course you can. I do it all the time. Sometimes I pretend I'm a cultured man of the world. If you pretend long enough you can become anything you want." Margaret was looking at him in openmouthed amazement. "Well, perhaps 'cultured' is a bit of a stretch for me," Nathan conceded. "But I know you can be whoever you want."

"I don't want to be anyone else."

Nathan relapsed into silence until they were driving past the lake. A heron took unlikely flight low over the lake to the other shore. Margaret pulled up as Nathan watched it raptly.

"You see everything as though for the very first time."

He turned to smile at her, his eyes alight with sun and laughter. "But it is the first time."

"And if we drove by here tomorrow and you saw the same bird you would be just as delighted."

"Of course, because it would be new again."

"Where the devil have you all been?" Sir Owen, Matthew and Jeremy were just dismounting in the stable yard. Dicea awoke and Nathan hopped down to lift her out. She began working on Sir Owen even before Nathan had helped Margaret down.

"Look, we found him again. We found Sir Kaye. And this is a friend for him. Nathan said he is deaf and sure to die without care. Please, can they stay?" Dicea was so changed from the despairing child they had carried upstairs the previous day, it would have taken a much harder heart than Sir Owen's to deny the child such a simple request.

Chapter Five

There ensued a week of comparative peace at Gaites Hall. Dicea, Nathan and Margaret spent more time together. Jared was sullenly quiet since he had been threatened with having his allowance cut altogether unless he kept the peace. Matthew, Jeremy and Sir Owen were absorbed in the training of Ember, the horse Matthew intended to race. Eleanor and Cristine were occupied by the choosing of patterns and fabrics for gowns for Cristine's come-out.

"Of course we shall have to buy some silks for Margaret, as well. She desperately needs some new evening gowns," said Eleanor as Nathan was passing through the morning room.

"Did you say you wanted silk?"

"Yes. We may be able to find some in Bath, but we may have to make at least one trip to London for fabrics."

"I have trunks of silk just sitting in Bristol at Captain Hewitt's house. I will send for them."

"We cannot expect you to do that."

"But they are no good to anyone molding away in the attic. There's no guarantee they will be what you want, but if I send now you'll have them in a few days. Then you can decide."

Dicea poked her head into the room. "Ready to go, Nathan?"

"Where are you children off to?" Eleanor asked benignly.

"Berry picking, another thing I have never done before. Do you want to come, Cristine?"

"No, thank you." She smiled. "They dragged me out there last year and wore me out. I hope that is not a good shirt you are wearing, for it is sure to be ruined."

"I will be careful for Fields's sake."

They walked to the pastures lined with the berry brambles something over a mile away. Nathan carried the basket with their lunch and Margaret carried the berry baskets while Dicea skipped ahead.

Nathan and Margaret had not argued since the quest, but they also had not made any progress that Nathan could see toward becoming closer. They talked of Dicea and everyday things, but Margaret was still only distantly pleasant. He began to wonder if playing the buffoon had not hurt his chances with Margaret. How to get her to take him seriously now he did not know. It popped into his head to ask her to marry him again, but looking at those brooding eyes, he knew what the answer would be, and he did not want to ruin the day.

"Rather a strain to be polite to me for so long at a stretch, is it not?"

She choked on a laugh. "Is it so obvious?"

"For you, yes. And it is telling on you. You had something quite awful to say to me last night at dinner. I'm sure that if you keep biting it back, you will make yourself ill."

"Is that how I appear—spiteful, vicious?" Margaret seemed truly concerned.

"I didn't say that," Nathan denied. "Well, only at first. Once a person knows you he realizes you are a victim of your own wit and intelligence. Too bad only Jared appreciates it fully."

"And how is it that you know this?"

"You mean one has only to go to sea to be regarded as a witless oaf?"

"The words are yours, not mine."

"Ha, there now, feeling better?

"Hardly. You have been making game of me ever since you came here."

"Perhaps, but I do it with a smile, so hardly anyone realizes. You should learn to school your expression into a more pleasant mode when cutting at people."

"I am not two-faced like Jared."

"True, and I suppose there would be little satisfaction in slashing someone to ribbons who doesn't even know he's under attack."

Margaret's smile disappeared suddenly and Nathan had a shocking glimpse of the frightened, uncertain girl within. "You don't know what it's like for someone in my position. I'm trapped here, perhaps for the rest of my life."

"Then perhaps you should not snarl so much at someone who is trying to get the cage door open," he said softly, and reached out his hand to her.

She shook her head and took a deep breath. She was, unfortunately, back in control. "I can never marry you. I told you that before."

"That's odd. I don't recall asking you lately."

She rounded on him and swung the empty baskets at his head, but he caught her wrist. "Where would you go, what would you do?" he asked, "if you had a choice?"

"Let go of me." She pulled away.

"Answer me then," he said passionately.

"I have found it useless to think of such things," she said, gathering up the baskets."

"Think of them now."

"Why?"

"I have said I want to help you." When she straightened up, he suggested, "Perhaps you would like a house of your own."

"No—I don't know."

"Think then," he said as Dicea came running back with the first handful of berries.

Nathan had no idea this berry picking was such a solitary business, but he worked his way through the patch allotted to him. He kept at it faithfully long after he could no longer blink the red and purple spots away from his vision. He checked on Dicea occasionally to make sure she was not getting too much sun, but she scoffed at his suggestion that they had enough berries.

As another tendril reached out and caught his shirt, Nathan refrained nobly from cursing. The jungles of Brazil had nothing on the tenacity and impenetrability of these vines. He tied his handkerchief around his forehead to keep the salty sweat from stinging his eyes. He must be getting soft, he thought, to consider this a hard task.

He was at the far corner of the field when Margaret called him for lunch.

"Nathan, you cut your face," Dicea observed as he set his baskets down.

"I don't feel anything. Are you sure?"

"Let me see." Margaret wet her handkerchief and wiped his face, which he submitted to like a small boy. She seemed disappointed to find that it was only a large smear of berry juice over a small scratch. The sudden shift in her manner from warm concern to cold disdain was like walking down a river valley and stepping into the chill layer of air at the bottom. It reinforced Nathan's notion that she could handle only physical complaints, not emotional ones. If he was sick or injured she was the most tender of companions, but whenever he was feeling fine there was no way to reach her. What he could not fathom was why she had such difficulty with a healthy rapport.

Well, he certainly had no intention of spending life as an invalid just to stay close to Margaret. There had to be a way to get through to her. Nathan strongly suspected he could not use the same tactics he had on his grandfather. For one thing she was smart enough to recognize them. Plus, he feared what damage he might do without knowing what all her problems were. That she had been hurt there was no

question. Until he could determine why she was so barri-
caded within herself he would have to tread warily.

They ate slowly and talked little. Conversation took too
much effort in the heat. Nathan could have lolled in the
shade for another hour, but when Margaret and Dicea resumed their task he doggedly followed them.

Margaret watched Nathan struggling with two separate
vines that were trying to annihilate him and laughed.

"Ouch! You would think they were alive. Next time I will
bring a machete."

"That would be stupid," she chided, helping to disen-
tangle him. "If you chop them down we won't have berries
next year."

"Another hour, and I quit," he warned her. "We'll be
lucky to carry all these back as it is."

Margaret finished freeing him and picked near him for a
while. His shirt was dripping with sweat and there was
something piratically attractive about the white handkerchief bound around his fair head. She could not deny she
found him handsome. Before Nathan had come, she would
have said there was not the smallest chance of her ever
marrying anyone. That she even toyed with the idea now
said much for the impression he had made on her.

He was so different from any man she had ever known.
He was worldly-wise in some ways, but innocent of even the
clumsiest sort of flirtation. There was no level on which she
could deal with him. She ended by either laughing at him or
giving him a blistering setdown. One way or another he took
more abuse than a man with any pride should tolerate.

The thought of accepting him as a husband she thrust
away from her when it intruded on her mind. Let alone
people would think Sir Owen had arranged the marriage,
which was no more than the truth, Margaret did not really
wish to dominate a man. And that would certainly be the
case with Nathan.

She almost felt sorry for him, illiterate, unable to truly
succeed to what was his due, through no fault of his. She

found herself wondering how he would have turned out if he had been raised with Jared and Matthew. She almost did not like to think of what all those years of exposure to Jared would have done to him. Matthew was big and bluff enough to threaten Jared physically if he went too far. Nathan would not have fared as well, she finally decided.

The alternative to marrying Nathan she hardly liked to think about. Sir Owen would bludgeon Nathan into marrying Cristine. Eleanor would talk Cristine into accepting, making Matthew miserable. She had watched Cristine teaching Nathan to dance and had to admit that they looked well together. It had given her heart an odd twist to realize that she was jealous of her own sister. If that marriage came to pass, her position in their household would become one of a mere pensioner. Never could she tolerate that. She would find a way to leave no matter what it took.

A carriage appeared in the lane—Matthew come to carry their haul home.

"Matthew, you lifesaver. I was just dreading having to carry all this back." Nathan squinted up at him.

"Grandfather sent me, when he found you were still out. Let me take that."

Sir Owen insisted that Dicea dine with them that night in honor of the first berry pie of the season. Dicea was actually a prudent addition to the dinner table. With everyone behaving, Sir Owen noticed a certain dullness in the conversation of late, and he hoped Dicea would liven the table up a little. True enough, her recounting of the quest for Sir Kaye, whether Dicea intended it to be humorous or not, kept them chuckling through the meal. And the entry of the fabled pie led her to tell of Nathan's trials in the berry field. She finished with, "I suppose Nathan is a wonderful navigator, but he doesn't know much about quests or berries." Nathan took this condemnation well.

"Navigator?" The one word seemed to catch Jared's attention. "Doesn't that require the reading of charts?"

"Only numbers," Nathan said blithely. Sir Owen chuckled and Jared thought it was because he was powerless to attack Nathan. Margaret did not have as much faith in Jared passing up the temptation so she changed the subject to ask if Cristine's new dress pattern had been fitted yet. She kept conversation in a safe arena until it was time for the ladies to withdraw, then looked meaningfully at Matthew, but she was not sure he was nimble-witted enough to parry Jared's barbs away from Nathan. Having hurt Nathan twice on this score herself, she was sensitive to shield him in the matter of his illiteracy.

Her concern, however, was unnecessary, for the talk had turned to racing, and even Jared participated in a quiet way, giving his opinion on Ember's chances at the racecourses near London. Matthew and Sir Owen also spoke of the work going forward on their own acres. Nathan had ridden out with them almost daily, paying close attention to the crops, the cattle, and the woodlot. He tried not to ask stupid questions and patently avoided embarrassing ones, but he had to confess he was more interested in the people they encountered than the land or animals.

The local residents didn't seem to be in desperate want compared to many in the country since the end of the war, but he could see repairs crying out to be made to cottages on the entailed lands, and feared things were worse on the lands on short leases. He knew little about it, nor how his grandfather stood for being able to afford to keep things up. He saw money being spent on horses and stock, but little on maintenance. Was the money not there or did his grandfather just not notice things falling to ruin as the church had been?

That's when it hit him that he actually had plans, albeit vague ones, for the Gaites property. He wanted the people who lived and worked here to be prosperous and healthy. He wanted them to like his family and think them fair dealers—his family. In his efforts to win Margaret he had entrenched himself here to the point where he could not bear to leave. Even if Margaret never agreed to marry him, he had a stake in the place and he meant to do what he could to improve things, even if it meant offending his grandfather.

They had another musical evening and Nathan was just feeling mellow after his second cup of coffee when Dicea asked on her way to bed, "You are coming with us again tomorrow, aren't you?"

"Yes, of course, where?"

"Berrying, of course."

"Again?" He nearly choked. "Surely we picked them all today." He looked despairingly at Margaret.

"Oh, there will be more ripe tomorrow," she said mercilessly.

"Just how long does this go on?" Nathan demanded.

"With no rain, another two weeks," Margaret answered cheerfully.

"I will never make it," he said, staring sadly into his cup.

"That's all right, Nathan." Dicea patted his shoulder. "If you are too tired, we'll go without you." She shook her head and, on impulse, went over and kissed Sir Owen on the cheek, then made her exit.

"I'm not sure, but I think I have been patronized by a ten-year-old," Nathan remarked.

"I'm sure," said Margaret, her dark, slanting eyes smiling up at him.

"That little minx." Sir Owen chuckled. "I will wager she gets you out there again tomorrow."

As it happened, Nathan endured only two more days of indenture in the berry fields before Mrs. Tomlin vouchsafed that she would not know what to do with another berry if it came into the house. Dicea seemed disappointed, but the arrival of the carrier from Bristol with Nathan's trunks and all manner of seafood, fruits and other delicacies more than satisfied her.

The trunks were carried into the morning room, where Nathan unlocked them and threw the larger two open for inspection. He then stood back and laughed at the exclamations of female delight over each new treasure. Many of the pieces would have been more suited to fairer women, but Eleanor thought that with cream lace or scallops they could even make use of these. There were exquisite deep greens and blues that she put aside for herself and Margaret. Cristine could wear nearly any color well, not just white, cream and primrose, but also pinks and blues. There were patterned silks, as well, which Nathan thought would be too daring, but Eleanor conceived the notion of designing some shawls from them, and was in such a state of excitement over the idea that she sent a groom to the village for her dressmaker.

Dicea sat quietly on the sofa, looking on in wonder at the pageant of color unfurling before her. She was, perhaps, feeling a little left out, since there was nothing unearthed that would be suitable for her, but she smiled at the rare delight the others took in the anticipation of so many new dresses. While Eleanor began a list of sundries for their new wardrobes, Nathan knelt to unlock the smallest trunk.

"I'm not sure why Captain Hewitt sent Father's trunk, but there might be something in it. Oh, look, Margaret, Belgian lace. I had forgotten about this." Dicea carried the rolls of lace over to Cristine and Eleanor. Nathan handed Margaret bundle after bundle of lawn and figured muslin.

"Dicea," Margaret said softly as she hugged the child, "we can make you such lovely dresses out of this. It's time you learned to sew, too. You can help us." At the bottom of the trunk were a few books, a packet of letters, a very large conch shell, which Nathan handed to Dicea, and a painted miniature in a carved frame. Nathan's eyes no more alighted on the picture than his face underwent a terrible change.

"Who is it, Nathan?" Dicea asked from behind him.

"My mother," he said with an effort. "Do you want to see her?"

"She's beautiful," Dicea said unreservedly.

That Nathan was being tortured by some distant memory Margaret had no doubt, but she did not know what to say to him. He got to his feet, excused himself numbly and left through the conservatory. After a moment's hesitation Margaret followed him. He paused outside the conservatory, looked uncertainly around him, as though getting his bearings, and began to walk slowly around the house and toward the home wood.

Margaret had no trouble catching up with him. "Opening all those trunks must have brought back a lot of memories. Did you buy all that for your mother?"

"Yes—no. It's a little hard to explain. My mother died long before I ever went to China. I suppose I bought them because they were the sort of thing she would have liked—or the sort of thing I imagined she would have liked. I am glad they are going to be used at last. It did not make any sense keeping them."

"You pretended you were buying them for her, so that you could feel closer to her."

"Yes, I suppose that's it." He turned to Margaret, rather surprised that she could verbalize something he hardly understood himself. "When I was away I didn't have to face her death. It was only when I came back to Bristol and she was not there, that I felt I had lost her."

"She would have been very proud of you."

Nathan searched her face for understanding and found something approaching comfort. "That sort of thing didn't matter to her. She would rather I had stayed and run the ship chandler's shop. I wanted her to have everything Father had promised her." Nathan changed to his story voice. "All the treasures she could imagine. Also I thought somehow that I would find my father. I was so stupid." He came back to his normal tone.

"You never found him."

"Not a trace. It's a big ocean," he said helplessly. "She died of a fever while I was away. I remember her begging me not to leave, as she had begged my father. She didn't care for silks or treasures, only for us. And I robbed her of that, just as Father had."

Margaret felt his hurt then nearly as much as he did. "If you had stayed you might not have been able to save her."

"True, but, at least, she would not have died alone." He raised his eyes to her for a second, but what he needed was not there. He turned away and walked on alone toward the woods.

Margaret's every feeling was to go after him to comfort him. His confession spoke of a trust, a faith in her that she did not deserve. Why she could not reach out to him, forget about words and just hold him, she did not know, but she was closer to being able to do such a thing than she had ever been before.

"Where's Nathan?" Dicea came out, carefully carrying the pink-and-peach-colored shell. "I wanted to ask if I could play with this."

Margaret knelt to her. "He went to be alone in the home wood. He's a little sad about remembering his mother."

"I will go to him. I know where he will be. He won't mind if I see him cry." Dicea put the shell in Margaret's hands and ran off toward the wood.

Margaret rose and went into the conservatory, marveling at the child's understanding. Margaret made it a point never to cry if she could help it. She considered it a weakness, but she could not stop herself when she thought of what Nathan had endured and would continue to endure. He could not change the past, or escape it, or even accept it. That was why he seemed so numb to snubs and censure. It was not possible to hurt him more than he hurt himself. And whatever other people did to him, he would dumbly submit to it.

Dicea found him sitting on a limb of the ancient willow tree watching the low-hanging fronds drag in the water of the lake. She climbed up to sit in silence beside him as though they were both in a scrape together and were ruminating on the injustice of life. When Dicea judged it was time, she said, "I wish I remembered my mother. Grandmama said she never got over having me and I was probably the death of her."

"Oh, no. That's not right," Nathan roused himself to say. "You were a year old by then and I'm sure she died of influenza."

"Well, that's a comfort. What did your mother die of?"

"I used to think it was a broken heart, but perhaps it was just the influenza after all. Still, I should have been there."

"Would it have mattered?"

"It would have mattered to me." He looked strangely at Dicea then as though what he had said surprised himself. He slid down from the limb. "Time to go back, I think. Margaret may be worried." He helped Dicea down and they walked hand in hand as they had so many times and talked of less significant things. Margaret was pacing outside the conservatory but attempted to look unconcerned at their approach, especially since they were both smiling.

"I forgot to ask." Dicea retrieved the conch from Margaret. "May I play with this shell?"

"Oh, you may keep it. If you carry it to Miss Prin, she may be able to tell you about the creature who made it." Dicea ran off on her new mission.

"I'm sorry if I frightened you," Nathan apologized. "I thought I had better control of myself than that."

"Your grief does you credit."

"Not really. You are right in thinking it would have made no difference to my mother if I had been with her. The only one it mattered to was me. A very selfish kind of grief, don't you think?"

Margaret stared at him and finally understood. "But one you can live with?"

"I shall have to."

* * *

Nathan and Margaret resumed their early-morning rides and Nathan felt that she was more reachable than ever.

"It's such a fine day," he said one morning as the sun was pulling the dew up off the grass, "why don't you marry me?"

"What did you say?" she asked suspiciously.

"Marry me?"

"No. It's too fine a day," she said, and urged her mare into a canter.

"Is that one of the hundred reasons?"

"It may as well be." Margaret had almost ceased to take Nathan's proposals seriously now, they came so often and in such odd contexts. Always she had an excuse. She practiced her excuses and they were as flippant as his proposals. It had become a game and so long as it continued Margaret had neither lost Nathan nor given in to him. Why she could not give in to him, she kept wound up in her mind with his freedom, but this reasoning was beginning to be so at odds with her inclinations, she spent her time with him in a pleasant reverie and her time out of his company thinking about what they had done together. So the summer passed, day after glorious day, but the days were only delightful because of Nathan and the odd way he was getting her to look at her world.

On some days Nathan rode out with Margaret early, then with the men after late breakfast, and again with his grandfather and Dicea. Although he still rode with too slack a rein, he did not slouch, and Sir Owen was beginning to think that he would not embarrass them unduly during the hunting season if only he would refrain from talking to his mounts.

A mere "good lad" or "well done" was never enough for Nathan. He kept up a running monologue that the beasts, judging by their ears, actually attended to. Sir Owen also put

Nathan on some of the younger horses and he handled these delicately enough to satisfy the most critical horseman.

Nathan was the only one who could get much work out of Samarkand. The party came to the bridge across the end of the lake one afternoon and Sir Owen turned to tell Nathan he would have to ride around and meet them on the other side.

"Go on ahead. I want to see if I can get him to cross."

The others did ride across, but Sir Owen paused within sight of the big gray. If Samarkand ever crossed a bridge for someone, he wanted to see it. Most likely Nathan would get tossed off.

"You can do it. I know you can." Nathan straightened the horse and urged him toward the bridge. "Look how far ahead the others are. You should be ashamed! A great brute like you afraid of the sound of your own feet." Every time Samarkand tried to turn aside, Nathan pointed him back at the bridge. "We could be here all day," Nathan threatened. "I give you fair warning, I am far more stubborn that you are."

Finally, with a heavy sigh, Samarkand set one foot on the bridge and, in response to a "good lad" from Nathan, tip-toed across and cantered up to the others.

"How the devil does Nathan get him to do things like that?" Matthew complained. "I can't even make him mind me with a whip."

"Haven't you been listening?" Jared asked. "He talks him into exhaustion. I would do much to get away from that voice myself." They all laughed.

"I have a notion," Sir Owen said as Nathan rode up patting his mount, "I may set you at training one or two of the young colts."

"Me? I know nothing about it."

"Since when has that stopped you doing anything?" Jeremy chimed in.

"You are wearing a hat today," Margaret remarked next morning.

"It's going to rain. Are you sure you want to ride?"

"It is not going to rain," Margaret denied as Kerry gave her a leg up onto Titian. She cantered down the driveway and Nathan followed meekly after. They were as far from home as possible when Nathan pointed to the dark blue wedge of storm front darkening the sky and crushing the life out of the summer day. "How did you know?" Margaret asked in exasperation.

"I have an instinct for heavy weather. Can we make it as far as the village? We could wait it out in the coffee room at the inn."

"Too far. Let's at least get under some trees."

"Too dangerous. Is there anyplace hereabouts to take shelter?"

"Not even a farmhouse. There's a stone shepherd's cottage down that way, if it's still standing." Nathan followed her through the quickening rain to the tumbledown structure. He slid off and helped Margaret dismount. He had no trouble forcing the half door open. The building's latest occupants had been sheep. Margaret led Titian in and Nathan tried to follow with Samarkand, but the big horse's ears brushed the webby ceiling. That and the sheep smell, plus the lack of a window, made him roll his eyes and flare his nostrils as he analyzed the stale smells in the dark building. Only Titian's presence and Nathan's cajoling resigned him to entering. Margaret held her mare quietly by the head while Nathan carefully turned Samarkand to point toward the open door. Just then a clap of thunder almost sent him overtop of Nathan, and even Titian jumped. They stayed by the dancing horses until the storm had resolved itself into a steady downpour and the horses had relaxed enough to look about them for stray bits of hay. Nathan closed them in with the half door and gathered up from the corners what hay looked clean enough for them to eat. He even unearthed a stool from one corner that Margaret could sit on if she propped it against the wall.

"Well, you are right. This has it all over the coffee room at the Half Keg."

Margaret choked on a laugh. "If I were with Matthew or Jeremy, they would be ranting at me for getting their coats ruined."

"Fields is used to it by now. Besides, my coat is scarcely wet." On a thought he felt her sleeve. "But yours is pretty well soaked through. Take it off and wear mine until yours dries."

"Certainly not."

"Oh, I was forgetting how much you resent comfort."

"Very well, if it will make you happy, but then you will be cold."

"Nothing of the sort. I am used to being wet," he said as he dropped his coat over her shoulders. The touch of it around her shoulders, still warm from his body, was strangely comforting, and she perceived that Nathan was, in fact, sweating. He tied his handkerchief around his forehead and crouched on the floor next to her, but a stray clap of thunder made him jump more than either of the horses.

"What's the matter? Are you nervous about being here alone with me?"

"No." Nathan grinned sheepishly. "The problem is we are not alone." He tried to lean nonchalantly against the wall beside her. "Those two won't take a fancy to start jumping around, will they?"

"Why, no, why should they?"

"We had one go crazy below decks once. I was the one who managed the loading of them, so they sent me down with a pistol to either calm the beast or kill it before it stove in the hull."

"Did you shoot it?"

"No. I'm not that good a shot, either, remember?"

Margaret smiled.

"It must have caught me with a hoof when it reared. When I woke up there was this hot breath blowing on my face and huge eyes staring right at me. I nearly yelled."

"That might have set it off again."

"Fortunately, that did occur to me. When I tried to move, it stepped over me, turned and came back to sniff me some more. What I could not make out was why it didn't trample me to death, and why it calmed down with me lying there helpless."

"A horse may knock down a man standing or step on his feet, but it will do its best not to step on someone on the ground. Too soft, you see. It might slip and fall."

This piece of information did not seem to comfort Nathan. "I never looked at it from their point of view before."

"How did you get out?"

"I kept turning over slowly until I could slide under the bars. What a ribbing I got, too."

"That's why you are ill at ease with horses."

"Let's just say I don't trust them overmuch."

"Was it very bad? Your life at sea?"

"No such thing. Not a bad life really while you are young enough to stand it. But I begin to worry about Captain Hewitt, even though he is mostly retired."

"He is a great friend of yours."

"Yes, would you like to meet him sometime?"

"Of course, why not?"

"I think he would like you."

"Why is that?"

"Because there is no nonsense about you. You say exactly what you think."

"Except when I am in a temper."

"Oh, especially then."

"But I do say things I don't mean."

"Things you don't mean to say," Nathan corrected, "but they are true for all that."

Margaret was looking very soft and lovely in the dim light. Her voice was low and vulnerable for once. "You, at least, have a choice. You can go back to your old life if you can't stomach this one. I'm stuck here forever."

He moved a step closer and asked, "What would you do if you had your freedom?"

"I dare not even think," Margaret said desperately. "I have never let myself dream about it." She leaned past him to look out the door.

"It's still raining," Nathan confirmed. "I know. Play the make-believe game with me, like Dicea does. I will start. A rich relative has died and left you a vast fortune. What will you do with it?" He knelt beside her.

"That will never happen."

"It's possible, the way our relatives fairly litter the countryside. What would you do first?"

She thought for a full minute, then said, "I would buy Tenwells."

"Tenwells? Of course. And then what?"

"And set the workmen to repairing it."

"Where would you live until then?"

"I think I would travel, now that the war is over—Paris first, then Italy."

"And would you take your Cousin Eleanor for propriety?"

"Oh, no, she would be far too busy with Cristine's come-out. I might take Jeremy with me, though."

"He would like that," said Nathan, noticing sadly that he did not figure in this imaginary future.

"And when I returned he could help me run the farm and the mill."

"What if Jeremy got married someday and left you?" Nathan asked, concentrating on the piece of straw he was breaking. "Would you stay there alone?"

"Having once gained my freedom, why would I want to be trammeled by anyone ever again?"

Nathan sighed. "For company, I suppose."

"That's the one thing of which I have had quite enough."

"Thank God, it's slacked off. You won't have to be afflicted with me any longer," Nathan observed dryly.

Margaret thought he was joking and laughed at him, but his face was unsmiling and a little hurt as he helped her into her jacket and led her horse out for her.

"You never got to tell your story. What would you do if you inherited a vast fortune?"

"Give it to you," he whispered.

"Don't be stupid."

"It seems I can't help myself where you are concerned." For once he led the way. He guided them cross-country as unerringly as she could have. This surprised her at first until she remembered what he did for a living.

They had all walked up to the lane that ran to the cow barns to watch Ember race. Matthew was on Ember and Jeremy on his four-year-old. It was an uneven race since Ember was carrying half again as much weight as Weaver, but Ember still ran away from his half brother with ease.

Cristine danced up and down like Dicea, and Nathan thought he had never seen her look so pretty and alive. But he had a notion it was Matthew she was enchanted with, not Ember.

"You should come riding with us. We would love to have you."

"Unlike you, I'm afraid I don't take criticism well." She held her straw hat on against the stiff breeze down the hill.

"Ride with Dicea and Grandfather then. I promise you he has not said one unkind word to her."

"Oh, but..."

"That's right. What would be the point with Matthew off doing something else?"

"Are we so obvious?" She blushed.

"You are not, but Matthew fairly devours you with his eyes. Only an idiot...or a Gaites could not notice. Why don't you marry?"

"We want to someday, but Eleanor wants me to wait until Margaret is settled. Also, Matthew says I should have at least one season in fairness to me."

"It's going to be torture for him, and God knows how many other young lads. You have no doubts, though?" Nathan surmised.

"I think I have been in love with him since I first laid eyes on him. I was only ten then, and Jared had just given him such a beating he could hardly stand. I will never forgive Jared."

"They are not much alike, are they? But the shoe's on the other foot now. Matthew outweighs him. I fancy Jared has not picked any fights since that came about."

"Now that you mention it, no, but he gets at Matthew in other ways, mostly through Sir Owen. Sometimes he even turns Jeremy against Matthew. It frightens me when Jeremy acts like Jared. Now that you are here he has another interest."

"I hope he doesn't imitate me. I'm the one who's still learning."

"Your dancing, at least, is progressing well. But I am no judge. I have been to only two country balls myself. Margaret should be teaching you."

"I think so, too. It would keep me out of trouble."

"What do you mean?"

"Matthew says I hold you too tight."

"Nonsense. You hold me quite properly. When did he say that to you?"

"Just yesterday, after he saw us waltzing. And if Matthew says I hold you too tight, then I had better mend my ways. I can't afford to be at outs with him. Besides, I have no desire to torture him. Look at him pushing Ember off on the groom to walk, so he can find out what we have been talking about."

"He cannot be jealous. He must be as sure of me as I am of him." Cristine smiled sweetly.

"He may be sure of you. It's me he has his doubts about. Be kind to him," Nathan said as he left her side to go talk to Dicea and Margaret.

If Cristine had concerns about Jeremy, it was nothing to Margaret's fears for his future. She could not bear the thought of him hanging on Sir Owen's sleeve like Matthew and Jared, anymore than she could like that kind of future for Nathan. Sir Owen had sent him to school, but Jeremy did not seem to have gotten much use out of it. He claimed they didn't teach anything he was really interested in. When he came back home he talked of reopening the mill, but the loss of Tenwells had put a stop to that. She was not sure Sir Owen would have encouraged such an ungentlemanly occupation anyway.

With the marriage settlements Sir Owen promised for Cristine and Dicea, they would do well enough when the time came. For herself she could imagine no future at all, not one she wanted to think about anyway. She would take Eleanor's place if Eleanor died before Sir Owen. In either case Nathan would have Gaites Hall eventually. If he did not choose to live here and left Matthew in charge, as the latter had hinted, she would still be Nathan's pensioner. No doubt he would use her kindly. The thought gagged her.

The one escape that Eleanor kept throwing up to her, the temptation to accept Nathan's offer, teased at her mind. He was handsome, easy to manage, even tempered and undemanding. He was neither as innocent nor as ignorant as he originally pretended, and he got on well with Dicea. If she were to marry she had less objection to him than anyone. That was the clincher, then. It did not seem like a particularly good reason for marrying someone, the fact that he was the least objectionable man she had met. Best not to think of it at all and keep him for a friend if she could.

* * *

Nathan had the misfortune to encounter her in this frame of mind while he was strolling about the garden looking for her. The worried look she cast at him almost made him flinch.

"What have I done now?"

"Nothing. That's the problem." When Margaret was upset, she always spoke to Nathan as though he were privy to her thoughts. "You, all of you, hang on Sir Owen's every whim. It's disgusting."

"I think that's why he likes you so much. You never give in to him."

"You have sold out like the rest of them, for a pretty horse and some new hats."

This irritated Nathan since he didn't like the hats above half anyway. "Do you really imagine he could keep me here if I did not choose to stay?"

"You plan to go back to sea then?"

"Do you want me to go?"

"I would like to think one of you has some fortitude."

"Unfortunately none of us have as much as you."

"If I were a man..."

"What? What would you do?"

"I would leave here."

"You would take the children with you?"

"Of course. Somehow I would make a place for them."

"Yes. I'm sure you would." Nathan nodded sadly. And then, as though he were talking of something else, he asked, "How can I help you?"

"You can't." She subsided and began to feel guilty about ranting at him.

"But you are extremely unhappy and I don't want you to be."

"Yes, but I am used to it," she said courageously, and left him.

He had already decided to buy Tenwells for her. It might not be proper for her to live there alone at her young age, but he rather thought Jeremy would fall in with her schemes and set up house with her. Besides, it was the only thing she said she wanted, and he could easily afford it. Of course, once she was secure there she would have no incentive to marry him. In the end he knew her happiness, even without him, was essential to his own peace of mind. He would free her and take his chances on his own merits. They did not look to be good.

Nathan usually took care of his correspondence very early in the morning room. Margaret was certainly aware that he got mail but must have assumed that Fields read the letters to him and wrote his replies. Nathan was just writing Captain Hewitt to find another navigator and to expect a visit from him that week when Margaret entered the room. She pulled up stock-still at the sight of Nathan dipping his quill and filling line after line of writing paper. He made reference to something in another letter lying by him and went back to writing.

"You can write!" Margaret said bluntly.

Nathan jumped slightly and looked around at her. "I can read, too, but I'm sure there's nothing extraordinary about that."

"You are left-handed," she said unnecessarily.

"And you are up early. I'm sure Captain Hewitt is sorry my hand has healed. He has to puzzle over my terrible scrawl again."

"It never even occurred to me . . ." She came up behind his chair, blushing furiously, a thing she hardly ever did. "Why didn't you tell me?" She sounded almost angry at being fooled by him.

"I don't suppose this means you will marry me?" he asked without looking up from his labors.

"No, of course not," she said over his shoulder.

"I didn't think so."

"Who is Mary Anne?"

"Do you mind?" Nathan laughed, covering the letter and turning to look at her.

"I quite see now why I can't write your letters for you anymore, if you must make arrangements for your *chère amie.*" Margaret flounced to a sofa and sat down to ignore him.

"My what?" He glanced at what he had written.

You shall have to make provisions for someone for the *Mary Anne* if you have not already done so.

"Mary Anne..." He stopped himself. If he told her *Mary Anne* was a ship she might still be angry or she might laugh about it as the mood struck her. But Nathan rather liked this start Margaret had taken. It was the first spark of jealousy she had ever shown over him. *"Mary Anne* is none of your affair," he said firmly.

"No need to tell me that," she said coldly. "How many are there?"

"Four," Nathan answered truthfully. He rose and walked ponderously toward the back of the sofa as though ashamed to face her. Captain Hewitt did indeed own four ships.

"Where are they, besides Bristol, I mean?" Her eyes snapped fire at him.

"Right now—" he leaned over the back of the sofa "—South America, the Indies, and...I'm not quite sure where *Jessica* is at the moment," he said provocatively.

Margaret rose on a tide of wrath. "How dare you flaunt them before me?"

She caught him a ringing slap. He retrieved her hand and kissed the palm of it, laughing. She snatched it away and fled the room. He directed his letter and slipped it into his pocket for posting in Whetstone later in the day.

When he had made all tidy and moved into the breakfast parlor, Eleanor accosted him, "What could you possibly have done to put Margaret in a passion so early in the morning?"

"I scarcely know. I seem to have a natural talent for inflaming her."

"I should call it an art," Eleanor snorted, "rather than a gift."

"Dear Eleanor, you always see through me." He kissed her hand and escorted her in great state to her chair, then took a seat on her right to receive a cup of coffee from her.

"You are pleased with yourself this morning," Eleanor said suspiciously. "What have you been up to?"

"I was just thinking," Nathan said playfully, "if Margaret won't have me, perhaps you will marry me." He flashed her a boyish grin. "We are not, after all, related by blood. I'm sure there could be no impediment . . ."

"Don't be ridiculous," Eleanor said, recovering from too large a gulp of tea. "I'm old enough to be your mother. And I wish you would not joke about such things. Margaret will have you if she's a sensible girl."

"Don't say that. A sensible girl would most certainly reject me. Margaret is the most passionate one among you. You just don't realize it because she keeps such a tight rein on herself." The effect of this statement was lost since a crash from above stairs and Margaret's shouting could be heard throughout the house.

"That," said Eleanor, looking heavenward, "does not speak to me of any sort of control."

"Well, but we were speaking of us," Nathan went on undeterred. "Don't you see how it would solve all our problems? If we marry, I can adopt Jared and Matthew. Jared will be the heir again and all will be tidy."

Eleanor snorted with laughter and choked on a bit of biscuit. The picture of Jared coming to Nathan for his allowance kept her chuckling and coughing so long Nathan was beginning to worry.

"You rogue," she finally managed, wiping the tears away. "And I suppose Jared and Margaret will marry?"

"Oh, no, that would never do," he decided. "Why, he would not last a week. No, I foresee that Jared will remain a bachelor and Matthew will find himself with Cristine."

"And what of Margaret?"

"Why, my mistress, of course," he said innocently.

This set her off coughing again, "Stop! You are terrible."

"What in the world is so funny?" Cristine asked as she and Dicea entered for breakfast.

"Why, I just offered . . ."

"Nathan, no, not the girls."

"I just offered to drive Eleanor to Bristol to go shopping and she does not think I can manage it."

"Well, you had best ask Sir Owen before you take out one of his teams," Dicea warned him seriously as she spread jam on her toast.

"Perhaps you are right."

"We have no need to go to Bristol," Eleanor asserted, trying to recover herself.

"But surely you need some extra laces and ribands for all those dresses that are being made. But perhaps we should take the carriage so that all the girls can go."

"Oh, may we, Eleanor?" Dicea begged.

"I'm sure I have no objection to a trip to Bristol, so long as Sir Owen does not."

"Does not what?" Sir Owen surprised them by asking from the doorway. His presence was so unprecedented at the early table as to startle even Eleanor.

"So long as you don't object to us taking your carriage into Bristol," Nathan supplied as Sir Owen seated himself.

"Yes, yes, do as you wish. I should be glad of some peace and quiet for a day. There's Margaret above stairs, ranting at her maid so loud a fellow can't sleep. What could have set her off?"

"I'm sure I don't know." Nathan looked up innocently, and then asked for more coffee.

Eleanor choked back a laugh and poured for him. "When are we to go on this shopping trip?"

"What say you to Thursday, right after breakfast? We can lunch at the Half Moon."

It took rather longer to reach Bristol in the lumbering carriage than in Matthew's smart curricle, but Jeremy and Matthew rode patiently beside. Margaret had managed to arrange the seating so that Dicea was between her and Nathan. She could be expected neither to converse with him nor trade looks with him. He was almost beginning to regret making her jealous. They left the horses and carriage at the inn, bespeaking a private parlor and luncheon for the noon hour. Nathan then escorted them to the streets of shops and unexpectedly abandoned them to Matthew's care on the excuse of urgent business. Jeremy capered off with the promise not to fail to meet them for lunch.

Nathan called at the office of the land agent whose address Captain Hewitt had supplied to him. He did not make himself appear to be overeager about acquiring a country estate. In fact he gave the impression that it was on a whim he stopped and inquired at all. He found something amiss with the several sites suggested to him and was beginning in fact to look a little bored. The agent knew his name well enough to know that despite Nathan's youth, he had done well for himself, and he did not want to lose such a client. At the complaint that the houses suggested were all too grand for someone with a taste for farming, the desperate man suggested Tenwells farm, described the house, mill, the sixty acres surrounding, and was about to set a day for a visit.

Nathan said it sounded perfect, hesitated enough over the price to get it down by two thousand, if the seller would agree, and left a check for hand money until the deal could be confirmed. Well satisfied with the morning's work, he repaired to the inn parlor to be regaled with tales of the finds the ladies had stowed into the carriage and to enjoy steamed crab and lobster, light ale and pineapple chunks.

"Are there any ships in port that you have sailed on, Nathan?" Jeremy's eyes were alight, so Nathan guessed he had been crawling about the quays.

"I'm not sure. We can walk down to see after lunch, while the girls finish their shopping. Margaret, would you like to come with us?"

Margaret opened her mouth to snub him, but hesitated to leave Jeremy in his company in such a state of excitement.

"On the other hand, best not," considered Nathan. "You would be bound to get your clothes dirty, and who knows what language you would hear."

She rose to the bait as Nathan knew she would. "As if I care for that. I will come, thank you."

Eleanor was on the point of refusing consent, but Nathan cast her a speaking look and she merely lifted her eyebrows. She had no desire to drag Margaret from shop to shop in her present mood, not when she was having such a good time helping Cristine and Dicea select trimmings for their dresses. Besides, if anyone could charm Margaret out of the sullens, Nathan could.

Nathan led Jeremy and Margaret down to the docks and along the pier to where a tidy three-masted schooner sat at anchor. The foremast was newly installed. "Captain Hewitt," Nathan called to a well-dressed old man with a pipe. "May we come aboard, sir?"

"Yes, my boy, of course."

Jeremy hopped up the gangway. Margaret was negotiating the springy plank when she saw the name on the bow of the ship, *Mary Anne,* and nearly lost her balance. Nathan grabbed her around the waist with what she thought unnecessary eagerness and scooped her up onto the deck. *"Mary Anne,"* she said after the introductions had been made. "Have you a ship called the *Jessica,* as well?"

"Yes, a bit larger. She's in the Carolinas now. The *Forthright* should be on her way home from the Indies, and the *Marivelle* is outbound for Guiana. Would you like to see below?''

"Oh, yes, please." Jeremy was so wrapped up in asking questions and Captain Hewitt so amused at the boy's excitement they both missed the sharp punch in the arm Margaret gave Nathan and her muttered threat to get him later. Nathan cringed in mock terror as Margaret refused his aid in getting down the companionway.

"I take it you have ambitions to go to sea," Captain Hewitt commented to Jeremy.

"Yes, well not perhaps as Nathan did," Jeremy said out of his sister's hearing, "but I would like to have my own yacht someday."

"Captain, do you still keep that small sailboat?"

"Why, yes, she's tied up by Jim Simpson's house. There's a fair bit of wind today. Why don't you three take her out on the river?"

"Oh, can we?" Jeremy was enchanted, but Margaret scowled.

"I think there's just time, unless Margaret would not care for it," Nathan consulted her.

"I can swim," Margaret said bluntly.

"Ouch," complained Nathan.

Captain Hewitt cackled with laughter. "You don't appear to have much confidence in Nathan. He won't capsize you, I promise, at least not in these calm waters."

"I'm beginning to be sorry I suggested it," Nathan said, but led them to the small boat. Jeremy had learned enough to help him unfurl the sail and cast off. Jeremy stayed in the bow as Nathan told him to and Margaret sat beside Nathan in the stern. He said this was to properly balance the boat, but she did not at all look as if she swallowed that one.

"You are really going to be in Sir Owen's black books when Jeremy goes back spouting all that sea talk. He won't give him a moment's peace."

"Yes, but I shall come about. Besides, I had to get Jeremy out here to find out about something."

"What?"

"We'll see."

Margaret studied Nathan's handling of the sail and rudder while Jeremy chatted happily from the bow until they were far enough out to feel a hint of the wash and drag of the tide coming up the river. Margaret had leaned back and was enjoying the salt smell, the seabirds veering overhead, and the slap of the small waves against the side of the boat. Her reverie was interrupted by the unmistakable sounds of her little brother throwing up. That sound had often roused her from a sound sleep and always moved her to compassion. She would have gotten up, but Nathan laid his hand on her shoulder and shook his head.

"Let him be, Margaret. I was afraid of this when you talked about him being queasy in closed carriages. I just wanted to know for sure."

He took them in then and rowed the last hundred yards to the dock. Captain Hewitt was waiting for him, and tied up the line Nathan tossed ashore himself. He gallantly gave Margaret a hand out of the boat. "I see you have a casualty."

Nathan took Jeremy's arm to steady him and made him sit on the edge of the pier with his eyes closed while he packed up the sail.

"I think I'm feeling better now," Jeremy said valiantly.

"Yes, and the dizziness will go away once you walk about a bit, I promise you," said the sympathetic old man.

"You don't suppose it was something I ate, do you?"

"It's possible, lad. Do you feel like going out again?"

"No, that is, not today anyway. Do people sometimes get over seasickness?"

"Not that I ever heard of. The first few weeks of a voyage would always be like that for you, I'm afraid. Don't take it so hard, lad. Better to find out you have no stomach for the sea like this than on a six-month voyage."

"I suppose you are right, sir." Jeremy stood and walked steadily enough up the dock.

Captain Hewitt kindly invited them to his house, but Margaret declined gracefully. "I fear we shall be very late already, but I would like to come to visit you another time. And I did enjoy the boat ride." She said this last to him out of Jeremy's hearing.

"Come anytime, anytime at all. I'm usually about somewhere."

"Thank you, sir. I would like that."

After that Nathan picked a fair day every week to go into Bristol with Margaret and Dicea. Margaret was an excellent whip and drove them there as quickly as Matthew could have. Captain Hewitt and Dicea were enchanted with each other, but that was no surprise to Nathan. Dicea bombarded the old gentleman with enough questions to convince him she was Jeremy's sister. They often lunched with him, and Dicea regaled the captain with the tales of Nathan's adventures since he had come to Gaites Hall.

Nathan's letters had glossed over the more dangerous and embarrassing of his escapades and concentrated on Margaret and Dicea. The captain could see that Nathan was in love with the girl, but how to win such a determined lass was a puzzle to him, as well. He did recommend Nathan not give up for she was worth ten of any other young miss he had met. "A girl of rare courage," he judged her.

On fair days they sailed on the river. Margaret picked it up as naturally as she rode, and before long Nathan was relegated to being the crew. Dicea was safely tied by the waist such that even if she tumbled out by hanging over the side they would be able to fetch her back. Nathan had to row them back when the tide was against them. Margaret rather enjoyed feeling the pull of the boat through the water, knowing that his effort was causing the movement. It was almost as though he were physically tugging at her yet never getting her any closer no matter how the sweat soaked the back of his shirt or dampened the hair hanging over his brow. He could not pull her in.

To be worshiped from afar by someone with no particular hold over her was pleasant enough. Nathan never asked for anything in return except, occasionally, for her hand in marriage. This more amused than angered her now. With this state of affairs Margaret would have been content forever. What she did not realize was that it would never be enough for Nathan.

"I was afraid of this," Nathan said as they left the curricle at the inn yard one day.

"What?"

"It's clouding up. There's a storm brewing."

"You say that every day that there is not bright sun."

"I am usually right."

When they got to Captain Hewitt's, he welcomed them into the sitting room. "No sailing today, I'm afraid. There's a storm on the way."

"How can you tell?" Dicea asked.

"Wind's coming from the wrong quarter. You'd best shelter here with me this afternoon until the worst is over. This won't be just a shower. When the wind backs around to the northwest like this we get our worst weather."

The prediction proved correct, but the party ignored the rain driving against the windows of the snug sitting room. Mrs. Beckley had outdone herself with steaming coffee and chocolate and an array of foreign fruit that the Westons could now name, as well as eat. The captain spoke of his voyages, not in an organized way, but in tantalizing bits and snatches as he proudly displayed the relics of his many years at sea. He did finally settle into his chair with his pipe and relate their encounter with a French frigate.

"Bit of fog rolling along just on top of the ocean, not enough to hide in, mind you, but it did disguise how low we rode in the water."

"We could never have outrun that ship," Nathan inserted.

"What did you do?" asked Dicea.

"Had the gun ports pulled open and turned the ship."

"You attacked?" Margaret was surprised.

"No, we bluffed," Hewitt said, puffing on his pipe.

"Captain had the signalman running flags up and down telling the rest of our party we were going in for a kill."

"You were not alone then?" Margaret questioned,

"Of course, we were, but the French didn't know that." Hewitt chuckled.

"Did they fight you?"

"They thought about it, then came about and ran for cover."

"From a merchant ship?"

"There is not a great deal of difference to be seen at a distance."

"Now I know where Nathan gets it."

"What?"

"His recklessness."

Margaret conveyed from Captain Hewitt to her grandfather an invitation to join them on their next excursion to Bristol. Since he acknowledged this with no more than a grunt, she was surprised then when he appeared mounted to go with them. Nathan felt strangely nervous at the meeting, like a bridegroom introducing in-laws to his family. He reflected that this was very much the position he would like to be in. Sir Owen declined sailing but walked the quays and talked to the captain.

"Has Nathan livened things up for you in the country?" Captain Hewitt asked, puffing his pipe and smiling with his eyes.

"More than a little." Sir Owen chuckled. "What a strange boy he is. I must admit, at first I thought him rather stupid. Then I came to realize what a mischief maker he is."

"Always one for a joke, is Nathan. We never had a dull voyage with him."

"He has made such a difference for us, especially Dicea." Sir Owen cleared his throat. "I am not unmindful of the debt I owe you for taking care of him."

"The boy has been a joy to me and he is my heir as well as yours, but I did not like the thought of him being alone once I am gone. I knew he would charm you into liking him."

"Who could not like Nathan?"

"Sweet Margaret has him fair hobbled. She is a rare challenge for him."

"I hope they make a match of it."

"Nathan has endurance and he's stubborn. I think he will win her in the end."

They all met for lunch at the Half Moon. Nathan never knew what Captain Hewitt and Sir Owen had said to each other. He did not know why it was so important to him, but he desperately wanted the two old men to like each other. Sir Owen later declared Captain Hewitt a capital fellow and announced the captain would be spending Christmas with them, if he could not tear himself away from his work sooner than that. Nathan smiled. His family was drawing together. If he could only bring Margaret up to scratch.

From one of these expeditions they returned with a large bolt of hemp cording, which Dicea informed Jeremy they would use to knot hammocks. The four of them spent so many hours that hot afternoon down by the lake tying and retying these flimsy structures, and picking out just the right pairs of trees to hang them on, that Sir Owen wandered down with his fishing tackle to see what they were up to.

Margaret and Nathan were still working over Dicea's tangle of lines, but Jeremy had hopped out of his hammock to swing Dicea on the large one Nathan had completed. Sir Owen laughed at the contraptions, refused to try one and merely warned them not to leave them hanging in the trees overnight since the birds would get caught in them. He then threw his line contentedly into the water and listened to the sound of Dicea's and Jeremy's laughter. If it had not been for Nathan's coming he would not have known what a nice lot of children they were.

When the deal for Tenwells was arranged to Nathan's satisfaction, and a time appointed to settle the affair, Nathan merely rode Samarkand into Bristol without telling anybody. It was a nice feeling going somewhere purposeful on a horse, rather than just hacking about the estate or running to the surrounding villages on errands. When he presented himself at the estate agent's office, no one would have known him for a sailor. He was dressed meticulously in top boots and riding leathers. He even sported one of Matthew's stylish hats, which he handed over to the clerk with his gloves as suavely as he had seen Matthew perform such a simple act.

He shook hands with Captain Vilard and was introduced to him as Mr. Gaites.

"What?" Vilard let go Nathan's hand as though it had burned him. "You are a Gaites? I thought your name was Nathan."

"Yes, that's right, Nathan Gaites. Do you know the family?"

"Not…that well." Vilard swallowed and pushed his fears of exposure to the background as Nathan sat down calmly in one of the armchairs provided for Mr. Larch's clients.

"Neither do I," Nathan lied, blank-faced to the harsh-featured dandy in his forties. "But I thought it would be amusing to purchase part of the property. Who knows, I might even take a fancy to farming. But then," Nathan said in a bored tone, "if I don't, I suppose land is always worth something."

"Not as much as some of us had hoped," Vilard seethed as Nathan read over the agreement of sale.

Nathan looked up after a moment, seeming to recollect that Vilard had spoken. "Second thoughts, sir? If you would rather not sell, after all, I'm sure Mr. Larch can find me another prospect.''

''No...the property is much too far from London to be of interest to me,'' Vilard said quickly.

''Very well then.'' Nathan smiled innocently and signed the agreement. Vilard scarcely read the document before scrawling his name with a flourish and accepting the obligatory glass of sherry to seal the bargain. Mr. Larch heaved a sigh of relief.

''Oh, by the way,'' Nathan said, as he descended the steps of the office alongside Vilard, ''I should appreciate it if you didn't tell any of the Gaites, should you meet them, who bought Tenwells.''

''Why should I?'' Vilard's eyes narrowed in speculation. ''What do you mean to do with it?''

''You know, I'm not quite sure yet.'' Nathan cast him a dazzling smile and wandered off to tell Captain Hewitt of his latest adventure.

The first inkling Margaret had that Tenwells had changed hands was seeing Mr. Kendall's wagon pulled up in front. He and his sons were checking the mortar and crawling up a ladder to look at the roof. ''What is it, Margaret?'' Nathan asked, guiding Samarkand up to her mare.

''Tenwells must have been sold. The Kendalls do a lot of the repair work hereabouts.'' She took a brave breath but still looked as though she were about to burst into tears.

''Don't be upset. I bought it.''

''You?'' She looked dumbfounded.

''Come, I have not been inside yet. Let's see what needs doing.'' He rode up to the stone house and tied his horse to a post. Margaret followed numbly and even let him help her down.

''Good morning to you, Mr. Gaites. I have made a list for you with an estimate. Not in bad shape, really, for having sat a few years. No mice or rats at least, Miss Weston,'' he assured Margaret kindly.

"Thank you, sir. I'm sure we'll be contacting you in a day or two with notice to start work, if it's convenient."

Nathan dragged Margaret inside once the Kendalls had left, and got her to show him the rooms. There was a fair-size drawing room and dining room, both with great stone fireplaces reaching to the ceiling, a large friendly kitchen with a rather modern stove, a small study, a breakfast parlor, and a sewing room. Upstairs were four large bedrooms and three smaller ones. Margaret had never seen most of these, nor did they look to have been used for decades.

"A lot of work to be done, even after the repairs are complete, I mean in the way of decorating," Nathan said, turning his hat around in his hands nervously.

"Grandfather will be very proud of you," Margaret said rather hollowly.

"This has nothing to do with Grandfather. This is the one place you seemed to hold some pleasant memories of, I suppose, because nothing bad ever happened to you here."

"Yes." She cast her mind back. "And Mrs. Morton was such a comfortable sort of woman. She treated everyone as though they were ten years old." Margaret was regaining her composure and walked over to look through the dusty window down into the herb garden. "It will be nice having you living so close."

"I bought it for you," he said softly from beside her.

She turned sadly, shaking her head. "I know you mean well, and I still don't understand how you can afford it, but I won't marry you, even for Tenwells."

"How could you think I would try to bribe you? I had the deed transferred to your name, along with enough funds to provide you an income to restore it as you like." He pressed the documents on her and she stared at them in disbelief. "I bought you your freedom, Margaret. Now no one can force you into anything."

"You don't mean to live here, then?" she asked dumbly.

"Well, no." He laughed shakily. "Not unless you decide to marry me. People might think it odd."

Her eyes flew to his face, trying to read his intentions.

"Just joking. There are no strings attached, I promise you."

"I can't accept it," she said, flushing hotly. "I won't be pitied, even by you!"

He did not let go her hand, but held it fast as he searched her eyes intently. "It's not just for you," he said desperately. "It's for Dicea and Jeremy, as well. Do you want them to be trapped at Gaites Hall as you are? Think about what your life has been." He felt almost guilty calling up those doubts and horrors to flicker in her staring eyes. "You cannot let that happen to them. And there's no other way I can save them from what you have suffered. You must take the house to make a home for them."

Margaret drew in a breath and trembled slightly. "I have worried about what is to become of them when I have been able to stand to think of the future. But what about you, spending your life savings to make a place for us?"

"Money, like silk, should not be left moldering somewhere. It should be used for something." He smiled sadly at her. "Please, Margaret, if I can't make you happy, at least let me make you comfortable." He let go her hand then and said lightly, "I expect you have some lists to make, also, wallpaper and drapery fabric, and such." He backed away, looking about the bare room. "So I will leave you to get on with it. Don't be too late, though." He turned back at the doorway. "You still have to live at Gaites Hall for a time yet. And even this won't keep Grandfather from ringing a peal over you if you hold up dinner." He was gone then and Margaret watched him ride away through the film of dust on the window and the blur of tears in her eyes.

Nathan thought he had managed the thing pretty well. Once Margaret got used to the idea of owning Tenwells, he was sure she would be happy there. He did walk on eggs for a few days in the fear that she would fly into a passion, tear the deed up and throw it into his face. Her subdued attitude caused Sir Owen to wonder if she was not feeling well, so she pulled herself together, commented that it was just the rainy weather, and tried to act like her usual self.

"Nathan," she called to him on the next clear morning as he walked to the stable.

"Oh, good, you are riding today. When you were not at breakfast, I was not sure."

"It just occurred to me that I never even thanked you. I was just so surprised, I couldn't quite take it in for a while."

"I'm sorry if I gave you a nasty shock." Nathan smiled roguishly at her. "What tears me is how I'm going to break the news to Grandfather that I'm not the pauper he thinks I am. There's a lot I could help him with on his own place if he would let me."

"Just what are you worth?" Margaret looked at him narrowly, with a returning hint of her former playfulness.

"Now, now, girl. Don't be mercenary." He mounted Samarkand and turned him down the driveway. "You'll get your fair share."

"Nathan! Just because you have money doesn't mean you can get by with that." She cantered after him, and they raced cross-country to the farmhouse, with Nathan leading most of the way but Margaret winning because she put Titian over the yard fence.

"Well, Miss Weston of Tenwells," Nathan intoned solemnly, "What say you? Do we put the Kendalls to work?"

"Yes," Margaret said firmly with a nod, and they carried on like a couple of schoolchildren as they raced to the village.

Margaret was walking about the garden, toying with a rose, trying to get used to the idea of being free. She felt that she could breathe, really breathe, for the first time in her life. The project of refurbishing Tenwells stretched before her like a happy dream. She had a future, a place, and time enough to do as she pleased. She must have been smiling rather foolishly when the shadow of Jared fell across her path.

Margaret recognized him, sighed that he was not Nathan, then smiled at him anyway. That brought a crease between his brows, for she had the look of one besotted and Jared had just about decided that Nathan would never manage to get her.

"I see you are not so careful to disguise your intimate little walks with Nathan anymore. Does that mean you will have him?"

"Why, no, Jared. Nathan and I are the best of friends." For once Margaret spoke from a position of strength. "He may still joke of marriage, but he has accepted the situation."

"Perhaps he's just playing deeper than any of us know. You may live to—"

"Stop it, Jared," she said tiredly, as though to a naughty child, "I won't listen to any more of your lies about Nathan."

"He's only human to want to be left as well-off as possible. He may even have a genuine affection for you. To have endured all you have dealt out to him argues, at least, for his patience."

"He has given up the idea, I tell you. He has provided for me and Dicea and Jeremy so that I need not marry anyone."

"Whatever promises he has made in the expectation—"

"His are not empty promises," she interrupted Jared ruthlessly. "He has deeded Tenwells over to me and given me an income to maintain it." Jared's eyebrows crashed into his face and Margaret chuckled.

"Are you drunk?" he asked her incredulously. "Nathan can't have bought it. He has no money."

"You have been a fool, Jared. Nathan has plenty of money. He arranged for the purchase this summer."

"Then he knows—" Jared blurted out. "He plans to use it—"

"What are you talking about? Knows what?"

"What does he expect in return?" Jared asked her desperately.

"Nothing." Her voice softened. "He simply wanted me to be free to raise Dicea and Jeremy as I see fit. That's all." Margaret could not make out why Jared was looking so horrified, but she was too human not to enjoy it. "I believe Nathan is right. You are rather amusing, after all."

Jared swore at her and stalked off with the ripple of her laughter rending what little was left of his composure.

For Jared it was the last straw. Bad enough to contemplate losing everything to an ignorant sailor, now to find out Nathan had been deceiving them. He probably meant to expose Jared's part in the Tenwells' scheme to Sir Owen. Why else would he buy the farm back and simply give it to Margaret?

He must have been mad to lure Talbot into that trap. He had no idea it would cost Talbot his life, but who would believe that? Not Sir Owen, who believed the very worst of him after the incident with the cat. This tore at Jared worse than all the rest. As much as he might contemplate his grandfather's eventual demise, he did not want that to happen anytime soon, for he had a very real regard for Sir Owen.

Nathan and Jeremy were just coming back from the lake with some fine trout for dinner when Jared encountered them in the white heat of his anger and despair.

"I believe I have been remiss in my share of your education, Nathan. I think I was promised to teach you to box."

"Will you teach me, too, Jared?" Jeremy asked hopefully.

"You can watch, little one," Jared said as he started stripping off his coat.

Nathan could see from Jared's color that his real purpose was to vent his wrath. But Nathan was so used to Margaret turning angry for no reason that he did not even bother to inquire into the cause of Jared's sudden interest in beating on him. Penning up so much ill nature was bound to cause an explosion sooner or later. Nathan was just glad Fields would have to clean the mud from his suit only once. Nathan slid off his coat, folded it over a willow limb and was turning resignedly when Jared hit him in the mouth.

Nathan cursed, more at his own stupidity for being taken by surprise than at Jared's villainy.

"You haven't even told him the rules yet," Jeremy complained as Nathan brushed his hand across his split lip and squared up to Jared. Nathan was concentrating on not hitting with his left so as not to break his hand again. He blocked Jared's right blow to his stomach and deflected a left to his face that caught him on the brow ridge over his left eye. He was momentarily stunned and went down on his left knee. Nathan could not see for the blood running into his eye, and when he shook his head to clear it, he spattered blood across Jeremy's white shirt. The fear and shock in the boy's face convinced Nathan that it was Jeremy who had been hit, not himself.

"Jared, you forgot to take your ring off," Jeremy shouted.

Jared's low chuckle made something boil up in Nathan. Jared may have been walking over to help him up. In any case, Jared was unprepared for Nathan's right fist flung around at him like a hammer on the end of his arm. Nathan staggered to his feet and looked down at the unconscious Jared whose nose was bleeding copiously.

"Oh no," Nathan whispered as he staggered back to lean against the willow. He tried to brush the blood out of his eye, then rolled his own coat to make a pillow for Jared's head. "Keep his head turned, Jeremy, so he doesn't choke. I better go get his valet."

"Maybe I should go," Jeremy said as he knelt beside Jared, "I don't think you can walk."

Nathan staggered into a tree but assured the boy that he was all right. On the way to the house he wiped the worst of the blood off his face and made a pad of his handkerchief for his eye. He cursed himself for losing his temper, even with Jared. But he had genuinely thought Jeremy had been hurt, and Jared's laugh—he hated it. That was no excuse. He may be a Gaites but he didn't have to act like one.

As he passed through the stable yard a groom looked at him openmouthed and when Nathan saw the lad gaping, he shouted, "You, Fletcher!"

"Yes, sir."

"Ride and get Dr. Stewart. Jared's been hurt." The groom hesitated an instant before tearing his gaze away, but Nathan's "Move!" sent him running to saddle a horse.

Nathan was making for the back of the house when Margaret saw him from the terrace. "Nathan, your face is bleeding, let me see."

"Oh, for God's sake, Margaret, leave it alone." Nathan was not feeling like being mothered.

"Well, if you think I care whether you live or die…" She was still at his elbow and he looked vaguely down at her out of one eye. "Nathan, I didn't mean that. I do care."

He wanted her so badly he succumbed to her attentions. "It's just a cut."

"It goes pretty well to the bone," she judged. "What happened?"

"Jared was showing me how to box and he forgot to take his ring off."

"Are you sure he forgot?"

"Actually I think it was an accident," Nathan admitted.

By this time Margaret had made a pad of her handkerchief as well. "Press on that tightly."

"I have to find Timms."

"What do you need him for?"

"Jared's a mess. I never saw so much gore. I caught him in the face."

"Good for you," she said, walking at his side.

"You are as bloodthirsty as your little brother. Where is the fellow likely to be at this time of day?"

"In the servants' hall, I suppose."

They invaded the kitchen area without ceremony, surprising the staff at their tea. "Timms, you are needed down by the lake. Jared's been injured—not too seriously, I hope, but take a basin and plenty of linen. Take someone with you in case you have to carry him back. I have already sent for the doctor." Nathan had only to issue these clipped orders to send half a dozen servants running.

Fields came around the table to him looking genuinely concerned, but Nathan was not sure if it was over him or the bloodstains on his shirt. He went on through the house with both Fields and Margaret in his wake and had the misfortune to meet Sir Owen in the hall. "What the devil's happened now? You have not put your eye out?"

Nathan looked at him out of one eye and imagined the old man was scared by the bloody rag he was holding. "Boxing lessons, remember, sir?" Nathan said with mock cheerfulness. "I'm afraid I made a mess of it though. Sorry to tell you this, but I'm pretty sure I have broken Jared's nose."

"Have you, by God?" Sir Owen chuckled. "That's a surprise."

"You are all alike," Nathan said in horror. "I'm the one who will catch it from Dr. Stewart this time."

"Let me see." Sir Owen pried Nathan's hand away with Margaret's help. "That will take a stitch or two to close. You two stay with him. Where's Jared?"

"Down by the willow tree at the lake. Jeremy is with him." Nathan thought he actually saw his grandfather rub his hands together with relish as he set out for the lake.

Nathan, lying in a darkened room with Margaret and Fields in attendance, and a wet compress on his head, was much relieved to hear Jared and company stamping up the stairs sometime later. Jared was complaining in a nasal voice that Nathan had not gotten one in over his guard, but had tricked him. Margaret giggled and Fields smiled sympathetically.

"This is not funny," Nathan complained. "Like as not I will never get on terms with Jared now."

They heard Dr. Stewart on the stairs then and Nathan told Margaret to take him to Jared first, so she could find out how he was.

Eventually Dr. Stewart moved over to Nathan's room, had the curtains thrown back ruthlessly for light, and probed the wound. All Nathan felt was a dull ache in his head.

"This will leave a scar," the doctor said cheerfully as he squinted to thread his suture needle, "but then you have not improved Jared's looks much, either."

Nathan awoke the next day without even much of a headache, but he was so tired and depressed he did not bother to get up. Besides, he saw no reason to haunt the early breakfast table with his ghastly appearance, so he went back to sleep.

"How is he?" Margaret slipped into Nathan's room to ask Fields.

"All right, as far as I can tell," Fields informed her, "but he had a bad night. I slept in the dressing room in case he should need me. He woke up shouting orders, which I have never known him to do before, even when he was feverish."

"A dream?"

"I suppose. It took me a few minutes to convince him where he was."

When Nathan became aware that the whispering was not the wind or ocean but Margaret and Fields talking together, he opened his unbandaged eye and tried to focus on them.

"What is it?" he asked thickly. "How's Jared?"

"Gone," Margaret said, coming toward the bed.

"Dead?" Nathan sat bolt upright. "I didn't think he was hurt that bad."

"No, silly, he packed up and left," she said, trying to push Nathan back against his determined efforts to rise.

"I have to go after him."

"Don't, I assure you we are all most grateful to you."

"You may say good riddance to him, but I cannot let him go with a quiet mind."

"Why not?"

"Let alone I have mutilated him and hurt his pride, he can be damned dangerous."

The other two looked at him blankly as he searched for his clothes. "He knows a lot of people in London. Have you any idea how much damage he can do me there?"

"I had not thought of that," Margaret conceded.

"If Sir Owen insists on me going to London in the spring you are all going to have a damned uncomfortable time of it. Now go and order me a horse," he told Margaret. "Better yet, the carriage."

When Margaret left he began to dress himself and ordered Fields to pack for him. He had never ordered Fields to do anything before, and the young man was so shocked he began to comply. But Margaret was made of sterner stuff than that. She did not go to the stable, but ran straight to Sir Owen and laid Nathan's intentions open without compunction. Sir Owen met a most determined-looking young man on the stairs and physically blocked his path.

"Let me go, sir. I must stop him."

"I'm sending Matthew to do that. At least people are used to seeing those two at odds. Besides, have you any idea the picture you present? You look like you have been in a war. And I scarcely think Jared will show his face about town for a few weeks, not with two blackened eyes. Now back to bed with you."

"Oh, I'm all right," Nathan said, much deflated as he slid down to sit on the stairs.

"Then come and have breakfast with me and no more nonsense. It was inevitable that you and Jared would come to blows. I'm just glad you finally put him in his place."

Nathan shook his head, but followed his grandfather meekly down to the breakfast parlor and ate mechanically what was put before him.

Sir Owen excluded Nathan from the ride that day. He flatly said he did not believe Nathan felt fine. So Nathan moped about the terrace and gardens. When Margaret approached him with the suggestion of a nap he looked at her scornfully.

"What's wrong?" She looked hurt.

"Just blue-deviled," he said, relenting. She waited patiently for an explanation so he said in a hard voice, "I lost my temper. That never—almost never happens to me."

"Is that all? I think it was past time."

"Yes, it's perfectly all right for you to storm and rant at each other. That's all that comes of your braggling." He paused, then continued in a different tone, "On board ship a mistake like that can cost someone his life."

It was not what Nathan had meant to say and it sounded oddly hollow to Margaret as Nathan was never anything but truthful. Margaret knew he was hiding something.

That Nathan was being tortured by some past tragedy Margaret had no doubt. But because she would have kept such a mental wound guarded against everyone's prying, she assumed Nathan would resent her questioning.

"Not quite your domain, is it?" he asked, and walked off toward the lake.

Nathan was right, she thought. She was no good at healing anything but physical hurts. If she had reached out to him with a word or a gesture, he probably would have told her the whole. So simple an act. Dicea would do it on impulse. But Margaret was feeling strangely fragile herself just then. She had never made such an overture before, least of all to a man. If Nathan spurned her just now, even if he did not mean it, she would stop ever trying to reach out again. She waited.

* * *

Nathan resumed his normal activities but in a subdued way, as though sadness were always at the back of his mind. Dicea's efforts to lift his spirits were touching. Sir Owen forbade his riding until the doctor came to remove the stitches, on the strength that riding with one eye was more dangerous than riding one-handed. So Nathan walked practically all day in a desperate effort to tire himself out so he could sleep.

Every night he tried to redo the events of his dreams and make them come out so that his mother lived. In his dreams he came back to her a wealthy man who lifted her from her tiresome occupation and treated her like a queen. She forgave him for going away once he had come back and made everything right. He had done what even his father could not do.

Then he awoke to remember that he had done to his mother exactly what his father had done, left her in tears and loneliness.

Nathan slammed himself against the black wall of his depression for a week before he came out of it. Whether it was Sir Owen's threat to have the doctor out again, Dicea's quiet understanding, or Margaret's pleading looks, even Nathan could not say. He had lost weight and looked more bone weary than when recovering from his fall, but the lines about his eyes had relaxed and he could laugh at the antics of Sir Kaye and Sir Gawain as they locked in a mock deadly embrace while they fought and tumbled about the terrace.

He found Margaret by the lake one hot afternoon and realized that he had actually gone there looking for her.

"I think I have been damned rude to you lately," he said bluntly. "I cannot exactly remember. But if I said anything awful, I'm truly sorry."

"I didn't regard it," she said softly as they walked to the middle of the bridge. "I don't see why getting angry upsets you so."

He was silent for a few moments, then said with an effort, "When I left home I didn't just slip off. I argued with my mother about it. They were the first cross words we had ever exchanged and they were the last ones we ever spoke to each other."

"Oh, Nathan."

"The things I said to her, they are engraved on my mind. The look on her face, that I could hurt her so. I can never forget it."

"And you can't ever take those words back."

"No," he said simply, beginning to marvel at Margaret's ready understanding. He had been right to tell her.

"But from what you have said of your mother she would have forgiven you. No doubt, she did forgive you. I am sure of it. Now you have only to forgive yourself."

Nathan looked at Margaret, so sincere in her efforts to convince him. He saw the likeness to Dicea when she was telling him something important. To make Margaret feel better, if not himself, he smiled and nodded. Once he had embraced the idea he began to believe Margaret might be right. "How do you come to know so much?"

"I am an expert at being miserable."

"But that terrible hopelessness I was feeling..."

"I get into black moods myself," Margaret confided.

"Nothing like this has ever happened to me before. I cannot explain it."

"Neither can I. It's like coming to the end of time. Like there is no future." Nathan looked at her in fear and compassion. "You see," she said, "it happens to me all the time."

"Margaret, how do you bear it?" He suddenly hugged her to him as though he did it every day. "I have never felt so alone in my life."

His embrace at that moment had nothing to do with sex. It was not a calculated effort to get close to her. Margaret sensed this and did not stiffen in his arms as she might have done. He looked at her, trying to get behind the pain in her eyes, and she smiled sadly at him.

"A day at a time. By waiting for the passage of time to carry you beyond the dark place. You cannot depend on anything else except time. Sooner or later it will change the things you cannot. I should have told you that, at least, but you would not have believed me."

"What can I do? I don't want this to happen to you ever again."

"Perhaps it won't, now that you have given me a future." She looked in the direction of the farm and he released her quite naturally as they began to walk that way. She had liked the hug from this warm and compassionate man with the confused boy hidden away inside. So long as it was given only in friendship she would let him do it again, Margaret thought, not realizing that friendship was the heart and soul of a relationship.

"I have put Jeremy in charge of the mill," she said more lightly. "Do you want to walk over to see how he's doing?"

Chapter Six

Margaret and Nathan had just returned from the mill at Tenwells and were dusting off their clothes as they went through the hall.

"Do you think he will ever get it back together again?" Nathan asked.

"I don't know, but he did see it in operation, and he seems to know what he's about," Margaret said. "Even if he doesn't, I don't care. This is the first time I have seen Jeremy really interested in something since Sir Owen gave him his colt to train."

"Oh, there you are." Sir Owen came out of the library. "Nathan, I need to see you for a moment." Nathan followed him into the room and braced himself for bad news. "I just got a letter from Matt. You were right about Jared. He's been spreading his poison all over town. Matt is doing all he can to counter it, but without you there, he's in a weak position. That's why I have decided not to wait until spring. We move up to London now."

"Unless I'm mistaken, there are not many people staying there in July and August. Maybe we should wait until spring for it to blow over," Nathan suggested.

"All the more reason to go now. There are some year-round residents. The others will take their cue from them and either accept or reject you. Either way, your future is decided in the next few weeks. If we go there presenting a united front I think it will weigh in your favor."

"But I—excuse me, but were you ever in the army?" Nathan interrupted himself to ask.

"Joined when I was sixteen in the teeth of my father's opposition and rose two ranks before he finally bought me a commission."

"Just the sort of thing you would hate for one of your sons or grandsons to do," Nathan mused.

"I'm not ashamed of having been young once."

"To put it in military terms then, I am at your complete disposal, sir, but I hesitate to throw the ladies into the breach. Margaret is all tied up with Tenwells right now. Eleanor would certainly mind being shunned in London on my account and it could ruin Cristine."

"We will leave that up to Eleanor's judgment. By the way, when is the wedding to be?"

"Wedding?"

"You have got Margaret fixing up the farm for you. I don't know when I have seen her in such looks. She's obviously accepted you."

"Actually, I dare not press her on that point for a while."

"What? Do you mean to have her or not?"

Nathan smiled sadly and approached his grandfather to keep him from shouting and making everyone privy to their conference. "I have probably asked Margaret to marry me more often than I have said good-morning to her. It is she who will not have me."

"She's a damn fool then and so I shall tell her."

"No!" Nathan said firmly. "I won't have her coerced into it. My position has been made a damn sight more difficult by someone already telling her that she must marry me." Nathan looked keenly at Sir Owen.

"What? Well, it was not me," blustered Sir Owen. "I would never do such a thing if she couldn't like the idea. Why, I'm fond of the girl."

Nathan nodded as his suspicions were confirmed. "If it was not you, then it is all Eleanor's doing. Margaret said they argued, but I had supposed you to be at the bottom of it."

"Why should she mind what Eleanor says?"

"Does Margaret always obey you?" Nathan asked.

"No, and I can't but think the better of her for that."

"And the worst that happens is you trade gibes with her for a few days and that's an end to it."

"Well, it's never over anything important anyway."

"But she has always minded Eleanor up until now. Eleanor can make her life here miserable in a thousand ways we can not even imagine."

"Are you implying I'm not master in my own house?"

"That's for you to decide, sir. All I can tell you is that if I ever win Margaret I won't be master in mine, and the thought does not upset me overmuch."

Sir Owen's eyebrows shot up. "What's to be done?"

"I'm going to speak to Eleanor. Perhaps it's not past mending."

"You are going to lock horns with Eleanor? Well, why not. Just remember we need her for an ally in London, and we must leave within the week."

"Yes, sir!" Nathan gave a mock salute that made Sir Owen chuckle. "But brace yourself for a late dinner. I'm going up to face her now."

Nathan carried the attack into the sanctity of Eleanor's dressing room. In fairness, he did announce after knocking, "It's Nathan. I must see you."

"I am dressing. I shall see you in the drawing room," Eleanor replied in irritation.

"Put something on. I must talk to you now."

Neither Nathan nor anyone else had ever spoken to her in that tone before, so she treated the visit as an emergency and threw on a dressing gown before sending her maid away.

"What is it then?" Eleanor demanded quellingly.

"You have been telling Margaret that she has no choice but to marry me," Nathan accused.

"Yes, it's no more than the truth. She must be married before anything can be done with Cristine."

"I see, and I'm the only alternative."

"Jared flatly refused and Matthew is afraid of her." The image of Eleanor proposing Margaret to Jared made even Nathan stare. "You, at least, overlook her tantrums. For some reason she does not scare you, and neither do I." Eleanor looked at Nathan appraisingly. His chin seemed firmer than ever. The scar through his left eyebrow gave him a more serious look.

"Am I to take that as a compliment?"

"At first I thought you too stupid to be wary, but now I realize you are simply a very good actor."

"What?" Nathan cast her his most innocent look.

"That won't work on me, Nathan," Eleanor said with a satisfied smile. "You had us all convinced you were a poor, ignorant sailor, but by what Miss Prin says, you are better read than any of us."

Nathan smiled sheepishly. "One does have such a lot of leisure on those long cruises. I really could not help myself."

"All the more reason for Margaret to swallow you with a good grace."

"She will not so long as she feels she is being forced."

"Well, how else was I to get it accomplished quickly? We have only until spring, or Cristine has to wait another year." Eleanor paced the room much as Queen Elizabeth must have done as she argued with her military advisors. "Do not pretend that you are indifferent to her." She flashed him a look.

"I'm not. I love her. But she will never come to love me so long as she feels she is being backed into a corner. She will hate me rather. You must tell her she is under no constraint to marry me or anyone. It must be her choice." Nathan said this so firmly Eleanor was taken aback.

"But surely this is all settled. She is decorating your house."

"You mistake the situation. I bought Tenwells for her."

Eleanor stopped short. "What can you mean?"

"I deeded it over to her, plus an allowance to maintain it. I had the devil of a time doing it, too, so that it was not thrown back in my face."

"But surely now she will accept you."

"No, but I do not mean to give up on her. Whatever else she needs, she must have her freedom and some time by herself. She means to live there with Jeremy so he can help her run the place. So far as I know, Cristine stays here. I do not know if Margaret really means to steal Dicea away, either, except for visits, unless you make the child's life too miserable here."

Tears started to Eleanor's proud eyes. "We have come to care for her so much. I don't know if we could bear to part with Dicea, even though she would be so close. Is this really what Margaret wants, Nathan?"

"I don't know. I don't think Margaret knows yet what she wants. But she has been happier these past few weeks than I have ever seen her."

"What about you?"

"I will live here if that's all right with you. Matt will always have the running of the place. I have plenty to occupy me in Bristol."

"I meant, will you marry someone else?"

"No. It's Margaret or no one."

"The young ladies in London may change your mind."

"Not me and not Cristine, either. She means to marry Matthew and she is nothing if not constant."

"You seem to have taken care of everyone except Jared," Eleanor said sadly, thinking of her eldest born.

"I have something in mind for him, but he is as hard to reach as Margaret. I'm pretty sure he would turn the idea down coming from me right now."

Eleanor shook her head. "You amaze me."

"My gall?"

"I would call it resourcefulness. What do you want me to do?"

"Set Margaret free. Tell her she need not marry if she does not choose to."

"Will it do the trick?"

"Not in and of itself. But it will remove one obstacle from my path. The hell of it is I don't even know what they all are yet."

"What do you mean?"

"Margaret has ranged herself about with a lot of defenses to protect herself from being hurt. Unfortunately they shut her off from love or any other good thing that might come her way. I believe in time I can reach her."

"I believe you can, too," Eleanor said sincerely.

Nathan nodded and turned to go. "Oh, I was almost forgetting," Nathan said with his hand on the door. "Sir Owen wants to carry us all up to London now to stop your son from vilifying me. Are you and the girls game for a fight? It could mean dangerous play. It could ruin you all, in fact."

"How much time have we?" Eleanor looked at the clock on her bureau as though their departure were that immediate.

"A week, no more."

"We shall be ready."

Once the decision was made to go, Eleanor pressed her troops onward like a good general. Nathan was touched by the loyalty on his behalf, not only from the family, but from the servants, as well. They worked far into each night to make all the preparations for moving a large household to a distant city. One week from the day, the carriages were drawn up in front of the house.

There was only one check. Dicea would not leave Sir Kaye and Sir Gawain. And Eleanor, fatigued after an extremely trying week, refused to ride with both a queasy Jeremy and a basket of kittens. Sir Owen emerged from his library to find Nathan unsuccessfully trying to mediate.

"Who is hurting Dicea?" he demanded.

"Oh, please, Sir Owen." Dicea clasped his hand with tears in her eyes and Sir Kaye clutched to her breast. "Say they may go with us."

"Is that what this is all about? How much trouble can a basket of kittens be? They can go in my carriage. Nathan will look after them." Nathan blinked but nodded compliance. "And Jeremy, you ride with us, too. I think half your trouble is having restoratives forever waved under your nose, and women constantly asking if you are sick."

Jeremy flushed, but was so glad not to be relegated to the women's carriage that he got over his embarrassment quickly enough. He even endured the first few hours of swaying with brave fortitude. He had brought his plans for renovating the mill with him, and he and Nathan had their heads together over these for a good part of the trip. Sir Owen too raised his glass to scrutinize the drawings.

"So this is what you learned in school?"

"No, sir, we did not do anything nearly so interesting at school. Vicar Denning has been helping me. We think at full operation the mill can employ at least a dozen men. Of course, at full staff we will have a manager," Jeremy said, turning to Sir Owen. "I am only interested in the mechanics of it."

"I see," was all Sir Owen said at this reassurance that Jeremy was not undertaking anything approaching trade.

They broke for lunch at Chippenham, where Dicea was reunited with her cats and they all dined quite merrily together. Nathan noticed that Jeremy ate sparingly and secretly admired the boy's determination not to be ill.

"I think you may be crowded in your carriage," Sir Owen told Eleanor. "Let Dicea come with us for the afternoon."

"Are you sure?" Eleanor asked.

"I know she can be a bit wearing with her questions, and I do not want you tired to death before we even reach Lon-

don. Besides, Nathan can teach her history to amuse her."
Actually, Sir Owen was rather missing the child.

They were no sooner on the road again than Dicea liberated the kittens from the large hamper full of straw Nathan had provided for them. They were passed around to various laps, and when Jeremy was feeling his worst, Dicea laid Sir Kaye on him with the assurance that a purring cat was a great comfort when you were not feeling well. Whether this was true or the animal distracted Jeremy, he made it to their lodgings at Reading without asking them to stop.

What the servants at the George thought of a family who traveled with a basket of kittens was of no concern to the Gaites and Westons. They had a merry evening in their private parlor and Dicea slept with Sir Kaye and Sir Gawain curled up on her bed.

Jeremy was not faring as well the second day. He had made a good dinner the night before but had skipped breakfast and was beginning to look a little pale when Nathan asked, "Do you know anything about foundries?"

"Only what I have read. I have never actually seen one in operation. Why?"

"Just a thought. Forged goods are much in demand where I trade. You can get some quite ridiculous prices for them in terms of goods, and we can not always come by a good supply in Bristol. I was just wondering if our area would be a good place to start a foundry."

"Transporting raw materials might not be a problem. It depends where you put it. The roads would have to be improved drastically and that takes a lot of labor."

"But that is the one thing we have in abundance, with all the soldiers released from the armies. How many men could such a business employ?"

"I don't know. Fifty perhaps, once it got going."

Sir Owen listened abstractly to these grandiose plans and then began to take a sharper interest, for while Jeremy was intensely interested in the technology that would have to be employed, both boys seemed concerned with how many men they could reasonably keep at work, and he began to wonder if such philanthropic notions also originated with Vicar Denning. Once this crisis was over he would have to take a look about him, he decided, and get in touch with what was going on.

"Will I like London, Nathan?" Dicea asked.

"Oh, I should think so. There are so many things to see—museums and picture galleries, markets and fairs. There's a wild-animal collection..." Nathan noticed Sir Owen looking at him rather suspiciously "... or so I'm told," he finished lamely.

"Who wants to waste their time on such stuff?" Jeremy scoffed.

"Will you take me to see everything?"

"One of us will. Do you want to see the foundry if Jeremy and I can find one that will let us in?"

"Oh, yes."

"I would not mind seeing one myself. Must keep up with the times," Sir Owen informed them. Nathan and Jeremy traded conspiratorial looks.

Matthew had primed the household to expect them. All the rooms had been opened and cleaned, not just those he and Jared used when in town. The staff had been temporarily increased so that the weary travelers were able to wash, change and sit down to a hot dinner within a short hour of their arrival in Gloucester Place. Jared was conspicuous at the dinner by his absence, so the cheerful trading of news was unmarred by any cutting remarks. Sir Owen was musing contentedly on the difference Nathan had single-handedly wrought upon the family.

The only talk to break the mood was Matthew opening up the council of war by warning them, "I'm afraid Jared has done his work well. At this moment there is not a house in fashionable London where Nathan would be received, nor a club where he would not be blackballed."

"It's all right, Nathan—" Dicea turned to him "—we all like you."

"That's all that matters, Dicea. Of course, there is nothing to prevent me from taking the ladies shopping or to the theater or opera. And I imagine there are dozens of other public places where I can be seen not to have two heads."

"Right," confirmed Sir Owen, "a good plan of attack. Be seen everywhere you can. I can take you into White's as my guest, or Matthew can. It would not hurt Jeremy to come along, too."

There was no sign of Jared before the tea tray was brought, and everyone turned in directly after that. He must have slinked in during the small hours of the night. Whatever reception he was expecting, the reality at late breakfast the next morning could not have been more mundane. Nathan said good-morning and noted that Jared's nose was a little more aquiline than before.

Jared noticed that Nathan was sporting a damned attractive scar, one that would grab the attentions of the ladies if Nathan ever got near any of them. If Jared was expecting a dressing-down, he was reprieved. Sir Owen asked Jared to accompany him and Nathan on a tour of the house, since Jared had the keys.

One room, which Jared reserved for his exclusive use and kept locked at all times, was a small study off the library. Sir Owen commanded him to open it. It was decorated in the Chinese style and contained a desk, a few armchairs and a glass cabinet with a quite remarkable collection of Chinese antique vases, jars and bowls.

"Jared!" Nathan said in genuine surprise, "I never knew you were interested in china."

"I'm sure there's a great deal you don't know about me," Jared said, not taking the comment as a compliment. "Please don't ask me to unlock the case."

Nathan spent several silent minutes scrutinizing the contents of the cabinet. It was an excellent collection for its size. Nathan recognized several of the pieces as having been handled by himself. He resolved at that moment to mend matters with Jared one way or another. He could use the man's expertise, for one thing, not to mention wanting to weld the family back together. But he was not above having a little harmless fun.

"Remarkable collection," Nathan finally said as though he knew what he was talking about. "Except, of course... well, never mind." Nathan shook his head sadly in a manner that sent Jared back to the cabinet after the other two had left to look searchingly at each piece. Then he caught himself and fumed. He could not believe he had been gullible enough to be disconcerted by that fool, Nathan. What could he possibly know of such things?

Dicea's lessons had been suspended for the duration of the visit to London so that she could take advantage of the opportunities offered. Margaret and Miss Prin pored over the guidebooks and Nathan escorted them on an expedition nearly every day to a museum, garden, park or other point of interest. What few people they met that Margaret knew were introduced to Nathan. They all seemed surprised that he spoke English. Even though he was not getting much exposure, he enjoyed these trips more than playing cards at one of Matt's clubs, strolling Bond Street, or shooting at Manton's.

It was easy enough to secure a box at the opera in the off-season, although there was not much of interest going on. But the plays and operas were all new to the Gaites and Westons so they went to one or the other nearly every evening. Nathan attracted attention everywhere he went and caused a great deal of comment. It said much for his composure that he ignored even the most obvious of the snubs dealt him and always kept his good humor. The only thing that really bothered him was the realization that the rest of the family, except Jared, were becoming outcasts for his sake.

As they were leaving for the opera one night, he asked Cristine point-blank, "Would you rather not be seen with me? I can stay home. I know it embarrasses you to have everyone staring at our box."

"No, I think it's good for me to get used to people staring. It will help me get over being so shy. Besides I like going with you. Who else would explain the story to me?"

"Not me," avowed Matthew. "I just go to hold your fan."

"I like going with you, too," Margaret said as he helped her into the coach.

"Yes, I was forgetting. Anything that draws stares of disapproval in your direction would naturally recommend itself to you."

They all laughed and made a merry party in spite of their isolation. No one visited them during intermission, so there was plenty of time for Nathan to explain to Cristine what had happened so far, and what to expect in the next act. His summaries of the dramas brought in humor where it was not intended, and he kept his party laughing until the curtain rose again.

"I wish I knew Italian," Cristine whispered to him.

"Better off not. It's much prettier when you imagine what they are singing instead of finding out they are hawking fish or something."

It suddenly occurred to Margaret that, in spite of his upbringing, Nathan was cultured in a way they would never be. He was multilingual to at least some extent. It was a shock, but a delightful one.

"Just how many languages do you speak?" Margaret asked as they rose to go.

"Fluently? According to Jared, none."

"Seriously."

"Bits and pieces of a dozen, I suppose, enough to get by in trade."

Margaret's attitude toward Nathan had done a complete turnabout since that first uncomfortable dinner, but she had supposed her acceptance of him would fly in the face of society's opinion. She now realized he was much more cosmopolitan than Matthew or even Jared. Instead of being an embarrassment to the family, he was a credit to the Gaites, or could be if not for Jared's gossip. If Nathan had engaged in trade, well, she did not have the same scruples about that as Sir Owen. She was, in fact, very proud of how well Nathan had done for himself in spite of being a cast-off.

She would not have hesitated to marry him on that score anyway. She began daily to examine the reasons for her refusal, and they began to seem more and more trivial. Other men, the few she had known, wanted something from her. Nathan had no ulterior motives. He had given her Tenwells, then made it clear he expected nothing in return. Also, he did not make her shudder. His touch, his looks, his words were honest and open. Margaret enjoyed being with him, and she realized that if he ever left, there would be a sad void in her life.

The family had been in town a week and Jared had avoided them as much as possible. He scarcely ever ate at home, but he was in no position to afford lodgings of his own. Plus, he strongly suspected his funds would be completely cut off if he moved out. He was drinking more heavily and playing very deep with Vilard. Since Vilard had made no mention of Tenwells, Jared finally brought it up at White's one afternoon. "I hear you sold that farm," Jared said in his tight-lipped way.

"Yes, at last," Vilard said almost casually.

"Well, did you have to sell it to my cousin?" Jared snapped as he threw down a card and drained his glass.

"How the devil was I to know who the client was? Besides, it's the only offer we had," Vilard complained. "He will never figure out it was you who lured your uncle into that card game. What a fool Talbot was to think he could best me at cards."

"Are you sure Nathan doesn't suspect something?" Jared asked. "He's not as stupid as he pretends to be."

"How could he unless you have been fool enough to let something slip? How do you want your share?" Vilard asked casually.

"Cash, of course," Jared heard himself say.

"It will be a week or two before everything clears the banks," Vilard lied.

Jared's distraction was such that he accepted Vilard's assurance blindly. It had not seemed to Jared such an evil undertaking. Talbot would have ruined the farm anyway, or sold it and gambled the money away. But that was before Talbot shot himself. Had he really been trying for a fresh start? Would he be alive today if Jared had not tempted him to London with the promise of easy pickings? There would never be any answers to those questions. Bad as the situation was, Jared had felt safe enough until Nathan started dabbling in Gaites matters. Now Nathan was something of a hero for bringing the property back into the family and Jared felt like some predatory bird.

"Are you sure he's your cousin?" Vilard asked. "He doesn't look a bit like you, or any of the rest of your family for that matter."

"You noticed," Jared said, refilling his glass from the bottle on the table. "His papers are in order but there's no telling whose by-blow he is. The hell of it is my grandfather has accepted him and there is not a damn thing I can do about it." Jared was still complaining about his upstart cousin when Nathan walked into the club with Matthew and Jeremy.

Nathan saw Vilard's hand arrested in the deal and Jared's half-drunken scowl brought to bear on him.

Suddenly Vilard raised his voice. "So you suspect him to have no Gaites blood at all. I shall certainly blackball him." Nathan pretended not to hear, and Jared looked at Vilard in some confusion. It had never occurred to him that his drunken mutterings would be publicly quoted in front of Nathan.

"I would not have thought it of Sir Owen Gaites to try to foist a bastard onto us," Vilard said loudly, swinging around to stare at Nathan.

Two dozen pairs of eyes in the room shifted from Vilard to Nathan to see how he would take it. Nathan's eyes swung around to assess the speaker. Nathan smiled, gave a small snort of contempt and went back to talking to Matthew and Jeremy. Nathan's masterful and wordless dismissal of Vilard was not lost on that gentleman, nor on Jared nor the rest of the members present. It was so well-done, in fact, that Jared found himself wondering for a stunned moment where the boy could have learned such subtlety.

Vilard rose from his table like a stiff-legged dog ready for a fight. "You must have heard what I called you."

"It is not my habit to eavesdrop, sir."

Nathan's eyes glittered in a way Matt had never seen before. Now that Vilard had confronted him, Nathan looked positively dangerous.

"Bastard!" Vilard said to his face.

Nathan surveyed him with apparent calm, "Vilard, is it not?"

"Captain Vilard."

"Oh, yes, I was forgetting. Well, I suppose I have been called worse by better people than you." There was a snigger from the gathering throng. "But I fancy that's an appellation put into your head by my cousin." Nathan glanced scornfully at Jared.

"What do you mean by that?" Vilard growled.

"I don't send my dog to fight my battles."

Jared slid his chair back and stalked up to Nathan. "I am quite capable of fighting my own battles." He had not bargained for a public confrontation, but now that it was started he had no choice but to face Nathan.

"Have we a quarrel then?" asked Nathan, his eyes narrowed to slits.

"I tell you to your face, you are no Gaites."

A dangerous smile touched the corners of Nathan's mouth, and he clenched his fists. He ignored the restraining hand Matthew laid on his arm. "Meaning that my mother was a whore."

Jared blinked a little at this implication but said, "Yes."

Without losing his smile, Nathan grabbed Jared's neck cloth in an iron grip and did no more than give him a good shake. But it had the effect of bashing Jared's head into Vilard's face, which was exactly what Nathan had intended. Matthew and Jeremy grabbed Nathan to restrain him then, but the damage was done.

"You'll meet me for that," Jared growled.

"Of course, was that not the whole object?" Nathan asked bitterly.

The rest of Vilard's face reddened to match his nose, for some such notion had been in his mind if it could be managed. If Jared lay dead or even grievously wounded, he would not need to be paid. If Nathan were killed, Jared would have to fly the country and, also, would not need to be paid. Or if Nathan were wounded, Jared would be grateful and would continue to play cards with him.

It was all quite simple really. He could not lose unless Nathan had challenged him, but he had sensed that if he could anger Nathan that anger could be turned against Jared. Oddly enough, the ease with which it had been done convinced Vilard that Nathan was a Gaites.

"Name your friends," Jared ordered, straightening his cravat.

"A simple matter, since I appear to have only two, Matt and Jeremy."

"Will you act for him, against me?" Jared asked his brother.

If he had expected some spark of loyalty from Matthew, it had been extinguished a long time since. "I see no impediment since it is you who are so eager to break the family connection," Matthew stated flatly.

"Much good all your bootlicking will do you. You won't keep Gaites Hall, either."

Matthew started forward, but Jeremy grabbed him. "You cannot, Matt," Jeremy said. "Not till his quarrel with Nathan is settled."

"Captain Vilard and Mr. Hollis?—" Jared received nods of acknowledgment from Vilard and the younger man "—will act for me. It will be pistols."

The meeting was set for dawn on the edge of Hounslow Heath. Nathan bowed stiffly and preceded his seconds out into the street. He sighed then and shook his head. "I have done it again."

"What?" asked Jeremy.

"Let my temper get the better of my judgment."

"You could not let such talk go unanswered," Jeremy consoled him.

"I suppose you are right," Nathan said with resignation.

Jeremy thought it was ill timed of Matthew to say, "You ought to know, Jared is accounted to be a crack shot."

"Yes, that does not surprise me."

"I cannot understand why he picked a quarrel with you. Even if you are not wounded, word of it is sure to reach Sir Owen," Matthew reasoned.

"Now that I recall, Vilard is the one who picked the quarrel," Nathan said, thinking back over the past few minutes. He stopped then and shook his head.

"What?"

"Today we have witnessed something I thought never to see," Nathan said in amazement. They both stared at him. "Our Jared being manipulated, and not realizing it."

"What do you mean?" asked Matthew.

"Jared may be an annoyance, but Vilard is dangerous. He wants one of us dead and I'm not sure he cares which one."

"Well, I do not think Jared will make it a killing matter," Matthew reassured him.

"Neither do I." Nathan laughed, finally seeing the lighter side of it. "Jared would be in a pickle if he killed me. After all the talking he's been doing, he would have to fly the country.''

"That's right!" All Jeremy's worries seemed to vanish. "He will probably just delope, or perhaps graze you," Jeremy said cheerfully.

"When you think about it," Nathan mused, "Jared is the one in real danger. Jeremy never did manage to teach me to shoot, not that he did not try.''

"I forgot about that. You cannot delope. You are in the right," stated Jeremy flatly. "And you might accidentally kill Jared, so you better not try to wound him," Jeremy cautioned.

"No?" Nathan looked innocently from one to the other in a way that would have made Margaret suspicious.

"Nathan, I have seen you shoot," Matthew said sadly. "You had better fire over his head, way over. No one will blame you for missing.''

"So I have only to miss . . . and everyone to come off all right?''

"That's it. Fire over everyone's head," said Jeremy in a voice that still turned boyish when he was excited.

"I suppose I don't have to warn you two to keep this quiet," Nathan cautioned.

Even at dawn, with the fog still crouching thick in the hollows of the ground, the air was warm and smelled of smoke from yesterday's cooking fires. Fields knew that Nathan was getting up early to attend a duel but his cheerful countenance would not have led the most suspicious of souls to conclude that he was himself one of the principals. In fact, Nathan left for the meeting ground with a much lighter heart than his two seconds. Nathan's problem, when he was plotting a joke, was that he took very little account of the consequences for himself.

Nathan kept a straight face through the formality of comparing the pistols. One of the spectators, who thought it worth looking in on his way home from a late night of cards, whispered to another that the "bastard," as they called Nathan, looked damned cool about setting himself up as a target for Jared Gaites.

After they had paced off the twenty steps and turned to face each other, Nathan waited for Jared to fire. He merely looked him in the eye and dared him to put a bullet through him. The shot grazed his shoulder so slightly he barely swayed. Nathan seemed to hesitate. Half the men there expected him to fall, not knowing how badly he was hurt. Nathan's pistol wobbled. It discharged prematurely and the bullet sped right past Vilard's ear, causing that gentleman to throw himself onto the muddy ground in a most undignified fashion.

"Oh, I'm sorry," Nathan said as he examined the pistol curiously. "Did I hit you?" This brought such a roar of laughter from the witnesses after the tension of the previous moments that any reply Vilard would have made was lost.

"Are you hurt?" Matthew asked as he examined Nathan's sleeve.

"No, but Fields won't be pleased. Another coat ruined," Nathan pronounced sadly, and Matthew chuckled. "What about some breakfast?" Nathan asked. "I saw an inn on the way."

"The Downy Bird," someone informed him.

"That's it. Everyone to the Downy Bird for breakfast," Nathan shouted. "I am buying." Jared and Captain Vilard did not accept the invitation to join this raucous band although Nathan would gladly have bought them breakfast.

Oddly enough, Nathan's credit rose more from this encounter than from all his careful posturing in public. For if there was one thing that was more admired by his contemporaries than skill, it was his brand of raw and unconcerned courage. Every man who went away replete and half-sprung from the Downy Bird had a good word to say for him. The tale of the morning's adventure lent Nathan more credit than Jared, and Captain Vilard, none at all.

When Jared returned early from the meeting ground, Sir Owen was lying in wait for him. Apparently Gregson, the butler, had gotten wind of the duel from Master Jeremy's young valet and had felt it his duty to prepare his employer for possibly grim news. Gregson was no meddler, but he had a sincere affection for Nathan and a growing one for Sir Owen, who was becoming almost human under the boy's influence.

The resulting tirade, once Sir Owen determined that Nathan had not been killed by his hapless cousin, could be heard by the entire house and possibly the neighbors as well. The ladies sat at early tea, too worried to talk about the duel. Margaret's angry face was masking a pounding heart and wretched fear. If only Nathan would come so she knew the extent of his hurts. The sounds of laughter in the hall did much to assuage the ladies' frayed nerves, but only served to exacerbate Jared and Sir Owen's tempers.

Nathan, Matthew and Jeremy were had in before Sir Owen, but since these three had drunk a great deal of ale with breakfast, there was little sense to be gotten from any of them. It did seem that a capital time was had by everyone except Jared. Matthew, who stood to bear the brunt of the remaining reproaches, entertained his grandfather with the picture of Vilard groveling in the mud after Nathan's misfire. Sir Owen chuckled grudgingly.

Jared slunk off to his room. He would have liked to have slammed out of the house but, in truth, he had no place to go. If Jared had been calm enough to analyze his resentment toward Nathan, he would have realized it went beyond the honeyfall the boy was likely to come into now that he had charmed Sir Owen. Jared's contempt was aroused by Nathan's simplicity, his innocence and his honesty—the very traits that endeared him to others.

It was with a shock that Jared realized Nathan could not possibly lose in their recent encounter. The boy could not be as stupid as he pretended to be, and Jared began to suspect him of being a rather skillful actor playing a very deep game.

Vilard's part in the incident he had originally put down to an excess of wine and friendship. Vilard was on his side. He had faced up to Nathan, yet somehow Jared had been the one caught in the middle. And he had no real desire to kill Nathan or even fight him again. Even that day at the lake he had only intended to give him a good thrashing. Anything beyond that would completely disgrace him with Sir Owen.

As Jared thought it over, the whole episode took on the aspect of a nightmarish plot. Yet it could not have been planned. Vilard was his friend. Even as he thought this, his reaction was one of disgust. Vilard was also ruthless and mercenary. If he stooped to fleecing drunken men, would blackmail be beyond his touch? The whole situation had thrown Jared into a mental sweat.

"What's to be done?" Eleanor asked in despair after she had been fully apprised by Jeremy of the circumstances of the duel. "Nathan will never be received now that his birth has been called into question."

Eleanor's unexpected lapse in appealing to Sir Owen in the face of social disaster prompted the old man to spit out, what was for him, a remarkable solution. "Throw your own ball and be damned with the rest of them."

"But no one will come."

"Oh, they will come all right. Don't you think they are all agog to see him, though not one of them with the courage to receive him? Send out the cards. I will stand the nonsense for anything you dream up."

With the help of Margaret and Cristine, Eleanor did as she was commanded but continued to predict disaster until the hour of the event, when the carriages started lining up in front of the house. Whether they came because they were curious, because there was nothing else going on, or merely because it was a fine cool night, Eleanor did not stop to question. Nathan stood in the receiving line beside her in immaculate black evening dress. His skin was still unfashionably brown, which made his white teeth and blue eyes look even more striking. He greeted untitled people with the same friendly politeness he showed toward the peerage, and did not seem overly impressed with anyone, just eager to get to know them.

When the dancing began, he let Eleanor drag him around to the least eligible girls so that he could invite them onto the floor. He had a knack for putting the most blushing damsel or confirmed spinster at her ease with a joke, and he danced extremely well. None took back a bad report of him.

Their mothers all knew where the wind lay when it came to the Gaites fortune and began to disparage Jared for misleading them about his cousin. The boy was shy, certainly, but totally acceptable from the standpoint of looks, manners and fortune. They should have known Eleanor would not try to foist a common sailor on them.

Nathan had not been able to persuade Margaret to dance with him even once. She was too busy skirmishing on his behalf among the dowagers, answering all manner of questions about him. "Yes, the family had been agreeably surprised in him...yes, he was quite charming...yes, the family did all adore him, except Jared, of course. But then Jared didn't like anyone very much."

Margaret could feel the tide of opinion running in Nathan's favor by the time he managed to steal a dance with Cristine. They both seemed to sparkle as they laughed and joked companionably. Lady Windhurst, who had no daughters left to marry, remarked that they were the handsomest couple in the room. Margaret knew them both well enough to appreciate, without jealousy, the picture they made. Matthew, standing at her shoulder with a glass of champagne, was not as acute. "I still say he's holding her too tight." Margaret laughed. "Believe me, you have nothing to worry about where Cristine is concerned." Matthew looked so pathetic, she added, "I'm her sister. I should know these things."

More than one mother of a marriageable daughter began to suspect Eleanor of a deeper game, dangling Nathan in front of them to gain acceptance for him while planning to marry him off to his distant cousin. Not only were many dinners and impromptu picnics planned that night, but Nathan caused the launching of plans for at least three balls.

What people liked most about him, even the gentlemen, was his lack of conceit and his good humor, even when the joke was at his expense. Nathan was busy that night but did not appear to be hard-pressed. It was as though the meeting of many divergent people in a short space of time, and the diplomatic handling of them, was second nature. That they were skills his line of work had honed to an art did not occur to any of them. Nathan was fast enough on his feet to extricate himself from a group and be at Margaret's side when supper was announced. She laughed at him but did not tease him by refusing when he blurted out, "Rescue me. If you do not go in with me, I may be torn limb from limb by these women."

Sir Owen led Eleanor in to the meal in triumph. She could not have been more pleased with Nathan and the efforts of the whole family to make the evening a success. She could only count Jared's conspicuous absence a blessing. Sir Owen had been smiling benignly throughout the evening, which surprised his cronies. He informed them that he was well enough pleased with the boy's progress in learning what would be expected of him as a member of the landed gentry. His further mention that he had no qualms about Nathan maintaining his various shipping interests in the spice and coffee trade so long as the boy did not sully his hands with the day-to-day work, gave rise to a good deal of speculation about what Nathan was worth in his own right.

The next morning there was a stack of invitations by Nathan's plate larger than anyone else's. They all looked at him expectantly and laughed at his despair when he asked, "I have to answer all these?"

"We'll help you after breakfast," Margaret offered.

After Sir Owen left with Miss Prin and Dicea to go driving in the park, and Matthew and Jeremy had escaped to a boxing salon, Nathan and the ladies set to work. They had barely finished their itinerary for the next few weeks when Lady Banks arrived on a morning visit with her daughter Clarissa. Morning callers had been nonexistent before. Now it looked as if they were to suffer a veritable flood of them, many of them mothers and daughters, all delighted to find Nathan dancing attendance on his aunt and cousins.

Nathan was as gallant and easygoing in the morning room as in the ballroom. He managed to draw the girls out without showing partiality to any of them. He only spoke of his travels when questioned about them, and then almost as though he had been a passenger rather than a seaman. Except for Jared's vicious rumors, everyone would have taken him for a gentleman from the start.

Everyone was startled when the Dowager Duchess of Leighton was announced. She had attended the ball and had come to thank Eleanor for a pleasant evening. This was a quite unnecessary formality but no one was about to say so. Since her daughter was already married and in the process of making her grace a grandmother for the third time no one quite understood her interest in Nathan. She engaged him in conversation a good quarter of an hour and seemed much more fascinated by what he knew of Spain than in his more exotic travels.

Cristine let slip somehow the problem of Nathan's intolerance for milk and Nathan blushed only slightly as he endured being the subject of so much solicitude that another young man might have skulked from the room. The dowager admired him for his good humor on this score almost as much as for any other reason. At the end of half an hour she seemed satisfied and took her leave, requesting that Eleanor bring Nathan and the girls to call on her in Grosvenor Square one day soon.

The Bankses were rising to leave when Lady Banks had the inspiration for Nathan to take Clarissa driving the next day so that she could introduce him to her friends.

"I'm sorry, but I am already engaged to take my young cousin, Dicea, to see the wild animals at the tower. I simply cannot disappoint her."

"Clarissa would love to go with you," Lady Banks said with assurance, much to the surprise of Nathan and Clarissa, if one could judge by their faces.

"Very well, then. We shall call for you at ten o'clock."

Sir Owen was duly impressed by a recital of the morning's progress and praised the participants. Then he bade them listen to Dicea's adventures in the hedge maze.

To everyone's surprise Jared presented himself in the drawing room that night hoping to join them for dinner. It was the first time he and Nathan had confronted each other since the duel and Jared said with mock grace, "My congratulations, Nathan. You seem to have taken the town by storm. How do you manage to pass yourself off so creditably?"

"It's been my experience that most people would rather believe the best of you than the worst."

Jared digested this morsel along with his dinner. He was now in the position of having the same doors that were closed in Nathan's face only a few days before not being held open for him with anything approaching glee. If he did not treat for peace with his family he might soon find himself a social outcast except for the company of ex-soldiers like Vilard who made their living gambling. He had also just had the shock of discovering the extent of his gaming debt to Vilard. The captain assured him there was nothing to worry about, since he still had his share of the money from the sale of Tenwells coming to him, and that far exceeded his gaming debts.

The money was termed by Vilard a "gift" for introducing him to the unwitting Talbot. Jared now suspected Vilard hoped to delay the giving of the "gift" long enough to let his gaming debts outrun what Vilard owed him. But Jared was in no position to pressure him, for to fall out with Vilard now would be disastrous. If he could have washed his hands of the whole mess, told Vilard he wanted no part of the Tenwells scheme, he would have done so. But his instincts told him this would be unwise. Vilard as a friend was daunting enough; as an enemy he could be downright dangerous.

Jared's only recourse was to avoid him. After dinner, he poised himself beside Margaret and tried to wheedle out of her the amount Nathan had paid for Tenwells, but it was a wasted quarter hour, since she blithely told him she did not know. The one thing Jared could not do was ask Nathan. He was thrown back on trusting Vilard, a course that was beginning to seem, even to Jared, a dangerous one to pursue.

Dicea was a little disappointed in the aged lion that was roused from a nap for her inspection. She did like the monkeys but was distressed that they had to be in such small cages. Clarissa spent the entire time with her face buried in a nosegay she had the forethought to provide herself with. The rest of her attention went to assuring herself that she was not brushing against anything dirty.

Nathan had another scheme for Dicea's entertainment, but he did not think Clarissa would approve so he offered to take her home first.

"Why? Where are you going now?"

"There is a fair just outside of town I thought Dicea should not miss," Nathan informed her.

"You can come if you like," Dicea offered generously.

They lunched on the way at a respectable inn, since even Nathan could not picture Clarissa eating a meat pie out of her hand at the fair. Nathan told the coachman and groom they would be there a matter of hours so the men could amuse themselves, as well. Clarissa sighed, put up her parasol and took Nathan's arm. Their desultory progress past the puppet show, the tumblers, the juggler, and the walking bear was slow enough to allow Dicea to drink in these delights to the full. There was also a fire-eater, two rope dancers and a menagerie tent, but Dicea was most impressed by a monkey, chained to a pedestal, who took the coins from those entering the theater tent to see the one-act play. He shoved the coins into a little box and tipped his cap each time to the delight of all. Dicea handed him one by one all the pennies Nathan had in his pockets just to watch the little hands at work.

"We are not going in there, are we?" Clarissa asked.

"Not unless you are interested in seeing them cut out the heart of Mary, Queen of Scots," Nathan said.

"No, really?" Dicea asked with interest as Clarissa repressed a shudder.

"Most likely it is a shadow play done behind a curtain with a beef heart from Smithfield being held aloft, then set aside for someone's dinner tonight." Dicea giggled and Clarissa looked reproachfully at her.

Neither Dicea nor Nathan let Clarissa throw a damper on the day. They flowed through the swimming crowds on a wave of medieval music and drank in the delicious smells from the food vendors. Other than warning Clarissa to mind her reticule, Nathan scarcely paid any attention to her and certainly made no effort to converse on anything except the delights laid out before them. Clarissa did not think Nathan should have brought her to someplace where she should have to mind her reticule, forgetting that she had insisted on coming.

Dicea sampled whatever of the food Nathan felt was safe to be eaten. Clarissa declined the sweet apple on a stick, the roasted chestnuts, the warm gingerbread, and even the pineapple chunks in a paper, no matter how highly Dicea recommended each of these. Nathan could see by her heightened color that Clarissa was either angry or hot from walking about so much. He was feeling a little guilty and was on the point of guiding Dicea toward the carriage when she had the inspiration to share her last treat with the monkey.

"You must ask his owner first if the monkey is allowed to have pineapple."

"May the monkey eat this, sir?"

"Lord, yes. If you've a mind to give it to him, he will sit on your shoulder."

Dicea was not sure she would quite like this, so Nathan took Jack on his shoulder while Dicea fed him. He would climb down Nathan's arm, take a chuck of pineapple, then go back to sit on Nathan's shoulder while he chewed away little bites of the sweet fruit, manipulating the pieces with his tiny hands.

"Nathan!" Clarissa said, "he is dripping all over your coat."

"It doesn't matter," Nathan said. "If I mistake not, this is the one Jared shot me in, so it has already been mended."

Clarissa's mouth dropped and Dicea finally found the courage to hold the monkey herself. He clung to her head, tickling her face and ears with his tiny hands and winding his tail around her neck. Clarissa gasped and Nathan shook his head.

"He tickles, but I think I could get used to it," Dicea said with delight.

"Unfortunately Jack has to go back to work," Nathan said, taking the monkey to his perch. He slipped the owner a coin for his indulgence.

They had very nearly made their escape when Dicea decided Nathan must try to knock over skittles for her. Rather than risk failure, Nathan secretly discovered from the proprietor of the event that it would cost only a pound for Dicea herself to be lucky enough to win the contest. The prize she picked after her successful throw was an articulated wooden monkey that hopped up and down a stick when you

moved another. She worked this the whole way back in the
carriage, playing on the already taut nerves of Clarissa.
When they delivered Clarissa to her home by late afternoon
she managed to thank them for the entertaining day, but not
the densest person could have supposed she meant it.

"Nathan," Dicea drawled in that appealing way she had
when she was wanting something.

"Yes."

"Does Clarissa have to come with us again?"

Nathan chuckled. "She did not look to be enjoying the
day much, did she?"

"She tried to smile as though she was having a good time,
but she was only pretending."

"You noticed that, did you?"

"Also she was afraid of getting dirty. Margaret never
worries about such things. Even Miss Prin does not worry
overmuch about it."

"Then next time we will take Margaret or Miss Prin with
us."

"Do you like Margaret better than Clarissa?"

"I don't care much for Clarissa at all and I love Margaret. I suppose I must have been pretending a little when I
met Clarissa."

"Is that wrong?"

"I don't know," Nathan said, thinking of the ruse he had
initially played out at Gaites Hall. "It is not nice to be rude
to people, but to pretend you like someone and discover
later that you cannot puts you in an awkward position, besides being unfair."

"It's difficult to know what to do. Must I still pretend to
like Clarissa? I'm pretty sure she does not like me at all."

"Perhaps she's just not used to children."

"But she has a little sister. She told me so. 'Sadie goes out
only with her governess,'" Dicea quoted.

"Poor Sadie. Perhaps we can arrange for you and Miss
Prin to visit her. You have no friends your own age."

"I have you and I would far rather be with you than with any little girl, especially if she might be like Clarissa."

Nathan laughed. "I see, you don't wish for the connection. Well, that is your privilege. And we shall not take Clarissa again. She is a spoilsport."

Dicea hugged him, getting him even more sticky than he was before.

Miss Prin shook her head over the condition of both of them, but smiled as Dicea followed her upstairs, pouring out her day's adventures.

The next day's post brought Nathan a dinner invitation to the dowager's town house. None of the rest of the family was invited, but this was not extraordinary since the dowager's parties were notoriously intimate. Nathan duly presented himself in Grosvenor Square with Eleanor's last-minute advice ringing in his ears. He made the acquaintance of his fellow guests in a well-appointed drawing room that managed to look cosy for all its size. These guests included Lord and Lady Haye, Lord and Lady Berkely, a Spanish attaché and his wife, the long-retired General Harding, and the dowager's sister, Lady Horton. Nathan now understood why the dowager had assured herself that he spoke Spanish for, although Senor Baeze spoke excellent English, his wife had none at all.

It worried Nathan very little to find he was seated between these two, since dinner conversation made no great demand on his vocabulary. He willingly conveyed the gist of the table conversation to the vivacious brunette on his left in an undervoice that would have worried her husband had he not realized how it freed him to converse with the other guests.

Nathan was certainly the youngest person at the table and he graciously accepted his role as translator, not bothering to initiate any topics of conversation himself. The late war had been thoroughly thrashed through during the first several courses, where Nathan was alert enough to notice a to-

tal absence of dairy products. By the dessert course, talk had
turned to the economic crisis the country was facing, so it
was inevitable that foreign trade would come into it as the
only possible solution to the worst of the woes.

"When will China be open to trade?" the general asked
him abruptly.

"It is now to some extent," Nathan replied. "We can
bribe the East India Company factors anytime we want in,
then the Chinese bureaucracy to get back out."

"I will have you know my son is with the East India
Company and that is not what I meant."

"Sad to say but the Company has long outlived its use-
fulness."

"You don't mean it should be dissolved?"

"You think England has the right to lay claim to conti-
nents for the sake of trading privileges?"

"I mean the trade is all one-way," the general said in irritation. "When will they buy from us?"

"Never, that I can tell you, and, yes, it has been on my
conscience for some time," Nathan replied with gravity and
took a swallow of wine.

"What do you mean?" the dowager asked with genuine
interest.

"The whole idea behind trade is an exchange of goods.
We ship cloth, forged implements and tinware to Guiana,
and now Brazil, in exchange for coffee, spices and chocolate. But even those farmers like to get a little hard money,
as well." He paused to convey this to Senora Baeze. "The
Chinese are not interested in our goods. They are convinced that everything they have is better than ours already.
So the only way to get porcelain, silk or jade from them is
to buy it. And the last thing England can afford to be doing
right now is exporting its gold and silver."

"Those barbarians do not deserve to be paid in gold,"
Lady Berkeley said. "You should use currency."

This stalled Nathan as the image passed through his mind
of Chinese merchants' astonishment when he handed them

bank notes. "They are not barbarians, Lady Berkely. If they were, I would not have got in and out so many times. Their civilization is at its height and very stable, while ours is still growing. I think they only sell us anything at all as a politeness."

"They should be made to take our goods," said General Harding.

"I could take a load there and dump it on the dock, but there it would rot. They are just not that interested."

"One thing will help. The East India Company has stopped using English silver. My son told me so."

"I know. They collect enough taxes in India to support their trade," Nathan said bitterly.

"Then they have found something the Chinese want."

Nathan looked at General Harding measuringly. "There is one thing, I am ashamed to say, the Chinese will pay money for—opium. It is already beginning to drain their economy and may destroy them in the end."

"Nonsense! The Company will soon put a stop to that."

"Lord, sir, it is the East India Company the little country ships obtain their opium from."

"I don't believe you."

"It is what I have observed."

"No Englishman would be a party to such a scheme."

"What is the difference between enslaving Africans to trade in America and producing opium with what approaches slave labor in India to trade to China? They are both heinous enterprises and put profit only in the pockets of a few. Rich shippers and merchants may buy country estates, but anyone who has built his fortune on human misery is not likely to feed hungry farmers even if they are English." Nathan realized that he had stopped General Harding, and pretty well shocked the rest of the table. He filled the embarrassed silence by translating the argument for the *señora,* whose assurance to him that he was correct needed no translation. Her taking Nathan's side even in another language broke the ice and there was a murmur of agreement from some of the others.

"But I know so little about England, that I have no idea what's to be done about it," Nathan said humbly.

"That accounts for your very un-English view of matters," joked Lord Haye.

"I suppose, but what awful things to be speaking of in her grace's dining room."

"Yes, they are things that rather should be addressed in Parliament," commented Lord Haye, who continued their discussion after the ladies had withdrawn.

"It strikes me that you may be in the same position as the rest of us, or will be, with regard to estates. Are things not as bad on your grandfather's lands as in the rest of the country?"

"We have plenty of men out of work, but it's not a case of starving yet, mostly because of Vicar Denning. He and his wife spent their savings on a cow so the village children could have milk. And Mrs. Denning spends all her free time baking and sewing for those too poor or tired to do it for themselves. I think they will be able to teach me how I may be of use. I plan to help reopen the gristmill and build a foundry. I know absolutely nothing about either of these things, so I expect to make plenty of mistakes, but I must at least try."

The dowager was not upset by having unpleasant topics discussed either in her dining room or in her withdrawing room. She was, in fact, pleased to find that Nathan was not just a pleasant young man, but a person with serious views who was not afraid to bring them forth. Whatever else he was, he was not the ignorant buffoon his cousin made him out to be.

The rest of the evening they talked of more pleasant things, such as the places Nathan had visited. But he disliked dominating the conversation so he adroitly switched the topic to agriculture in England and managed to learn something of estate management from Lord Berkely. He got

Lord Haye to brief him on what would be done in the next session of Parliament. Even General Harding unbent a little when Nathan questioned him about the transporting of horses, for Nathan was pretty sure he had gone about it all wrong. When the party broke up it was well after midnight, and all seemed pleased to have made Nathan's acquaintance.

"I must admit," Lord Berkely confided, "you are nothing like Jared described you."

Nathan smiled. "My cousin, Jared, has a most subtle sense of humor. It will get him into serious trouble one of these days."

"Good Lord, some of the things he said of you were positively libelous," Lord Haye put in with a grin.

"Yes, but he was a little provoked with me then. You see, I broke his nose."

"You?" asked an astonished Lady Haye.

"Yes, he was teaching me to box and I did not quite understand the rules. No use to apologize for something like that. He must have looked a mess for weeks."

"So that's what happened. He said he had an accident." Lord Haye chuckled.

"Well, it was really. I did not mean to hurt him. I suppose he will get over it eventually."

"You are an optimist!"

Once the cause of the quarrel between Nathan and Jared was circulated, not only was Nathan more generally accepted, but Jared's motives were not as suspect. To viciously attack Nathan out of pure anger was more excusable than to say the very same things out of jealousy or spite.

With the sponsorship of Lord Berkely and Lord Haye, Nathan had the entrée to White's. Although he went there occasionally with Matthew or his grandfather, he still spent most of his free time escorting the girls about. He would not, however, go shopping with then. He claimed it was the only time when they all lost their reason, including Dicea.

Nathan thought he had succeeded in putting a stop to Clarissa Banks's interest in him until he came back from driving with Matthew and Margaret. He had discovered that driving a team, provided they were well mannered, was not much more difficult than riding, since you had no more reins to manage. The use of the whip in anything like the style Matthew and Margaret practiced still confounded him.

They were just starting up the stairs when Eleanor appeared in the doorway to the morning room. "Nathan!"

Nathan jumped guiltily and Matthew cringed in sympathy.

"I want to know what sort of rig you were running when you took Clarissa and Dicea to that fair."

"Aunt Eleanor, I did not think you knew such language," Nathan said in mock astonishment.

"Don't give me that look. Clarissa seems to think you are some kind of imbecile." She consulted the letter she was carrying as Matthew chuckled. "She also speaks of your passion for monkeys." Eleanor waited for an explanation.

Nathan opened his mouth to speak, surprised innocence written large on his face.

"Don't bother to cozen me. I know your tricks by now. One of these days your playacting will get you into trouble."

"And has it?" asked Nathan, finally surrendering his pretense.

"Apparently not. She finds your innocence in the presence of a child touching, as do so many others." She rolled her eyes at him. "God grant they never discover what you are really like," she said in an undervoice, consulting the letter again. "She feels she would like to get to know you better..." Eleanor read.

"That's pretty bold of her," Margaret thrust in.

"Which I take it could be accomplished," Eleanor continued, "if you were to take her driving again, without Dicea, of course."

"Oh, no!"

"Well, what's the matter? Don't you think you could keep up the ruse that long?"

"Never, I shall have to get out of it somehow."

"Pretty thick with Clarissa on the strength of two meetings," Margaret chided on the way up the stairs.

"And I was only trying to give her a disgust of me."

"I'm not sure you could," said Margaret, thinking of Nathan's money.

"You have not seen me at my worst—well, yes, you have. What am I going to do?"

"You trapped yourself by dangling after her. You figure it out."

Margaret flitted into her room and slammed the door in Nathan's face, leaving him talking to the oak panels. "I never encouraged her—nothing like the lures you throw out to Malvern at any rate."

"I have no need to throw out lures," Margaret said from within, her voice muffled by clothing.

Nathan stood a moment, picturing her undressing, and sighed. "No, you don't," he whispered. "They flock to you like moths to a flame."

Nathan dared to smile at Margaret at the breakfast table the next morning and got a glare in return. Everyone was so used to him being in her black books that they were both ignored until Margaret overturned a cup of hot tea on Nathan's thigh. Sir Owen merely rolled his eyes in sympathy. "That's quite enough, Margaret," Eleanor reprimanded. This sent Margaret away from the table. Nathan left after a safe interval to change, and Dicea begged to be excused.

"Nathan, what happened between you and Margaret?" Dicea asked. "You were getting on so well."

"I made a mistake. I made her jealous. And this time there really is another woman, not just a ship with a woman's name."

"But who is it?"

"Clarissa."

"But you don't even like her. It's silly for Margaret to be jealous of her."

"That is perfectly clear to you and me, but there is one good thing about it."

"What?"

"If Margaret is jealous of me, then she must love me just a little."

"If she loves you as much as she is angry with you, then she must love you a lot," Dicea said in wonder.

"I had not thought of that." Nathan chuckled. "Come, I have been neglecting you and I intend to make up for it today. Choose anything you want to do in the whole of London, your majesty. I am at your service."

"Very well, Sir Nathan, first we must walk the cats on their ropes in the square. Then I wish to review the wild beasts at the menagerie. Then, in the afternoon, I think the market at the West India Docks—oh, I forgot, you don't like to shop."

"This is your day, my queen. It will be as you command." Nathan bowed and Dicea inclined her head gravely and they went off to apprise Miss Prin of their itinerary.

Watching the two of them was as good as seeing a play, Miss Prin always thought. She joined them to the extent of being Dicea's lady-in-waiting and carrying the ridiculous parasol and other silly toys Nathan bought her. Miss Prin, as much as anyone, wanted Nathan's suit to prosper, not for the sake of her future employment, but because she could not bear the thought of him leaving them. It would break Dicea's heart if he did go off to sea again and that was just where Margaret's tantrums were likely to send him.

Dicea's last acquisition was a pair of lovebirds in a large wicker cage.

"Don't you think Sir Kaye and Sir Gawain might get into trouble over these?"

"If they have birds to watch in the schoolroom they may stay out of the home wood," Dicea explained.

"Excellent idea, your majesty."

When they returned, Dicea tripped off to tell Sir Owen of her adventures, leaving her court to convey her treasures to her room.

"Sorry, Miss Prin," Nathan apologized as he set the cage down on a table by the window. "I am such a soft touch the schoolroom will soon be a menagerie."

"I like animals. I do own to some apprehension lest we had run across a monkey for sale."

"Do you think that was what she was looking for?"

"Oh, yes, for she has talked of nothing else since your last expedition."

"What a narrow escape we have had then," said Nathan, grinning with relief.

"You would have bought it for her? You are spoiling her, you know."

"Yes, but no child deserves it more. I shall have to be more careful where we go next time I make her queen."

Cristine had pretty well found her feet in London society, and Margaret certainly did not want Nathan dancing attendance on her. He was free to wander as he pleased at the Humeses's ball the next night.

Besides being eligible and attractive in a boyish way, Nathan was every hostess's dream in that he did not retire to the card room after a few dances, but made himself available in the ballroom to stand up with anyone his hostess introduced to him.

He did not often get to dance with the diamonds of the first water, nor did he aspire to, but in an awkward moment Juliana Sedley was making her way through the ballroom when Lady Humes trapped her and presented Nathan. Juliana inclined her blond head and made a polite pretense of being pleased to dance with him, but once Lady Humes had left them, Nathan said, "Don't worry. I won't trip you. They have taught me to dance, at least." She looked at him in some surprise. "Or, if you would rather not, I can take you out of here."

"No, of course, I want to dance," she said, momentaril fascinated by Nathan's clear blue eyes. Her own blue eye had been praised by more than one amateur poet, but sh could not help thinking Nathan's eyes were wasted on man. For such a shy young fellow, Nathan seemed to Ju liana to take her through the waltz with unaffected grace an confidence.

"That was not so bad, was it?" he said to her as thoug he had just administered a dose of foul medicine.

She laughed. "You wretched boy. You make it imposs ble for me to say anything polite to you." He smiled an walked her toward the refreshment salon.

"Who is that staring at me? If looks could kill, I think would be dead."

"Lord Warburton and he is not staring at you. He i watching me."

"You know him then?"

"Yes, and in spite of what he thinks, he does not ow me."

Nathan looked at her inquiringly, then nodded. "I wil remember that."

"I don't know what is wrong with me to involve a com plete stranger in my affairs."

"He has tried your patience, that is all."

"How did you know?"

"I have seen that look before."

"Something tells me you have provoked it, too."

"To no good end. She will not have me."

"Who?"

"Margaret Weston," Nathan said, looking toward Mar garet, who was dazzling in emerald silk.

"I do not believe I have met her, but that silk is Chi nese."

"You know your business."

"You are laughing at me."

"Never. What other business have you than to displa such finery?"

"Do you know where she got it?"

"I brought it back from China. There is no more to be had unless I go there again."

"Why does that make me covet it even more?"

"I have often wondered why rarity adds value to objects. A beautiful gem, or a piece of cloth, even a spice, should have an intrinsic value."

"I never thought about it."

"The music is starting again. Are you promised for this next dance?"

"Yes, to Warburton, but you may fill in for him."

Nathan was on the point of refusing her, but felt a strange compulsion to humor her by obeying her command. It seemed harmless enough.

She waltzed so close to him it almost seemed indecent, and the adoring looks she cast at him made him wonder if he should have given her wine. He was relieved when the dance ended and she seemed to lose her intimacy, glancing noncommittally around the ballroom. "Are you looking for someone?"

"My partner for the next set. Don't worry. He will find me."

Juliana was right. Lord Malvern greeted Nathan briefly before whisking her away. Nathan wondered absently what the woman would do if men stopped acting so predictably.

Even Margaret, whose head Nathan thought could not be turned by flattery, had several attentive suitors, Malvern among them. Yet he could not grudge her such success. Being the object of attention by more than one gentleman had done Margaret a world of good. It was not that they were interested in Tenwells, either. It was being free that made all the difference in Margaret. Nathan could see that. She could toy with these men, trading witty repartee, then snap her fingers in their faces if she chose. She did not need them. For the first time in her life Margaret was enjoying herself with no more serious thought in her head than what to wear to the next party. *This is what she is really like, Nathan* thought, a woman of fire and passion, not an icy citadel. Nathan basked in her radiance like a beggar warming himself before someone else's fire.

He must have been gazing at her in his hangdog way when he was clapped on the shoulder. "I want to talk to you."

"Oh, Lord Warburton, is it not?"

"You know very well who I am. Who in hell do you think you are?"

"That sounded like a rhetorical question."

"What?"

"I only danced with her."

"What were you talking so long about then?"

"Cloth."

"What?"

"Silk, to be exact. I am by way of being a...connoisseur." He had almost said *merchant.* "It was the only common ground I could find with her."

"You would have me believe you only talked about dresses?"

"Well, you know, I'm not very good at this sort of thing yet. Does it get any easier as you go on?"

Warburton's mouth dropped open and he looked at Nathan in a disbelieving way, then suddenly laughed. "Yes, it becomes second nature unless you happen to be unfortunate enough to fall in love."

"Your warning comes a bit late."

"Juliana?" Warburton asked in a panic.

"No."

"She was only toying with you. You do know that?"

"I should rather say she was using me."

"What do you mean?"

"To make you jealous."

"Why did you let her then?"

"I suppose in my own way I was using her for the same thing. Unfortunately Margaret did not take the bait."

"You mean Margaret Weston?"

"Yes," said Nathan, casting her an admiring look.

"They say Malvern will have her."

"He doesn't deserve her."

Warburton shrugged. "And you do, I suppose."

"I have made a study of her, as I do of anything that intrigues me. Still I cannot read her. There is too much going on inside. I sometimes blunder up to her and take a cut for something Jared has said."

"Why do you want her then?"

"I'm not really sure, only that I do want her and no one else. Margaret is deep. She's like the sea, a thousand dark mysteries tossed together and stirred about, sometimes beautiful, always dangerous."

"That's right. You are that sailor."

"I imagine everyone has heard of me. I'm not used to being such a novelty. I hope no one minds me having fun with it."

Lord Warburton laughed. "I see Lady Humes looking this way."

"I wonder if she needs me again," Nathan said, putting down his glass. "Happy to have met you." Nathan nodded and made his way to his hostess.

By the end of the evening it occurred to Nathan that his initial appraisal of women as a whole might not be that far off the mark. It was merely a matter of how much they sold themselves for, or rather how much their parents asked. Cristine and Margaret he regarded as rare exceptions. He found the whole scheme of things rather depressing and it strengthened his resolve never to marry unless it were to Margaret.

Nathan was well on his way to being comfortably established when his reputation took its next blow, but this was not, for once, at the instigation of Jared. It was Matthew who invited him to the Carlton Club in Clarges Street. Jeremy could not comfortably be excluded, but Matthew warned him the play was high and he better just watch. The rooms were well-appointed, what could be seen of them through the smoke, and Nathan concluded that the place at least smelled better than most of the other hells he had been in, but not that much better. Vilard was present, winning a great deal of money from a young man who had obviously been served too much wine.

The proprietor was a lively little man named Pico, whose country of origin even Nathan could not name. The little man frowned on Vilard, then conducted them around the four rooms. One contained an EO wheel, and Jeremy enjoyed losing small amounts at it. They then went to watch half a dozen gentleman play at French hazard, but Matthew restrained Jeremy from getting involved. There appeared to be no entertainment in the way of female singers, the place being strictly given over to the vice of gambling. Nathan did note that those present were either hardened gamesters or green young men being fleeced. Perhaps it was just that he was in such a brown study over Margaret's coldness that nothing pleased him.

They were standing talking in the card room preparatory to leaving when Nathan happened to glance over Vilard's shoulder. He stiffened and stood watching the game intently for several minutes. The hand was over and the loser had gotten up to leave, so Vilard looked about for new prey.

"Care to play?" Vilard said silkily, evidently forgiving Nathan for their previous encounter.

"Cards is not my game," Nathan said coldly.

"What exactly is your game?" Vilard asked.

Nathan's jaw hardened and his eyes glittered. "Perhaps exposing cheats," Nathan said loud enough for the whole room to hear. Matthew's eyes widened. Captain Vilard rose so abruptly he upset his chair and let loose a stream of oaths at Nathan.

Jeremy bristled and stepped forward as did Nathan. "Jeremy, hold!" Matthew shouted. "Now, Nathan," Matthew warned, turning to him, "I know that look."

"Credit me with having been about the world enough to recognize such tricks, Vilard, however skillfully they are performed," Nathan said menacingly.

"You'll meet me for that!" Vilard shouted in genuine outrage. Several of Vilard's supporters, or perhaps they were accomplices, spoke in his favor.

"If you like," Nathan promised, with glittering eyes. "But since you have informed me I am not a gentleman and you are certainly not one, do we need to arrange a formal meeting?" Nathan had deftly extracted his wallet and tossed it to Pico who, sensing trouble, had gotten between the two men.

"What is this for?" asked the proprietor.

"Damages."

"What dam—"

Nathan interrupted him by knocking Vilard onto the card table, which broke under his weight. Since Nathan's accusation merely confirmed the suspicions of several other players, these ranged themselves against the young profligates who formed Vilard's supporters, and before long a raucous brawl had erupted, which Jeremy threw himself into with glee.

Matthew was in the thick of it, as well, but no one disputed Nathan's right to keep Vilard for himself. When the older man was fairly spent Nathan collared him against a wall and delivered an additional threat.

"You have not paid Jared his share from Tenwells yet, have you?"

"You and Jared? But you hate each other."

"He's family. Not so easy a mark as Talbot, of course, but I won't have him cheated."

"You would not dare call in the law."

"No, and neither will you. If I have to come after you again I will take the price of Tenwells out of your hide." Nathan dealt Vilard one last blow by way of a sample, then let go of him and watched him slide to the floor.

Nathan had long suspected Jared's complicity with Vilard but was not happy to have his guess confirmed. He had much rather Vilard had laughed at him or denied the conspiracy, even if the denial had been a lie. Nathan's opinion of Jared was that he was not the sort of man to stoop to such a scheme. Jared must have been drunk, desperate or in flat despair to have considered it. Not for the first time Nathan thought about Jared's prospects. They had not been good even before he arrived. Kept to heel by a domineering grandfather who was likely to live another ten or fifteen years, Jared's intelligence and resourcefulness were being wasted. It was no wonder they had gotten him into trouble.

But Nathan could put him to work, and at an occupation where he would thrive. If only Jared still had a conscience left. Nathan would find out. When Jared finally received his ill-gotten gains, how would he feel? What would he do? Nathan hoped he knew the man well enough to guess.

Jared's arrival at the Carlton Club coincided with the combatants being hauled off to the roundhouse. Matthew looked to have gotten the worst of the fight. Jared chuckled when he saw his brother dragged out, bleeding at the mouth and nose and still resisting between two constables. Jared was not quite so amused at the sight of Jeremy excitedly describing his part in the fight to Nathan while he dabbed at a cut over his cheek.

Jared entered the club and was stunned at the extent of the destruction. He found several other fellows being patched up preparatory to arrest. Captain Vilard was still unconscious and Pico was presiding over the rubble. "That cousin of yours is the very devil. But what a fight!" Jared thought the proprietor looked extremely cheerful for someone who had just had his place of business broken up. Jared stayed only long enough to make a brief assessment of the damages, then ran straight to Sir Owen.

Sir Owen may have thought Jared was carrying tales when he was roused from a sound sleep, but Jared had not enough money by him even to rescue the combatants. Although he would not have minded the thought of Nathan and Matthew languishing in a cell all night, he did not want Jeremy exposed any longer than necessary to the inhabitants to be found in a London jail.

Sir Owen himself felt much inclined to leave the three in the lockup the rest of the night. But the thought of bringing them home in broad daylight in he knew not what shape induced him to change his mind. He finally dressed, grumbling the while about stupid boys' tricks, and commanded Jared to accompany him. Jared would not have missed it for the world. The charm of the situation was that he really was an innocent bystander this time.

They arrived at the roundhouse to find Matthew pacing the squalid cell in embarrassment and chagrin. Nathan was crouched against a wall placidly conversing with another prisoner. Jeremy was following their talk raptly since it embraced some expressions entirely new to him. Nathan slipped a coin into the fellow's hand as he rose and grinned rather sheepishly before the crucifying stare of his grandfather. Matthew began a well-thought-out explanation but was cut short by Sir Owen, "Not a word until we get home."

The silence in the closed carriage was uncomfortable for all but Jared, who looked from one to the other of the three young men sitting across from him in rueful silence. He had not felt so close to Sir Owen in weeks.

"Go to the study," Sir Owen commanded. The recalcitrants filed into the room, Nathan and Jeremy standing very much at attention before the desk and Matthew sitting on it sideways with one hand to his head. Jared stationed himself in an armchair from whence he could observe Nathan and began playing with a glass paperweight. Sir Owen paced the room. "Matthew!" he yelled. Matthew winced. "You were supposed to prevent this sort of thing. Now I find out you are the one who took them to this gaming hell. What have you to say for yourself?" Sir Owen continued in this vein for several minutes, asking rhetorical questions and expounding on the evils of gambling. Matthew's bruised head began to ache in earnest.

Sir Owen moved on to the corruption of children as part of his discourse and Jeremy visibly blushed, for he thought he had given a good account of himself. But he held his peace, merely shifting uneasily to take the weight off a trampled foot.

"And you, Nathan. I am disappointed in you. I thought you had some sense." He spoke to Nathan as though he had dug around the winter apple barrel and gotten to the rottenest fruit at the bottom. "No doubt you have seen the inside of a prison before. You seemed quite comfortable there. I promise you Jeremy and Matthew were not. What have you to say for yourself? Nothing, I see." Nathan squinted at him out of a swollen eye, but snapped back to attention when Sir Owen paced in front of him.

Jared's enjoyment was temporarily disrupted when his grandfather wrenched the paperweight out of his hands. "I want to know what started a brawl that destroyed most of one floor in a house in Clarges Street." There was dead silence for a few moments as Sir Owen paced and the cousins eyed each other uncertainly.

Jeremy spoke up first. "Captain Vilard used such language on Nathan that there was no bearing it."

"You started the fight?" Sir Owen asked in surprise.

"No, but I might have if Matt had not stopped me."

"Matthew stopped you." Sir Owen was sounding sarcastic as he rocked back on his heels, his hands clasped behind his back.

"Vilard was cheating at cards. Someone had to do something," Matthew said. Nathan watched Jared's face and was comforted to see a look of shock come into it. Jared had not known about Vilard.

"Matthew, don't tell me you attacked Vilard," Sir Owen demanded.

"It was my fault," Matthew admitted. "I should have been able—"

"I started the fight," Nathan said abruptly. "In fact, I provoked the whole thing. It was the only way to expose Vilard."

"You say that with a certain amount of pride. Did it occur to you that your cousins might be injured, that you would destroy your reputation?"

"I lost my temper," Nathan mumbled.

"You what?"

"I'm afraid I lost my temper, sir. It was the way Vilard asked if I wanted a game of cards, as if I could not see that he had never made an honest guinea at cards in his life."

They had then to listen to a homily on the evils of hotheadedness from Sir Owen Gaites. Nathan was feeling so wretched the irony of the lecture did not at first occur to him. But as it went on, Nathan had to compress his lips so hard to keep a straight face it made his bruises hurt. Matthew might have contained himself, but one giggle from Jeremy set him off and Nathan had to cover his face. Since the situation looked soon to be beyond even Sir Owen's control, he yelled, "You are drunk, the lot of you. Out of my sight!"

Sir Owen stared at the door that closed behind the miscreants and waited to hear them laugh their way up the stairs before turning back to Jared with a chuckle escaping him. "What a mad bunch. I don't know what Eleanor will say to this mess, but I can hardly wait to get a full account of the fight from Jeremy."

Sir Owen could not help noticing that Jared was not smirking. He had, in fact, dropped his usual bored expression and was looking rather "human," the only way Sir Owen could think to describe it.

"Don't take on so, Jared. I doubt you could have stopped it even if you had been there."

"What?" he rasped. "Stop Nathan? I'm not sure anyone could. But I might, at least, have kept Jeremy out of the thick of it."

"That's true. The boy has not taken any hurt fighting shoulder to shoulder with Matthew and Nathan, but when it comes to keeping him out of trouble it's plain I cannot rely on them."

"I have made an awful mess of things." Jared shook his head sadly.

"Yes, but it was not past mending until Nathan took it into his head to tear up London. Do this for me. Patch things up between the two of you. Let people see you don't hate each other. I'm sure Nathan would be willing."

"Nathan would shake hands with the devil himself."

Nathan awoke the next morning with a thumping head and an aching conscience. "Fields," he moaned, "what time is it?"

"Nearly nine. I didn't wake you for early breakfast. I thought you needed the sleep."

"I doubt the ladies would have appreciated seeing me." Nathan rolled out of bed with a moan to assess the damages in the mirror. These included not only a puffy eye and swollen lip, but a badly bruised shoulder and back where someone had broken a chair.

"Would you like me to get you some coffee?"

"I don't deserve any coffee."

"No," Fields said, and chuckled. "But you look like you need some."

"While you are downstairs, see if there's any liniment in the house," he said as he walked with Fields toward the door, "and anything you can think of for a headache."

Nathan had no sooner closed the door on Fields than Margaret burst in, hitting him in the back with the door hard enough to make him grunt and send him staggering.

"How could you? After all we have done to make you respectable." Nathan watched Margaret's fists clench with something like alarm and retreated toward the bed.

"Margaret, don't you ever knock?" Nathan grabbed his dressing gown and threw it on over his nightclothes.

"I have seen you in less than that."

Nathan's retreat, unfortunately, gave her the pick of objects on the dresser and washstand to throw. He managed to duck two books and a shaving mug, which went to pieces against the wall.

"When? And what is the matter with you?"

"Never mind that. How dare you start a brawl in a gaming hell?"

"I couldn't help it. I am a Gaites, you know," Nathan said lamely, trying to get a chair between them.

"A what? A what?" Margaret, in her incoherence, sought expression in destruction and hefted the huge porcelain ewer. Nathan sprang forward and wrestled for possession of it.

"Listen to me," he pleaded.

"Do you expect me to excuse you taking my little brother into a place like that?"

"Let go, Margaret. I didn't mean for Jeremy to get involved. I thought it would only be me and Vilard. It was an accident..."

"An accident!"

Nathan had difficulty talking to her with the huge pitcher clenched between them but refused to loose his grip on it. "I was so angry I didn't realize what might happen to Jeremy."

"That is worse, not to even think of Jeremy." Margaret let go suddenly and Nathan fell backward into the wall. "Ow." He lowered the pitcher to the floor slowly and crouched to the bed.

"Your shoulder! It's hurt again—but you deserve it. Oh, let me help you off with that. Where is Fields?"

"He went for liniment."

"Tell me the truth. Why did you start the fight? You must have known it would ruin you."

"Why, to discourage Clarissa, of course."

"Could you just for once not make a joke of everything?" Margaret demanded impatiently. "How bad is your shoulder? You have hurt it again, haven't you?"

"It felt pretty fair until you clouted me with the door."

"Let me see."

She began to undo his dressing gown and unbutton his nightclothes as he sat on the bed. Against his better judgment, he let her. Even a solicitude provoked by injury was better than her anger or her coldness. He felt nothing when other women touched him. Margaret's slightest brush brought up the gooseflesh. He drank in the intoxicating scent of her hair, and his pain was gradually replaced by a gnawing hunger for her. He trembled with the struggle against his desire, and his breathing grew heavy as he lost control of himself. Almost against his will he pulled her to his bare chest, raised her chin and kissed her with a passion he had never felt before. It seemed to him that for a long moment she did not resist, that she was under the same spell. Like a fool he thought he had finally won her. Then she started like a sleeper in a dream and dealt him such a blow to the ribs that it knocked the wind out of him. As he lay helpless on the bed, Margaret deliberately picked up the pitcher and dashed it to the floor. Nathan recoiled from the flying chips of pottery. He was still sitting on the bed brooding when Fields returned.

"I see Miss Margaret has been here."

"I have weathered hurricanes better than this."

After Fields doctored his wounds, Nathan washed and managed to shave around the cuts and bruises on his face while he had his coffee. For some reason the hot steaming brew brought everything into perspective. By Dicea's gauge of measuring love with anger, Margaret must be fairly besotted with him.

Nathan appeared in good time for the midday meal. To Nathan's surprise, Jared joined them at the table. There was no evidence of Matthew emerging as yet. Nathan glanced apologetically at Cristine and Eleanor, but they both smiled at him. Knowing that he was forgiven made him feel that much worse.

Sir Owen looked at Jared expectantly. Jared rose and offered Nathan his hand. "I want to apologize and call a truce if it's not too late."

"Never too late for peace in the family." Nathan shook his hand warmly, wincing a little. "But it looks like your original assessment of me may be borne out. I am a disgrace."

"Oh, things may not be as bleak as you think." Jared sat down and received a cup of tea from Eleanor. "I have had a look in at White's and the comment, at least among the younger set, is running in your favor. The older gentlemen don't even condemn you for the stand you took. They merely feel you could have conducted your complaint in a more...organized manner."

Nathan was looking at him openmouthed. "I thought you were going to say 'gentlemanly.' You mean to tell me I'm not ruined?"

"It might be a good idea to lay low for a few days, until you are a little more presentable, but I fancy your credit can survive this, if we all stick together."

"I had a word with Lord Haye," Sir Owen said. "He seems to think your youth and the fact that you have inherited the Gaites temper could be held as an excuse for the manner in which you...er...expedited justice, so to speak."

"You all mean to stand by me?" Nathan was almost overcome.

"Well, of course, Nathan," Dicea said. "What did you think?"

"Brazen it out as we always have," said Sir Owen gamely. "We have nothing to lose."

Chapter Seven

Nathan was standing about at the Eversons' ball feeling a little lost. Lady Everson did not attempt to push Nathan onto anyone as a partner since she was not sure how he was going to be received after his recent notoriety. And Nathan himself was hesitant to ask any but the boldest of damsels to risk their characters by being seen with him. He was content enough to watch Margaret dance, but when the set had finished he got up the courage to walk over to her, thinking that she would not likely swat him in public.

"Getting the cold shoulder?" she asked icily.

"Only from you, but I'm used to that. Let's just say I'm too much of a coward to risk rejection. If you refuse to dance with me, I will be done up."

Margaret was on the point of refusing him. She was still angry with him about the brawl, but she had come to realize that Jeremy had only been an excuse for her anger. It hurt her much more to see the marks of the fight on Nathan's face than on Jeremy's. She now knew she was angry that Nathan had let himself get beat up. Didn't he realize he could be hurt or killed? Didn't he realize how it made her heart sink when he was in pain? None of this could be read by Nathan in her face, only an uncertainty that caused him to look at her with his most helpless, hopeless expression. Suddenly she relented.

"All right. But promise me you won't do anything outrageous."

"I will be good," Nathan promised, smiling and leading her into the waltz.

Nathan forgot about everyone else in the room and reflected that his recent disgrace was worth the pain if it got Margaret to dance with him. She was a never-ending puzzle to him. He could never look into the wells of those dark eyes and have any inkling what she was thinking. To get to the bottom of her mystery might take a lifetime. Like the sea she could start at a dead calm and be in a raging tempest in minutes.

"People are staring more than usual tonight," she commented as though on the weather.

"Perhaps you are just looking particularly lovely tonight."

"More likely it is because of that brawl you instigated," she said ruefully.

"No doubt you are right," Nathan said absently, laying his cheek against her hair.

"Must you always agree with me?" She pushed him away from her, but he held her tightly.

"I have always found that to be the wisest course. I have no wish to anger you. That happens often enough without my doing."

"Well, of all the unkind things to say, when I have not so much as ripped up at you all day."

"Your forbearance has been rather amazing."

"What do you mean?" Margaret eyed him suspiciously.

"For you to act so out of character for such a long time."

"Out of character? How do you know what my normal character is? You have only been around me since I was under a constraint to marry you. And that would put anyone in a passion."

"Yes, I quite see that, but I have it on good authority that you used to be very nasty tempered."

"How dare you?" She snatched her hand away to strike at him but he caught it in a iron grip.

"Not to mention your punishing right."

She tried to wrench away from him, but he pulled her even closer to finish the dance. "Please let go of me," she said in a measured way that warned of dire consequences.

"So that you can run off the floor and disgrace yourself? Better to hold your tantrum in until we are alone. Then you can hit me as hard as you like."

"You think I won't?"

"I'm pretty sure you will. But then you will be sorry, for your compassion is as ready as your temper."

"You, sir, are the only one who exercises both of them to the full."

"I do seem to drive you to extremes. I have from the first day we met and I'm damned if I can figure out why."

"You do it on purpose. You say the rudest things, and then when I am ready to bite your head off you do something nice."

"Surely not on purpose. It's just my nature to be kind. Did I ever tell you how magnificent you look in red when you are angry?"

Margaret laughed in spite of herself. "You are hopeless. And you can let me go now. The dance is over."

"Do you still want to hit me?" he whispered. "I will take you out on the balcony."

"Don't push your luck, Nathan."

"Oh, right."

As Jared had surmised, the brawl in Clarges Street did not ruin Nathan after all. The younger gentlemen proclaimed it famous sport. After the initial shock, the older ones tended to chuckle over his boyish exploit and recall all the outrageous things they had done in their youth. The women were, on the surface, shocked, of course, but many were secretly pleased to find he was not such a shy innocent.

In fact, he was now pursued by the few really dangerous young ladies left in London, debutantes of one or two seasons who thought it might be fun to bring Nathan to heel, even if they decided not to marry him. There was something about his blue eyes. He could make a woman want him without even looking at her, what was worse, without even being aware of his effect on her. Once Juliana Sedley perceived that Nathan was being pursued by others she determined she must have him. Nathan was not startled then to have her rush up to him and possess herself of his arm. "Please, take me into supper. I have quarreled with Warburton again."

"Are you trying to get me shot?"

Juliana did not know how to take Nathan. He addressed her as he might a sister and it was difficult to be ardent with someone so critical.

"How can you abandon me? Do you know how wretched it is to be left alone at one of these affairs?"

"No, and I do not think you do, either. You have only to raise a finger to bring half a dozen fellows to heel. Can't you let me alone?"

"I don't feel safe with—"

"That tears it. There goes Margaret on Malvern's arm and she's looking daggers at me again."

"So she is a little jealous of me."

"With Margaret there is no such thing as a little jealous. The last time she knew I was with another woman she dumped hot tea in my lap."

"But why? Everyone says she will have Malvern."

"I'm not everyone." By this time they were seated in the supper room, but Nathan was in such a foul mood that he would not humor Juliana even to the extent of fetching her cakes and ices. She was left to her own devices to lure passing gentlemen over and request what she wanted. She began to wonder if Nathan was worth the bother since he had eyes only for Margaret, but she was not one to admit defeat. The brooding Lord Warburton she did not even notice.

It was a relief to Nathan when the dancing resumed and someone came to take Juliana off his hands. He could not think what she had been saying to him the past half hour, but it had dulled his senses and he could not recall that he even replied to her. Malvern made off with Margaret again and Nathan was about to go in pursuit when Warburton collared him.

"I thought you said you were not interested in Juliana."

"I'm not. Let me pass."

"Then why do you look so serious when you talk to her? Do not expect me to believe you were discussing fashions."

"I have no idea what she said. I was not attending." Nathan once again tried to pass Warburton, who still restrained him. They were beginning to attract notice and one or two of the younger set thought they might be fortunate enough to see a brawl in the middle of a ballroom.

"You what?"

"I have no idea what she was going on about. My mind was elsewhere."

Warburton laughed in some relief. "We may be the only two men in the room guilty of not hanging on her every word."

"Then you think her tiresome, as well?"

"Yes, often, but dear to me for all that."

"After the way she treats you? Why?"

"Because I knew her before she was fashionable and bored. She was not boring in those days, but as bouncy as a puppy and rather round."

"You mean . . . fat?" Nathan asked in disbelief.

"I have known her since she was ten. She used to get so excited about things and it was genuine then."

"Is there any of that Juliana still left in her?" Nathan asked.

"There must be! I have to believe there is. Sometimes she does look at me in that old way and all the tortures in between fade away."

"You have been in love with her all this time?"

"It seems forever."

"I admire your endurance if nothing else."

"I don't know what I shall do if she marries someone else. My life will be over."

"I know the feeling."

Nathan got nothing but a frosty stare from Margaret the next morning and he prudently chose a seat across the table from her. They both ate in silence and he followed her from the room.

"Margaret, please talk to me. What have I done?"

"You know very well what you have done."

Nathan looked at her so dumbly she turned back from the stairs. "Don't pretend to be so stupid. How do you think it made me feel to see you throwing yourself at Juliana all evening?"

"I don't even like the girl."

"No, you flirt with all of them impartially. I have my eyes open now. I see what you really are."

"What are you talking about? If it comes to that, you have the whole town taking bets on whether you will have Malvern or Belleceour. That can scarcely have happened without some dalliance on your part. It cuts both ways, you know. You are going to have to decide if you will have me or no."

Nathan knew he had blundered as soon as he had said it. That Gaites temper again. He prepared himself for a blistering.

"As you proposed so gallantly this time, no, I will not have you." She turned on her heel and started up the stairs. Nathan stared at the spot on the carpet where she had stood. He had ruined all. He had pushed her and now she would most likely fall into Malvern's arms.

Margaret looked down at him from the landing and hesitated. She could imagine the hurt on his boyish face. She had caused it often enough. She was not sure why except that she used to hurt so much herself. He became aware of her regard and glanced up with some desperate flame of hope alight on those blue eyes.

"But then I will not have any of the others, either." She did not know what made her say it, except that it was the truth and Nathan deserved that, in so far as she knew it.

Why would she not marry him, she wondered as she walked to her room. There was no question of his suitability. They got along well—most of the time. He was, in fact, everything she could have wanted in a husband, if she wanted one. That was the rub, for once tied, the knot could never be undone. In a world where there were so few difficult decisions to make, marriage was the most irrevocable.

Nathan stared up at the landing in bafflement long after she left him.

Sir Owen had been able to extract from Jared a confession of the worst of his debts, which he duly covered, and even advanced him next quarter's allowance, a generous enough amount to make Jared very much at ease with the world. A prudent man would have banked it against the needs of the next fourteen weeks, but Sir Owen's generosity had never taught Jared to be prudent.

Jared was not a hardened gambler, but merely a desperate one. He only lost great amounts at cards when he was in debt and trying to recover, which was when he could least afford to play. On this particular day a circular from Foley's auction house had arrived in the post for him. When he announced at lunch that he thought he would have a look in there, Sir Owen merely grunted in resignation, but then had a thought. "Why don't you take Nathan with you? It would do him good to be seen in your company."

"Why not, if you do not think you will be bored?" Jared offered to Nathan.

"In your company, never," Nathan replied, but smiled so ingenuously that Jared shook off the suspicion he was being made game of. "Mind if I stop at the bank for some money? You never know when you might see something you want."

"Yes, of course, we can stop on the way, but I hardly think this is the sort of auction you are used to."

"Why? I imagine they are all about the same."

This made Jared smile, but he said nothing.

The viewing rooms were not crowded and were rather conspicuously guarded. Nathan seemed absorbed in examining the jewels on display in the cases, so Jared went to look at the porcelain. There was only one piece there that he coveted, a Ming vase with a blue coiled dragon crouching on it. He just might get it, too, if none of his regular competitors showed up. Nathan came to look over his shoulder.

"What do you think?" Jared asked him in some amusement.

"I would not risk it, not if it goes above a few hundred. It is hard to tell in this light, but it does not seem to have the right translucence. The painting is first-rate, of course, so as art it certainly is worth something. If it pleases you, buy it. But it may not be as old as you are."

Jared's mouth gaped. "Just how much do you know about Chinese porcelain?" he asked suspiciously.

"I can tell hard-paste from soft, but so could any child. I noticed your collection ran toward the severe firings. Captain Hewitt favors the mild hard-paste, because of the satiny look."

Jared was staring hard at Nathan when one of the proprietors came over. "Mr. Gaites." Jared half turned to discover that Mr. Trowby was greeting Nathan rather than himself. "Odd seeing you at the other end of the business."

"Oh, this is a pleasure trip, sir," Nathan reassured him. "I assume you know my cousin, Jared Gaites?"

"So you are related?" Trowby shook Jared's hand warmly. "I did not realize that. I am surprised you two do not deal together directly."

"We have only lately discovered our mutual interest," Nathan said kindly.

"We have nothing left that you brought us, Nathan, so you won't be able to see how we have been cheating you," Trowby said, and chuckled.

"I do not pay your outrageous prices." Nathan laughed. "I see you list this piece as possibly Ming."

"Yes, do you feel that to be incorrect?"

"I feel that to be safe." Nathan smiled at him knowingly and Trowby put on a look of supreme innocence that rivaled Nathan's best efforts. "It is a lovely piece anyway." Nathan finally turned away from the vase and asked, "Can you tell me any more of the history of this set of rubies?" Nathan indicated a ruby necklace and earrings in an antique gold setting of Spanish design.

After another twenty minutes the clients filed into the auction room. Jared had not thought that Nathan would have the patience to sit through the entire afternoon, but he seemed to amuse himself well enough studying the other bidders. He expressed no interest in anything until the ruby necklace came up, then it seemed he must have it. He upped his competitor's bid by a hundred each time, and Jared was beginning to feel uncomfortable and conspicuous. He turned and opened his mouth to remonstrate with Nathan, who stopped him by saying, "Don't worry. This fellow won't go much higher. He bids for Lord Avery."

"How do you know that?"

"I have dealt with him. He is almost at his limit. This will look much better on Margaret than in a display case."

Although Nathan paid far above the actual worth of the stones and gold, Jared supposed the age of the piece must add something to the value, but he was not himself a connoisseur of gems. Nathan practically stole the earrings, since no one wanted them without the necklace.

The bidding on the vase quickly ran beyond Jared's means, since more clients had entered the salon by the time the vase came up for bid. This relieved Jared of trying to decide whether or not to trust Nathan. "If you really want it..." Nathan started to say.

"I think not," said Jared, more from a reluctance to borrow from Nathan than because he doubted the piece's authenticity.

Nathan paid for his purchases in cash and pocketed them as though it were no great thing to be carrying such baubles about. "You know, I rather like this," Nathan said in a satisfied way. "I may have to come more often." Jared turned away to hide his expression of disgust. "You know you really should come out to China some time," Nathan mentioned offhandedly. "I think you would do quite well for yourself there."

"Me? In trade?"

"Considering the profit on genuine Ming is seven or eight hundred percent, plus the excitement of finding it..." Nathan wisely left the proposal unfinished. The last thing he wanted from Jared was a flat refusal. Jared merely looked at him dubiously, but could not deny it was the most exciting idea he'd heard in years. When London started to bore him, he thought nothing would ever excite him again. Nathan might as well have thrown a treasure map in his lap.

The Gaites family was entertaining at home that night, not a ball, but a very large dinner with dancing after, a sort of appreciation party for all those who had been the kindest to Nathan. Nathan invited Lord Warburton. No use to ask him unless Juliana Sedley was to be there. It was Eleanor's idea to invite the Bankses and, of course, Malvern had to be included. Nathan found himself juggling people such as the Hayes and Duchess Leighton, who thought him intelligent, at the same time as those who thought him halfmad or stupid. It was not an easy task. There was enough conversation at dinner to cover his ambivalence of character, and his family was used to his blank looks and silent lapses. But later, when the Duchess Leighton demanded what was wrong with him, he hardly knew how to answer.

"Just blue-deviled, your grace."

"Any other young man would be pleased to be pursued by so many women, even such noddies as Juliana and the Banks girl. It amazes me how a lad of such good sense in the ordinary way could have got himself so trapped."

"Not willingly, I promise you. And the only woman I want either takes no notice of me or bites my head off."

"Margaret seems to be good-humored enough tonight."

"But for how long?"

"I should say as long as you can avoid the other two."

"Precisely."

Nathan was acute enough to claim the first dance with Margaret even though it was not a waltz.

"Everyone has commented on my rubies."

"Are you not glad you accepted your birthday gift early? They are perfect for that dress," Nathan said, glancing at the scarlet silk. "Do you realize how few women can wear red and get away with it?"

"What do you mean by that?" asked Margaret, looking up from under her lashes.

"Nothing!" Nathan said, giving her a frightened glance. "I think I had better keep my mouth shut."

"You are sweating," she observed unkindly.

"It's a tight corner."

"Of your own making."

"You know how I blunder into things."

"Yes."

"I can almost handle Juliana because I know she does not really want me, but Clarissa . . . is a dangerous woman."

"Blunder out again then," Margaret advised lightly.

"That is what I have been trying to do."

"To the amusement of your friends."

"I don't mind being laughed at."

"No, you never did. You have no pride at all, in fact, or you shed it mighty easily to play the fool."

"Pride is a very encumbering thing. That's the advantage of being driven as low as you can go. It is the first thing you jettison in order to survive."

"You think I have not?" Margaret challenged.

"I do not know what keeps you afloat. I don't really understand you and it's not from want of trying."

"How could you?" she asked, her eyes wide and vulnerable all of a sudden. "I don't understand myself."

"You said some such thing to me once, and it was a revelation to know that I was not the only one at sea."

"You think too much, Nathan," she chided. "Believe me, it's dangerous."

"I also talk too much. Anything I say tonight may be dangerous."

"That's your own fault for cozening so many people."

"I was warned. If I do my duty and dance with the rest of these women, do you think you can keep your temper?"

"So long as you don't make a fool of yourself."

"What are the odds of that?"

"Slim."

"Well, did she give you your congé?" asked Juliana, sailing up to him with her fan fluttering. "What did Margaret say to you?"

"To watch my step."

"With me? I would never try to manage you like that."

"No, you would torture me like you do poor Warburton."

"Well, he asks for it."

"Can you not be kind to him this once?"

"I had much rather be kind to you."

"I only asked you here for his sake."

"Why are you not like the others?" Juliana demanded.

"I am. I simply do not pretend as they do. It is a game with a definite end."

"You are wrong. They love me. They all do. You just did not invite any of them tonight."

"Your court? Why should I?"

"No, when you want me for yourself."

"Now you are wrong. I invited you to keep Warburton from going insane wondering about you."

"Why do you care about him?"

"Fellow feeling. I also am spurned and ridiculed by the woman I love. I know what it can drive a man to."

"Margaret? Did you really give her that necklace? I would have loved to have that."

"Forget it, Juliana. Rubies would never become you." He left her speechless and hoped Margaret noticed her bereft face.

"What are you laughing at?" Nathan asked Matthew as he downed more wine in the hope of cooling himself.

"You, flopping about like a landed fish."

"London is getting very much too hot for me," Nathan complained, trying to loosen his neck cloth without destroying it.

Even to Jared's jaundiced eye, Margaret was the most striking woman in the room. He solicited a dance with her, and in the spirit of peacemaking, she agreed. "Nathan was right," he said, holding her off to look at the necklace. "They do become you."

"Thank you. They are very old, are they not?" She glanced down at the rich crimson and gold lying on her creamy breast.

"Yes, Spanish, he says—I suppose he would know."

"Nathan is quite remarkable, considering his start in life."

"I'm only just beginning to discover that. You will be careful, won't you? You have something over five thousand pounds hanging around your pretty neck."

Margaret gasped slightly and touched the stones to make sure they were still there.

"Don't look at me so. I did not tell you out of malice, only so that you would know to have a care with them. I was pretty sure Nathan didn't think to warn you."

"No," Margaret said, the color returning to her face. "He dropped it onto my dressing table like it was a string of beads from the Bartholomew Fair." She smiled then at the recollection.

Jared chuckled. "He does have style. I begin to like him in spite of myself. And his taste, whether in jewels or in women is impeccable. I wish I had valued you as he does. What is the matter? You look so surprised."

"I was just trying to recall if you had ever said anything nice to me before that didn't have a barb buried in it."

"Perhaps I'm just not myself tonight. I may be back to normal tomorrow."

"I hope not."

"Nathan is not the pauper we imagined him."

"I know."

"Don't you see. If he offers for you, it is not because of Gaites Hall."

"He has offered."

"You may as well marry him then."

"It's not the money. It never was."

"For the rest, you can make him. He's malleable enough."

"Don't let's speak of it anymore," Margaret begged in confusion.

Jared looked at her in a puzzled way, but obeyed her request.

Nathan and Jared were invited to dinner at Lord Haye's country home near Watford. It was not an hour's drive from London, but Nathan still thought it odd them being invited there rather than the London house. When they arrived there were two girls still playing at lawn tennis under the fond eye of their governess.

"Jared," they called and waved. Jared smiled and waved back at them.

Nathan looked askance at his sophisticated cousin. "You know the Hayes pretty well."

"Lord Haye's brother and I were at school together," Jared said reminiscently. "And because he was my closest friend they have stood by me through all my stupid escapades."

"I'm glad."

Besides Lady Haye and the daughters of the house, Constance and Maria, there was only one other person to dine, Mr. Garvy, a quiet gentleman with a West Country accent, who glanced at Nathan sharply from time to time in the course of the meal. Nathan thought it an odd party, even for a family dinner, but he enjoyed the lively conversation of the twelve- and fifteen-year-old daughters and found himself looking forward to Dicea growing up. Was it possible she would become even more charming with the passing years? After Lady Haye and her daughters retired, he found out why they had come.

"Agriculture can no longer support the country," Lord Haye was saying. "That much is clear. The bad harvests the last few years have people starving here, let alone having anything to export."

"Manufactured goods will carry the load one day," Garvy stated, "but it takes investors, and knowledgeable ones, to start such enterprises."

Nathan grinned and told them about the plans for the mill and the dream of opening a foundry. Garvy gave him the name of a foundry owner in the Midlands who would be happy to advise him.

"Much as it pains me to say it, the only temporary solution is higher taxes on imported goods," Nathan said, "not foodstuffs, you understand, but things only the wealthy would buy."

Jared looked up over his glass. "Such as silk, lace, china and the like?"

"Precisely." Nathan laughed.

"I have never watched someone cut his own throat before," Haye said in amusement.

"Won't that just increase the smuggling trade?" Garvy asked.

"That's not entirely bad," Nathan said, disregarding the stares cast at him.

"What?" Jared gasped, afraid where Nathan was heading with this.

"The land guard will provide honest work for a lot of ex-soldiers who know no other kind of occupation."

"I see. Watching the coasts will keep the navy at full strength and in good repair should we need them again," said Garvy as the idea settled in.

"Exactly," Nathan replied. "It takes a great deal more time to retool a ship than raise a brigade of soldiers."

Nathan was just pondering how much he and Garvy thought alike when that man suddenly said, "I'm satisfied."

"With what?" Nathan asked.

"With you," Garvy said. "Lord Haye wants to run you for Commons in my district. I'm retiring, you see, and we want to make sure we have the right man."

The way Nathan gaped at them, they might have had second thoughts had Jared not spoken up. "There's a sight I thought never to see, Nathan speechless."

"You are serious?"

"Nathan, you can do it," Lord Haye assured him, "and make a better job of it than many I know."

"Yes, there was only the question of residence, but if you mean to stay at Gaites Hall that is no problem, and whether you might be too…colorful for our purposes," Garvy said.

"I am honored, of course, but my affairs are rather up in the air at the moment."

"We do not need your answer today. Take some time to think about it."

Nathan was thoughtful on the way home. "You knew what they meant to do?"

"Haye might have said something of the sort to me," Jared conceded. "Believe me, if I can succeed in China, you can certainly find your feet in the House of Commons."

"You are interested in China then?"

"Yes, I admit you have piqued my interest. I used to think you such an innocent. You don't do anything by chance, do you?"

"Not if I can help it. By the way, that encounter with Molly was an accident. Nothing actually happened."

Jared laughed. "You must have realized later that she was looking for me in that bed. Why didn't you give me away?"

"I think I had already started to like you."

Jared rolled his eyes at Nathan and Nathan chuckled.

"Here, drink this." Jared offered his flask of brandy. "There is something I must tell you."

"Is this to brace me for a shock? There is no need."

"You know then?"

"I mean there is no need to tell me anything."

"I'm responsible for Tenwells being lost."

"No, I don't think so," Nathan said thoughtfully. "Vilard would have found another way to get at Talbot if you had not helped."

"But it was my idea, my plan. I must have been mad."

"So glad you have come to your senses then," Nathan said as he handed back the flask.

"You did know."

"I'm not stupid."

"You give a very good imitation of it."

"I regret now that game I played on all of you. It has caused me no end of trouble."

* * *

The family had been in town something over a month by this time and everyone, with the possible exception of Nathan and Margaret, was enjoying this little season they had created. Only one person in London would have been glad to see them go—Captain Vilard. He had enough money to pay Jared, but it went against his nature to part with it if he did not have to. And only Nathan could make an issue of it.

Vilard racked his brains to discover some way to discredit Nathan, and eventually remembered one very damaging item that would probably send him packing forever: Nathan could not read or write. Vilard distinctly remembered Jared complaining of that vehemently. Jared was not even drunk at the time, so it must be true. How to unveil this required a week's intensive planning and the assistance of a London hostess. He found just such an accomplice in Lady Chamborne. Her husband had married for money, she for a title, and she was never so self-assured as when she was tearing down someone else.

The Gaites family were not particular friends of Lady Chamborne, but when they all received an invitation to a musical evening with a specific request for Margaret to play, it sounded like a harmless and rather amusing outing. All the entertainment was to be provided by the guests. A fair number of the ton accepted. Lady Chamborne rubbed her hands in malicious glee as she planned the evening. No one but the few gentlemen who were being asked to read would know that the evening would turn literary. If Nathan refused her impromptu suggestion to read for them, she intended to ask if he did not know how. Vilard knew Nathan well enough by now to surmise that he would not lie.

Nathan enjoyed the evening immensely, but he did not think either of the other two girls who had played was a match for Margaret and he told her so. She accepted his compliment very prettily. After supper the guests filed back into the large salon where the young poet Lang was requested to read some of his favorite pieces. Lord Haye read an excerpt from one of his speeches from Parliament and Mr. Talon read Coleridge's "Kubla Khan."

It was about then that Jared, sitting on Nathan's other side, turned his head to discover who was entering so late, and saw Vilard taking a seat in the rear of the room. The look that then flashed from Lady Chamborne's eyes shot a bullet of fear through Jared. "Nathan, a word with you outside." Jared grasped his sound shoulder and tried to compel him to rise.

"What? Now? Are you ill?"

"Vilard is here, and he means mischief. For God's sake, come away with me," Jared whispered fiercely.

"Why don't we hear from someone who has actually been to such exotic places? Nathan, you read something for us," Lady Chamborne said, as though the thought had just occurred to her.

"I have nothing prepared," Nathan laughed, forgetting for the moment that Jared was still under a misapprehension about him.

"But you have such a marvelous voice. Among all these books I'm sure you can find something to take your fancy."

Nathan saw she was going to insist, so he rose goodnaturedly to perform. It was only when he glanced back and saw the tragic look on Jared's face that it hit him what Jared was thinking. Then he saw Vilard smirking in the last row. The look of slightly arrested surprise that passed across his face merely whetted Lady Chamborne's appetite. She led him to the book-lined corner, where Nathan bit his lip while ostensibly making careful choice of a volume.

To do him justice, Jared never thought of getting up and leaving the room. It even ran through his mind to compose some speech in Nathan's defense.

Nathan picked up *Romeo and Juliet,* laid the thin volume on the table and leafed through it one-handed until he found the passage he required. "I think I should dedicate this reading to Captain Vilard, who will appreciate it more than anyone else.''

All those who had seen Vilard enter turned to gaze at him, drawing everyone else's eyes in his direction. Things were not going according to plan.

"Act 3, Scene 1, the duel between Tybalt and Mercutio with Romeo intervening." Nathan read each voice differently: Tybalt, belligerent; Romeo, placating; Mercutio, teasing and, later, desperate. He tagged the first few lines of dialogue in an undervoice, after that there was no need. The speaker was obvious. Jared's eyes lifted to Nathan's face in rapt amazement. He was not just speaking from memory. He was reading, and extremely well. Jared stole a look at Vilard and observed their nemesis actually trembling with rage. Lady Chamborne did not look best pleased, either.

Nathan finished magnificently:

> " 'Now, Tybalt, take the "villain" back again
> That late thou gavest me; for Mercutio's soul
> Is but a little way above our heads,
> Staying for thine to keep him company.
> Either thou, or I, must go with him.' "

Nathan closed the book on the genuine applause that resounded. He nodded, but to demands for more, he merely said, "No, I have done my turn. Give someone else a chance." Vilard had slipped out. Lady Chamborne did not have that luxury.

"Nathan, you dog," Jared said, shaking his head. "If knowing you is going to give me heart failure every other day, I'm not sure I can handle it."

"Why, what do you mean?" Nathan's innocence was belied by a faint smile.

"Don't give me that! What will you do when everyone sees through you?"

"Actually, I would have set your mind at rest, if I had thought about it."

After that night's work, Vilard had one less friend in London and he was being markedly cut by people. If he had picked up and moved himself abroad, even without discharging his debt to Jared, Nathan certainly would not have pursued that matter. All Nathan really wanted was Jared weaned away from Vilard's influence, and he thought he had accomplished that.

Vilard, however, credited Nathan with a ruthlessness he did not actually possess, and decided that his ultimate act before leaving the country would be to revenge himself on Nathan. It would be honorably done, of course. And no one would think it odd for him to fly after wounding someone in a duel. He even pictured some sympathy on his part for the exile he would have to suffer. He had only to get close to Nathan one more time to challenge him. Nathan was a Gaites, so provoking him would be an easy matter.

Nathan, in happy ignorance of the plot being hatched against him, wandered into the library of the town house to find Sir Owen in a brown study. He was about to excuse himself again when his grandfather detained him. "This actually concerns you as much as Margaret. Sit down." Sir Owen seemed to hesitate.

"Bad news?"

"I have had an offer for Margaret's hand, and a very flattering one—young Lord Malvern. Do you know him?"

After the initial shock, Nathan found his voice. "We have met. I like him very much. Actually—"

"Damn it, Nathan. I don't want your opinion on his character. I want to know what you intend to do about it. I'm sorry. It's just that I would so much rather you married her."

"Yes," Nathan said ruefully. "So would I. Actually I'm surprised you have not had a host of men beating down your door. She's pretty well the most desirable woman in London."

"I hardly knew what to say to the man, except that Margaret is at liberty to do as she pleases. That was as good as giving him a license to pay his addresses to her. You must make some kind of push if you mean to have her."

"I have blundered so frequently with her of late I would not give much for my chances."

Sir Owen swore softly.

"But she says she does not want any of the rest of them, either. So there is that."

"What are you going to do?"

"At one time I had thought to go back to sea, if my case was indeed hopeless, but it would worry Dicea too much."

"She is not the only one."

"Thank you, sir. It may be awkward having me about if Margaret will not have me."

"And what family rubs along without any squabbles?"

"Captain Hewitt was right. Having a family means ev'rything."

"Good man, Hewitt. I thank God you fell into his hands. When I think of what might have happened to you it frightens me."

"I will speak to Margaret tonight," Nathan finally decided without having any real idea what to say to her.

"I thought you were all going to a dance at Vauxhall."

"I should be able to find a few minutes alone with her. Thank you for telling me first."

Except for Nathan, they made up a gay party that night. Even Margaret was in one of her lighter moods. Jared had acquired a supper box for them to retire to between dancing and other entertainments. Since it was a less formal atmosphere, Nathan could steal as many dances with

Margaret as he wished, and Matthew kept Cristine to himself the whole of the evening.

Eleanor was left to chat with passing friends and be embarrassed by Jared's first lessons to Jeremy on the art of flirtation. Since the two talked quite candidly about various women in front of Eleanor, she was kept in stitches. She tried to be disapproving, especially since she considered Jeremy too young to be thinking of such things. But he was nearly as good a tease as Jared, so they reduced her to tears of hilarity again and again.

Nathan sat with them for a while, and although he smiled at the jests, his distraction showed. Finally Eleanor escaped to visit Mrs. Farley in another box, in order to compose herself. Jared and Jeremy went in search of fresh game. Margaret was just coming back from dancing with Lord Malvern. Nathan thought Malvern smiled at her in a very possessive way before he released her hand. He wondered mutely if his own face looked so totally entranced when he was with Margaret. She caught him frowning at her, smiled dazzlingly and returned to sit beside him. "You have been very quiet tonight," she chided.

"You like Lord Malvern?"

"Well enough," she teased.

"Well enough for what?" Nathan asked desperately.

Margaret had not often seen Nathan jealous, so she could not help torturing him a little. "He asked me to marry him, you know." She tilted her head up provocatively.

Nathan looked away as all the blood in his body seemed to collect in his chest, impeding his breathing. "And what was your answer?" he whispered at last.

"I said I would think about it." Margaret saw him only in profile, that liquid blue eye staring off into space, the faint lines around his eyes and the set mouth. She was about to relent and tell him she was only joking when Nathan seemed to cross some kind of threshold. He took a deep breath and looked back at her, trying to see through her, it seemed.

"I meant what I said about there being no strings attached. If you should choose to marry someone else, I will understand." He said no more then, but the color returned to his face and he watched the other dancers bleakly for a while before excusing himself to go for a walk.

Margaret realized then what he had been doing. He had been giving her up and it had not been easy for him. She wanted to run after him, to tell him that she had no intention of marrying anyone else. But she could not do that, not unless she was willing to become his wife.

Why not? she asked herself. She certainly loved him. She tried to picture what their life would be like together, and it seemed such a gay dream until she imagined their first child. That's when it hit her. It was nothing to do with Nathan or marriage. It was the thought of having children that terrified her. It seemed so simple a truth when she was on the other side of it. She had been so distracted by other problems that her deepest, darkest fear had lain dormant, waiting to spring when all the others had been banished. She began to wonder if she would slip into one of her black moods, but when she checked she found that she still had a future. It just did not include a husband. What had she done to Nathan? She had to confront him, to explain, to assure him that he was not the problem. She was just rising to go look for him when an oily voice said in her ear, "Care to dance?"

"No more than I would care to play cards with you, sir," she said into the leering face of Vilard.

Although Nathan had not been anticipating any more trouble from Vilard, he had not been idle with respect to the captain and had made some careful inquiries about him through the young officers he had become acquainted with. These were none of them Vilard's contemporaries, though, so all they could say about him was that he had sold out early in the Peninsula conflict.

It was Lord Haye who came up with the intelligence that Vilard had not even seen foreign action, and had been forced to sell out to avoid court-martial. No specific reason could be discovered, but Nathan thought he could make a good enough guess to bluff Vilard if need be. It was something, anyway, if Vilard ever threatened to incriminate Jared. Nathan mused on the loose ends of his life, which he seemed to have set in order. If he had failed irrevocably to win Margaret, well, it certainly was not for want of trying. This was small consolation to him as he dragged himself along the paths lit by colored lanterns, with the gay music of the dance rolling across the summer night at him.

Juliana had been watching Nathan and had sensed he was out of spirits. His abandonment of his box seemed to indicate a breach with Margaret and she threw herself into it.

"Walk with me!" she commanded, blocking Nathan's path. "Please," she pleaded as he made to brush by her.

"What is the point?"

"I like you. I cannot imagine why, but I do like you."

"I meant what is the point of all this, the intrigue, the torture. Sometimes I think you and Margaret are two of a kind. What if when you are done with all your little games, there is no one left?"

Juliana shrank from his angry words. "There is always someone."

"This year. What about next year? You fritter your life away. Do you think you will be young and pretty forever?"

"I do no one any harm," she claimed.

"You are more stupid than I thought. What about Warburton?"

"He will always be there."

"Are you so sure?"

"He loves me. He would never marry someone else."

"If he were sensible he would have washed his hands of you years ago. You are a spoiled, selfish little cat. You don't care about anyone except yourself."

"That's not true!"

"Look at him watching us, poor devil! Was it a serious quarrel?" Nathan's voice had softened when he spied Warburton.

"He says I flirt too much." Juliana pouted.

"Particularly dangerous in a place such as this. Another man might have taken advantage of you. You are lucky to have your watchdog about you."

"He has no claim upon me," the girl complained, tilting her head up.

"But he doesn't realize that. He has loved you these ten years or more, poor fellow."

"Why poor fellow?" Juliana regarded Warburton now with a pretty frown.

"Because you are torturing him and you don't even realize it. I used to think women very cruel, that they did such things on purpose. Margaret informed me that women are just as confused and frustrated by these affairs as men are. Think of the opportunity for miscommunication. It's a wonder people ever get together."

"You seem to know a vast deal about it." She looked at him with awakening interest.

"I was not born to this life, but I learn fast. When I am alone he will ask me what we talked about, what you said, like a hungry beggar trying for a few crumbs from the king's table."

"He's coming over. What should I do?"

"If you don't make it up with him, he will go away downcast again. Show a little compassion for once."

"I don't think he's so fragile," she said doubtfully.

"So hard to tell when you have pushed a man too far," Nathan mused. They both watched the hesitant approach of the young lord with his half-angry, half-hopeful expression.

"Have you forgiven me then?" Juliana caught Lord Warburton off guard and his face was transformed. "I was being silly," she said, taking Warburton's arm and leading him off. Nathan watched them go, hoping he had fright-

ened the girl into taking her lover seriously, and with half his
mind wondering if he had really done Warburton a favor.

When he thought he could face Margaret with any kind
of composure he forced himself to go back to the box. He
was startled to see Vilard insinuating himself with Margaret and her looking flushed and angry. He sprinted the last
distance, vaulted over the edge of the box and was about to
grab Vilard by the throat when Margaret got between them.

"Don't start a quarrel, I beg of you," Margaret said.

"You coward, to pester her just because I was fool
enough to leave her."

"You can't call me that and expect not to meet me," Vilard said, tapping Nathan lightly on the chin. Nathan col-
lected himself for a swing, but Margaret interposed herself.

Jared had just wandered up with Jeremy. "What's going
on?"

"Nothing," Margaret claimed, holding Nathan back by
throwing all her weight against him.

"Your cousin has insulted me," Vilard informed him.
"Do you act for him?"

"Not again!" Jeremy complained.

"It would have come to this sooner or later," Nathan
said. "I leave you to make the arrangements. Hold out for
sabers, not pistols," he whispered to Jeremy. "Tell Eleanor
I have taken Margaret home." With that he picked up her
wrap and guided her away from the center of attention.

Nathan was strangely silent as they walked along the gaily
lighted paths toward the carriage. Vilard had done it to him
again. How could he have blundered into the same trap
twice? Nathan could not bear the sight of another man
touching Margaret, but he might have to someday. Vilard
would pay for that liberty. He must have thought Nathan
would be an easy victim. Nathan remembered his unful-
filled threat to Vilard about the Tenwells money. That had
to be at the back of it, unless Vilard merely wanted revenge. Nathan could not think the man would take even the
smallest risk unless there was some monetary gain to be had.

Vilard must only plan to put him out of commission, not kill him. Well, Nathan knew how to disable a man, too, and it would not be pretty.

"I'm sorry I left you," he apologized as he handed Margaret into the carriage. "I should have had more sense."

"You cannot fight him! You may be killed!" she burst out passionately now that no one could hear.

"Don't worry. Do you think I would be fool enough to set myself up as a target for Vilard when I don't stand a chance of hitting him with a pistol? I imagine Jeremy will be able to sort things out." He sat on the seat beside her.

"How can I not worry? I care about you so much."

He noticed that she did not say she loved him. "I meant that I have been taking care of myself for a long time. I know what I'm about."

"I owe you an explanation."

"Lord, I'm sure you did not invite him into the box. He came for one reason only—to provoke me. And, of course, it worked. I'm sorry I made it possible for him to use you in that way."

"That's not what I meant. Nathan, I would never marry anyone else."

He looked at her with a sudden flash of hope, and it hurt her to watch it die stillborn in his eyes. He turned his face away. "I know. That's why I said it. I want you to be happy, even without me."

"There is a reason I cannot marry you. I just did not properly understand it myself."

"Oh, that—one of the hundred reasons. Don't worry yourself over it. I told you, you owe me nothing, except, perhaps, your friendship."

"I don't want us to be friends," she said so vehemently that Nathan looked hurt and confused. "I want to marry you, but I can't. I simply cannot bear the thought of having children."

Nathan searched her face, still not understanding her, so he went on in a rush. "Don't you see? I have already been through it all. I almost delivered Dicea. I had to nurse them through all their childhood illnesses. Now I'm having to let them go. I just cannot face it all again."

"I had no idea. All this time, it was not me at all."

"No, it's me. I just did not realize it. I don't think I can ever change."

"But it's you I want."

"No, you want some sweet innocent girl who will fall willingly into marriage and motherhood without having the slightest idea what is entailed."

"I cannot accept that there's no way for us to marry. We have torn down the walls one by one. What keeps us apart now?"

"I don't want children and you want them more than anything else."

He could not deny the truth of this and waited a minute before saying, "If I thought I was strong enough never to ask—I would want to marry you anyway."

"That would not be fair."

She could just barely see the emptiness in his face as he sat beside her.

"Friends, at least, then?" The words almost choked him. He took her hand and locked his fingers in hers with a heavy sigh. She was so near tears she dared not answer him. "There's just one thing," he said with an effort.

"What?" she whispered.

"You will tell me if you change your mind?" He said it lightly enough and even laughed a little shakily.

"Nathan, you don't mean to wait for me?" Margaret asked in despair.

"Why, yes, what did you think?"

Chapter Eight

When they got back to the house it was after one o'clock.

"You are all right?" Nathan asked to reassure himself. "Vilard didn't hurt you?"

"I can handle the likes of Vilard."

"Good girl!" With that he gave her one quick desperate kiss and was gone to his room. It was a spontaneous act and Margaret thought he never would have attempted such a thing if he had not been so distracted. It was the sort of parting kiss he would have given her if theirs had been a normal relationship. And that was what Margaret longed for now, to be able to marry Nathan without fear or care. But she was not a stupid child. She knew better than Nathan what lay before them. And she could not face it again, not even for him.

Nathan dreamed he was drowning again and could get no air. But he was so tired he could barely struggle. Some freakish ocean current was rolling him over, pushing him up to the surface of consciousness. He awoke with a gasp, his heart pounding heavily in his chest. The face that had loomed before him in his dream this time was not his mother's but Margaret's. He was drowning and the only thing that bothered him was the grief it would cause Margaret. No wonder she could not bear to marry him. Her tantrum over the fight was not anger but love. He had frightened her with his stupid stunt.

If anything went awry with this duel it might destroy Margaret. Nathan decided he did not deserve such a woman, but that did not stop him wanting her. He thought over the previous night. It had been a setback to be sure, but at least he now knew the extent of Margaret's fears. He was not about to give up on her. He had years to convince her to be his wife, the rest of his life if that's what it took. For now he had to keep out of her way lest she get wind of the fight. It was not fair to worry her. He dressed and crept to Jeremy's room to wake him.

Margaret had wrestled with the problem most of the night and only fell asleep toward dawn, which made her miss early breakfast and the chance to talk to Nathan before he went out. She wanted to assure herself that he did not mean to go away, that they could go on as they had before. Their friendship was the most meaningful thing in her life and if they found themselves at odds with each other from time to time, well, making up was fun, too.

Margaret paced the morning room waiting for Nathan to return. She wore such a deep scowl Cristine only smiled sympathetically at her and even Eleanor did not attempt to talk to her. That's when Margaret discovered what a comfort Dicea could be. Margaret was staring numbly out the window when Dicea walked over and took her hand. "Let's go for a walk. Nathan will be back for dinner."

Margaret was on the point of spurning the idea, but found she could not do that to the child. She and Dicea walked in companionable silence for a time. "You miss Nathan even when he is gone for half a day, don't you?"

"Yes, of course, I do. We have been together so much lately."

"I have seen everything in London. I wish we could all go home together now."

"Yes, so do I. There is something I should tell you. I'm not going to marry Nathan." They sat on a shady bench.

Dicea thought for a while. "It's because of me, isn't it? Because you had to raise me. You don't want to be tied down again."

Denial was on Margaret's lips. Instead she said, "I wish we had talked a long time ago. I want you to know that I would not trade my life for anything. That I love you very much." She took Dicea's small hand. "It's not that I don't want children. It's just that I'm afraid to be so helpless and not able to do anything. And then there are so many things that children can catch." The tears stood in Margaret's eyes. "I'm just too afraid to face it again."

"But it would be different this time. I mean you would not be alone. I'm never afraid when I'm with Nathan. He would always take care of me. He would take care of you if you would let him."

"I never even thought of that," Margaret said numbly as she tried to picture not being alone in everything. It was an idea that was quite foreign to her, counting on someone else and liking it.

"Because you are not used to depending on anyone. You have always been the one to take care of us." Dicea looked out from their shady spot into the glaring sun and it made her eyes hurt. "If you don't marry Nathan, does that mean he will go back to sea?"

"No, I don't think so. He loves you all too much for that. At least I hope that will keep him with us. But I have hurt him very much. I wish there was something I could do to make it up to him."

"I know," Dicea said brightly. "Let's do something to cheer Nathan up."

"What?"

"Let's buy him a present," Dicea said in a conspiratorial way that would have put Nathan on his guard.

"Yes, that is an excellent idea," Margaret said, checking her reticule for cash. "What would he like?"

"A monkey."

"A what?"

"You know how much he misses the jungle and all the animals from his travels. A monkey would be just the thing to make him feel at home."

"If you are sure," Margaret agreed dubiously.

"He really liked the monkey at the fair, but I suppose it is gone now, not that the man would have sold Jack."

"Where on earth would we be able to buy such a creature?"

"We could look at the West India Docks. You can buy almost anything else there. We'll go to the booth where I got my birds. That man might know where we can get a monkey."

"Very well, we will get a hackney and go at once." As Margaret handed Dicea up into the coach and gave their direction, she asked. "You are quite sure Nathan would like such a present?"

"More than anything. I know he would."

"I expect you are right. But we have to sneak it into the house and give it to him before Eleanor sees it."

"Why?" asked Dicea innocently.

"Because it's easier to get forgiveness than permission."

Dicea giggled at the conspiracy.

What Margaret had in mind was a kitten-sized monkey who would live in a bird cage and take treats out of your hand. What Dicea found, being sacrificed by a seaman ready to leave port, was a grown spider monkey for a mere twenty guineas, who doffed his little cocked hat when anyone said his name, Napoleon, and stood at attention with his tiny hand thrust inside his little coat just like Bonaparte. This sent them both into gales of laughter.

"This is the one, Margaret. You know how Nathan holds Napoleon in contempt."

"But it's so big. How will we get it home?"

"''E's used to going on a leash, miss," the sailor assured her. "Look how the little girl is taken with him. What say you to eighteen guineas? I have to sell him today and I want him to have a good home."

"I can manage him, Margaret," Dicea assured her sister. Indeed, when she reached for Napoleon, the monkey went to her and sat on her shoulder quite willingly, holding on to her hair and making her laugh.

"''E don't ever bite, miss, and 'e's very clean. What say you to fifteen guineas?"

"Please, Margaret."

The combination of Dicea's plea, Napoleon's natural charm, and getting such a bargain convinced Margaret. "Done."

Nathan was just coming up the outside steps of the house carrying a long, thin parcel when he heard screams and pounding footsteps from inside. Nathan flung open the door and stood transfixed as first Sir Gawain and then Sir Kaye fled up the hall toward him and made the turn into the dining room with a monkey in a blue coat in pursuit. Dicea and Margaret came running after it. Nathan stood gaping at Gregson and the butler gaped at him. The doors must have been open from dining room to drawing room and from there to the hall, for the cats, monkey and flushed girls made another lap, leaving another round of screams in the drawing room as they passed through.

"Nathan, help us," Dicea begged as she jogged past.

"We must catch him," Margaret gasped as she ran by, her long dark tresses trailing about her shoulders. This was a Margaret Nathan had never seen before.

Nathan laughed, tossed his package to Gregson, then sprinted in the opposite direction, adding the thump of his boots to the din. Had Sir Gawain not run up his leg and Sir Kaye not gotten between his feet and tripped him, Nathan might have grabbed the monkey on that round. Dicea leaped over Nathan and Margaret paused only long enough to pull him to his feet. She laughed and Nathan ran laughing after her, up the hall and through the dining room.

The parade charged into the drawing room amid more screams and what looked like the remains of a tea party. Nathan scarcely noticed who was there, for he saw only a bunch of women standing on sofas, holding their skirts up. Sir Kaye and Sir Gawain shot under the furniture and made it through the door just as Gregson had the presence of mind to slam it, cutting off Napoleon's escape. This sent the monkey up the drapes and onto the bookcase. Margaret and Dicea ran along below, catching most of the statues and vases he dislodged as Nathan jumped and grabbed for the leash he saw the monkey trailing.

Nathan was just congratulating himself on getting hold of it when the beast made a fantastic leap toward the center of the room, pulling Nathan off balance and over one of the sofa backs. He somersaulted onto the tea table, smashing it and the tea service in the process, but did not let go of the lead. Amid continued screams, shouts of joy from Dicea and a "Well done!" from Margaret, Nathan reeled his captive in and tried to calm the chittering monkey.

Suddenly the door was thrust open and the astonished face of Sir Owen looked down at Nathan, groveling amidst the broken cakes and china. The situation put both of them so much in mind of the incident with Molly that neither of them could speak for a moment.

"I suppose I know who I have to blame for this," he shouted finally.

Margaret took Dicea's hand and pulled the child protectively toward her. The room had fallen silent except for continued gasping and exclamations from the ladies and the chittering of the still-terrified monkey.

"It's my fault, Sir Owen," Dicea said bravely. "It was my idea to buy Nathan a monkey."

"And did you want a monkey, Nathan?" Sir Owen taunted, bending over and addressing Nathan as though he were an eight-year-old.

"Oh, yes, more than anything," Nathan said, by now clutching Napoleon about his middle. "Ouch!" he said as the monkey nipped his hand.

"Really, it is all my fault," confessed Margaret. "I paid for the monkey, but I had no idea..." She scanned the destruction in amazement.

"Out! Out!" shouted Eleanor, coming down off her perch. Nathan looked up to see Clarissa and her mother and grinned broadly. They shuddered. Cristine lost her composure and giggled, drawing a glare from Eleanor.

"It's really all my fault," Nathan began, "for showing Dicea a monkey."

"Stop!" demanded Sir Owen. "There is enough blame to share among the three of you."

Sir Owen cast an admonitory eye over the three young faces before him. Dicea was round eyed with excitement. Margaret was looking magnificent and childish at the same time. Sir Owen thought she could not have been lovelier. Nathan was his innocent, inquiring self.

Since the screaming had died down and Nathan had ceased to grasp Napoleon so tightly, the monkey was quite content to sit on Nathan's chest and look nervously about.

"Perhaps," Dicea said sadly, "Nathan does not even want Napoleon."

"I do, I do," Nathan vowed, just as Napoleon, having heard his cue, doffed his hat, put it back on and stood to attention with his hand in his coat front. Nathan gasped, Sir Owen guffawed, Dicea and Margaret went into whoops. Only Eleanor managed a tight-lipped composure, until the offended guests had huffed their way out of the house.

"Dicea," Sir Owen finally managed, "do you think you can keep the monkey under control and away from the cats?"

"Oh, yes. Napoleon can stay in Nathan's room." Napoleon did his routine again, sending them into whoops again when they had only started to recover from his previous performance. Sir Owen had to sit down to catch his breath.

"Yes, and I think we will give him a shorter name," Nathan said, "and only use Nap—his full name for special occasions."

"Good idea," Sir Owen managed.

The three carried Napoleon into the hall, past a line of concerned servants, whom Gregson was calming with orders, and upstairs to be tied to the leg of Nathan's writing table. Dicea went off to fetch him some fruit, and Margaret, catching sight of herself in the mirror, went to put her hair up.

When she returned to Nathan's room, there was only Dicea feeding Napoleon orange slices and a wary Fields, preparing a basket of straw for the new resident and hoping he would not have to ride with the monkey on the trip back to Gaites Hall.

"You know, I begin to think Vilard might split and run if he supposed you to have any skill with a saber at all." Jeremy looked across at Nathan as he sauntered down the street. "Well, have you any?"

"You don't imagine we just turned our cargoes over to the French cutters, do you? We probably saw more hand-to-hand than most of the navy, since we did not carry much in the way of cannon. Plus the French would have preferred to capture our ships and cargoes, not sink them."

"You ran the French blockade?"

"Into Italy and Spain for as long as Napoleon's Continental System lasted. Seems a bit foolish now when I look back. All that risk for the sake of some coffee and chocolate. But Captain Hewitt didn't like to let Boney own the seas. And if we were willing to take the risk he would throw in his ships."

"Did you never carry arms?"

"No, because they might fall into the wrong hands. We did have a passenger now and then. What they were up to I didn't know and didn't care to know."

"Nathan, you are as good as a smuggler. This is wonderful."

"Not under English law." Nathan laughed. "We always paid the duty on our cargoes. After Napoleon took Spain and Italy and our navy got him bottled up in Europe, we traded as we pleased in the rest of the world."

"But there were French fleets about."

"Yes, and they were formidable in battle, but as for France being a naval power we never took Napoleon too seriously."

"Why not?"

"For France to gain any kind of supremacy on the seas Napoleon would not only have had to know what the British navy was going to do next, he would have had to have some kind of notion what the French navy was apt to do."

Jeremy chuckled. "Did you never think of joining the navy?"

"Conditions were much worse on navy ships than ours. More men died of fever than in battle. We often had to run from our own navy to keep them from pressing our men. Besides, guarding ports would have seemed dull compared to what I was doing. Chances for advancement were slim unless you were lucky."

"Will you be a captain someday?"

"I suppose, when Merrow retires, if I want. I have a heavy choice to make there."

"Why did you never tell me any of this before?"

"Margaret did not wish it."

"Does she think that's all it would take to make me run off to sea?"

"I think perhaps she doesn't know you very well since you have grown up. She still thinks of you as her little brother."

"At least you have always treated me like an adult."

"I suppose I am in awe of your superior knowledge of, uh, gears and whatever all those other things are."

Jeremy chuckled.

"Where do you fancy dining?" Nathan asked. "I don't mean to return to the house tonight. I don't want to risk Margaret finding out about the duel."

Nathan left Jeremy to order their dinner and went into the lounge to write out some instructions for Matthew and a threatening note to Vilard. He informed Vilard, quite untruthfully, that he was leaving a written account of the affair behind for Sir Owen in case anything should happen to him. He chuckled as he dispatched it to Vilard's lodgings via a waiter.

He and Jeremy enjoyed an excellent dinner while they talked over their plans for the mill and the foundry. Over the port, Nathan said, "If anything should go amiss, I have provided the means for you to continue these projects. There is one thing yet undone. I have not made Jared known to Captain Hewitt. I think Jared is the man to handle our interests abroad. He seems to be agreeable to do so in any case. But if I cannot, I rely on you to get them together."

"You are not worried, are you, Nathan?"

"No, but I don't like to leave things to chance. Here are some instructions for Matthew. You know enough to take care of the rest of it."

Jared was called away from the dinner table at home by Gregson, who informed him that Lieutenant Tilden waited for him in the library. The officer presented him with a package from Captain Vilard and expressed surprise that Jared did not know about the duel. After informing Jared of the time and place of the meeting, he excused himself. Out of the bundle slid a pile of bills that would previously have made Jared's eyes light up. Now the sight of the money turned his stomach, just as Nathan guessed it would. He had almost absolved himself of guilt in the theft of Tenwells, since he had not profited by it and had confessed to Nathan, but the heinousness of his crime was again brought home to him. Bad enough to milk the estate, but to steal from it! And he still believed his greed had cost the hapless

Talbot his life. He sat staring bleakly into space until Sir Owen entered the room, as Jared knew he would.

"What's all this?"

"Blood money. My share from the theft of Tenwells. Nathan never said anything to you, did he?"

"No, but do you think I'm stupid?"

"No, I think I am, or insane. I as good as murdered Talbot."

"Talbot tripped and fell on his shotgun because he was drunk, as I already told you. He didn't give a damn about Tenwells or the loss of it, and he certainly didn't court suicide. It was an accident that would have happened sooner or later no matter what you did."

"Thank you. You know I didn't like Talbot much, but the thought that his death was my fault has weighed on me more than anything." Jared took a deep breath. "I'm going to pay you back the rest of the money."

"There is no need for that, boy."

"I will sell my collection."

"Jared! No. You must not. I don't know much about it, but Nathan says some of your pieces are pretty well priceless."

"I will give them to you then. They were all bought with your money anyway."

"I don't care about that. There is only one thing I want to know from you. Did you mean to shoot Dicea's cat or not?"

"Lord, no. I didn't even know it was there. What scared the hell out of me at the time was that I might just as easily have killed the child. If I had been paying any attention to her at all, I would have known she was always in those woods. It did set my back up to have Nathan defending me. The irritating thing about Nathan is he always expects the best of you and you find yourself tempted to behave . . . out of character."

"I have noticed he has that effect on people."

"I don't suppose you know Nathan goes to meet Vilard tonight?"

"I want to go with you."

"Very well."

Jared went to the drawing room and made a sign to Matthew, who came out into the hall to talk to him. In the dim light neither noticed Margaret slip out to stand in the corner.

"Nathan meets Vilard at ten. Is that where Jeremy is?"

"It must be. Lord, I thought that was over with. Can we stop it?"

"If we get there in time—Margaret! What are you—?"

"I'm going with you, and don't try to stop me," said Margaret, her fists clenched. "How could he lie to me, just when I have finally decided to marry him?"

"You have?" they asked in unison.

"Yes, I would have told him so if he had only come home."

"You wait here," Matthew comforted. "We will bring him to you."

"If you don't take me with you, I am going myself."

"I don't think..." Jared began.

"What if he should be wounded?" she said desperately. "I will be more use than any of you."

They looked at each other and realized she was right. Sir Owen had heard the last of this as he came back from ordering his curricle.

"Best let her go or we will be here all night arguing. Jared and I will get started. You and Matthew can catch up as soon as his team is harnessed."

"All right," agreed Matthew. "Get your cloak, Margaret, but I am driving."

Jeremy drove Nathan to the appointed place with time to spare. The youngster would have preferred to talk his nervousness away, but since Nathan seemed inclined to curl up for a nap, Jeremy held his peace. There was no moon, and a light rain was beginning to fall. At any rate, Vilard's men were to bring torches. Nathan roused himself after no more than twenty minutes and got out of the carriage. He stretched and walked about, limbering up as though he were rising from a restful night's sleep.

Just then two carriages arrived, one with Mr. Samuel and a surgeon, one with the lieutenant and Captain Vilard.

"So, he did show," Jeremy said in some surprise.

"I had a feeling we could count on the lieutenant to bring him up to scratch," said Nathan.

Nathan was in better frame than Vilard, who had drunk away part of the evening in the company of Tilden. Jeremy opened the package with Nathan's two sabers in it and offered it for Vilard's inspection.

The man looked thunderstruck. "I thought . . . I thought you meant swords."

"No, military sabers is what I chose," Nathan assured him, grinning as he divested himself of coat and hat and tied his white handkerchief about his head as he would do if he were going into battle. "Being a military man, you should know how to use one."

By now the torches had been lit, and the lieutenant recommended they get on with it before someone got curious about the lights.

Vilard had removed his coat and waistcoat, so that his white shirt and pale face stood out starkly in the dim light. He picked up one of the weapons at random. Nathan hefted and flexed the other one, then took a few practice cuts in the air.

"You are left-handed," Vilard complained.

"What of it?" Nathan asked.

Vilard lunged, but Nathan parried easily. Nathan seemed to have the advantage for the first few minutes of the fight while they studied each other. The clash of weapons rang sharply amid the increasing downpour. Vilard took a slight wound to the forearm and Nathan paused to give him time to see to it, but Vilard made a desperate charge instead. Nathan retreated slightly, but kept him at bay easily enough. Vilard looked likely to exhaust himself until Nathan had the misfortune to slip on a wet tree root and fall backward. He managed to turn aside Vilard's thrust to his body, but took a deep gash on one thigh.

Jeremy gasped as the blood poured out. Nathan himself seemed hardly to notice the wound, since he rolled and sprang back up while fending off two hammering blows from Vilard. But the wound was bleeding furiously, making the already muddy ground even slicker. Vilard would not give him time to tie it up.

Nathan went on the attack then and managed to give Vilard a cut across the hip, which brought him down for the moment. This gave Jeremy time to run in and tie his handkerchief tightly about the wound. Vilard was on his feet again. It was a more even fight after that, with Nathan's loss of blood and mobility weighed against Vilard's age and lack of condition. But Vilard seemed only to continue out of desperation, like a cornered animal, and Nathan still fought with some purpose. Nathan scored Vilard's ribs to bring him back to attention. Vilard's rushes were becoming frantic, his breath rasping awfully. Nathan moved little, just waited patiently for the charges that were quickly exhausting his opponent.

Vilard rushed in with a desperate swing that jarred Nathan when he blocked it and made him dance to regain his balance. Vilard had drawn back quite suddenly. Here it comes, Nathan thought. Vilard spun and brought the saber around two-handed like an ax. Had Nathan not been able to stop the blow directed against his left side it might have cut him in two.

The clash of steel and the now drenching rain covered the approach of a curricle and pair, but neither combatant could ignore the chestnut team that drove straight at them, forcing them to fall apart to keep from being trampled. Nathan tripped again and fell full-length, knocking the wind out of

imself. He was still struggling to recover when Margaret
eaped from the curricle and threw herself on him.

"How dare you lie to me?" she demanded.

"Margaret!" Nathan said plaintively, like a little boy
whose mother is embarrassing him in front of his friends.
"What the devil are you doing here?"

"She made me bring her," Matthew confessed. "She also
made me pass Sir Owen on the road and he won't be best
pleased about that."

"Don't worry, Margaret. I won't kill him," Nathan as-
ured her as he thrust her aside and struggled back to his
eet. "Matt, have you run mad to bring her here?"

Jeremy was hastily trying to get the lieutenant to con-
ince Vilard to surrender. "Never!" Vilard gasped and
ressed his attack again just as Margaret threw herself on
Nathan.

"You said you wouldn't fight," Margaret accused. "You
promised." By an effort of will Nathan hurled her aside and
met Vilard blade for blade with such force that the guard
roke on Vilard's saber, and Nathan's blade cut into his
and. Vilard dropped his weapon. The battle was at an end,
o too any fancy card tricks in the near future.

"You silly girl. You could have been killed," Nathan said
ondly as he took her in his arms.

She punched him in the chest, almost oversetting him.
"How could you worry me like this?"

"I said I wouldn't fight him with pistols," Nathan com-
lained. They were all drenched by this point. Sir Owen and
ared had just pulled up and alighted.

"You tricked me then, and just when I was going to marry
ou."

"What?"

"I want to marry you," she shouted above the rain,
ringing conversation to an end. "I want to have your chil-
ren."

"Margaret, show a little discretion," Matthew complained. "Bad enough you come chasing out here at all, let alone to be announcing that."

"I don't care who knows," she wailed.

"Neither do I," Nathan said, folding her in his arms. "You're not just saying this because I'm bleeding all over your skirt? You know how you are when I am hurt."

"Are you wounded?"

"You precious girl. You didn't even notice. You really do mean it." He cast the weapon away, vowing never to touch another one, and spent all his remaining energy kissing Margaret without fear of retribution.

Nathan and Margaret treated the assembled gentlemen to a kiss so passionate it made the duel seem like the comedy before the real play. That's very much how Margaret felt. Her whole life up until then had been a frantic comedy of errors. Nathan was the real thing. It was all just beginning for them. Their future expanded in her mind with all its possibilities and for once she saw only the good things.

"I have never seen you like this." Nathan brushed the tears off her cheeks. "Matt, you owe me an explanation. Why did you bring her?"

"She would have driven herself if I had not."

"I will marry you, Nathan. I cannot bear the thought of being without you."

"Do you forgive me for frightening you so?"

"Yes, if you promise not to do it again."

"I will make it part of our marriage vows."

Since the doctor was giving all his attention to Vilard's hand, Jared came over to tie his handkerchief over the sluggishly bleeding wound on Nathan's thigh. Sir Owen looked on in satisfaction. These children made such a piece of work out of a mere engagement. And it had all come out just as Eleanor had planned. They should have listened to their elders in the first place and saved everyone a lot of trouble.

Jeremy thrust himself under Nathan's armpit. He was still pale with shock at the violence he had seen and the fear that Nathan would be killed, but he had recovered himself to the extent that he could help Nathan into the curricle. Matthew had to suffer through the couple's lovemaking the whole way back to the house.

Nathan slept the night through and well into the next day. He awoke almost dreamily, vaguely aware that something good had happened or was about to happen. There were no sea dreams any more, only Margaret, and he awoke with her name on his lips. She was by him to stop him getting up.

"Why are you struggling?" she asked, pushing him back.

"We need a special license. You might change your mind."

"You want to be married from your bed?" she laughed.

"I don't care, so long as you are mine. Get that box for me out of the nightstand."

She did as he asked and came back to sit on the bed. He took out a ruby ring set in worked gold. "Last chance to back down."

She took the ring from him and placed it on her finger herself. "Will you be quiet now? If you keep twisting round, you'll set your leg bleeding again."

"You are not marrying me just because I'm wounded?" Nathan was assailed by a momentary doubt.

"No, I want to marry you. Now are you satisfied?"

He pulled her down to steal a kiss. "It will be as you want," he said rather huskily. "No children. It's enough if I have you."

"Don't be an idiot. I want to have your children. Before I always thought of myself as having to go through everything alone. Dicea pointed out that you would be with me this time. It has taken me awhile to get used to the idea of depending on someone other than myself. And I begin to like it. It just had not occurred to me that I would not have to do it all myself. I won't be afraid with you beside me."

There came a soft tap on the door as Jared entered. "Are you awake?"

"How is Vilard?"

"He will live. He won't be playing any cards for a while. There was something I wanted to ask you."

"About coming into the business?"

"As to that, yes, I would like to travel for you, if you think I could handle it."

"You would need to learn a bit of Chinese from me and a few other dialects—nothing that would tax your mental powers. And I think you would do well for us and yourself."

"I accept then, but that was not what I wanted."

"Oh, of course, your collection. I forgot to tell you. That is probably the cruelest jest I have ever played on anyone. So far as I know your pieces are all genuine."

Jared heaved a sigh of relief and Margaret only laughed.

Epilogue

It was full summer, and sweat streaked the men's shirts as they tried to lever the big waterwheel into position.

"A little more to the right," Jeremy commanded from someplace inside the stone structure. Nathan, perched precariously on the windowsill nearest the great wheel, relayed Jeremy's order to Mr. Kendall and his two groaning sons. Margaret, the vicar and Captain Hewitt looked on anxiously. Finally Jeremy sent out the two lads he had helping inside to put their shoulders to the beams being used to lever the great wheel into position.

"Is this the last step?" Captain Hewitt asked as he pointed with his walking stick.

"Yes," Vicar Denning answered. "Jeremy convinced us we should change it from an undershot wheel to an overshot one to gain more power, so we have had to retool a bit and turn the thing around."

"Also, they had to build a dam and stone sluice upstream to raise the water level," Margaret explained. "Jeremy planned to do it with a wooden sluice, but I didn't think it would look right, besides not being permanent."

"That's why it's taken us the whole winter and half the summer to get this far," explained the vicar. "But it was worth it. You can barely distinguish the new stonework from the old."

"If part of the object was to employ as many men a
possible, I thought we should do it right," Margaret said
"We had up to twenty at a time here for the dredging."

"Are those the fellows working on the road now?" aske
Captain Hewitt.

"Yes. If we want farmers to bring their grain here, w
have to make it passable in all weather—it's moving!" Vica
Denning shouted suddenly and went forward to keep
closer watch.

"Looks like another inch will do it." Nathan, who wa
the only one who could see much on the outside, finall
leaned too far, lost his balance, and fell into the small pon
below the wheel just as the wooden giant slipped into place
Margaret started forward but Nathan came up laughing.

"This is nice. Come for a dip, Margaret." He grabbed th
hand she reached out to him and tried to pull her into th
water.

"Tempting, but it will have to wait until later." She pulle
him out. "The wheel's in place."

Nathan crawled up to sit on the bank, dripping as Jer
emy appeared, much streaked with grease, to check on th
wheel. Jeremy saw Matthew riding up and hailed him.

"What's the verdict?" Matthew asked. "Will this thin
grind wheat this year or not?"

"That's what we are about to find out," Jeremy said a
he disappeared into the building. He called out to have th
sluice gate opened, and suddenly the huge wheel shivere
into operation. The noise was incredible. The workmen al
scrambled inside to watch with pride the first grain bein
ground.

Jeremy came back out wreathed in smiles. "It's work
ing! You should hear it inside. I had no idea it would vi
brate the whole building. No wonder they made it fron
stone."

"That's good news and I have some, too," Matthew said
"I just came to invite you all to dinner. Jared is home. Yo

ould see him. He's brown as a nut and he's brought Di-
a a mate for Napoleon."

"How is Grandfather taking that?" Margaret laughed.

"The monkeys can stay for all he cares," Matthew said,
smounting, "so long as Dicea keeps them in the conser-
tory where they can't molest the cats."

"This is good news," said Captain Hewitt. "We were not
oking for the *Marivelle* for another two weeks."

"How are Cristine and little Gaylen?" asked Margaret.

"Fine. Cristine is coming down to dinner tonight. It will
quite a party."

"Especially if the monkeys are invited," suggested Na-
an. "You know you didn't have to name your son Gaylen
st because Dicea suggested it."

"No, I rather like the name myself," Matthew said
oudly.

"Come, we had better hurry and change, or we will dis-
ace ourselves by being late," Margaret said as she reached
r hand down to Nathan. He pulled her into his lap and she
uealed, "You are getting me all muddy."

Matthew was laughing at the mock struggle between Na-
an and Margaret. Jeremy turned and shook his head in
sgust. "Sickening!" Jeremy observed. "It's a wonder I get
y work out of Nathan at all when Margaret is around. It's
most more than I can stomach, the way they carry on."

"We must make allowances," said Vicar Denning. "They
e still practically newlyweds."

"Race you to the house," Margaret taunted, and took
f.

"Not fair. I swallowed gallons of water." But Nathan
ught her halfway through the hay field and threw her
wn in the sweet-smelling grass ready for the harvest.
There's mud on your face," he said, kissing it away.

"What do you think? Do we have time before dinner?"
e asked provocatively. He kissed her again, then grew
oughtful.

"No. Besides, it is about time this month we quit doi[ng] that or you will end up with a baby before you are ready f[or] one." Nathan pushed himself up, but Margaret grabbed [his] shirt and pulled him back to her.

"I want a baby. I have wanted one since the moment I sa[w] Gaylen."

"You mean now?"

"Yes, now, silly," she said as she began undoing his bu[t]tons.

"You are mad, not in the middle of a field." He laughe[d.] "We have scandalized Jeremy enough. You want a bab[y?] Race me to the house." He took off and ran. Margaret r[an] laughing after him.

* * * * *

Harlequin® Historical

Nora O'Shea had fled to Arizona seeking freedom,
but could she ever find love as a mail-order bride?

MARIANNE WILLMAN

From the author of THE CYGNET and ROSE RED,
ROSE WHITE comes a haunting love story full of
passion and power, set against the backdrop of the
new frontier.

Coming in November 1993 from Harlequin

Don't miss it! Wherever Harlequin books are sold.

**Fifty red-blooded, white-hot, true-blue hunks
from every State in the Union!**

Look for MEN MADE IN AMERICA! Written by some
of our most poplar authors, these stories feature fifty of
the strongest, sexiest men, each from a different state in
the union!

Two titles available every other month at your favorite
retail outlet.

In November, look for:

STRAIGHT FROM THE HEART by Barbara Delinsky
(Connecticut)
AUTHOR'S CHOICE by Elizabeth August (Delaware)

In January, look for:

DREAM COME TRUE by Ann Major (Florida)
WAY OF THE WILLOW by Linda Shaw (Georgia)

You won't be able to resist MEN MADE IN AMERICA!

Harlequin® Historical

From *New York Times* bestselling author

Elizabeth Lowell

Reckless Love

The powerful story of two people as brave and free as
the elusive wild mustang which both had sworn to
capture.

A Harlequin Historicals Release
December 1993

1993 Keepsake

CHRISTMAS

Stories

Capture the spirit and romance of Christmas with KEEPSAKE CHRISTMAS STORIES, a collection of three stories by favorite historical authors. The perfect Christmas gift!

Don't miss these heartwarming stories, available in November wherever Harlequin books are sold:

ONCE UPON A CHRISTMAS by Curtiss Ann Matlock
A FAIRYTALE SEASON by Marianne Willman
TIDINGS OF JOY by Victoria Pade

ADD A TOUCH OF ROMANCE TO YOUR HOLIDAY SEASON WITH KEEPSAKE CHRISTMAS STORIES!

Relive the romance...
Harlequin and Silhouette
are proud to present

by Request™

A program of collections of three complete novels by the most-requested authors with the most-requested themes. Be sure to look for one volume each month with three complete novels by top-name authors.

In September: **BAD BOYS**
Dixie Browning
Ann Major
Ginna Gray

No heart is safe when these hot-blooded hunks are in town!

In October: **DREAMSCAPE**
Jayne Ann Krentz
Anne Stuart
Bobby Hutchinson

Something's happening! But is it love or magic?

In December: **SOLUTION: MARRIAGE**
Debbie Macomber
Annette Broadrick
Heather Graham Pozzessere

Marriages in name only have a way of leading to love....

Available at your favorite retail outlet.

REQ-G2

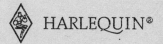 HARLEQUIN®

 *Silhouette*

When the only time you have for yourself is...

STOLEN *moments* ™

Christmas is such a busy time—with shopping, decorating, writing cards, trimming trees, wrapping gifts....

When you do have a few *stolen moments* to call your own, treat yourself to a brand-new *short* novel. Relax with one of our Stocking Stuffers— or with all six!

Each STOLEN MOMENTS title is a complete and original contemporary romance that's the perfect length for the busy woman of the nineties! Especially at Christmas...

And they make perfect **stocking stuffers**, too! (For your mother, grandmother, daughters, friends, co-workers, neighbors, aunts, cousins—all the other women in your life!)

Look for the STOLEN MOMENTS display in December

STOCKING STUFFERS:

HIS MISTRESS Carrie Alexander
DANIEL'S DECEPTION Marie DeWitt
SNOW ANGEL Isolde Evans
THE FAMILY MAN Danielle Kelly
THE LONE WOLF Ellen Rogers
MONTANA CHRISTMAS Lynn Russell

HSM2

 **WORLDWIDE LIBRARY**